LITTLE
BONES

Sam Blake

twenty7

First published in Great Britain in 2016

London WC1X 8RE

www.twenty7books.co.uk

Copyright © Sam Blake, 2016

All rights reserved

A CIP catalogue record for this book is
available from the British Library.

Paperback ISBN: 978-1-78577-023-4
Ebook ISBN: 978-1-78577-024-1

3 5 7 9 10 8 6 4 2

Typeset by IDSUK (Data Connection) Ltd

Printed and bound by Clays Ltd, St Ives Plc

Twenty7 Books is an imprint of Bonnier Zaffre,
a Bonnier Publishing company
www.bonnierzaffre.co.uk
www.bonnierpublishing.co.uk

LITTLE BONES

Sam Blake is a pseudonym for Vanessa Fox O'Loughlin, the founder of The Inkwell Group publishing consultancy and the hugely popular national writing resources website Writing.ie. She is Ireland's leading literary scout who has assisted many award winning and bestselling authors to publication. Vanessa has been writing fiction since her husband set sail across the Atlantic for eight weeks and she had an idea for a book.

Follow Vanessa on Twitter @inkwellhq, @writersamblake or @writing_ie.

For everyone who has ever wanted to write a book
and get published: you can – just keep writing.
This is for you.

PART ONE

Coming Apart at the Seams
*In clothing: where two pieces of material come apart and
the garment can no longer be worn. Often caused by
a weakness or break in the thread.*

1

The door to the back bedroom hung open.

Pausing at the top of the narrow wooden stairs, Garda Cathy Connolly could just see inside, could see what looked like the entire contents of the wardrobe flung over the polished floor-boards, underwear scattered across the room like litter. The sun, winter weak, played through a window opposite the door, its light falling on something cream, illuminating it bright against the dark denim and jewel colours of the tumbled clothes on the floor.

Cathy's stomach turned again and she closed her eyes, willing the sickness to pass. There was a riot of smells up here, beeswax, ghostly layers of stale perfume, something musty. She put her gloved hand to her mouth and the smell of the latex, like nails on a blackboard, set her teeth on edge.

Until thirty-six hours ago Cathy had been persuading her-self that her incredibly heightened sense of smell and queasiness were the start of a bug. *Some bug.* But right now her problems were something she didn't have the headspace to deal with. She had a job to do. Later, when she was on her own in the gym, when it was just her and a punchbag, that was when she'd be able to think. *And boy did she have a lot to think about.*

Pulling her hand away from her mouth, Cathy impatiently pushed a dark corkscrew curl that had escaped from her pony-tail back behind her ear. Too thick to dry quickly, her hair was still damp from her early-morning training session in the pool, but that was the least of her worries. She folded her arms tightly across her chest and breathed deeply, slowly fighting her nausea. Inside her head, images of the bedroom whirled, slightly out of focus, blurred at the edges.

When the neighbour had called the station this morning, this had presented as a straightforward forced entry. That was until the lads had entered the address into the system and PULSE had thrown up a report from the same property made only the previous night. The householder, Zoë Grant, had seen a man lurking in the garden. Watching her. Cathy would put money on him doing a bit more than just watching. One of the Dún Laoghaire patrol cars had been close by, had arrived in minutes, blue strobes illuminating the lane. But the man had vanished. More than likely up the footpath that ran through the woods from the dead end of the cul-de-sac to the top of Killiney Hill.

And now someone had broken in.

It was just as well Zoë Grant hadn't been at home.

Cathy thrust her hands into the pockets of her combats and fought to focus. *Christ, she was so sick of feeling sick.* The one thing that Niall McIntyre, her coach – 'The Boss' – drilled into her at every single training session was that winning was about staying in control. Staying in control of her training; her fitness; her diet.

Staying in control of her breakfast.

And she'd got to be the Women's National Full-Contact Kick-boxing champion three times in a row by following his advice.

Below in the hallway, Cathy could hear Thirsty, the scenes-of-crime officer, bringing in his box of tricks, its steel shell reverberating off the black and white tiles as he called up to her.

'If this one *is* Quinn, O'Rourke will be delighted. Have a look at her shoes; he's got a thing about bloody shoes. Lines them up and does his thing . . .' The disgust was loud in his voice.

Trying to steady herself, Cathy took a deep breath. DI Dawson O'Rourke might be dying to nail 'Nifty' Quinn, but she knew he wouldn't be at all impressed if he could see her now. Dún Laoghaire was a new patch for him, but they went way back. And . . . *Christ, this wasn't the time to throw up.*

Shoes. Look for the shoes.

'The place is upside down, there's . . .' Her voice sounded hollow. But what could she say, there's a bad smell? No question that would bring guffaws of laughter from Thirsty. And she was quite sure no one else would be able to smell it; it was like the kitchen back at her shared house. If Decko, their landlord, or one of the other lads she rented with had left the fridge open or the lid off the bin, she couldn't even get in the door. *Thank God they hadn't noticed.* Yet. Decko fancied himself as an impersonator and there was no way she was ready to be the butt of his jokes.

Taking a deep breath, Cathy edged through the door, the heels on her boots echoing on the wooden floorboards. Downstairs she heard another voice. The neighbour this time, calling from outside the front door.

'How are you getting on?'

'Grand, thanks. A member of the detective unit is examining upstairs.' Cathy could tell from his response that Thirsty had his public smile in place. 'Any sign of Miss Grant?'

'Zoë? Not yet. I'll try her again in a minute. It's going to be an awful shock. He didn't take that big painting, did he? The old one of the harbour? I've always loved that.' The neighbour paused, then before Thirsty could comment continued: 'Is there anything I can do? Can I get you a cup of tea?'

Listening to Thirsty making small talk, Cathy focused back on the room. She needed to pull herself together and get on with this. They couldn't hold Nifty Quinn for ever. She could hear O'Rourke's voice in her head.

What had he been looking for? Cash? Jewellery? Or some sort of trophy? This didn't feel like a Nifty job to Cathy, and she'd seen enough that were. Whatever about him being picked up in the area this morning acting suspiciously, and his thing for single women, this felt different, more personal. But only Zoë Grant would know for sure if anything was missing. A lipstick? A pair of knickers?

Cathy had seen worse, but standing here in the ransacked bedroom, her six years on the force didn't help make her feel any less unclean. How would the woman who lived here feel when she got home? Someone had been in her *bedroom* . . .

Cathy scanned the tumble of fabrics on the floor. The cream silk was a misfit with the blacks, purples and embroidered blue denim. The colour of sour milk, it looked like a . . . wedding dress?

Bobbing down on her haunches, Cathy let the folds of milky fabric play through her fingers. The disturbance released more of the ancient perfume, the scent jangling like a set of keys. The silk had torn where it had caught on a nail in the wardrobe door, minute stitches unravelling along the hem, opening a deep cleft in the fabric. Tugging gently, Cathy tried to lift it from the pin. The seam widened and she caught a glimpse of something dark inside.

What the feck was that?

Whatever it was had fallen in deeper as she moved the silk. Leaning forward, Cathy teased the two edges apart with her fingertips, trying to get a better look.

She needed more light.

'Thirsty, have you got a torch down there?' Cathy's voice was too loud in the stillness of the room. Then she heard Thirsty's footsteps on the stairs and a moment later his greying head appeared in the doorway, a heavy rubber torch in his hand.

'Got something?'

'Not sure.' Frowning, she stood up to take the torch. 'There's –' A voice calling from downstairs interrupted her.

Thirsty rolled his eyes. 'Jesus, it's the bloody neighbour back. Call me if you need me.'

Cathy flashed him a grin and, crouching down again beside the pile of clothes, played the torch over them, double-checking before she went back to the dress. Looking for *what*? She wasn't sure. Fibres? Blood? She shook her head half to herself.

This was something different. She could feel it in the pit of her stomach, could feel the hairs rising on the back of her neck.

What was she expecting to find? Had the guy who had been here left some sort of gift? Like Nifty? Christ, she hoped not. Normally she could take all of that in her stride, but today she wasn't so sure.

Cathy suddenly realised she was feeling nervous – which was stupid. *What could possibly be in an old dress, in a room like this, that was making her heart pound?* She'd been in the force too long, had seen too much for this to spook her. But for some reason it was, and spooking her badly. Cathy could feel her palms sweating, absorbing the talc on the inside of her blue latex gloves. Were her hormones making her supersensitive? This was crazy.

Clearing her throat, she swung the beam of the torch onto the gap she had made in the creamy silk. There was definitely something there. Cathy eased back the seam, opening the fabric to the torchlight.

Pale grey shards. Hidden deep within the folds.

Shards of what? Something old. The rhyme took off like a kite inside her head. *Something old, something new* ... Shaking it away, she lifted the weight of the silk and, holding the torch up, slipped her fingers into the seam, prising it apart. The stitches were minute, little more than a whisper along the hemmed edge.

Then she saw them. More shards. Tiny, twig-like, tumbling as the fabric moved. And in a moment of absolute clarity she realised what they were.

And the nausea came like a tidal wave.

Bones. Tiny bones. The unmistakable slant of a jaw, the curve of a rib.

'Thirsty, I need you up here now!'

This was going to make O'Rourke's day. First the FBI – and now this.

2

'And tell me about this one?' Max Igoe indicated three canvas panels hanging on the smooth white wall of his loft office in the heart of Dublin's Temple Bar. From his art gallery below, the strains of Mozart were filtering through the polished boards, the hubbub of voices indicating that it was already getting busy. Max took a step backwards, a step closer to a young woman who was nervously fiddling with the loose ribbons on her white gypsy blouse, her ringless fingers stained blue with indigo pigment.

'It's a triptych. Three panels telling different parts of the same story.' Answering tentatively, as if she was skating on a frozen pond, Zoë Grant avoided his eye, instead focusing on the cobalt and phthalo blue-green of the tumultuous waters that raged across the canvas, iridescent white illuminated by a shaft of sunlight from the Velux window above.

'And the embroidery?'

'Originally I trained in textiles. I use a lot of stitching to add texture and life to the pieces. There's embroidery in all of them. In this one it's text.'

'*In the dark blue sea, an open shell, shy and sure. Under closed eyelids, thunder.* Nice.' Max pulled up the sleeves of his deep purple cashmere sweater and crossed his arms, looking speculatively at the pieces Zoë had brought. 'And they're all of the sea?'

The triptych was the only unframed piece, the other twenty or so paintings captured in broad, brightly coloured frames. Max rubbed the designer stubble on his chin. Zoë could feel him watching her. She'd pulled her waist-length chestnut hair back from her face with a glittering butterfly clip this morning and every time she moved her reflection was caught in the picture glass, her grey eyes two pools in pale unfreckled skin, picking up the dusky ripe plum of her long velvet skirt like the sea reflected the sky.

'Yes, always water.' It took Zoë a moment to answer Max's question. 'Everyone says a writer's work is autobiographical – it's the same with an artist. With me I suppose it's a way of getting to grips with my phobias. I've been terrified of water for as long as I can remember.' Zoë's sudden laugh was hollow. 'I'm not good with spiders either, but people prefer pictures of the sea.'

It had been after midnight the night before when she'd finally finished the last, most important piece in the collection: the triptych. Trying to blank out the roll of the waves hitting the rocks beyond the end of her garden, the sound magnified by the darkness, nagging at her like a schoolyard bully, Zoë had plunged the needle back through the painted fabric, pulling the thread taut, a blue so dark it was almost black, its triple strand parting slightly as she knotted it off. Standing, stretching her cramped body, she'd laid the final section beside its sisters, taking a moment to admire it, a maelstrom of emotions whirling in her stomach. *Would her work be good enough? Would Max Igoe like it?*

Beyond the long windows of the timber-built studio, naked trees in the neighbouring wood cast grotesque shadows on the grass. Zoë couldn't see the trees from inside – beyond the windows the garden was black, deep black. Mars black. But she knew they were there. Could feel them watching her through the glass, making the hairs stand up on the back of her neck.

Zoë had shivered. There always seemed to be someone, something, watching, waiting for her to trip. At school it had been the nuns who had hovered like great black birds ready to swoop on the smallest transgression; but they were nothing compared to Lavinia, her grandmother, her pencilled-on eyebrows raised in permanent disapproval. Nothing Zoë did was ever good enough for her.

It had been at that moment, as the shadows of the trees outside moved gently in the night air, that she'd felt rather than seen the movement in the garden. She'd reached, puzzled, to dim the studio lights and had clearly seen a man's outline stark against the weak light from the street lamp. *In her driveway.*

And she had known for sure that whoever he was, he was between her and the back door of the house.

For a moment she hadn't been able to breathe, had just stood there staring, terrified. Then she'd grabbed her phone, dialled 999, her voice shaking as she'd relayed her address to the controller.

The Guards had arrived fast, had searched the overgrown bushes with torches and nightsticks, but the man had vanished into the night as quickly as he had appeared. Part of her had begun to wonder then if he'd been there at all, if maybe it had been a trick of the shadows or of her overanxious mind. The Guards had made sure she was safely inside the house, doors and windows locked, before they left, but she hadn't been able to sleep.

Zoë pushed a stray strand of hair from her face; between that and her nervousness at the prospect of this meeting with Max, at the chance of having her first solo show in one of Dublin's most prestigious galleries, it had been a stressful twenty-four hours. And even now, even hearing – incredibly – that he liked her work, her pleasure was tinged with a sadness that ached. Even if she did have her own show, the one person who would not be there to see her success was the one person she wanted there the most – her mother.

Lavinia had made it perfectly clear right from the time that Zoë had been old enough to ask that there was no point in trying to contact her. Despite Lavinia's money, her influence, she had always refused to help whenever Zoë had brought it up. '*She didn't want you, Zoë, didn't give a damn about either of us. She's gone and that's that.*'

Her mother had abandoned her, and the pain of facing up to the reasons why had stopped Zoë from searching for her when she'd become old enough to do it on her own – up till now. Now she had a real reason to find her. Hurt and resentment swirled inside her like acid. Lavinia thought she was God and Zoë hated her for it.

Max turned to his desk to pick up his mug of coffee.

'And how long have you been painting?'

It took Zoë a moment to clear her thoughts and find an answer. Shrugging, she avoided his eye. 'Since I was in school, I suppose. My mother was an artist . . .' For a moment Zoë faltered, then, gathering herself, banishing the bad thoughts, she turned a dazzling smile on Max, her words coming out in a rush. 'My life's all about colour, how it affects your mood, how it influences behaviour. I think we all have our own palette and if you get on with someone it's because your colours complement each other – does that sound mad?'

'I'd say eccentric rather than mad, wouldn't you?' Max grinned. 'But then I'm in the image business.' He paused, his eyes meeting hers for a second before she looked away. 'What colour am I?'

'A green, I think.' Her cheeks flushing, Zoë screwed up her face in thought. 'Emerald or cobalt green perhaps.'

'The colour of money. I like it.' Max's laughter was spontaneous. 'And so tell me why you haven't had a solo exhibition up to now. Your work's really superb.'

Zoë blushed.

'I've done group shows, but I haven't had the confidence, I suppose. We're so busy at work, and I'm a bit of a perfectionist. It takes me ages to complete a painting, to be happy enough to let people see it.'

'So you've been arranging flowers for celebrity weddings, instead of focusing on your art?' There was a hint of amusement in Max's voice. He managed to make her job sound like something silly.

'No.' Zoë's voice was firm. 'I paint when I can, but the flowers are art too. My arrangements are about colour and form and matching the right flowers to the occasion. Historically there is a whole language in flowers; I like to draw on that, even if it's only in a subtle way. The type of people who come to us have huge budgets, I get to use the most beautiful flowers, to create the most amazing displays – and when we deliver them I get the satisfaction of seeing how delighted our clients are.'

'If I hadn't spotted that painting, would you have got a full collection together?'

Zoë tried hard not to look affronted. But he was right, the shop had got so busy recently that the chances of her focusing her energies to draw together enough work, and then, more importantly, getting a meeting like this, were virtually non-existent. She still couldn't quite believe it had happened, that Max Igoe of all people had seen one of her pictures and liked it so much he'd wanted to see more.

It had been such a crazy day and she'd been on her own in the shop, the phone ringing constantly. And then he'd rushed in out of the rain, soaked to the skin, needing a bouquet made up as fast as she could do it. One of her newly framed seascapes had been leaning on the wall behind the cymbidium orchids, waiting for her to get a chance to bubble-wrap it and bring it home. And while she'd been concentrating on selecting stem roses and trying to find out what colours he wanted in his bouquet, he'd started asking questions about who the artist was and where they'd exhibited and she'd found it hard to concentrate on the bouquet at all. And then, as he was paying, he'd slipped his business card in front of her and she'd found herself speechless, had just looked at him stupidly as the pieces had suddenly fallen into place.

'Eventually I would have.' Zoë smiled. 'Really. I'm sure I would. Phil loves making frames that match my paintings, from driftwood and stuff he finds on the beach, using natural dyes. It's just a slow process, and I like things to be right. The painting you saw was heading for a group show in Blackrock.'

'Well, God bless Foxrock Flowers and Framing – and God bless my inability to remember birthdays, otherwise I might never have walked in . . .'

Zoë grinned. It hadn't been the way she'd expected to land her first solo show, but as Phil had said, serendipity must have been playing a part . . .

Without warning, behind them the office door burst open with a clatter, shoved unceremoniously by the front wheel of a mountain bike. Zoë started, surprised at the interruption.

'It's all right, he's tame.' Max raised an exasperated eyebrow as a young man's head appeared in the doorway.

'You're going to have to get a lift, Maxie boy,' the new arrival cut in. 'Can't keep lugging the bike up here.'

Switching his grin to Zoë, he leaned forward to push his bike into the room, his body wedged awkwardly behind it. Rolling his eyes, Max put down his cup and moved to help, deftly pulling it inside, wheeling it across the polished wooden floor with one hand into the only corner not stacked with canvases. From the black scuff marks on the wall it looked like it was left there regularly.

'Zoë Grant, Steve Maguire.' And then by way of an explanation: 'Steve won't leave the bike downstairs in case it gets nicked.'

Steve shouldered off his pea-green messenger bag, throwing it onto one of the huge white leather sofas set on either side of a low coffee table in the middle of the office.

'Steve Maguire, owner-editor of *Scene* magazine, Dublin's hottest guide to what's happening in the city.' He said it without pausing. 'Good to meet you. I look after Max's PR for his various enterprises.'

He reached out to shake Zoë's hand. His grip lingered longer than she expected, longer than she felt completely comfortable with. His fingers were cold, long and slim; writer's hands.

'These yours?' He gestured at the paintings. 'Wow. Really powerful. Max said you were good. He wasn't joking.'

Zoë blushed faintly. Steve Maguire hardly looked old enough to have an opinion on art; he had the fresh-faced look and short, spiky, badly bleached hair of a student. And he was dressed like one too, the jeans, tatty baseball boots and denim jacket hardly appropriate for the time of year. Before Zoë could reply, Max cut in, 'Thank you, Steve, for your artistic opinion. We were rather –'

'Busy? I bet. But we need to get an interview done today. And pictures. We go to print Friday.'

'Grand, well you'd better have a quick chat with Zoë now because we're going to be busy working out the details of her exhibition for the rest of the day.'

'So, you like them?' She hardly dared say it.

Max laughed. 'I love them. And I want them in my gallery. All of them.' He paused. 'If that's OK with you?' Zoë opened her mouth to speak but before she could answer properly, somewhere on the floor behind her, a phone began ringing.

'Oh goodness, sorry, that's mine.' Zoë turned and dropped to a crouch beside her bag. The crescendo stopped just as she found the phone. Zoë rolled her eyes and was about to cram it back into her bag when it piped to tell her she had a voice message.

'You'd better get that. Sounds like someone needs you.' Max shot her an encouraging grin. 'I'll organise some more coffee while you sort yourself out. Are you OK to hang around here this afternoon so we can work out the details?' Zoë nodded. 'Of course, I'm not working today.'

'Perfect. Go ahead, pick up the message.'

Punching her keypad, Zoë put the phone self-consciously to her ear. For a moment, she looked confused. Then, as she heard the message in its entirety, Zoë's face paled.

'I'm so sorry,' she said. 'That was my neighbour. My house has been broken into. The Guards are there.' She put her hand to her forehead, not quite grasping the message.

Max's face creased with concern. 'You'd better call back, right now.'

3

One thing Cathy Connolly was absolutely sure of was that the Irish state pathologist Frank Saunders despised women. In fact, he didn't really like people full stop. He certainly didn't like dead people, or their relatives, friends or lovers. It was as if the bodies he saw every day were an inconvenience, slabs of meat on a block that had to be dealt with, rather than people with real lives, money worries, children to collect from school. So, perhaps not surprisingly, having been dragged away from his afternoon contemplation of the day's papers, the remnants of a hearty lunch distributed between his lapel and his tie, Professor Frank Saunders was not in a good mood.

'So how'd you find them, these bones? Sixth sense is it with today's Ban Gardaí?'

As he eyed Cathy over his half-moon spectacles, Professor Saunders's voice was rich with sarcasm, his use of the outdated '*Ban*' – woman – deliberately derogatory. She stared right back at him, battling the overpowering stench of pipe smoke that hung around him like the spectre of death itself, and resisted a sudden urge to give him chapter and verse on what the *Ban* Gardaí thought of short balding men with bad breath. Instead she smiled innocently.

'Just good policing, *Doctor*, exactly what they teach us at Templemore.'

Humphing like a camel with indigestion, Saunders looked away from her with thinly veiled distaste and bent to pick up his bag. Over his head Detective Inspector Dawson O'Rourke threw Cathy a congratulatory wink before turning, his face straight, to the pathologist. She grinned to herself. *Just like the old days.* It felt like a hundred years since they'd worked in the same station, but nothing had changed.

'So what can you tell us, Professor?' For a big man, O'Rourke's Monaghan accent was surprisingly soft: pasture and meadow, betraying no hint of the border violence that had spilled into his childhood.

Narrowing his eyes and puffing himself up as only a grossly overweight man of five foot two could, Professor Saunders surveyed the back bedroom of the cottage, now lit by the intense beams of two free-standing arc lights, and, turning towards the door, let loose a typical shotgun reply.

'Time of death is it you want? Do I look like the Wizard of Oz? I'm not a magician, Inspector, I can't pinpoint time of death to a plus or minus of five minutes, you know, even when we have got an intact cadaver.'

Behind the pathologist's back, O'Rourke ran his hand across his forehead, and rolled his eyes. Cathy could almost hear him saying, *Give me strength*. She stifled a smile.

'I was thinking more of a guideline on species,' O'Rourke persevered. 'Animal, vegetable, mineral? It would be a help to determine whether this is a serious crime scene, or a bride with an unusual take on the whole lucky rabbit foot thing.'

The pathologist cleared his throat noisily, a disgusting removal of mucus that sent Cathy's stomach into a neat spiral. She could feel herself turning pale again.

Choosing to ignore O'Rourke's own brand of sarcasm, Saunders stumped towards the door, throwing his answer over his shoulder like a Tudor king tossing a chicken leg. 'Human, without a doubt. Less than three months old, I'd guess. Impossible to tell gender at this stage, but we'll put everything together back at the lab and see what we have.' A shiver ran up Cathy's spine – *he made the remains sound like a jigsaw*. 'Can't tell you more than that at the moment.' He scowled at them, his face taut. 'Let's see if we can do *this one* by the book, will we, Inspector?'

The pause was too long, the air between the pathologist and O'Rourke suddenly charged with electricity. Cathy started, looking at each of them, wondering if she should hit the deck, get herself out of the crossfire she was sure was coming. *What the –?*

But O'Rourke wasn't getting it either. His eyebrows had shot up like Saunders had jabbed him with his scalpel. Saunders gave O'Rourke a hard look.

'You were probably in nappies, weren't you?' Saunders shook his head, his face relaxing marginally. 'Nineteen seventy-three, Inspector. Look it up. And let's see if we can maintain a chain of evidence, not lose anything, will we?'

A few moments later, with Saunders safely at the bottom of the stairs, O'Rourke rubbed his hand hard over his military-style buzz cut.

'What the feck was that about?'

Cathy shook her head. Nothing Saunders did made much sense to her. 'Maybe Thirsty knows. He must have joined in the seventies.'

'Whatever it was, it's got Saunders's goat.' O'Rourke grimaced and shook his head. 'But good call. They looked like rabbit bones to me.'

'Thanks, Cig.' The familiar Irish term for Inspector rolling off her tongue, Cathy hid an embarrassed smile.

'Just like old times, eh?' Relaxing, O'Rourke grinned. 'Drop the "Cig", Cat, makes me feel like a dinosaur.'

'That's what happens when you start heading for forty, it just all falls apart.'

Cathy fought to keep back her laughter. They'd met on her first night in Pearce Street Station, when straight out of the Templemore Garda Training Academy she'd been assigned to his patrol car as a rookie observer. If he'd had any qualms about partnering with a student, a girl at that, even one who stood five-nine in her socks and who would soon be powering through the WAKO full-contact kickboxing tournament circuit, Sergeant Dawson O'Rourke hadn't shown it, a fact that Cathy had always been grateful for. And she'd never forgotten his comment that night, delivered with a wry grin as he had buckled his seat belt.

'Welcome to Pearse Street. There's Templemore and there's the real world. This is where your training really starts. No smoking in the car, no country music and you'll do grand.'

Of course O'Rourke had been right; nothing could prepare you for the real job. Most nights it was same old same old: dealers and working girls, stolen cars and assaults, whiling away the quiet hours making small talk, swapping filthy jokes. But it hadn't taken Cathy long to find out that working nights in a patrol car, you formed a bond with your partner, got to know them better than you knew yourself, that you looked after them when things did kick off. Like they looked after you.

'We'd better see how Thirsty's doing on the prints.' O'Rourke paused, his face creased in a frown, his focus back on the job. 'We'll set up the incident room in Dún Laoghaire, get in a team from Shankill and Cabinteely and a task force from uniform – they can get the house-to-house started now. Let's see if anyone remembers seeing a baby around the place, and while they're at it, the lads can check to see if there's been anyone suspicious hanging about over the past few days. Any idea about the girl who lives here?'

'I had a chat to the neighbour, she reported the break-in, saw the back door ajar. Householder is a Zoë Grant, early thirties, lives alone, works in a florist up in Foxrock and she's an artist – there's a studio in the garden. Thirsty spoke to her briefly. She was in town, said she'd come straight out but she's probably got stuck in traffic.'

O'Rourke nodded. Even in his navy pinstripe suit he looked like a boxer, had the square jaw and shoulders of a street fighter, the broken nose; but that was where the similarity ended. He'd transferred out of Pearse Street before Cathy, but she knew he'd made his mark in the Emergency Response Unit in Harcourt Square, had gone on into the Criminal Assets Bureau. At thirty-six he was the country's youngest DI, and only a week into his first posting outside the city centre, it was obvious to everyone in the district why he was on the fast track, that he had the makings of Commissioner.

'Right so, let's get this show on the road.'

4

Downstairs, the cottage's front door stood open; beyond it, blue and white crime-scene tape was draped across the garden gate like a ceremonial ribbon, cracking in the stiffening breeze. Cathy shivered, but it wasn't just the November chill that was bothering her. The memory of the scent of stale perfume lingered at the back of her throat like a bad taste.

Before O'Rourke could comment, Thirsty appeared from the kitchen behind them, followed by three white-suited SOCOs from the Garda Technical Bureau in Dublin's Phoenix Park. Gathering at the foot of the stairs, they acknowledged O'Rourke with a nod. Old faces. In this job you knew everyone, had either trained with them or worked with them at some point during your service, and if you hadn't, you knew someone who had – it worked like a big puzzle, the team slotting together into a different shape on each case. O'Rourke greeted them with a grin.

'Afternoon, lads. Thanks for getting here so fast. The action's upstairs. Looks like the neighbour disturbed him before he could get down here. Lots of photos and bag the dress. You might get some prints off the fabric back at the lab – it's a good surface and it's been kept dry up there. There's a building in the garden needs looking at too.'

'No problem, Cig. Thirsty's given us the heads-up.'

O'Rourke nodded his thanks. 'What do you think, Thirsty? Reckon the break-in was Quinn? Could have been him here last night, checking her out?'

'Doesn't look like it, he was in that gouger's pub in Ballybrack until closing time, was totally langers apparently.' Thirsty grimaced. 'This guy was systematic, went through the kitchen drawers, then seems to have gone upstairs.' He paused, shaking his head. 'And her shoes are all over the place. Nifty always lines them up before he . . .'

O'Rourke rolled his eyes. Nifty Quinn's predilections were well documented. 'Get any good prints?'

'Gloves, but I'll run what we have got through AFIS. We might get lucky.'

'Grand so. Cat and I are going to have a little chat with this Grant woman as soon as she gets here. I need a quick word first, Thirsty, if you've got a minute.'

O'Rourke's conversation with Thirsty was short, the team heading upstairs with their equipment behind them. Cathy knew he'd want to find out whatever it was that Professor Saunders was alluding to quietly. The lads could be like girls with gossip, and until O'Rourke had the full picture and its impact on his investigation, he'd want to be discreet. Out of the corner of her eye she could see him nodding, his head close to Thirsty's, framed by the doorway of the living room. Moments later they were finished. O'Rourke's face was grim.

'Good to go, lads?' The SOCO waiting at the bottom of the stairs nodded. O'Rourke turned to Cathy. 'Come on, Miss.'

Outside, ducking behind the Technical Bureau van parked across the entrance to the drive, O'Rourke pulled off his gloves and the blue plastic footies covering his shoes. Following his cue, Cathy bent to peel off the plastic covering her own boots.

'I don't want to spook Miss Grant. As soon as the lads have processed the studio, we'll use that to question her. I want you to get her relaxed, establish a rapport.' O'Rourke's voice was so low Cathy could hardly hear him, but she nodded. Standing in her khaki combats, her black polo-neck sweater pulled down low to conceal the 9mm SIG Sauer and the Smith & Wesson handcuffs clipped to her belt, Cathy shivered again. 'She must know something. Is it too soon to caution her?'

O'Rourke paused, his brow furrowed. 'If she implicates herself then obviously we need to, but we'll see what she has to say first.'

Cathy nodded. Then, her voice barely a whisper, 'Reckon it was hers?'

O'Rourke balled up the plastic footies and pulled open the back door of the van to toss them inside. 'Who knows? . . . Christ, what a day.'

Cathy didn't say anything, crossed her arms tight across her chest. She had a feeling he was going to tell her exactly how bad his day had been. She was right.

'The FBI tracked this bloody Yank to Dublin airport. They've got CCTV their end of him using the victim's passport to board his flight.'

'What happened exactly?' They'd been so busy this morning Cathy had only caught snippets of the story from Thirsty and the other lads as they'd arrived.

O'Rourke paused, his scowl deepening. 'He shot a guy at the Holiday Inn near JFK, close range, body was locked in the guy's boot in the car park. Could have been there for weeks if some woman's dog hadn't gone mad – he was supposed to be on a business trip.'

'And they've got a positive ID on the suspect already?'

O'Rourke nodded. 'The FBI has been developing state-of-the-art facial recognition software. They matched the CCTV image of our man checking in to their database, but the ballistics match was the clincher. Guy's name is Angel Hierra, plenty of previous: aggravated burglary, GBH – just the sort of tourist we need.'

Cathy nodded, taking it in. 'He shot his father?'

O'Rourke rubbed his palm over his eyes. 'Yep. Old man was in his seventies, had the shit beaten out of him, then a shot to the back of the head. Execution style. Very angelic. FBI reckon Hierra went straight from there to New York and found his mark. He probably thinks he's safe for a few days at least – apparently the father lived miles from anywhere, was a bit of a recluse. He might never have been found either if he hadn't made an appointment for his life-insurance rep to call out.' The irony wasn't lost on O'Rourke. 'God only knows why he's come here though. I'd have gone to South America. Warmer.' He paused again, shaking his head half to himself.

'Angel? What sort of name is that?'

'Mexican, from Las Vegas. They've all got bloody mad names out there. Must be the sun.' O'Rourke pulled a face. 'Did Thirsty give you his description?'

Cathy nodded. 'Six foot, dark, freaky eyes. I'll check the photo when I'm back at the station. They sure he's here?'

'He got sloppy, or maybe he's just overconfident. I very much doubt he'd have expected the father's body to be found or for the Feds to get involved so quickly.' O'Rourke half-smiled, she could almost hear him thinking – *sometimes the cards fell in their favour*. 'So we know the second victim's passport and credit card were used to hire a car at Dublin airport. We picked the vehicle up going over the toll bridge. Card was used again to purchase coffee and a map at the service station on Rochestown Avenue this morning and, wait for it, to buy a kitchen knife in Tesco's. The lads are going through those CCTV tapes now.'

'How the hell did he get through immigration?'

O'Rourke stuck his hands in his trouser pockets, jangling his change, his face clouded in thought. 'Feds were quick but not that quick. Victim was Hispanic, same weight, age about right. You know what passport photos are like.' He paused. Cathy could almost see the connections forming in his brain. 'I want everyone on the alert.' He shook his head. 'Jesus, we've got no bloody DS with Griffin injured, I've got every spare mule out looking for this Angel character, and here we are with a whole new case. I haven't even got the plastic off my office chair yet. And,' O'Rourke drew the word out, 'you were right. Thirsty knew what Saunders was on about.'

Cathy could tell from the look on his face that the news wasn't good.

'In 1973 the body of a newborn baby was found in an alley in Dún Laoghaire.' O'Rourke paused, turning pale as he sucked in his breath between clenched teeth. 'It had been stabbed forty times with a knitting needle.'

'Feck it.' Cathy's hand shot to her mouth, the details of the case tumbling into her head. 'The Murphys. They lived in White's Villas. Three of the kids committed suicide, in the end. Jeez, I never even thought of it.' She paused. 'One of them jumped off the cliff at Killiney, body was found wedged behind a wall at the DART station. I'd only started secondary school then.'

'That was one of the brothers, wasn't it?'

Cathy nodded. The body had been found by workmen, had raked up the whole story again. 'Do you think this is connected? The abuse? The parents were touting their kids, all of them.'

O'Rourke frowned. 'The girl was eleven, the one that had the baby? Those bones looked old to me . . . What age do you reckon Zoë Grant is?'

'Early thirties?' It wasn't much more than a whisper. 'The Murphy girl claimed she'd had another one afterwards, that they'd buried it in the garden.'

O'Rourke nodded. It had happened a long time ago but it was one of those cases. And not just because of the horror, the abuse, but because no one had ever been brought to trial, and then, when the mother of the child had turned up to spill the whole story, the files had gone missing . . .

'I don't care what we find here, Cat, this investigation is going to be run right. Nothing gets lost, nothing mislaid. Nothing.' O'Rourke was talking more to himself than to her, had his eyes fixed on the ground like he was running the press reports, the internal gossip through his head. 'I don't know why I didn't make the connection before Saunders said it. The press won't be so slow – they'll have a field day if they hear that the bones of a baby have been found in Dalkey again – they're going to give us enough of a pasting over this bloody Hierra character walking right through immigration.' O'Rourke's steel-blue eyes met Cathy's. 'This goes nowhere. I'm going to have a chat to Thirsty, to the Techs – the details of this one are need-to-know only. I don't want any leaks.'

Nodding, Cathy bit her lip. During her four years in uniform and two as a detective, she'd seen plenty of dead bodies in various states of disrepair, sights that would haunt most people, but the Dalkey baby case, as the press had dubbed it, had been about as bad as it got. Like this one, when she'd first heard about it, it had creeped her out, made her feel incredibly sad. Children trusted the adults around them to provide food and warmth, love and protection. *And when that trust was betrayed . . .*

Older officers often muttered about every detective having a weak point, a case that gave them nightmares. Cathy crossed her fingers behind her back, hoped to God that this case wasn't it for her.

'If it was Zoë Grant's child and something similar happened, she'll be pretty badly damaged.' O'Rourke's voice was low, communicating his own struggle with the situation.

'Assuming she knew the bones were there, she obviously didn't expect us to find them or she'd have got here a whole lot quicker when she heard about the break-in.'

O'Rourke grimaced. 'Indeed. And quite how or whether the break-in is connected to the bones, God only knows. Can't see how though, more likely a bizarre coincidence.'

Cathy bit her lip. She didn't believe in coincidence. But then again, the last place they'd think to search after a forced entry was the hem of anything, let alone a wedding dress.

'But what's with the dress?' Cathy's voice came out sounding more desperate than she intended. She shuddered – *maybe this was better than ending up in a plastic carrier bag in an alley, or being buried in the garden . . .* the thought of a tiny corpse dumped into cold damp soil sent chills up her spine . . . *but a wedding dress?* 'Why stitch a baby's bones into the hem of a wedding dress for God's sake? Whoever did it must be an absolute nutter.'

Before O'Rourke could answer, the Guard who was stationed in the front garden appeared around the side of the van.

'She's here. Just drove up, looks like she's having a panic attack.'

5

It was cold in Bethnal Green. And grey. A sort of non-stop greyness that covered London like a dirty woollen blanket. Emily Cox pulled the front door of their four-storey Georgian terraced house behind her and hooked her straw-coloured bob behind her ear. Despite the hooded, fur-lined parka she was wearing, Emily felt chilled. *Who'd have believed that the weather was so much better in Boston?* Gritting her teeth against the spectre of depression that followed her like a shadow, Emily reached determinedly for the positive.

For now London was home; and it had plenty to offer to make up for the damp, dreary weather. Bethnal Green was a wonderful hotchpotch of colour and culture that billowed across the grey like a multicoloured sari. She'd found a job easily – occupational therapists were always in demand – and Tony was really happy too in his new role as consultant psychiatrist at St Thomas's Hospital, which had been the ideal next move for him. She'd made friends, everything was perfect. Almost.

Hitching the leather handles of her basket onto her shoulder, Emily headed across the road, past Bethnal Green Tube station, and on down to the bright lights of the street market that crowded along the Whitechapel Road.

'Morning, Mrs Cox. What can we do you for?'

The fruit and vegetable seller greeted Emily with a huge smile as she reached his stall, striped red and white plastic sheeting flapping noisily behind him in the stiff breeze.

'My old mum said to say hello when I saw you,' he said. 'She's doing salsa dancing now, says she's going to knock 'em dead when she goes on her coach tour.'

Emily laughed out loud, her mood lifting. 'Make sure she doesn't overdo it or she'll need to get the other hip done too!' Her Donegal accent was distinctive against the cadences of the East End.

'That's what I keep telling her, Mrs C, but will she listen? "Super Gran", my boys call her.'

His boys. A sense of longing clawed at her heart. Emily skirted swiftly around the thought. 'Would she come and do a demonstration for the lunch club? Show them what a difference doing the exercises makes?'

'No problem, Mrs C, I'll ask her.' Leaning over, the fruit and veg man picked up an orange from the display in front of him, spinning it high into the air, catching it easily in his huge hand. 'How about some of these lovely oranges today? Sweet enough even for you I reckon, Mrs Cox. Oi! What are you –?'

Without breaking for breath, the fruit and veg man switched from flirting to roaring, and dodged out from behind the stall. Emily spun around to see him pounding after a youth in a hooded sweat top who was weaving through the oncoming crowd, making for Whitechapel Tube station, an old-fashioned handbag shoved under his arm.

The whole event must only have taken a second, but Emily felt like she was watching it in slow motion, the sight of the fleeing youth sending a chill to her core. In a series of freeze frames Emily's mind flicked through images stamped onto her memory: *leaves falling at her feet, the boy in the hoody bumping into her, jostling, grabbing her bag. Then the pain. Waking in the hospital, dazzling white, the odour of bleach sticking in her throat.*

Dizzy, feeling the crowd close in around her, Emily steadied herself on the edge of the stall. Dark shapes, dark and pale faces merged into one. Then an elderly Indian gentleman was heading towards her, helping an even older lady through the tight knot of onlookers. The old lady was trembling violently, her pale blue eyes full of tears, unfocused.

It took Emily a moment, but then she recognised her.

'Mary? My goodness, what happened?' She hurried to slip her arm around the old woman's waist; her body was featherlike, so fragile that Emily felt she might snap.

The fruit and veg man's assistant took charge. ''Ere's a chair, let's get 'er sat down. That's right, mind the boxes. Don't want you having a tumble.' He briskly pulled out a folding canvas chair, guiding them into the back of the stall. Moments later another stallholder appeared with a polystyrene cup of hot tea.

'That's the ticket; need something sweet after a shock like that.'

Lowering the old lady into the chair, Emily slipped her basket off her shoulder and bobbed down in front of her, her brown eyes filled with concern. She blew on the steaming tea before guiding it to Mary's lips. After a few seconds, the colour began to return to her cheeks, but Mary's face remained bewildered, her fear raw. And Emily was sure Mary didn't recognise her from the church, from the flower-arranging group Emily had been running as part of their outreach programme for the elderly. Taking the half-finished cup, Emily put it safely on the ground, gently rubbing Mary's freezing hands in her own.

'My bag, he took my bag. I need to find it – my keys . . .' Mary tried to struggle up from the chair, her eyes wide with panic.

'Don't worry about that now, just sit down for a minute; you've had a bad fright.'

'Is this it, Mrs?' The fruit and veg man appeared behind them, a blue vinyl handbag in his huge hand. Mary's relief was palpable.

'Oh, thank you, thank you so much. What's your name?'

'No problem, Mrs. And it's Johnny – Johnny Rotten they call me down here. Think they're being funny, with the fruit and that.' If she hadn't been so worried about Mary, Emily would have laughed. Johnny continued, 'Got him down by the Tube – couple of bobbies have him now. I don't think he had a chance to open it.'

Looking up at him towering above her, Mary's voice was suddenly smaller, exhausted. 'Oh thank you, thank you.'

'No problem, love. Just you have a good look and make sure nothing's missing.'

Her hands still shaking, Mary manipulated open the worn silver catch on the frame of the bag, slipping her hand inside to check the contents. 'Oh thank goodness, I think everything's here. Thank you so much, young man, you don't know what it means to get it back.'

Surprised by her soft ladylike accent, Johnny gave Mary a curt nod, blushing. 'Better get you home, I think. Are you nearby?'

'You're just on Roman Road, aren't you, Mary?' Emily looked to Mary for confirmation. 'We'll get a cab.'

'Goodo. I'll pack you up a box. Bit of vitamin C's what you need after a scare like that.'

Mary started to refuse, but he shook his head.

'No arguments.'

As the black cab pulled up outside Renmore House, a squat red brick building, railings council blue, Emily reached for her purse, but the cabbie shook his head.

'No need for that, I'm a pal of Johnny's and I heard you fixed up his old mum right proper with your exercise classes. I'll bring that box of fruit in.'

Helping Mary slowly through the door of the flat, Emily could hear the cabbie putting the box of fruit down in the kitchen, the slosh of water as he turned on the tap and filled the kettle. He stuck his head out as they passed the kitchen door.

'Kettle's on, I'll leave you to it, love. I'll let Johnny know you got home safe.'

Emily smiled, about to thank him again, but a moment later she heard the front door close gently, the lock clicking into place.

Helping Mary into a worn velour armchair, so big it seemed to swallow her up, Emily was surprised to see that the living room of the one-bedroom flat was almost bare. Apart from the sofa and chairs and a tiny portable television in the corner, there was little to suggest that anyone lived here at all. Before Emily could think any more about it, she heard the kettle click off.

'Let me get that tea, it'll warm you up.'

Leaving Mary clutching her bag to her chest, Emily discovered that the kitchen was as spartan as the living room. And Mary's fridge was empty too. A small carton of milk in the door, a piece of cheese and a pork chop congealing on a plate. Turning to look at the crate of fruit and vegetables on the table, Emily felt a tear of gratitude prick her eye. Johnny didn't know it, but if the fruit could keep that long it looked like it would feed Mary for a year.

Suddenly Emily felt a hand on her arm. Mary had followed her into the kitchen, her face flushed, eyes bright.

'He was here again, I can smell his cigars.'

Surprised, Emily looked around, sniffing the air. *Damp, the stale odour of unwashed floors. Definitely no cigars.* Before she could reply, Mary chuckled, 'He's a devil, you know, with those cigars, and that hat, my goodness, such style.'

Taking Mary's arm, guiding her gently back towards the living room, Emily sat her down again in her chair, bobbing down beside her. 'Who was here, Mary?'

Mary shook her head and a flash of anger crossed her face. 'It doesn't matter now, does it? It's all finished now. It's her fault. She wanted him for herself, sent me away.' Then, her voice cracking with bitterness and despair, 'It's all her fault, all of it . . .'

'It's OK, Mary; I'm here, it's OK.' Concerned and slightly shaken, Emily stroked her arm, worry pricking at her like a needle. Mary had been a bit confused when she'd met her at her class. It wasn't unusual amongst the elderly people she dealt with, but she had never been this bad. It was as if the attack had triggered her memories to tangle themselves with the present, like reels of thread unravelling in a box.

The moment passed and Mary became calm, as if her frayed edges had been neatly turned in, hidden from view. When Mary spoke again, she was coy, confiding, her voice soft, wistful. 'He's French, you know. So charming. A *count*. The society papers love him.' Then, as suddenly as she had slipped from the here and now, she was back as if nothing had happened, shivering, her face fearful again. 'Could you bring my shawl, dear? It's in the bedroom.'

'Of course.' Her brow creased with worry, Emily patted Mary's arm. *She'd need to get Tony to see her.* She was quite sure the trauma of being attacked in the street was doing nothing for Mary's obviously delicate mental state.

'I'll be right back with it and we'll get the tea in the pot.'

Crossing the narrow hall to the bedroom, her mind half on the lack of food in the flat, half on Mary's attack, on her talk of cigars and a French count, Emily pushed the door open. And stopped dead, a gasp of surprise caught in her throat.

The tiny room was dim, illuminated by the light falling from the hallway behind her, from a crack in the thin curtains where weak sunlight shone through. But it was enough to see that the floor was piled with hundreds of plastic bags, crammed full with a jumble of what appeared to be clothing. Patterns and plains, chintz and brocade, the stench of stale fabric made Emily gag for a moment, the contrast between the meagre contents of the rest of the flat and this room, stuffed to bursting like the back room of a charity shop, somehow shocking.

Fumbling for the light switch, Emily turned her focus from the bags, looking for Mary's shawl. Covered with a patchwork quilt, the bed huddled against the far wall. As Emily forced a path through the bags of fabric, she could see a pair of rag dolls, tucked in beside the pillow, their faces exquisitely embroidered with stitches so tiny that they looked almost alive. One was dressed in a smart pinafore, yellow wool plaits ending in matching ribbons, the other, its hair a mass of short lengths of chunky wool, wore matching dungarees. And in the middle of the pillow lay a circular nightdress case, cream silk, its embroidered cover a riot of flowers and leaves intertwining. As she studied it, Emily realised that the trailing fronds formed letters written with a flowing hand, each letter linking with the next to form a word – it looked like 'grace'.

The verse on the terracotta wall plaque her mother had positioned just inside her hall door sprang straight into Emily's mind: *Plenty and grace be to this place.* Was Mary hoping for grace, for elegance and good manners, or for forgiveness?

A soft green shawl lay across the end of the bed. Emily picked it up and retraced her steps through the bags of fabric to the bedroom door. The old lady had returned to the living room, was sitting on the edge of the armchair, her arms crossed around herself.

'Here we are, Mary.' Emily wrapped the shawl around her shoulders.

'Thank you, my dear.' Mary smiled. 'But my name's not Mary.'

6

Angel Hierra leaned against the cheap ply door of his hotel room and let out a deep breath. A breath laced with tequila and anger. He'd never been good at keeping his temper. How often had he heard his father say that he had his mother's Latin temperament; that he only got away with half the shit he got himself into because he had her dark good looks as well?

His father. Hierra could feel his lip curling, the bitter taste of bile rising in his mouth. Even now the thought of his old man made Hierra mad. Worse than mad. Something inside him lurched, the memories of that day rising like a foul tide, rancid and stinking. How long had he lain paralysed with fear, huddled beside his mother's unconscious body, sure she was dead, the temperature inside the trailer increasing until he was almost suffocating, his bruised body aching with despair and helplessness?

Hierra had never dreamed he'd be glad to hear the landlord pounding on the trailer door, grateful to see his pockmarked face leering through the window.

But angels come in many guises. His mother's voice came to him now like a draught, chilling his skin despite his heavy coat, the hand-stitched wool suit. Automatically, he crossed himself. That was the day he'd started hating his father. Really hating him. The day he, Angel Hierra, had decided to get even. It had been his fifth birthday.

Hierra balled the saliva in his mouth and spat onto the stained grey carpet, wiped the back of his hand across his mouth.

Getting even had taken a bit longer than he'd planned, but he was glad about that now. He'd never have gotten the full picture if he'd done it sooner. His mom had loved the bastard until the end. *Santa Maria, how fucking stupid was that?* Through the beating and the whoring, she'd loved him.

Hierra closed his eyes, trying to push the memories aside, to focus on the plan. But what he'd seen today had made him hate the old man all over again. What had he and his mom had? A fucking beat-up trailer in the worst part of town ... *Holy Mother* ... Hierra shook his head, and pushed himself away from the door.

The room he was in now was cheap, basic, the carpet stains blackened with age, the paint chipped. But he wasn't after luxury, or a sea view. Just anonymity. And tucked away in the back streets of Dún Laoghaire, this place was perfect. Clarinda Park had been grand once, but now the Georgian terraces were divided into flats and bedsits operated by faceless agencies, populated by a transient population of foreign students and migrant workers. *Exactly what he needed.*

He'd parked in the centre of the square watching people coming and going, their heads down, minding their own business. The sign outside, faded and peeling, said 'Hotel' but it was stretching the point. Inside, the reception area stank of damp and BO, the fat tart slumped behind a dimpled glass partition hardly turning her head from the TV when he'd walked in, barking out the price and pointing to the register, a biro attached to it with tape and greying string. She never once looked him in the eye.

Fine by him. Oh yes. Fine by him.

The Samsonite suitcase was still on the bed where Hierra had thrown it when he arrived. He hadn't gone through it properly yet, had just had a cursory glance, pulled out the suit he was wearing, made sure the basics were in there – a change of jocks, clean pants – before slipping out of the room to find the fire escape, to get his bearings. He knew he didn't have much time before the cops caught up with him, wanted to get things moving as fast as possible, didn't intend to be in Ireland any longer than was absolutely necessary to get what he needed.

Throwing back the lid, Hierra pulled out a couple of shirts, identical to the one he was wearing, threw them onto the nylon bedspread. Crisply folded and ironed, under them corduroy pants, a turtleneck sweater, a pair of loafers, clean socks balled inside. *The guy's wife was good, had thought of everything.* Hierra checked the size, couldn't resist a grin. A half-size too big, but very serviceable. He'd chosen his mark well. The heavy woollen overcoat was a perfect fit too, and just as well – he shivered – it was fucking freezing in this miserable damp hole of a country. It was easy to see why so many Irish left.

At the bottom of the case, Hierra spotted a black leatherette washbag. He doubted the cops would be on to him yet, but if they had spotted him coming through customs they'd have him on camera with the moustache and goatee he'd been growing for the past few days. If he got rid of that and shaved his thick dark hair down to a buzz cut, used the cheek pads, he knew he could alter his whole appearance. Unzipping the washbag, he checked the contents. Deodorant, shaving soap, razor. And at the bottom of the bag a single gold ring. Hierra pulled it out.

A wedding ring.

Now why had he taken that off? Amused, Hierra rolled it in his palm, the gold heavy, chunky, engraved on the inside. Slipped it on, admiring his hand. He could sell it later, but until then it might come in useful. *So the guy must have had some other business here as well as the conference.* Now that was a bit of luck. Hierra grinned – he'd wondered why the guy had been coming over so soon: according to the crap in his briefcase, the conference didn't start for another week. So no one was going to miss him for another few days at least, and whoever he was meeting was hardly going to call his wife and ask why he'd been delayed. Neat.

In fact, finding the mark had been pretty neat altogether – Hierra had hung around the Holiday Inn looking for someone going to London, had reckoned that it would be easy enough from there to get into Ireland by ferry or on a fishing boat. And then he'd heard the guy talking about Dublin, about some con-ference . . . *Angels come in many guises.*

Hierra slipped the ring off and tossed it in his hand. *It gave him all the time he needed.* He'd collect the cash tomorrow and get out. Things had gone well today, better than he'd expected. The moment he'd started talking to the old bitch, mentioned a few names, Hierra had known he had plenty of leverage. The old man had spilled the whole lot already, but he was a two-faced lying bastard, and Hierra wouldn't have been surprised if he'd been lying even then, on his knees, with a gun to his head and no place to run.

A little bit of Hierra still couldn't believe it, but the pieces were coming together like patchwork. As soon as he'd shaved and fixed his hair, he'd get back over there to keep an eye on things. He had the keys to the houses now, both of them, could let himself in any time, but it was the cash he needed. He didn't have the time to start fencing a load of stuff, even if it was top quality like that painting. He'd only had time to glance at it but had known immediately that it was the same one the guy doing the interview for *Vanity Fair* had almost pissed himself over. He'd schlepped on and on and on about it in the article. But the painting would be a last resort. What he needed was cash and maybe a bit of jewellery and then he could get over to Bogotá and set himself up. There was no way Kuteli would find him there.

He'd have to sort her out first, of course, but that wasn't a problem.

La revancha. Payback.

7

It was four o'clock by the time the scenes-of-crime team had finished processing the studio, and it was already beginning to grow dark. O'Rourke's phone rang as Cathy escorted Zoë Grant past the back door of her cottage; he waved them on ahead, holding up a finger indicating he'd only be a minute. Above them a security light flicked on, making the shadows blacker, the trees whispering above them as if they were trying to speak. For a moment Cathy wished she'd grabbed her leather jacket from the car, but it would stink of Thirsty's fags by now and Cathy didn't think she could handle smelling like an ashtray, no matter how cold she was.

The studio was surprisingly warm considering the temperature outside, and inside the scents were just as strong as in the house; different, but enough to make Cathy recoil as she entered. Sour paint, overlaid with something chemical, heady; turps or white spirit maybe. And lilies. A huge bunch of white lilies dominated the counter at the far end of the studio, their strong perfume adding to the overpowering mix. *She really hoped this wouldn't be a long interview.*

'Inspector O'Rourke won't be long.' It sounded odd to her ear, 'Inspector'. Formal, stiff. Back in the day she'd called him O'Rourke and he'd called her Cat – Kitty Cat when he was teasing her. Cathy sighed inwardly. They were friends, had shared stuff that no one could ever understand. In a moment her mind was back in a badly lit industrial estate, a confusion of sounds swamping her: shouting, gunshots. Pain. Cathy took a shaky breath, pushing it from her mind. She couldn't go there now, she needed to focus on this case, on this moment. On getting it right.

This was the first time she and O'Rourke had been in the same station since Pearse Street, but she wasn't surprised to find they'd slotted right back in where they'd left off, easy in each other's company, each understanding what the other was thinking. Promotion had come fast for him and they'd moved into different divisions – they'd kept in touch, been out for drinks a couple of times, talking late into the night in the secluded corners of hotel bars, had met at parties. *Parties.* Cathy's stomach dropped; the last party she'd been to hadn't turned out at all like she'd expected. A dark shadow of regret began to grow inside her. *So much had happened . . .*

Fighting to bring her focus back to Zoë Grant, Cathy forced a smile, struggling to look friendly. Zoë was standing in front of a huge angled drawing board, tidying an already tidy pile of coloured papers, each one decorated with sketches and blobs of colour, with pieces of fabric that had been painted and stitched. As she moved, Cathy caught sight of an unframed painting under the drawing board, the canvas casually leaning against the end of the counter beside it. It was of the sea, predominantly pale grey, streaks of white suggesting breaking waves and clouds, seagulls smudges on the horizon. The brushstrokes captured the movement and danger of a storm so skilfully it almost took Cathy's breath away.

'Is that one of your paintings? It's amazing.'

Zoë looked to where Cathy had pointed. 'Yes. And thank you' – Zoë paused, her tone curt – 'but it needs more work.'

Needs more work? Cathy wasn't an expert on art but she knew what she liked, and she understood enough about proportions and balance to know a brilliant painting when she saw it. And this painting wasn't even about balance and proportion, it was about emotion, and, Cathy was sure, fear. Each brushstroke communicating part of a story about the power of the sea, about man's fragility. *What was Zoë Grant afraid of?*

Hardly aware of Cathy's reaction to the painting, Zoë's eyes darted nervously back to the house. 'My neighbour said there was a break-in. I don't understand – why are there so many vans and cars? Is it because of the man in the garden last night?' Zoë trailed off, and seeing the pile of papers she was fiddling with was perfectly aligned, turned to lean back on the drawing board, her arms crossed tight. 'I couldn't believe it when I picked up the message.'

'Why don't you sit down?' Cathy caught her breath; she needed O'Rourke here before the questioning started. She'd have to waffle a bit, give him a chance to finish his call. 'I'm afraid whoever it was left upstairs in a bit of a mess.'

'My laptop! I left it in the living room.' Zoë's hand flew to her mouth.

'I'll get the lads to check for the computer, but it doesn't look like he had time to get into the front room.'

Zoë nodded, her long earrings catching the light from the overhead spots. Then, almost in a whisper, 'Do you know who it was, last night? He was watching me, I'm sure.'

Cathy shook her head. 'We don't know yet. It's possible it's a coincidence.' *Better not to spook her too much, but there was that word again, 'coincidence'.*

As Cathy spoke, the security light flicked on and O'Rourke appeared winding his way down the garden, dipping his head under the branches overhanging the crazy-paved path. He held a steaming mug of tea in each hand, his pale pink silk tie flapping over his shoulder. Cathy turned to open the door for him. He handed Zoë a mug, passed the other to Cathy, catching her eye, a moment of understanding passing between them, then pulled out a stool from under the drawing board. Cathy took a sip. She hadn't realised how much she needed it. *And O'Rourke had remembered she took sugar.*

Hovering by the door, happier to stay standing, her hands around the mug, Cathy tried to keep her face open and warm. She wasn't sure what she had expected, but Zoë Grant had one of those exclusive south Dublin private-school accents she was very familiar with. Landing a full scholarship, she'd attended a school like it herself, as a day pupil, but she'd been the only girl in her year who lived in a council house. Her friends were great, but they were all 'Port Out, Starboard Home', as her dad always said when he picked her up from a hockey match before his shift started at the pub, his ancient Nissan no match for brand-new Jaguars and Mercs, however lovingly it was kept.

Cathy glanced at O'Rourke. By rights, he should be taking the lead, but he was relaxed, was quietly studying Zoë Grant, his almost imperceptible nod giving Cathy the go-ahead. *Start with the easy questions.* She could hear his voice echoing back from the past.

'This is a lovely place to paint; do you spend a lot of time down here?'

It took Zoë a few moments to reply; she sipped her tea before she spoke. 'I wish I could spend more time here. You wouldn't think the flower business would be busy at this time of year, but we seem to be non-stop.' Zoë paused. 'I play here too when I get a chance.' She nodded towards a musical instrument case dominating the space beside the filing cabinet, a double bass or a cello.

'Where do you work?' The neighbour had told Cathy pretty much everything there was to know about Zoë Grant: that she arranged flowers for South County Dublin's wealthy elite, that it was always her flowers that featured in *OK!* magazine. That there was no current boyfriend on the scene. But Cathy needed to hear it from her.

'I work in Foxrock, in the florist's shop there. We do a lot of TV and magazine work as well as weddings and events, anything you need flowers for really.'

'But you prefer to paint?'

Zoë pursed her lips as if she found Cathy's lack of understanding annoying. 'I love to paint, but I love flowers as well. An arrangement should be art too. It's like sculpture, three-dimensional – four if you design with scent in mind as well as form.'

Well, that put her in her place. O'Rourke diffused the hint of tension. 'Have you lived here long?'

'About ten years. I bought it while I was in college.'

Cathy felt her eyebrows shoot up. She'd been right in thinking there was money in Zoë Grant's family, and lots of it obviously. Dalkey was one of the most expensive villages in County Dublin.

'Old properties are a labour of love, aren't they?' O'Rourke made it sound like he knew all about it.

Zoë nodded distractedly. 'Everything goes wrong. The builders had to get all the plumbing redone as well as the rewiring. Then all the windows had to be replaced. And finding someone who could make new sashes took for ever.'

O'Rourke grinned in sympathy – *like he cared.* 'We noticed you had a dress upstairs. Cream silk. Tell me a bit about that.'

Cathy hid a smile in her mug. *He'd never been good at small talk.* He was managing to hide his impatience from Zoë but Cathy knew if he'd had a tail it would have been flicking from side to side, like a cat eyeing its prey.

For a moment Zoë looked blank, a shadow passing across her face. It took her a moment to answer.

'The wedding dress? It was my mother's.' She paused, her thick brows knitted together in a frown as her gaze flicked up to her bedroom window. Cathy waited. *What would Zoë say? Would she mention the bones, could she explain them? Did she even know they were there?*

'Have you had it long?' O'Rourke again, his voice casual.

But she wasn't giving anything away. 'I've had it for years. I don't quite know what to do with it.' She paused. 'I can't believe this has happened today. I was in the middle of an interview for an exhibition when I got the message.'

Cathy was getting the feeling that Zoë Grant was somehow disconnected from the here and now, in her head at least. Cathy knew that if a crazed stalker had just broken into her home, and into her bedroom at that, she'd be seriously pissed off – but maybe that was her fight instinct coming through, her ability to turn fear into anger one factor that had helped her keep her title. Zoë was different, but her reaction was still strange though. Cathy had seen a lot of people in shock: usually they became catatonic, staring into space, or talked incessantly. Zoë Grant was doing neither. Maybe she was just a good actress.

O'Rourke said sympathetically, 'I'm afraid the back bedroom got a good going-over. It's a bit of a mess.'

'That's my room.' Zoë glanced nervously up to the window again, watching intently as dark figures moved around inside.

'Do you have family nearby? You'll need to stay somewhere else tonight.' Cathy's turn, her cue unspoken. Sometimes she wondered if O'Rourke could read her mind as well as she could read his.

Zoë continued to look out into the garden as if she wasn't listening, then, snapping her head around, stared at them both intensely for a moment.

'No. I mean there's just my grandmother. My mother doesn't live here. She's . . . abroad. She lives abroad.' The words seemed to stall in her throat. Then, 'My grandmother said she's probably in Paris.'

'I see.' O'Rourke nodded. Cathy could tell he didn't see at all. How could Zoë Grant not know where her mother was living? From the way she was behaving, Cathy would put a week's pay on her trying not to tell them something. And O'Rourke was like a terrier when he caught the whiff of an untruth.

'Is there anyone else you could call – another relative or a friend?'

Zoë's jaw tightened. 'Just my grandmother . . . But look, I'm sure I'll be fine here. He's not going to come back, is he? Not now there have been Guards everywhere.'

Cathy hid her surprise. Whatever about not wanting to stay with her grandmother, most women would be terrified at the thought of spending the night alone in a house that had just been broken into. Never mind the fact that someone had been hanging about, in the dark, only the previous night. Didn't she have any friends, someone else she could stay with?

What was really going on here?

Cathy felt a blast of irritation. The studio was too warm and she was starting to feel claustrophobic. Leaning on the cool glass of the door, Cathy pulled out a fine-bead chain from the neck of her sweater and began to play its oval silver dog-tag pendant along the length, her eyes on Zoë. O'Rourke glanced at her, their thoughts crossing for a second. *It was time to crank it up or they'd be here all night.*

O'Rourke's face betrayed nothing as he considered the best way to give Zoë the bigger picture. He knew as well as Cathy did that there'd be no chance Zoë would get back into the house tonight.

'I would be surprised if he came back tonight. But we might not be able to release the house just yet; it might be the morning before we finish processing everything.' O'Rourke paused, watching Zoë's reaction. *Nothing.* 'You see we found something else while we were examining the scene of the burglary. In the hem of that dress we mentioned.'

Pulling at the ribbons on her blouse, Zoë looked confused, her eyebrows knotted, waiting for him to continue.

'There were' – O'Rourke chose his words carefully – 'some bones stitched into the hem.'

'Bones?' Zoë screwed up her nose. Then after a long pause she said, 'What kind of bones? I thought they used metal weights in the hems of dresses. Surely bones would be too light?'

Running her pendant slowly along its chain, Cathy could feel the hairs rising on the back of her neck at Zoë's reaction – had she rehearsed it? Had she spent ages working out a way of explaining away the murder of a baby?

A baby.

A real little person who hadn't asked to arrive in the world.

Cathy put her fingertips to her temple, trying to massage away the pressure she could feel growing there. *Oh holy God, how could she have been so stupid?*

It wasn't like she didn't know about safe sex, that she didn't know the pill's effectiveness could be affected by all sorts of things, like taking antibiotics – *or forgetting to take it*. It had only been one day, and instead of taking it in the morning she'd remembered late that night – well maybe technically it had been the next morning, but she'd taken the damn thing.

Cathy breathed deeply, trying to quell the panic that was starting to rise in her chest. Obviously they should have used a condom, that was the bottom line, pill or no pill. But sometimes you don't plan for stuff to happen, there's just a spark and it starts a fire and it's happening before you know it, too fast and intense to stop. She hadn't even thought of a condom at the time, had been so caught up in the moment *she hadn't even thought.* Niall McIntyre, The Boss, was always telling her she was too impulsive, that she followed her heart when she had a damn good head that she really should check in with more often.

Was that what had happened to this baby's mother?

Cathy pinched the bridge of her nose, glanced over at O'Rourke, who was looking hard at Zoë, waiting for her to answer – *what had he asked her?* Feck, she needed to get back with it.

'There's boning in the bodice.' Zoë shrugged her shoulders in answer to O'Rourke's question, like it was nothing to do with her. 'Maybe the bones slipped down into the lining?' She had her head on one side, her face puzzled. *Was she really not getting it or was she being deliberately evasive? Perhaps she really didn't know the bones were there?* In any investigation everyone was a suspect until they could be conclusively ruled out, and Cathy had a feeling it would be a while before they would be ready to take Zoë off the list.

'Maybe.' O'Rourke didn't sound convinced by Zoë's suggestion.

'So your mother gave you the dress?' Cathy tried to keep her voice relaxed, to hide her irritation. 'When was that exactly?'

'About ten years ago, maybe more, I'm not sure.'

'And was your mother living here then?'

Zoë faltered for a second. 'Well, actually no.'

'So she came home to Ireland and gave you the dress?'

Zoë seemed to be struggling with the facts. 'No. My grandmother gave it to me, but it was my mother's dress.'

'OK' – Cathy said it slowly, like she was talking to a child – 'and your mother was aware that your grandmother was giving it to you?'

'Look, I really don't know. Does it matter? It's only a dress.' Zoë's face was beginning to flush.

'We just want to establish the chain of events that brought the dress into your possession.' O'Rourke's voice had an edge to it.

'Your grandmother, does she live here in Ireland?' Striving to keep her voice friendly, Cathy moved to take her weight off the door as she spoke. Her gun was digging into her hip where it was sandwiched against the glass. It wasn't helping her mood.

Zoë seemed to know the answer to this one: 'Yes. In Monkstown.'

'And is she here in Ireland, in Monkstown, at the moment?' Cathy knew she sounded sarcastic but she was reaching the end of her patience.

'Yes. She lives there.' Zoë paused. 'She's Lavinia Grant.'

Cathy paused, working on keeping her eyebrows from shooting up, working hard to keep her face straight. She hadn't expected that. It only lasted for a second, but suddenly the silence in the studio was deafening. Cathy could hear her own heartbeat, the creak of O'Rourke's shoe leather as he shifted on the stool. She caught a faint whiff of his aftershave, suddenly sure it was CK One, the same one she'd given him that Christmas. He must be feeling the heat too.

'The Lavinia Grant of Grant Valentine?' Cathy fought to keep the surprise from her voice. She might not have the cash to throw away on designer gear, but she read *Image* and *VIP* like every other twenty-something, leafed through the social pages to see what the A-list were wearing. And Lavinia Grant was the doyenne of Irish fashion, Grant Valentine a chain of department stores that rivalled Harvey Nichols, whose name had been part of Irish culture since the fifties when no one had any money and children walked barefoot to school to save their shoe leather. In the heat of the Celtic Tiger's roar, Grant Valentine had opened up in New York and Toronto, already had stores in Belfast and London.

Zoë gave a sharp nod, her voice suddenly colourless. 'Yes, that Lavinia Grant.'

O'Rourke cleared his throat again – Cathy knew exactly what he was thinking. He could already hear the media banging on his door – this was all he needed.

8

Catching his breath, Consultant Psychiatrist Tony Cox shook mercurial raindrops from his shoulders and greeted his wife Emily with a hug and a peck on her cheek.

'So how has she been since the mugging? Any progress? It's been a few days.'

St Anthony's basement community hall in London's Bethnal Green was already filling up, the scraping of chairs and the chink of cutlery on china making it hard for him to hear her reply. But he could see Emily was frowning, her brown eyes clouded.

'She's still very confused. And I can't find anyone who knows her history. She told me she was from Dublin, and she sounds educated, but at the moment she's not even sure of her own name. You'll see for yourself.' Emily grasped Tony's hand, leading him through the increasingly packed trestle tables, the rich scents of cake heavy in the air. 'I've set her up over here where it's a bit quieter.'

Without make-up, her hair pulled back into a ponytail, Emily's jeans and trainers made her look like a teenager, made Tony, at almost fifty, wonder yet again what on earth she saw in him – and thankful, again, that his dark wavy hair was all his own. Even if it did need a good cut. Today Emily's pale skin was flushed from the rising heat as more elderly local residents arrived, looking forward to their monthly singalong and after-noon tea.

The hall, with its dusty parquet floor, always reminded Tony of his school back in Boston, of the gym at St Paul's, rank with sweat and smelly training shoes, with ambition and self-consciousness and fatigue, and the dull ache of homesickness. Tony felt a stab of regret, of guilt; old, but as familiar and impossible to shift as a stain on a favourite shirt. He could never detach thoughts of school from thoughts of his best friend, Anselm, and that intense, bitter sense of loss. Anselm had been so much more troubled than any of them could have guessed, his suicide something Tony knew he might never come to terms with. But Anselm was the reason he'd trained in psychiatry, and ultimately his job had been the reason he'd met Emily. Tony was sure Anselm had been look-ing out for him that night, the dinner party hosted by an Irish American physician a welcome break from his routine, the Irish girl he sat next to like a ray of sparkling light. And he'd been like a moth to her flame from that moment on. He still found it incred-ible that she'd agreed to a date – and he'd been full sure he'd never marry, not at his age, but she'd proved him wrong.

Focusing back on the busy room, Tony gently pushed the memories of school away. *Boys learned to survive* – most of them at least. And Tony was sure it had been the same for the people here when they had come to the basement of St Anthony's, sheltering from the Blitz, singing the same songs they would be singing after lunch, keeping up their spirits, yearning for the all-clear. Everyone here had a history – he wasn't alone in that.

Emily turned to him, keeping her voice low. 'I checked with the housing officer. She turned up at the council offices about a month ago – she'd been evicted from her bedsit because the place was being sold. She didn't have any ID but had a letter addressed to a Mary in her cardigan pocket, so they assumed that was her name. They found her a place in sheltered accommodation, and she's been coming over to some of my classes, but she's definitely becoming more withdrawn, more confused. And now with this mugging . . .' Tony nodded. 'Her thoughts seem to go round and around. She's talking about dancing a lot, and the sea. And lipstick. She's got quite a thing about the right colour lipstick.'

'Has she been seen by a GP?'

'She was assessed when she arrived at the housing office, and she's monitored through Renmore House, the sheltered accommodation, but honestly they're pushed to the limit. I thought it would be much simpler if you could just have a chat to her.' Emily threw a cheeky grin at him. 'No point in having connections if you don't use them, is there?' Tony smiled, amusement making his brown eyes shine. Emily had a knack for getting around bureaucracy, for ignoring red tape when it suited her. Emily had a knack for getting around him.

And, to be fair, skipping a few steps in the process might end up saving the NHS money in the long run. From everything Emily had told him, Mary's behaviour suggested a psychiatric disease, one perhaps causing dementia. Emily had worked with the elderly for long enough to recognise the symptoms.

'She's such a sweetie, but she seems to be locked inside herself, doesn't seem to be making any friends.' Emily inclined her head in Mary's direction. Sitting alone at one of the few empty trestle tables, her eyes were focused on the cup of tea in front of her.

Shouldering off his overcoat, Tony pulled up a chair beside her and sat down, giving the elderly lady a discreet but thorough appraisal. She huddled in a grey button-up cardigan, a maroon nylon shirt with gold sprigs peeking from the collar, and an unlikely overlong blue denim skirt. Mary's thick bottle-green tights formed rings around her crossed ankles, her legs ending inappropriately in a pair of scruffy trainers. She seemed hardly aware of his and Emily's presence. Owl-like, her short silver hair wavy and unbrushed, pale blue eyes rheumy and vacant, Mary was staring at something in the middle distance that neither Tony nor Emily could see, her only movement the anxious caress of a piece of fabric she clutched on her knee.

She looked exactly like one of Emily's strays. Tony almost shook his head, amused and touched all over again by his wife's compassion. Emily had been drawn to this place from the moment they had arrived in London six months ago, fresh from Boston. Whatever worries Tony might have had about taking up a new post, about Emily being stuck at home in a strange city, had evaporated as soon as she'd discovered that Tower Hamlets Social Care Team was crying out for occupational therapists with her experience. And she made friends easily, exuded an inner confidence that drew people to her. After six months she had already set up a book club, all 'blow-ins' as she called them, many from overseas who had made London their home. Passionate about local theatre and the arts, about supporting new talent, she dragged him out to meet her new friends at gallery private views and opening-night performances whenever he had an evening off. Too often, if he was honest with himself. Perhaps it was his age but he relished their time alone, loved nothing more than lighting the fire and closing the curtains and curling up on the sofa with her to watch an old movie. He sometimes wondered if she kept so busy so she didn't have time to think . . .

Leaning forward towards the old lady, Tony kept his voice low, unthreatening. 'Hello, Mary. I'm Tony, Emily's husband.' He searched her face for a reaction. She didn't respond.

'Do you remember I told you about my husband, Mary? He works at St Thomas's.' Squatting on the floor beside the old lady, Emily took Mary's hands in her own. 'He can only get down here to talk to my very special friends.' Mary's eyes seemed to flicker, perhaps registering the difference in their accents, but she still didn't speak. Tony tried again.

'Emily's asked me here to meet you so that we can find a way of making you feel a bit better, Mary.'

Mary turned to him, her blue eyes puzzled, almost transparent silver-white eyebrows raised in question. 'Better?'

'Yes, Mary; Emily's worried about you. She's noticed you've been a bit distracted.'

'Really?' There was a long pause as the old lady gathered her thoughts. Then, speaking slowly and deliberately, she said, 'Well, it's very nice of you to come, but I've been waiting. Why did it take you so long?'

9

Angel Hierra slipped the parking ticket onto the dash of the hire car so that it could be seen from the outside and slammed the door closed, peeling off the latex glove and dropping it into his pocket. He checked his watch. In his head it was sometime in the early morning, he wasn't sure. He'd been running on adrenalin but now jet lag was starting to catch up with him. He'd tried to sleep on the plane but the anticipation of customs, of passing through immigration, had kept him on edge. Laughter began to fizz in his head like Alka-Seltzer. He should have relaxed – as the guy in the bar at the Holiday Inn had said, one spic looks like another . . .

A shadow flicked behind him, made him start. Distracted, Hierra spun around, running his eye along the seafront, over the paved plaza outside the ferry terminal, to the old building to his right, straining to see into the shadows. Nothing. Hierra rolled his shoulders, trying to relax. *Must have been his imagination.* Lack of sleep was making him jumpy.

Had he been followed? The thought tumbled around his head like hogweed, sending up a cloud of dust that made it hard to breathe. He shook it away fast.

How could he have been?

He'd been planning this for weeks, had been so careful back in Vegas, taking the back roads to the old man's place. And he'd left his phone in New York, suddenly realising as he'd sat in the bar at the Holiday Inn that Kuteli and his monkeys might be able to track it through signals or GPS or something. He'd dumped the guy's phone as well, just to be sure, left it in the trunk with the body. His face twitched into a grin – there was something funny about the thought of the guy's wife calling him, the mistress too, leaving messages on the answerphone to deaf ears.

Pulling out the map from his pocket, crumpled where he'd refolded it, Hierra checked his bearings. It was a bit of a walk back to his hotel, but he wasn't going to take any risks on this one. Just in case someone knew he was here. The mark was expected in Dublin, so using his credit card here wouldn't arouse suspicion, would in fact be more likely to confirm that he'd arrived safe and well, but the hire car would be easy to track if anything had gone wrong. He had the cash he'd got from his father's stash in the condo to live off and he'd only be here a few days if everything went according to plan.

Bastard. That last win had been a big one, and the old man knew Kuteli was turning up the heat, calling in his loans. He knew them, could have helped him out, could have made the payment, bought him some time.

But he hadn't. Hierra felt a surge of anger building all over again. Why had he been surprised? His father had let him down all his life; why when his son's life was threatened should it be any different?

Hierra stuck his hands in the pockets of his overcoat and headed away from the car, his shoulders tense. His father had asked for it. Asked for everything he'd gotten, and then some. And he, Angel Hierra, was going to get the last laugh. After everything, after all the years of shit, Angel Hierra was going to get himself sorted. *The sins of the father.* He almost laughed out loud. *Now it was time to cash those sins in.*

10

In the studio, Zoë reached for a walkabout phone. O'Rourke's tone hadn't left any room for discussion. *'Can we call your grandmother perhaps? I think we need a quick chat with her as well.'*

'She's still not answering.'

Cathy detected a hint of irritation in Zoë's voice as she clicked off the phone and laid it back down on the desk. It had taken a while for Zoë to fully understand that they needed to speak to Lavinia Grant about the wedding dress and that she wouldn't be able to stay in her house tonight, would need somewhere else to go.

And now, after all the effort, Lavinia Grant wasn't answering.

In the heat of the studio Zoë had taken off her blue velvet coat, hanging it over the musical instrument case leaning in the corner; Cathy wasn't sure what sort of instrument it was, but it was almost as big as its owner. Now Zoë ran her slim fingers along her collarbone, an unconscious movement that made her silver bangles play down her bare arm, the sound like the high notes on a keyboard.

'Is your grandmother normally at home at this time?' Cathy asked.

'She usually has a rest in the afternoon, says she can't sleep at night. She's an insomniac; she just won't admit it to herself.'

'Does she have a mobile you could try?'

'She doesn't even have an answering machine.' Zoë laughed sardonically. 'She reckons mobiles are all bugged by the media, that if you need her badly enough you can seek an audience by making an appointment with her secretary.'

'Not to worry.' O'Rourke stood up decisively. 'We'll try her again in a few minutes. She might have popped out for a pint of milk or something.' Before O'Rourke could continue, Zoë interrupted him, her voice heavy with sarcasm.

'She has a housekeeper for that type of thing.'

Cathy couldn't tell if the tone was directed at O'Rourke or at Lavinia Grant, but it sure as hell didn't improve his mood.

'Naturally. We'll need to speak to her too.' O'Rourke forced a smile. 'Now while we still have the scenes-of-crime lads here I'd like to get some samples from you.' His tone was matter-of-fact, his steady blue eyes meeting Zoë's like she was an errant child brought in front of the headmaster. 'For elimination purposes.'

'I, er, I'm not sure . . .' Zoë paled, her eyes darting between them, her hand frozen at her throat.

'It's quite simple. Just fingerprints and a sample we can use so we can distinguish your DNA and eliminate it.' Cathy could see Zoë didn't have a clue what she was talking about. 'We can take a couple of hairs, or a blood sample, but the simplest is a small scraping from the inside of your mouth.' She summoned every remaining vestige of patience she had. 'It's called a buccal sample – it's Latin for cheek – and it really doesn't hurt at all.'

'I . . .' Obviously unable to think of a reasonable objection, Zoë nodded slowly, her hand fluttering, fussing with her hair, with the ribbon on her blouse. Before she could change her mind, Cathy had the studio door open, was breathing in the cold night air.

'I'll give Thirsty a shout, he's very nice. Won't take a minute. Do you want to try your grandmother again?'

Despite Cathy's assurance that the procedure was painless, Zoë winced as Thirsty scraped the inside of her mouth. In the close confines of the studio, Cathy could hear the rasp of Thirsty's breath, the rattle deep down in his lungs as he added the details in his notebook and slipped the sample into the job bag.

Sometimes she felt like stealing his fags and putting them through the shredder. He wasn't the only one who smoked; when you stumbled out of a crime scene, flashbulbs going off in your face, or had to witness the post-mortem on a child, those who smoked did so with gusto. But as Thirsty regularly pointed out, it was his only vice. He'd earned his nickname drinking orange juice, had joined the teetotal Pioneers group when he was eighteen, resoundingly making the decision to renounce alcohol around the time, Cathy reckoned, that he'd got married. Now he had four daughters, all settled down, none of them running around in the middle of the night getting shot at – or stupid enough to get themselves up the duff. Cathy rapidly curtailed that line of thought as Thirsty gave her one of his grins, a look loaded with experience and encouragement and *I know you're grand but look after yourself, lass*, and flipped the lid of his box closed, the catches rattling.

'That's me done.'

'Thanks, Thirsty.' O'Rourke said, 'It's getting late, so I think we need to pay a visit to your grandmother's house, Zoë.' He glanced at the battered diving watch that never left his wrist. It was way too big to be practical, gave pressure readings down to a hundred metres as well as about a million other things apparently. When they'd been in the car together Cathy had slagged him mercilessly over it, continually asking what the wind speed was, whether it gave the suspect's full name and address or just his date of birth. 'We need to talk to her. Let's see if she's in and just not answering the phone, will we?'

A shadow passed across Zoë's face. Cathy wasn't sure quite what it was – fear? There was definitely something amiss with Zoë's relationship with her grandmother. And by the sounds of things, her mother too. Zoë looked unsure. 'She hates people calling on her.' Then, as if the solution to the whole problem had suddenly presented itself, her face brightened. 'I could try Trish. She's Lavinia's friend. She lives at Oleander most of the time – Lavinia doesn't like being on her own.' Zoë paused. 'She's got a mobile. Her number's in my phone, in my bag.' She looked confused for a moment. 'I think I left it in the car.'

O'Rourke picked up her coat, handing it to her, and opened the studio door ceremoniously, his eyes cold, winter blue. 'Lead on.'

Cathy moved to follow Zoë but O'Rourke caught her arm, his voice low.

'Keep an eye on her. I want to catch up with the boys. Let me know what's happening.'

Cathy nodded wordlessly and, crossing her arms to fend off the chill, stepped out of the heat into the night.

The car was right where Zoë had left it, a patrol car now behind it, the Technical Bureau van still wedged into the mouth of the drive in front. Squeezing past the van's pristine white sides, her feet crunching on the gravel, Zoë headed straight to the passenger door, leaning into the front seat, searching through her handbag. It took her a few moments. A few moments in which Cathy exchanged glances with the guy stationed on the door, stamping to keep his circulation going. A few moments in which she heard a voice that lifted her right out of the darkness.

'Jesus, Cat, what are you doing here?'

What the . . . ? In a flurry of loose shale Steve Maguire had skewed his bike to a halt only feet away from her, his face blazing red. *So it should be.*

Jumping back out of the way, Cathy steadied herself on the stone gate pillar, her right hand flying to her hip, a reflexive action. Surprised by the suddenness of his arrival, and just a tiny bit shocked, it took Cathy a second to recover. It was six weeks since she'd last seen him, the night when . . . *Christ, why did life have to be so complicated?* She could feel herself starting to blush. Her rebuke was fast and acerbic.

'You better watch yourself, Steve Maguire. You can kill someone speeding on a bike.'

Steve looked back at her and stuck out his tongue, any confidence he'd lost from the surprise of seeing her returning with a vengeance.

'Don't be such a stuffed shirt, Cat; what are you doing here anyway?'

As Steve spoke, Zoë emerged from the car, her phone in her hand, and he shot her one of his devastating grins, one Cathy was very familiar with, a heady blend of little boy lost and successful magazine entrepreneur.

'Zoë.' He switched his tone, his voice caring, concerned. 'I thought I'd better check on you and see if everything was OK – you had to rush off so quickly.'

Zoë's hand flew to her mouth, her voice betraying her surprise at seeing him. 'I didn't get back to you. I'm so sorry. The Guards have been here all afternoon.'

'No problem, you've other things on your plate. Max said you can drop in when you're free to work out the agreements. He's planning to get the exhibition up at the end of the month – so there's no panic.'

So that was what he was doing here – he knew Zoë. Through Max and the gallery. Cathy inwardly rolled her eyes. *That would be right.* There were some days when Dublin was just *too* small.

Best pals since school, Max and Steve were her brother Pete's best friends, serial entrepreneurs all of them, who saw obstacles as challenges, who didn't take no for an answer. As Steve was always saying, quoting Dr Seuss, 'You're on your own. And you know what you know. And you're the one who'll decide where to go.' They were well suited. 'The three stooges', her big brother Aidan called them. And in that moment Cathy found herself back in the seemingly endless summer holiday at the end of her first year in senior school, to them all hanging out by the river. *Half-eaten orange ice lollies falling off the stick; red lemonade and ham sandwiches; flip-flops and cut-off jeans; sunburn; the rope swing; shrieking at the ice-cold water. Steve Maguire's fringe flopping into his eyes and her first kiss.* Oh Christ.

'So you two know each other, do you?' Sitting up, his hands in the pockets of his denim jacket, Steve looked innocently from Zoë to Cathy and back again.

'We just met today,' Cathy said. Then, speaking to him as if she was addressing a rather dim child, she jerked her head to indicate the Technical Bureau van behind her. *You could hardly miss it.* 'I'm working.'

Steve slapped the side of his head theatrically. 'Of course.' He ran his hand through his hair, ruffling the spikes, then, hanging over his handlebars again, grinned mischievously, blue eyes twinkling. 'So how's it going, Garda Connolly?'

'Grand, thanks, but we're a bit busy here right now.'

'Work away, don't let me stop you. I'll just have a quick word with Zoë and I'll be off. I need to set up an interview. She's going to be the next big thing this Christmas, trust me.'

'I'm afraid Zoë's not going to be available for a chat for a bit longer.' Cathy turned her attention back to Zoë. 'Your grandmother's friend? Will we try her now?'

'Maybe we can talk later?' Apologetically Zoë turned to Steve before she glared back at Cathy. 'If I'm allowed.' Then: 'Trish's a journalist; she always has her phone on.'

As Steve leaned over his handlebars fiddling intently with the brakes or something, like he wasn't listening in, Cathy tried to focus on Zoë Grant, on the reason why they were all there. Maybe Zoë really didn't know anything about the bones, or maybe she knew all about them but somehow didn't see that she'd committed a crime – concealing a death at the very least, infanticide at worst. The thought sent Cathy's hand to massage her stomach, a quick unconscious movement. Being a mother so wasn't part of her master plan, easily rated as the biggest shock of her life, and right now it was a shock Cathy wasn't sure she'd ever get to grips with – but there were ways of dealing with an unplanned pregnancy that didn't include stitching the bones of your baby in the hem of a dress, a wedding dress at that.

Cathy felt an unexpected stab of pity as she looked at Zoë Grant. She seemed to have everything: incredible talent, looks, money, a fabulous house; but teasing the ground with the toe of her boot, her free hand plucking at her blouse again then tucking her long hair behind her ear, she looked lonely and isolated.

'It's ringing.' Interrupting Cathy's thoughts, Zoë crossed her arms, pulling her coat around herself, leaning back on the side of the car, her grey eyes flicking over towards Steve, then back to the ground.

'Trish? It's Zoë.' Zoë's posture changed as she spoke, her face becoming animated. 'I need to speak to Lavinia. She's not answering her phone; do you know where she is?'

Listening for a moment, Zoë put her hand over the mouthpiece and turned to Cathy. 'She's at Lavinia's house now. Just got out of a cab. She's been out to lunch.'

'Would you mind if I had a quick word?' Cathy moved towards Zoë, her blue eyes questioning. Zoë frowned, then said into the phone, 'Trish? There's a girl here who needs to talk to you. She's a Guard. Yes, a Guard.' Zoë held out the phone to Cathy. 'She's had a lot to drink, you might get more sense out of her.'

Steve was still leaning on his bike, one foot on the ground steadying it. Straightening up, he raised his eyebrows, his face concerned. 'Was there much taken? In the break-in?'

Zoë shrugged, standing uneasily biting her lip. Cathy didn't catch what she said but Steve nodded as if he understood.

'Trish? This is Detective Garda Cathy Connolly. We need to speak to Lavinia Grant rather urgently. Is she at home?' Glancing over at Zoë, Cathy raised her voice, repeating herself, this time trying to say every word as clearly as possible. The voice on the other end was slurred. Obviously it had been a very long lunch.

'Course she is, my dear. Place is lit up like a bloody Christmas tree. Didn't bloody answer the door though, the silly cow. I've forgotten my keys ... I'm just looking for the back-door key.' There was a pause, the sound of scrabbling. 'Here it is. Be in in a mo.'

Cathy could hear the door being opened, had to hold her phone away from her ear as the next comment was shrieked.

'Lavinia? Where are you? Lavinia, PHONE!' There was a pause. 'Can't find her. She must be upstairs. LAVINIA!'

Cathy could hear the crash of a door opening and closing.

'LAVINIA! I know you're in,' then to Cathy, 'Maybe she's upstairs.'

A clicking sound, something banging on wood as Trish struggled up the stairs, her breath laboured.

'LAVINIA? Where are you? There's a girl on the phone ...' More puffing. 'Bugger these stairs.' A door banged. 'She's not in her room, Christ, she must be at the top. Do you really need her now?'

'I'm afraid so ...'

'Just call the Guards if I have a heart attack.' Trish began to giggle at her own joke. 'Here we are, almost there ...'

Cathy was about to speak when there was an animal shriek from the phone.

'Trish, are you OK?'

Another shriek. Choking, gasping for breath. Then hysterical sobbing. Pain, raw and pure. Even Steve looked taken aback. 'Jesus, what was that, a banshee?'

PART TWO

Adjusting the Tension

Tension refers to the pressure being placed on the needle and bobbin thread by the sewing machine. When the tension is correct the stitches will be even and neat. Your sewing machine manual will show you the appropriate settings and examples of what the threads should look like on the right and wrong sides of your stitching when the tension is correct, and what happens when it is incorrect.

11

It didn't take them long to find the body.

A patrol car and ambulance had already arrived outside Lavinia Grant's impressive Georgian end-of-terrace house when O'Rourke pulled up. One of the uniformed Gardaí, getting no response at the front door, had acknowledged O'Rourke's arrival with a wave of a long black torch, flicking the beam on as he skipped down the broad granite steps and disappeared out of sight behind a dense bush, heading for the back door. The two paramedics followed.

O'Rourke turned to Zoë Grant and Steve Maguire, huddled in the back seat of the car. 'Stay here, both of you, don't move until someone comes to get you.'

Steve had nodded silently. Zoë didn't appear to hear him; she was staring up at the house. She had been monosyllabic on the way to Monkstown, her grey eyes unfocused: her grandmother lived alone unless Trish was staying, the housekeeper left at three; Lavinia hadn't mentioned any appointments today.

Cathy had been surprised when O'Rourke had bundled Steve into the car along with Zoë, but his explanation made sense: 'He'll keep her entertained while we find out what's going on. I don't want any loose strands on this investigation, and we don't know what he knows.'

Cathy had nodded. He had a point. Zoë and Steve obviously knew each other – quite how well, they'd find out later.

Cathy pulled the collar of her jacket up against the chill as she got out of the car. Across the road a man slowed as he walked past, hands thrust into his overcoat pockets, hat pulled low over his eyes, looking at them curiously. Cathy half-glanced at him, would have moved him on if she had had time; they all hated rubberneckers.

As Cathy followed O'Rourke through the side gate, the sound of her heels bounced off the walls of the passage running to the back of the house like bullets ricocheting off a target. The bulbs had blown in the security lights along its length, the last one struggling to produce a weak pool that illuminated the gate at the end. The smell of cats was overpowering, dizzying, and for a second Cathy wondered if this was what dying was like.

They said you could see a light at the end of a tunnel.

The darkness whirling, Cathy reached for the wall, shutting her eyes, the raw stone cold and sharp against her palm. No one had mentioned if the tunnel to the afterlife stank like this one, but she could feel the hair standing up on the back of her neck. *She'd been there once – almost. The pain. The sound of shots bouncing off the walls like the sound of her boots on the concrete. Darkness and cold and pain. More pain. O'Rourke's voice calling her, then slowly fading.* Memories normally pushed to the deepest recesses of Cathy's mind bubbled to the surface like methane.

Shaken, as much by their reappearance as her physical reaction, Cathy tried to calm her racing heart. It had been a routine patrol: she'd been teasing O'Rourke about slipping the disc in his back when a driver had pulled out of a junction, swerving wildly across the road right in front of them. 'Pissed as a fart', as O'Rourke had put it. It should have just been a simple Section 49, but they had had no idea as they flashed him to pull over, as they got out of the car putting on their hats, what was going to happen next. And she still had the scars . . . Cathy felt her legs wobble.

Christ, she needed something to eat.

Missing lunch was normal on a normal day, but not now, not since that bloody blue line had appeared on the pregnancy test and wrecked her head.

Ahead of her, O'Rourke was through the gate, the sound of his radio cutting into her subconscious. She couldn't hear what was being said but saw him nodding.

'Get a move on. We need to suit up so there's no cross-contamination.'

Not looking at her, O'Rourke held out a white paper suit he'd grabbed from the boot of his car and pulled a pair of gloves from his jacket pocket. Taking the last few steps to the end of the passage, Cathy reached for it, shaking it out, taking advantage of the fact that he had his back to her as he pulled his on to lean on the frame of the gate and catch her breath.

'You OK?'

Glancing over his shoulder, O'Rourke gave Cathy a searching look. Her smile was fast, more of a flick of the corners of her mouth, her excuse feeble, even to her ears.

'Missed lunch.'

O'Rourke passed her a pair of gloves, pulling foot covers out of another pocket. 'The lads have probably got a couple of Mars bars in the car. Make sure you have something. I need you thinking straight.'

'What have we got?'

Arriving at the top-floor landing, O'Rourke's voice was calm, clear, with no hint of the fact he'd just run up about ninety stairs.

Behind him Cathy grabbed the banister, her stomach turning as she caught the cloying scent of heavy perfume. The Guard who had gone on ahead was standing back as the paramedics crouched over the body of an elderly woman. Behind them, a woman wearing a white trouser suit was sitting huddled on a large cardboard box pushed half in, half out of a doorway. Trish O'Sullivan, Cathy presumed. And she was still crying. Cathy wasn't sure if it was Trish's perfume she could smell, but it was beginning to catch in the back of her throat. The lead paramedic looked up, his face practical, emotion lost in years of experience.

'Can't find a pulse.'

O'Rourke nodded curtly. 'We'll need the doc to certify. Thanks, boys. Looks like we'll be needing Donovan's.'

Lavinia Grant lay on her back, her head almost at the top of the stairs, one leg twisted beneath her, a high-heeled patent shoe lying beside her. Eyes open, staring lifelessly at the single bulb hanging from the heavily painted ceiling rose, her skin was ghostly pale, two bright splashes of make-up vivid on her cheeks. Her smart Chanel-style suit was a garish purple in the harsh light, her arms splayed uselessly at her sides, like she was floating in a pool. But there was no way she was going anywhere in a hurry, on land or in the water.

The Guard nodded towards the woman sitting on the box. 'This is Trish O'Sullivan, Cig, a friend of Mrs Grant's. She found the body. Mal's checking the lower floors but it doesn't look like anyone else was here when Ms O'Sullivan arrived. The building was secure.'

Clutching a silver handbag covered in rhinestones with one hand, Trish pressed a tattered tissue over her nose and mouth.

Huge diamonds flashed from her fingers, her hands deeply tanned and heavily wrinkled, her nails an unnatural orange.

'I'm sorry you had to find her, Mrs O'Sullivan. I know it was a shock.' O'Rourke's voice was low, compassionate. 'Would you like to come downstairs? You might be more comfortable down there. We can get the boys here to check you out.' O'Rourke glanced at the lead paramedic for confirmation.

'She's dead, isn't she? I knew she was dead.' Trish didn't look at him, her eyes fixed on the body of her friend as if she was paralysed.

Trish's voice was gravelly, deeper than Cathy expected. She started sobbing again, the sound rasping, painful. Coming up past O'Rourke, stepping carefully around the body, Cathy squatted down beside Trish, putting her arm around her shoulders. The perfume was Trish's and it wasn't freshly applied. Cathy could feel the nausea building, fought to ignore it.

'Is there anyone we can call? A friend who can come and sit with you?'

Ignoring Cathy, Trish reached into her handbag for another tissue, the dozen or so gold chains and strings of pearls hanging around her neck clinking together as she moved. Then she shook her head, as if Cathy's voice had taken a while to register, her short hair, teased into a helmet of curls, remaining static despite the rapid movement of her head. Thick trails of mascara had formed long black stains down her heavily lined face.

'No. No, not now.' Another sob wracked her. 'I couldn't possibly see anyone looking like this.'

They heard Professor Saunders before they saw him, puffing and panting, his feet heavy on the stairs, his paper suit rustling. His mood hadn't improved since this morning.

'Do you really need me? The station doctor should be doing this.' He paused to catch his breath. 'She probably had a heart attack after that climb.'

Ignoring the jibe, O'Rourke nodded curtly.

'Thanks for coming out again. This is the grandmother of the girl whose house we were at earlier.' He shot Saunders a meaningful look. 'The two *events*' – he emphasised the word, implying he didn't want to elaborate – 'may be related. I wanted you to see her *in situ*.'

'So generous. I'm sure photos would have done the trick.'

'Open to interpretation, Doctor, as you know. I need your take on it if you don't mind.' O'Rourke paused. 'We're not leaving anything to chance on this one.'

Saunders glared at O'Rourke, thumped his bag down on the floor and leaned over the body. His voice was matter-of-fact. 'She's still warm to the touch and the limbs are flaccid, so she's probably not been dead for more than a few hours. A contusion to the back of her head and slight bleeding, consistent with terminal collapse, no other obvious marks of injury.'

'A blow to the head?'

'Possibly. Can't tell until we get her onto the table. Is there anywhere her head might have struck as she fell?' Saunders paused, reaching for his thermometer. 'What do you know about her – has she got any significant medical history or is she taking any medication?' His focus on the body, only half-listening, O'Rourke shrugged and immediately regretted it.

'I have no powers of telepathy or clairvoyance, Detective Inspector; I cannot give you a definitive cause of death without the fullest information. I suggest you make some enquiries.'

12

Mary pulled her cardigan around her shoulders, shivering, the first drops of rain pricking her skin. *Would he be there?* Images materialised and merged in her head like the colours of a kaleidoscope: *the Gresham Hotel, the warmth and light and laughter waiting for her, overflowing from the lobby, spilling down the steps like champagne.*

Unaware of the litter blowing around her feet, of the oily darkness seeping from the foul-smelling alleys separating the shuttered shops on Roman Road, the graffiti in this part of the East End Turkish and Bengali, Mary could feel butterflies dancing in her stomach, her mind in Dublin, the thrill of anticipation real again.

Could she bear it if he wasn't there? After last week, after he'd kissed her . . . he had to be there. Her cheeks flamed at the memory of last week, of his hands, of his soft words, his promises to take her away with him.

Ahead of her Mary thought she could see lights twinkling gem-like in the darkness; heard laughter, a shout, the roar of traffic. She pulled her cardigan closer, her slippers silent. The ground was cold and hard through the thin soles but she couldn't feel it, thought instead that she was wearing her dancing shoes, the silver leather shimmering. Ahead of her, silhouetted in the darkness she could see a tight knot of figures, the present converging with her memories to enhance her feeling of reality. *Was he there, chatting to someone he'd met?*

Mary caught a sound from the group ahead, straggling now across the pavement, a jeer, cruel, like hyenas at a kill. But it didn't register. *She knew her feet would be throbbing tomorrow after all the dancing, but she didn't have to get up for mass until nine.* The shapes ahead reconfigured, hands concealed in pockets. Nonchalant. Menacing. *He would be waiting for her . . .*

'Hey, Mrs!'

Mary started, the voice sending a jolt right through her body. Then the roar of an engine was on top of her, lights blinding. Lurching away from it, Mary stumbled, a hand gripping her arm, pulling her up before she hit the paving stones. Panic overwhelmed her, her heart racing. Then fear, ripping through her, raw and jagged.

Through his dreams Tony Cox heard Beethoven's Ninth Symphony begin to rise to orchestral proportions. It took a few moments for him to wrestle with the heavy layers of sleep and to fumble for his phone. He rolled over to reach for it, anxious not to wake Emily as she slept beside him. His movement dislodged one of her cats, which had settled down to sleep on his shoulder. It stuck its claws in his arm, catching them in the cotton of his pyjama jacket. Swearing under his breath, he struggled to unhook the paw with his free hand, swiping the phone screen with his thumb. He was quite sure they made a beeline for him because they knew he only tolerated them for Emily's sake. It was like some sort of bizarre feline one-upmanship.

'Hello?' Tony kept his voice down, glancing anxiously at Emily, but he could see from the rhythmic fall of her shoulder that she was still sound asleep.

'Dr Cox?' The voice was businesslike, far too efficient for the middle of the night.

'Yes, yes it is. What's the problem?'

'Sorry to wake you, sir, Limehouse Police Station here. An old lady's just been brought in – one of the traders from Whitechapel Market saw her wandering down the Commercial Road in her cardigan and nightie. He reckons your wife knows her, Dr Cox. And we found your card in her cardy pocket. She's very confused, not sure who she is, so we wondered if she was one of your patients. Duty doc's with her now.'

Tony closed his eyes for a second, gathering his thoughts. *An old lady? Commercial Road? She could be any one of a hundred of his patients, but one who knew Emily? And why the police station and not the hospital?* Tony felt himself starting to wake up. *At least if the duty doctor was on site she'd get seen quicker in the grand scheme of things.*

'I'll have to see her. I'll be with you in fifteen minutes.'

'That's great, sir, see you shortly.'

On the other side of the bed, Emily slept on, undisturbed by the telephone, her hair a halo against the pillow, duvet pulled to her chin. *Should he wake her? The cop had said she knew the old lady . . . but she looked so peaceful . . .*

Swinging out of the bed, his feet flinching on the cold boards, Tony looked for his slippers, reaching for them, both cats now awake, slinking in under the duvet behind him as he leaned forward, delighted to curl up next to their mistress.

'Morning, sir, Dr Cox is it?'

Tony almost laughed. The cold blast of air that had hit him as he climbed out of his car had thoroughly woken him up and now, struck by the wall of intense heat in the foyer of Limehouse

Metropolitan Police Station, he felt as if he was on a euphoric sleep-deprived high.

'What gave me away?'

The sergeant looked at him quizzically. 'Could be the fact that I called you fourteen and a half minutes ago.'

That would be it. 'Where is she?'

'Inside, sir. Duty doc got another call. He checked her over, said she's physically fine, needs to be kept warm, get plenty of rest.' The sergeant tutted to himself. 'Any longer out there dressed like that and it would have been a different story.'

Following the sergeant through the heavy security door and along the brilliantly lit corridors of the station, polished floor tiles and regulation cream walls reflecting the overhead fluorescents a little too brightly for Tony's liking, he could hear the echo of clanging doors deep in the bowels of the building, the occasional shout.

'Here we are, sir. She was lucky she was spotted – almost went under a van she did, walked right out into the road.'

The room was small, bare, a single steel-legged table and two plastic chairs the only furniture. The old lady was huddled into one of the chairs, a rough blanket, prison grey, wrapped around her shoulders, face pinched as if she was thinking hard, her eyes fixed on a spot on the lino floor.

It only took Tony a moment to register who she was, but before he could say anything, she started speaking, her voice agitated. 'She told you, didn't she? She told you I was going to the dance. Told you where to find me. Had to ruin it, didn't she?'

She was rambling. Tony pulled a chair over, settling himself in front of Mary as the door closed on the duty sergeant with a conclusive click. She was agitated but he'd seen a lot worse and she was so frail she didn't present a threat. Before

Tony could say anything, Mary continued, 'He'll come, you know. He'll come and find me. She said he doesn't love me, that he wants the money, but she's lying. I know she is. She just doesn't want me to be happy.' Mary shook her head, her eyes filling with tears, bottom lip trembling. Under the blanket Tony could see she was plucking at the thin rose-pink nylon of her nightdress, the fabric hanging from her painfully thin knees. Then suddenly Mary looked up, looked directly at him, her face confused, as if the music had stopped and she was the last one without a chair.

'Who are you?'

'I'm Emily's husband, Tony Cox. Do you remember we met the other day – at the lunch club at the church?' He kept his voice level, friendly and warm.

'The church?' Mary shook her head, a tear slipping down her cheek, her face fearful. 'Not the church.'

'It was the lunch club, Mary, we met at the lunch club. My wife's name is Emily. She said you had a bit of trouble in the market. She took you home.'

Mary screwed up her face, then it began to move, expressions passing like a breeze was blowing thoughts into her head, one minute angry, the next sad.

Behind him, Tony heard the door open. The sergeant was back.

'How are you doing, Doctor? We'd like to get her home.'

'She's not one of my patients, not yet at least, but my wife does know her. I think she lives near St Anthony's in Bethnal Green. I'll have to give Emily a buzz and get the address.' Tony glanced at his watch: *1 a.m.* The ring of his phone interrupted his thoughts, Beethoven bouncing off the bare walls. Pulling it out of the pocket of his coat, Tony held it at arm's length so he could see the screen clearly. *His eyesight was getting worse.*

'It's her.' He stood up. 'Excuse me for a moment, Mary.'

He kept his voice low, quickly explaining what had happened. 'No, you don't need to come down, stay in bed. She's fine. The duty doc's had a look at her. We just needed her address.'

Tony paused, turned to raise his eyes to the sergeant, who could hear Emily's voice, tinny but insistent on the other end. Tony clicked the phone off.

'My wife's on her way. We live in Paradise Gardens; it's only a few minutes.' His voice was apologetic.

'That's great, sir.' He smiled sympathetically. 'My wife's exactly the same. Doesn't reckon I can tie my shoelaces on my own.'

'How is she?' Emily Cox arrived through the front door of Limehouse Police Station in a whirlwind of cold air, cheeks flushed, her lime-green ski jacket zipped tight, a fuchsia scarf doubled over at its neck. 'I can't believe it. After getting mugged in the market, now this. And she's such a sweet old thing . . .'

Tony raised his eyebrows, pointed wordlessly to the door he'd just emerged from. The sergeant punched in the security code as Emily drew breath. Tony had a strong feeling he knew what was coming next.

'How on earth did this happen? She's supposed to be living in a warden-managed unit.'

Tony held up his hand like he was stopping traffic, his face half amused, his other hand on the handle of the door.

'Thanks, sweetheart, but all we need is her address.' Opening it wide, Tony continued, 'And the guy's a warden, not a jailer – if

Mary wanted to get out badly enough she would have given him the slip.' But Tony might as well have been talking to himself.

Emily didn't answer, instead went straight to Mary, sighing audibly, and bobbed down beside her. 'Mary, whatever's happened to you now?' Emily's voice was soft, her accent even more pronounced than normal.

For the first time that evening Mary seemed to show a flash of recognition, lifted her hand from her lap, gesturing for Emily to come closer.

'He's here.' Mary giggled, a girlish high-pitched sound totally incongruous in the harsh surroundings. 'I told you he'd come for me, and look – he has. Isn't he handsome?'

Emily followed Mary's eye. Glancing quickly at Tony, her eyes filled with laughter as she cottoned on.

'We need to get you warm and dry, Mary, and we need to get you dressed, don't we, love?'

Tony ignored her look. 'There's a squad car waiting to take her home. They just need to know where to go.'

Emily stood up straight, glanced at him anxiously then back at Mary, chewing her lip. When she spoke, her voice was so low that Tony could hardly hear her.

'She can't go home, love, not on her own. That flat's so, *so* grim.'

It took Tony a moment to work out what Emily was implying, then he raised his thick eyebrows, looking at her in horror. He'd seen that look before. But last time it had been the cats. *And he couldn't even pretend he was allergic to old ladies.*

'Oh, no. I have to be able to get away from my job, Emily. And you do too. We have to have a bit of space.'

'I know, but –'

'But nothing.' Even as he cut her off, she turned to look at him, switching on the glow in her brown eyes. Tony took a deep breath. 'And it's Thanksgiving.'

'Exactly. It's Thanksgiving.' Emily paused. 'It won't be for long, just a few days until she gets back on her feet.'

'I think it'll take longer than that.'

'But she's had a terrible shock. I'm sure that's what's made her wander. You're always saying yourself how much stress is a factor in exacerbating symptoms.'

'*Psychiatric* symptoms, Emily.' Tony crossed his arms, his no-nonsense, let's-be-practical, I'm-in-charge voice firmly in place. 'Mary's confused, rambling. I'm pretty sure she's suffering from auditory and olfactory hallucinations. She could be suffering from anything from dementia to schizophrenia. We've discussed it.'

'Exactly. Which is why she has to come home with us, just until she gets back on her feet. She needs medication and help. And she must have family somewhere . . .'

'And you're going to find them, are you?'

Emily didn't reply, pursed her lips stubbornly. 'We've got loads of space. The spare room's all made up.'

Tony looked at her stoically, trying hard to think of an objection. Mary wasn't his patient yet, so he couldn't even claim a conflict of interests. *Hell, why was Emily so stubborn?* He thought of the cats. *This was ridiculous. Why was he such a pushover?*

13

The changing room was empty when Cathy arrived, gunmetal-grey doors hanging open, the tiled floor beside the showers still wet from the last class of the evening. The odour of sweat was strong, and as she got to her locker she was hit by a choking cloud of body spray. Kicking off her boots, she changed quickly into her black Lycra vest top and shorts and slipped in her gum shield. She'd taken off her silver necklace in the car, hiding it in a black velvet bag in the door compartment, invisible to prying eyes. It was far too precious to risk getting pinched from the locker room. Rolling up her clothes, she grabbed her water bottle and phone and slung her kitbag into her locker, punching the code in to lock it.

Thank goodness she was the only person here. She wasn't up to conversation tonight; there was so much going on in her head she felt like it might burst.

As she headed through the double swing doors into the gym, her bare feet silent on the padded matting, she glanced into The Boss's office. There was no sign of him but she knew he was around somewhere, probably reorganising the equipment in the container out back. Ex-British military, Belfast-born Niall McIntyre had a need for order that was bordering on OCD, but it was his systems and schedules that had her at the top of her game. And they had a unique relationship, understood each other. He'd trained her brothers, all of them, and although Phoenix Martial Arts was on the north side of the city in Dublin's notorious Ballymun, a major trek daily for training, she wouldn't dream of moving closer to home.

Cathy's warm-up was as brief as she could get away with, tucks and press-ups alternated with skipping, the rope whistling through the air as she spun it faster and faster. Each set in short, sharp bursts, just like a fight. She wasn't in the mood for circuits, wanted, needed, to get into a rhythm with the punchbag.

The chain securing the navy and red PVC bag rattled as she hit it, the thud of her gloves dull. She could feel the power of each blow: left jab, right jab, left hook. She kicked high: front kick, then spun into a roundhouse kick, the noise reverberating off the raw red brick walls, cutting through the beat of chart music.

Out of the corner of her eye she caught a movement, saw The Boss raise his hand behind the etched glass wall that partitioned the office from the gym itself, the image of a phoenix, its wings extended, watching over them. He sat down at his desk. When his classes were finished he got on with his paperwork and Cathy knew he'd let her train on her own for as long as she needed. She'd escaped as soon as O'Rourke had let her go that evening, leaving Donovan's Undertakers to remove the body, the techs to process Oleander House, and Zoë and Steve to sort themselves out.

'We'll be in touch tomorrow,' Cathy had told her, 'to give you an idea of when you'll be able to get back into your own house.'

Zoë had nodded, still in shock. 'Steve said I could stay at his place.'

I bet he did. Cathy stopped herself from saying it, just.

Now she was at the gym Cathy had the space and time she needed to think – Zoë Grant could wait.

What the hell was she going to do? What a fecking mess. Before she could stop them, tears pricked like needles at the corners of her eyes. Turning, she lunged at the bag with an uppercut, sending it reeling away from her, hitting it hard again as it came back on the chain.

She was twenty-four, for God's sake. Twenty-four and doing a job she loved. Twenty-four and SINGLE. The word reverberated around Cathy's head like a ball bearing in a pinball machine echoing the sound of her punches. SINGLE. Very single. And absolutely not about to get hitched whatever the situation. *Jesus, why had she had so much champagne? What the hell had she been thinking? One fabulous red dress, one look from across the room and look what had happened . . .*

She'd always fancied him, but when his eyes had met hers – Christ, it was such a cliché – it had been like someone had switched on an electromagnet. He'd come over to top up her glass, said she looked gorgeous, and she'd just felt so good. They'd talked, and when he reached over to kiss her the charge was positively electric. She'd forgotten everything and just gone with it. And it had been amazing. Not that that was any consolation now – if it had been a bit less amazing she might have been a bit more sensible.

It wasn't like she was some slapper who specialised in one-night stands. Cathy danced backwards, her gloves under her chin, sweat running down her back. *Far from it – her relationship history was positively unspectacular.* Even Áine, her best friend from school who had already raced into marriage and motherhood, had seen more action than she had. Cathy drew in a sharp breath as she jabbed again, her conscience pulling at her. They hadn't been in touch for ages but she knew she should talk to Áine, tell her the whole thing. Part of her was crying out to, but

Cathy knew that even her best pal wouldn't be able to give her unbiased advice, wouldn't understand how it felt from her end.

Before Áine had had her twin boys she would have been the first person Cathy would have called, but now, despite the stress and the sleepless nights, Cathy knew there was no way, with her TV news anchor husband and her beautiful house in the Wicklow Mountains, her four-by-four and her Tumble Tots mornings, that she could possibly grasp how catastrophic this was. Maybe Cathy was underestimating their friendship, but Áine had proved you *could* have it all, and was one of those people who got on with things, always saw the positive.

The only positive Cathy had seen in any of this had been a thin blue line on a pregnancy test.

Everything had been going so right; she was the fittest she'd ever been, had taken gold for the third year running at the Kickboxing Irish Open in April. The Boss had raised her arm so proudly in the victory salute that his grip had hurt more than the fight bruises. She loved her job: she knew she'd walk the sergeant's exams, and her brother Aidan was engaged to the Assistant Commissioner, for God's sake, which couldn't hurt anyone's career. The lads in the house were brilliant – the new guy Eamonn hilariously driven demented by Decko's latest fad for astronaut impersonations, 'Houston, we have a problem' and Yuri Gagarin's 'I can see Earth. It is so beautiful' getting into every conversation. The boys were sound, just like her brothers, even if they didn't have any earthly idea how to clean a cooker.

She felt great, she looked great *and look what had happened. Jesus Christ. How could her life have changed so fast?*

Cathy struggled to stay practical, to assess the problem objectively. The thoughts that had kept her awake the past few nights reran in her head as she pounded the bag.

What had the ad said at the back of that magazine she'd got in London? Something about choices . . . single motherhood, adoption, abortion?

Were they *choices*?

Hardly able to say the words even to herself, Cathy flinched and, pausing, pulled at the Velcro on the back of her glove with her teeth, slipping it off and reaching for her water bottle.

She might not go to church, but Cathy had been dragged up a Catholic. *Abortion.* The word rolled around, picking up impact as it bounced off the sides of her head. Was it an option, honestly? Cathy doubted it. And if her mother ever found out, she'd never speak to her again. Ever. That was a given. *And how would she live with herself?*

Pushing her hair out of her face, she lay down on the matting, her abs pulling as she worked through her press-ups, hearing The Boss's voice in her head, *'sixty seconds, go!'* Jumping up, she pulled her glove back on and turned back into the bag with even more intent than before.

Could she give her child up for adoption? The very sound of the word made Cathy feel heavy, weighted down. She doubted that too, realistically. Would her mum let her? No, of course not. But her mum had worked too hard all her life to be saddled with a baby now. Theresa Connolly had kept down three jobs to keep them in school uniforms and shoe leather, and now her dad, Pat, was retired, they were starting to travel a bit for the first time in their lives, were right now in Lanzarote soaking up some budget winter sun. Which was probably a good thing, gave her time to think. Cathy knew her mum would help, of course she would, but it was so much to ask.

So how the feck was she going to manage? Garda pay didn't exactly stretch to nannies, Cathy didn't have any sisters – and

Niamh, Aidan's fiancée, was hardly going to be in a position to help, she had the whole bloody An Garda Síochána to run. And she lived with three lads – actually really enjoyed living with three lads – but what the feck would they say to sharing with a newborn? *Jesus Christ . . .*

Her arms were tiring now, her abs aching, sweat running off the tip of her nose.

Adoption, adoption, adoption.

And what on earth was she going to tell The Boss? The thought jumped into her mind like a sparring partner jumping into the ring. Niall McIntyre had an instinct for untruths that was almost psychic. *Thank God they were in the middle of a case.* The job was the only reason he'd let her miss training at Phoenix unless she was dying in her bed, and she had to make up any missed sessions with extra pool work, or at the gym in Dún Laoghaire.

An image of the bones flashed back into her head.

Tiny carpals and metacarpals. *Baby's* bones. Cathy felt her stomach turn, a potent blend of revulsion and despair.

Carpals and metacarpals. The words that sprang to mind whenever Cathy thought of bones. Words she'd learned by rote at school when she'd memorised the skeleton, words that had a sort of poetic ring to them. *The tiny bones of the hands and fingers. Tarsals and metatarsals. The tiny bones of the feet and toes.* It was mad, but of all the subjects Cathy had taken for the Leaving, biology had been the most useful, the one she recalled most often. Christ, that was ironic now.

Cathy slowed, shaking her arms out between volleys of punches, her mind distracted from her own problems by the case. Most of a baby's bones were soft, unformed, deteriorated fast. The bones they had found had been clean. Ribs and the jaw.

The stronger, formed bones. Old enough that the flesh had rotted away. So where had the body been?

Something wasn't right with this case. Something *really* wasn't right. And the memory of the feeling she'd had in Zoë Grant's bedroom took her straight back to a hot summer's day when she was twelve years old, a day when Cathy had learned to listen to her gut instincts.

Even when the Guards had asked her afterwards, Cathy couldn't remember what had made her look up from her magazine, what had drawn her attention to the little girl standing in the centre of the green across from their house, bald patches in the grass beaten hard from games of football. Denim pinafore; red and white checked blouse; toffee-coloured hair slipping haphazardly from plastic hair slides. Not more than four or five, she had appeared from nowhere, chasing a cat, or maybe just skipping along in the August sunshine, not watching where she was going.

But as she had turned in the middle of the huge green, her sandalled feet moving in a tight circle of distress, realising she was lost, huge tears had started to fall, waves of shock spreading from her tiny frame like a depth charge. Sitting straddling their low block garden wall in her cut-off denims and swimsuit, the stone hot on her bare legs, sun beating down on her tanned back, Cathy had watched the little girl for a few moments, looking for a big sister or a woman with a pram to take ownership of the child.

When had she noticed the car? Surely only moments after she had spotted the child. It had pulled up on the opposite side of the green, the sun glinting off paintwork shiny like a black beetle. Then the driver had flung open the door, glancing anxiously from side to side, thrusting his hands deep in his tracksuit pockets as he trotted across the road, shoulders hunched as if he didn't want anyone to see his face. Heading straight for the girl.

Cathy still didn't know precisely what had triggered her movement, exactly what it was about the scene that had rung all the alarm bells, but she'd thrown her leg over the wall and started running, trainers pounding like machine-gun fire on the baked earth, her voice trailing like a streamer behind her, yelling for her brothers to come and help, yelling at the girl to run.

That had been the day she'd decided to join the Guards. The day she'd realised that there were people in society who meant harm to others and who needed to be stopped, and others who needed to be looked out for, and how one small act could change the course of someone's life for ever.

'You good, miss?' The Boss's voice interrupted her thoughts. Cathy lowered her gloves; pulling at the Velcro with her teeth, she eased them off as he crossed the gym towards her, reaching for her water bottle again. Compact and wiry, he looked too small to be a soldier but she knew he'd had a colourful career, the tattoos on his arms like a map of the world.

'Got a case on . . .' She picked up her towel and rubbed the sweat from her face.

'Needed some thinking time?' He finished the sentence for her. She smiled, *he knew her so well.*

'Here, go have a shower, it's late. I want you back sparring as soon as that slave driver lets you go.' His face cracked into a grin. He'd patrolled O'Rourke's home territory from the other side of the border, had discovered their shared history the first time Cathy had invited O'Rourke to a tournament.

The Boss held up his hand for a high five as she walked past him. 'There's talk of an exhibition fight in Norway in February. Make sure you keep on top of your weight.'

It was just as well he couldn't see her face.

14

'So what do you think?' O'Rourke popped a chip into his mouth and shook the bag on his knee, redistributing the salt. Otis Redding filled the car, 'Sittin' on the dock of the bay . . .'

Back in the changing room she'd picked up her phone to see a text from him. One word. *Chips?* And suddenly she'd felt overwhelmingly hungry.

She'd texted back: *At the gym. U at the station?*

The reply had been instantaneous, like he'd been waiting. *Yep.*

It was past eleven by the time they pulled up at the end of Cathy's street and Cathy had hopped out of her car and into his so they could talk while they ate. It had started raining now, his windscreen gleaming with a million drops, magnifying the yellow of the street lights that marched into the darkness like a battalion of warrior angels.

'I reckon fish and chips are seriously underrated. Especially in the middle of the night.' Cathy tore off a strip of fresh cod and stuck it into her mouth, savouring the tang of vinegar on her tongue. 'This is heaven.'

'Better not tell McIntyre. He'll be after my guts.'

Cathy shook her head. 'Carbs are fine if I'm burning them – in moderation obviously. I've done two sessions today, was down at the pool before work, reckon I deserve it.'

O'Rourke grinned. 'I don't think a large fish and chips is moderation, do you?'

'It's all relative. Where's the water?'

'So?' O'Rourke rolled his hands. 'Lavinia Grant, what do you think?'

Cathy tore open the side of the bag on her knee, looking for the crispy chips at the bottom. 'There doesn't seem to be any love lost between her and Zoë. From what Zoë says she doesn't sound like the easiest person in the world to get along with. I detected a distinct coolness there.'

O'Rourke nodded. 'D'you reckon they had a row?'

Cathy stared thoughtfully out into the night. 'Zoë took an age getting back after we called her. She said it was traffic, but maybe she nipped to Monkstown on the way out of town. She'd almost have to drive past there to get to Dalkey – maybe they did have an argument and it ended badly.'

O'Rourke took a swig of his Coke. 'She said she came straight from the gallery when she heard about the break-in. We should be able to pick up her car on CCTV on the N11, work out the timing.'

Cathy wrinkled her nose as she thought. 'The traffic *was* bad.' She paused to chew. 'But I mean, really, what are the chances of this happening today of all days and it being totally unrelated?' She took another chip, continued speaking with her mouth full. 'Actually, I think they're all utterly nuts. Did you hear how that Trish one spoke to the housekeeper? Honestly, we'd get hauled up on a harassment charge if we bullied people like that.'

'She was stressed, and the poor woman was confused, couldn't remember if she'd double-locked the front door or not.'

Cathy grunted. 'Well, whether she forgot or Lavinia Grant opened it after she left, Trish didn't need to eat the face off her. How many times have you locked your car door and had to go back to check it? The mind has a weird way of erasing repeated actions.'

O'Rourke looked at her out of the corner of his eye. 'That has to be a woman thing. Never happened to me.'

Cathy thumped him.

'So you reckon Trish is nuts as well, do you? Could she have whacked Lavinia on the back of the head, or given her a good shove, tried to push her down the stairs?'

Cathy shook her head. 'She sounded genuine to me on the phone, and she was pissed, was having problems standing herself. She could have done it earlier in the day, of course, and then gone out and got ossified, I suppose. Maybe she didn't realise how bad it was until she got back.'

'I wish we had a clearer idea of Lavinia Grant's movements this afternoon.' O'Rourke stifled a yawn. 'We'll know more in the morning after the PM. Her purse was empty too, which is a bit strange. You'd expect there to be some small change in it.' He frowned, thinking. 'But maybe she needed to go to the bank. Trish will have to go through the house and see if anything's missing. Maybe she just went upstairs and her heart gave out, and she hit her head as she fell. All very clean.'

Cathy screwed up her face, thinking. 'D'you reckon she knew about the bones?'

'That's not a very attractive look; I'd avoid it if I were you.' O'Rourke paused, waiting for her to react. Cathy threw him a scowl, but didn't rise to the bait. He stuck a chip in his mouth, continuing, 'Honestly I've no idea. After what happened at the Murphys', I'm prepared to believe anything. I checked. The mother was in that one up to her eyeballs. When the Murphy girl turned up in the public office in Dún Laoghaire in 1994 she claimed her mother killed the child, then stuck the body in a plastic bag and took it to Dún Laoghaire to dump it down Lee's Lane. A hundred yards from the old Garda station.'

Cathy frowned. 'Weird.'

'Dumping it so close to the station?' O'Rourke put another chip into his mouth, spoke with his mouth full. 'I know. They could have chucked it off the pier. Might never have been found. Even if it had been washed up, a lot of the trace evidence would have been lost.'

'But the chain of evidence was dodgy from the start, wasn't it?' The more Cathy thought about it, the more she remembered. 'Cynthia Murphy claimed that there were no fingerprints taken from the bag, and then the body was released to be buried up in Glasnevin – in a foundling grave so they couldn't even be sure they had the right one if it ever needed to be exhumed.' It sounded unbelievable, like a badly written B-movie.

'*And* when they did reopen the inquiry, the original file had been lost.' O'Rourke scrunched up his face, as if the whole case gave him a pain. 'Which isn't going to happen here. What's that phrase they teach you in Templemore? *Absence of evidence is never evidence of absence.* So we keep Lavinia Grant in the picture as well as Zoë's mother – what was her name?'

'Eleanor.'

'Eleanor, exactly. We need to talk to her pronto, see what she knows, see if the dress was out of her possession at any stage before it arrived at Zoë's house. It's gone up to the lab – they're going to look at the thread that was used to stitch the hem, see if they can get DNA off it. Assuming we can find a match, that could give us our dressmaker. And we'll check Zoë's DNA against the bones too, see if anything shows up.'

Cathy nodded, taking it in. DNA might be a clincher if they could find any, but it took weeks to process and even then wouldn't tell them the exact chain of events that had led to the bones being stitched into the hem of the dress.

'I still don't get why she was up there.'

'Who? Lavinia Grant?'

Cathy popped another chip into her mouth, nodding. 'Hell of a lot of stairs for someone her age.'

'It could have been anything. The housekeeper said she'd been clearing the study ready for the decorators. A lot of the books were boxed up there. Quite possibly she wanted to find something in particular. Maybe someone followed her up, or perhaps the climb up those stairs was just too much for her and it *was* natural causes. According to the housekeeper and Trish she was a heavy smoker, had high blood pressure. Not a good combination.'

'Her doctor will confirm that. I'd still like to know exactly what route Zoë took home though.'

O'Rourke grunted. 'Bloody nuisance that we didn't get to speak to Lavinia Grant about the dress.' He paused, contemplating the rain running down the windscreen for a moment, was about to speak when his phone rang. Flicking on the speaker, he threw Cathy a glance warning her to keep quiet.

'O'Rourke.'

'We've found the car, Cig, the one this Angel Hierra hired.'

His face cracked into a smile. 'Was he in it?'

"'Fraid not. It was at the seafront, beside the Stena terminal. Maybe he got the ferry to Wales from there.'

'Let's hope so. Get Stena to pull their security tapes. If he was a foot passenger he'd have had to go through the terminal building to buy his ticket. Call me if you find him and alert Holyhead he might be on their side of the water. Anything in the car?'

'Clean as a pin. Still has the plastic on the seats from when he picked it up.'

O'Rourke nodded half to himself. 'Get the boys to check how far it's been driven. See if he went anywhere between collecting the car and arriving at the ferry.'

'Will do.'

'And assuming he didn't get on the ferry, get everyone out around the pubs and clubs tonight, show his picture about.'

O'Rourke clicked the phone off, his face thoughtful, working through the information. Cathy kept quiet. Angel Hierra was a double killer. A particularly vicious double killer – she knew his arrival in Dún Laoghaire had been on O'Rourke's mind all day. A moment later he snapped back to her.

'Where did Zoë say her mother was? Paris, was it?'

Cathy nodded. 'She *said* Paris all right but she didn't seem very sure.'

O'Rourke sighed, his irritation flaring for a moment, almost warm enough to clear the mist that had formed on the inside of the car windows. Cathy knew he was trying, but Zoë Grant had pissed him off. She was spiky, defensive. They'd found *human bones in her bedroom* for goodness' sake, but she didn't seem to be going out of her way to be helpful. Cathy knew with the parallels with the Dalkey baby case – the remains, the location – the alarm bells were ringing in his head. If Zoë had been abused too, it might account for her behaviour. It was one of the possibilities they had to consider. And one thing O'Rourke was known for was assessing the possibilities and following every one until it ruled itself out. Just like he was doing with this Hierra character.

'Any chance of a trip to Paris, d'you think? My passport's up to date.' Cathy screwed up the brown paper bag on her lap. She knew his answer before he even opened his mouth, the withering look he shot her met with a giggle. 'Right, that's me done. What time are we meeting tomorrow?'

'Eight sharp. Incident room. The techs are satisfied they have everything they need from the scene at Oleander House so we can release it, but we keep Zoë Grant's place sealed for the moment. Hopefully we'll have a positive location on this Hierra character by then too. It's a small town. We've really got enough nutters of our own without importing them. God knows why he wanted to come here in the first place.'

Cathy smiled, her hand on the door. 'I'll hit the gym at seven then. See you in the morning. Fancy a game of snooker before we kick off?' Whoever had designed Dún Laoghaire's state-of-the-art Garda station had somehow forgotten to include a designated incident room. The only space big enough to house a serious investigation was the kitchen and rec room where layers of ply turned the snooker table into a conference table. He caught her grin as she levered the car door open. 'Less of your backchat, miss. Now get moving, it's freezing.'

Slamming the car door closed, Cathy rapped the roof with her palm and headed for home. O'Rourke's tail lights blazed red, the colour reflected in the puddles that had formed on the pavements. *It was good to be working with him again.* She pulled her jacket close around herself, tugging at the collar to stop the freezing rain heading down her neck.

It had been one long day. And now . . . But she didn't get any further in her train of thought. Only a few steps from the path to her house, Cathy suddenly felt the urge to vomit. Quickening her pace, almost running down the narrow poured-concrete path glistening in the light from the street lamps above, she headed for the passage that ran beside next door's high wooden fence. She almost didn't make it. Wrenching open the top of the wheelie bin, Cathy felt her stomach contract, the contents reappearing, undigested, bitter with the taste of bile and regurgitated salt and vinegar. It only took a few moments for her stomach to empty, and then the tears came, falling freely, hot on her cheeks as she shivered violently, reaching out to the rough block wall of the house for support.

The face that stared back at Cathy from the bathroom mirror wasn't her own. Or at least it didn't feel like it. About three shades paler than normal, her eyes surrounded by a scattering of red pinprick broken veins – it happened every time she vomited – she looked like something out of a horror movie. *This felt like a horror movie.*

Steadying herself on the edge of the sink, Cathy could feel the rumble of the Xbox coming through the tiled bathroom floor. JP and Decko had been so absorbed when she came in that she'd been able to yell out a greeting and scoot straight up the stairs to the bathroom. As if everything was normal.

In her head, Cathy could see Sister Concepta, her Leaving Cert biology teacher, face taut, running through the parts of the human reproductive system like items on a shopping list. *Weetabix, sperm, baked beans, ovulation, milk and butter, and, of course, pregnancy.* Smothered giggles in the back row of the lab, flicking erasers off a ruler at Geraldine O'Mahony, and afterwards, behind the lavs, with Áine and their gang comparing notes on the real thing . . .

'Sister Immaculata says if a boy ever puts his tongue in your mouth you have to bite it off!'

'My sister says you definitely can't get pregnant if you do it in the bath.'

'Or standing up, that's safe too.'

'How can you do it standing up?'

And the same Sister Immaculata issuing reams of instructions before the debs dances began.

'Now girls, remember when we're dancing with a boy we must keep well back to allow plenty of space for the Holy Spirit.'

Sex before marriage? An abomination . . . who would want a girl who was sullied? You had to keep your virginity for your husband. Loose girls were fallen women, would be left on the shelf, ostracised by society. And then there was eternal damnation. Mustn't forget that. The fires of hell were already roaring in her ears.

Turning on the cold tap, Cathy pulled her hair back and splashed cold water onto her face. She needed to talk to someone. That was the bottom line. This was one problem she couldn't deal with on her own. But who?

She already knew what Áine would say. She'd be sympathetic but there'd be no question of 'options'. And her mum would be the same. There would be shock and embarrassment and lots of recrimination but the conclusion would be the same.

It wasn't that Cathy, deep down, didn't know that there was only one option here, but she knew she needed to explore everything, if only for her own sanity. Perhaps there was something she didn't know about, a miracle cure, a solution to the whole fecking mess.

Closing her eyes, Cathy leaned heavily on the sink, trying to focus on something other than her stomach. *Who could she talk to?*

Abortion was banned under Irish law, so her GP was going to be useless, she was sure. Not that abortion was really an option, a choice, but it had to be considered. Cathy was good at her job because she weighed up all the options. She might do mad impulsive things occasionally, follow her instinct completely, but one of the first things O'Rourke had taught her back in the day was that she needed to balance all the information. Especially when considering a problem as fecking meteoric as this one.

Cathy felt her stomach contract as another wave of nausea passed over her. She still didn't even know how long this puking business was going to go on for, or if it was going to get worse. *Could it get worse?* Christ, she hoped not.

So if she couldn't talk to Áine or her mum or a GP, who did that leave? A face loomed in her memory, hot kisses, too much champagne. Christ, she wasn't ready to talk to him yet. That was a *whole* other problem. No, she needed to be sure in her own mind what she was going to do before she went near him.

Pulling her phone out of her back pocket, Cathy turned around to lean on the sink. The Internet was slow in this corner of the house; she tapped the side of the phone with her fingernail, waiting for the bright colours of the Google logo to appear. She should have done this before, but she had been praying so hard that this problem might solve itself, that she might miscarry, that she hadn't had the guts to put the words 'crisis pregnancy' into a search engine. It would have made the whole thing a whole lot more real than she was ready for. Until today. Now she was quite sure this was a crisis and it wasn't going away on its own.

A moment later Google did its thing, dark blue text on white: positiveoptions.ie, giannacare.ie (what the hell was that?), standupgirl.com. Cathy tapped the last one, which sounded like her in more ways than one. She would have smiled but it wasn't funny. Really wasn't funny. The site was pink, with butterflies, at the top the words 'Pregnant, scared? Email Becky'. Cathy scrolled down the page. *Nausea and vomiting may come as early as a week into the pregnancy . . . Dizziness and fainting.* Helpful.

But it was an American site. They weren't even on the same planet as she was. She needed an Irish site.

Prolife.ie? She didn't think there would be a whole lot of unbiased advice there.

She scrolled down. Choiceireland.org. Maybe this would be it? Downstairs a cheer rose from the lads, whoops and high fives. At least someone was winning.

She tapped through to the site.

The 3 organisations listed below offer non-directive counselling sessions . . . they will talk openly about all the options available to you – adoption, abortion and parenting . . .

Oh. Thank. God.

The Well Woman Clinic.

Why hadn't she thought of that before?

15

His shoulders hunched against the chill penetrating his denim jacket, Steve Maguire looked blankly at the screen of his mobile phone, fiddling with the keys, selecting tunes, then deselecting, skipping to the next one, looking for ... *looking for what?* He adjusted his earpiece, wriggling it to improve the sound.

This was possibly the earliest Steve had been up in the morning since he sat his Leaving Cert, definitely the earliest he had ever tried catching the DART. Glancing above him, squinting through the curtain of mist-like rain billowing in from the sea, Steve could see the illuminated information board, its light glowing bright red against the winter darkness. Next train: 10 minutes. Dalkey was a good few stops away going south, but with the night he'd just had, right now Steve's priority was to get some air and some time to think, and to pick up his bike. By which time it would be light and would have stopped raining, and, hopefully, he would have got his head around the whole Lavinia and Zoë Grant thing.

Zoë Grant. Steve felt a rush of heat from somewhere deep inside as Zoë's name careered around his head like a character from *Super Mario Bros. Zoë Grant.* Fragile, brittle. Incredibly talented. And gorgeous with it.

But her world was quite, quite mad.

Her grandmother was Lavinia Grant. *Lavinia fucking Grant.* One of the wealthiest and most reclusive women in the state. A woman who never gave interviews. *And she wouldn't be giving any interviews any time soon.* The journalist in him facepalmed. Here he was, with an exclusive every paper in the country would be after, *and* with unique access to her granddaughter who also kept an extremely low profile. She could have been living it up on yachts in the Caribbean, hanging out in Lillie's VIP Library Bar every night, but what was she doing? Arranging flowers in Foxrock and painting the sea. *Very rock and roll.* There had to be a story there.

Shifting from one foot to the other, Steve leaned in against an advertising hoarding in an effort to avoid the worst of the rain, mentally back inside that house; back with the ghost of Lavinia Grant, with the distraught, foul-mouthed and utterly pissed Trish, back with Zoë.

It had seemed the thing to do at the time, to offer her his spare room for the night. Had he expected her to accept? Steve wasn't sure. But the Guards were crawling all over her place and would be at Oleander House for most of the night, and on top of all that, while they'd been waiting for O'Rourke to reappear from the house, Zoë had told him some guy had been skulking about in her garden the night before, that she'd been so worried she'd called the cops. What else could he have done? She couldn't go home, and her grandmother had just dropped dead – he could hardly leave her at a hotel for the night. Her mother lived abroad and, God knew how, they'd lost touch. And her closest friend was a picture framer called Phil who was away with his boyfriend this week collecting driftwood in Donegal.

Zoë had been exhausted by the time Cathy's lot had finished with her, had hardly been able to think straight.

Jesus. Zoë Grant.

Steve shoved his phone into his pocket and wiped away the trail of raindrops heading down his nose with his sleeve, remembering the events of the previous night.

She'd sat down at his kitchen table and put her head in her hands, her thick hair falling over her face.

'I can't believe this is happening.'

Nor could he.

Unsure what to say, he'd hauled open the fridge and pulled out a bottle of white wine. The questions had been jumping in his head, whizzing around like the lights on a slot machine. What were the chances of him, Steve Maguire, landing in the middle of the biggest story of his life and not being able to damn well do anything about it? Max wouldn't want anything to affect Zoë's show, and Steve couldn't compromise Cathy, they went way back. Her brother Pete was one of his best friends for Christ's sake, if he messed Cathy about Pete would kill him, literally as opposed to figuratively, assuming she didn't first. *'Step with care and great tact and remember that Life's a Great Balancing Act.'* Balancing act was right. Dr Seuss nailed it every time.

'Do you think they'll think it was me?'

Pulling her hair from her face, Zoë had looked up at him as he'd put the wine glass down in front of her, her grey eyes brimming with unshed tears. He'd frowned, not sure what Zoë was talking about. Did she mean they thought she'd broken into her own house? Or been involved in her grandmother's death? That had sent a cold chill down his spine. *She couldn't be, could she?*

'What do you mean? Why you?'

'Because the dress was in my house, in my wardrobe.'

Pouring himself a glass, sitting down opposite her, Steve had taken his time answering. But he wasn't getting it.

After everything that had happened, from finding himself sitting in the back seat of a cop car with an incredibly beautiful girl whom he had only met that morning, to them arriving at her (wealthy and famous) grandmother's house to find her dead on the stairs, Steve felt like he had definitely missed part of the story. After a few moments he'd given up. Zoë wasn't making sense, and life had taught him that rather than make a prat of yourself pretending you knew what someone was talking about, it was always better to be straight.

'What dress?'

Zoë had shivered then, taken a sip of her wine, her eyes fixed on the glass as she carefully put it back on the table, lining up one side of the base with the grain in the wood.

'The one in my wardrobe. The one with the bones.'

It had taken him a moment to register what she'd said. 'Bones?'

'They found some bones, they said, in the dress.'

Had it been the way Zoë said it, 'bones', that had made Steve realise that the bones were human? Or was it just that the whole cop thing had suddenly fallen into place? Ever since he'd found himself in the back of Cathy's boss's car he'd been wondering why there had been so much activity at Zoë's house, why Cathy had been so frosty. The last time he'd seen Cathy Connolly, at the launch of Pete's new Temple Bar restaurant, La Calèche, she'd been looking a million dollars in a very short, very low-cut red number and the highest heels he'd ever seen, and she'd been sipping champagne like it was water, giggling, confessing that she'd had a huge crush on him when she was a kid. But this afternoon Cathy had been in full work mode, focused and efficient, apparently not in the least bit embarrassed about the way that night had turned out.

How could he have been so thick? A complete eejit would have realised something serious was going on at Zoë's house. Behind him, Steve heard the kitchen clock ticking, the sound suddenly too loud, and with each movement of the hands it had all begun to click into place.

'Sometimes the questions are complicated and the answers are simple.' Dr Seuss had it right. With a regular break-in the forensic lads turned up, dusted and if you were lucky you got a follow-up call from whoever had taken your statement. But at Zoë's place there had been a Technical Bureau van, two patrol cars and that DI, Cathy's pal O'Rourke . . . and he wasn't the type you'd want to get into a row with.

Zoë Grant had the police crawling all over her house because they'd found *bones* in her bedroom. *Human bones.*

And suddenly Steve had realised, without question, that in her head at least, Zoë was definitely living in a different world – and it wasn't one orbiting in this solar system.

'What dress was it?' The words fell out, badly organised, *full marks for interview technique.*

'My mother's wedding dress.'

Her wedding dress? What the hell? *Her wedding dress?*

'And where were the bones?' Steve said it tentatively, disbelieving, not much more than a whisper.

'They said they were in the hem.' She took another sip of her wine.

Steve knew he was a bright guy, had scored ten A1s in his Leaving Cert, breezing into medicine like it was the easiest subject in the world – almost as easily as he'd breezed out of it, in fact. And that had been before he'd set up the band, or thought of developing the magazine. But he still wasn't getting it.

'Why on earth would there be a pile of bones in the hem?'

The shrug again.

'Can't you ask her – your mother, I mean? She must know what they are, where they came from.'

Zoë shifted in her seat, pulling at the ribbons on her blouse. Steve could hardly hear her when she spoke. 'I can't . . . I don't know where she is.'

Weird, and getting weirder. Maybe he'd wake up in a minute and it *would* all turn out to be a dream. 'You must do. She's your mother.'

'She went to Paris when I was little. To be with my dad, Lavinia said. I haven't heard from her since.' Zoë paused, her voice catching like a silken thread on a nail. 'I wanted to find her. I've always wanted to find her, but Lavinia said she hadn't wanted us, that she'd gone. She wouldn't help me find her.'

Steve could feel her sadness, dark blue, seeping out of her like spilled ink. Maybe Zoë wasn't bonkers, maybe she was just a lost child, running wild. The half-remembered words of a song came to him. He stood up to refill their glasses, using the moment to try and make sense of what she was saying.

'*Someone* must know where she is. Your grandmother must have had an address, even if they weren't in touch?'

'Maybe. I don't know . . .' Zoë sighed, a deep sigh that caught again as she exhaled. She rubbed her face with her hand. 'I don't think so.' She took a sip of her wine. 'I'd just like to talk to her once. Find out why she left. Find out what she's doing. See if I'm anything like her.' She paused. 'I really, really want her to come to the exhibition.'

The hoot of the incoming DART brought Steve back to his senses. He was really cold now, hands stuck into his jeans pockets, shoulders hunched against the dawn. He knew he should have said something when he left the house, but he'd knocked on her door gently, opening it a crack to see Zoë was fast asleep, the dreamless sleep of the exhausted, her hair splayed across the pillow like a streamer.

And Steve knew he'd have had no idea what to say to her. She was like porcelain, fragile, and with a hairline fracture running right down her centre.

So he'd scribbled a note, left it on the counter. Before she'd gone to bed Zoë said something about needing her cello, about needing to play if she couldn't paint. So Steve had left a note saying he would check with the Guards when he collected his bike, would put it in a cab if they let him have it. He promised he would be back in time for a late breakfast, leaving his mobile number if she needed him.

And he'd slipped out of the house praying she wouldn't wake, closing the front door firmly behind him, walking hard towards the DART station, trying to get his head together. How the hell had he got into this? Why the hell had he gone to Dalkey in the first place? But maybe he already knew the answer to that one. Max had sent him, but he knew he'd had his own reasons, had wanted to see Zoë again . . .

Relaxing into the caterpillar-green velour of the DART carriage, the interior lights comforting, bright, *normal*, Steve put his foot onto the seat in front and crossed his arms. *They had found bones in the hem of a dress in Zoë's house.* Images careered around his head like something from a horror film – they'd have to be small bones to fit in a dress, wouldn't they, so where were the rest of them? Where was the rest of the body? *And who . . . ?*

And *why* had he said he'd help her find her mother?

Whatever about keeping Zoë company yesterday, about giving her a bed for the night – he'd still only just met her. But she'd sounded so helpless, so lost, that it had just sort of slipped out. *'I'll see what I can do – she must be somewhere. I spend my whole life tracking down and verifying information about people. I'm sure we can find her if we try.'*

Lost in his thoughts, Steve hardly heard his phone ringing, felt instead the vibration in his top pocket, the movement making him start. Panic flashed through his mind. *Zoë must have woken up already, was upset that he'd gone. Was he ready to talk to her yet?* Hauling the phone out of his pocket, Steve checked the screen. And a surge of relief hit him. It was Max. Mad bloody Max.

'What the hell happened to you? I thought you were coming back here yesterday.'

'Sorry, mate, I was overtaken by events.' *That was an understatement.*

'You didn't sleep with her, did you? Already? You're some dirty dog, Steve Maguire . . .'

'*Me* a dirty dog? No I bloody didn't. And how can you talk?'

Max didn't let him continue. 'So what kept you?'

Jesus, where did he start?

16

'What's up with you?' From behind her, O'Rourke's voice cut through Cathy's thoughts like a blade. She was sitting alone in what would soon be the incident room, fiddling with her mobile phone. Looking up, her eyes widened in surprise, like a child caught with her hand in the biscuit tin.

'What?' Cathy tried to make her voice sound light, like she had no clue what O'Rourke was talking about, prayed he couldn't tell that her heart was hitting the floor, that a cold sweat was breaking out down her back. *Did he know?* The idea popped into Cathy's head like a bubble of methane heading to the surface of a murky pond . . . *surely not?* But it was the way that he said it, 'What's up with you?' Her Auntie Sinead could always tell when someone was pregnant just by looking at them . . . surely men couldn't do that too?

O'Rourke towered above her, his broad shoulders blocking out the glare from the fluorescents bouncing off the bright cream walls. He reached out and tilted her chin, his touch gentle.

'You look like you've been out on the tiles and are suffering for it, madam.'

Feck. Did she look that bad? After training this morning she'd put a load of foundation and extra concealer around her eyes to hide the broken veins. Thankfully there was rarely anyone else in the gym in Dún Laoghaire when it opened at six, so it didn't matter how shite she looked going in. It didn't exactly cater for competition athletes, but it had the equipment she needed to fill the gaps between proper training sessions over at Phoenix, and it was only five minutes from Dún Laoghaire Garda Station.

Cathy threw him a grin, sly and cheeky, she hoped. 'I wish. Couldn't sleep. Think the lads must have put a pea under my mattress.'

O'Rourke's face broke into a smile, blue eyes softening for a split second. Then he shook his head as though Cathy was a hopeless case and stuck his hand back in his trouser pocket, jangling his change as he looked around the room. The night shift had pulled two huge sheets of ply over the snooker table, had rolled the round white melamine tables, which usually spilled out of the kitchen, back inside. It was a bit of a squash, but when the concertina doors dividing the recreation room and kitchen were pulled closed it would give them a semblance of privacy, give the impression, at least, of a high-tech incident room.

'Anyone else coming, do you reckon, or are we running this one on our own?' There was an edge of impatience to O'Rourke's voice.

Cathy checked the time on her phone. 'You're early. It's only seven thirty.'

'You're here.'

'Yep, but I'm keen, I want promotion to ERU.'

He turned to look at her, surprised, his eyebrows meeting in a frown.

'Emergency Response? You don't?'

'Don't you think a Heckler & Koch would suit me? I look great in black.'

'You have to be sane, you know. It's a bit of a fundamental before they let you loose with a submachine gun.'

'You're right, and balaclavas give you terrible hat hair.' Cathy threw him a grin then, stretching, yawned. 'Christ, I'm knackered. Thought the walk from the gym and a bit of fresh air would wake me up.'

'Too much training, it's not natural. You know, you should dry your hair before you come up here. You'll get pneumonia.' He paused, a glint in his eye. 'And where's your car? Central locking broken again?' She scowled at him; he sounded like her mother. Her retort was prim. 'Life is too short to spend half an hour every day drying my hair. There are more important things to do. And my car is fine, thank you – the central locking works most of the time.'

O'Rourke grimaced. 'Right.' His pause was loaded. 'So, any more thoughts about our friend Miss Grant?'

''Bout her granny carking it, or whether she murdered her baby and stitched its remains up in a dress?'

'Either, both.'

Cathy slipped her phone onto the desk. She could feel his eyes on her. She pulled out her necklace, the dog tag catching the light, running the chain over her nose, considering what he'd said.

'Well, I'd love to know more about Zoë's relationship with Lavinia Grant – I can't figure that out at all.' Wrinkling his nose, O'Rourke nodded his agreement. 'And I'd *love* to find out what

the big secret is about Zoë's mother. I was getting a lot of vague-
ness when we mentioned her. Zoë wasn't comfortable talking
about it.'

'Reckon they've had a row?'

Cathy nodded, shrugging. 'Know my mother would have a
few words to say to me if I sewed the bones of *my* baby into
her wedding dress.' The words were out before Cathy realised
what she'd said. She could feel her cheeks turning, she was sure,
almost puce. Feck, why had she said that? And now her secret
was written all over her face.

O'Rourke didn't seem to notice. Sitting down sideways to
the desk, he had thrown one ankle over his knee, was focusing
on his sock, navy blue and red argyle, jiggling his foot up and
down impatiently. Cathy could feel his tension, knew he was
worried about the still-missing Angel Hierra as well as the
ramifications of the Dalkey baby case. Just because the Grants
had money didn't mean something similar couldn't have happened there.

'Saunders is doing Lavinia Grant's PM now – I just spoke
to him. He reckons, off the record, that it could be natural
causes.' O'Rourke paused, his contempt for Saunders and his
theories written across his face. 'But obviously the PM isn't
going to tell us if there were suspicious circumstances leading up to the onset of "natural causes".' He paused, scowling.
'I've asked him to send the bones over to the UK for DNA
analysis when the lads here have finished with them. He was
pontificating about them being too degraded to extract anything significant, but I'm pretty sure he was talking out of his
hat. Mitochondrial DNA was identified in bones found in the

sewer of a Roman bathhouse, so it's entirely possible that the guys in the UK will find something. With luck we should get enough to either identify or rule out Zoë as the mother, and find out the sex of the child too.'

'Any idea how long it'll take?' Cathy asked.

'Weeks, I'd guess. But I don't get the feeling that there's going to be a quick solution to this one.'

She nodded. It wasn't exactly a case that had presented a mass of leads. 'Has house-to-house turned anything up?'

'Nothing significant. They were going softly-softly but no one saw anyone acting suspiciously in the area prior to the break-in, and there don't appear to be any sightings of a baby in or around Zoë Grant's address, nor children unaccounted for in the immediate area. We've a request in with Missing Persons to see what the story is with missing babies. Can't say I remember any in the last twenty years to be honest. Be helpful if we had a more specific time frame, of course . . .'

Her head on one side, pulling at the roots of her hair, Cathy wrinkled her nose, thinking.

'Maybe no one knew.' She paused, a sick feeling worming its way through her gut. 'Maybe Zoë didn't go to the doctor, maybe she didn't tell anyone, delivered it herself, just like Cynthia Murphy. Or that woman in France – she had eight kids, murdered them all at birth, hid the bodies around the house.' Cathy paused, running her pendant along its chain once more. It helped her think. 'If Zoë was the victim of rape or abuse, she might have hidden the whole thing, pretended nothing was wrong until the baby arrived. It wouldn't be the first time. And there's always a chance it was premature or stillborn. Presumably the techs in the UK will be able to give us an idea of how old the baby was too?'

'Saunders said one of the bones was a femur, and a very small one at that. He reckons it was newborn.'

'Good.' *Was that good?*

Cathy shifted uncomfortably in her seat. *She needed to change the subject.*

'Any news on Hierra?'

O'Rourke was staring into the middle distance, ran his palm across his face.

'Nope. Seems to have disappeared into the ether. I'm rather hoping he's moved on.'

Before Cathy could answer, behind her the swing doors to the stairs banged open. O'Rourke looked up, flashed her a grin.

'Looks like the troops are here, let's get started.'

'Settle down everyone. I want to keep this short, get you all out there.'

A buzz crossed the incident room, fourteen carefully selected faces looking expectantly towards O'Rourke. It was a small team for this type of investigation, but a tight one, and that was how he wanted it. Behind him a whiteboard had been set up: date, incident and crime number written haphazardly across the top on one side with a dark blue marker. On the right-hand side, photos of the scene, of Zoë's bedroom, long shots of her cottage, close-ups of the wardrobe, of the dress. Of the bones. On the other side, photos of Lavinia Grant lying at the top of the stairs.

'Right, you all know why we're here. So first off, let me be absolutely clear: none of this goes out of this room. The press will have a field day if even a sniff escapes. We already look like prats after what happened at Whyte's Villas with the Murphys – those of you who are local will be familiar with it. Those who aren't, look it up. It's one of the worst cases of abuse I have ever had the misfortune to learn about and no one was prosecuted. And not only was no one prosecuted, but there were serious questions asked about the chain of evidence, lost files and the like. That doesn't happen here. We do it right.'

O'Rourke paused, letting his words sink in, looked around the room making eye contact with every single officer. He'd chosen them carefully, brought in the guys who had been at the scene yesterday, had done some digging and found other locals familiar with the Murphy case who were just as sick about the outcome as he was; supplemented by lads who wanted to make something of their careers, who were serious police officers on the fast track. Members who didn't want a fuck-up on their record.

'There will be comparisons when it all comes out, it's inevitable. But there will be no questions asked about the way in which we conducted this investigation. It's by the book. Anyone who can't manage that is off the team. Is that understood?' The ripple of nodding heads was like a Mexican wave. Cathy focused on her pen, on a doodle she was drawing on the pad in front of her. O'Rourke sounded bloody good. In control. In command. Even the smart-arses were like pussycats when he was in charge. He quickly outlined the facts of the case.

'Professor Saunders is doing Lavinia Grant's PM this morning.' He paused, leaned over to take a slug of the coffee cooling on the desk beside him. 'Our priority is to establish Zoë Grant's mother's whereabouts, talk to her about the dress, find out where it's been since it was made. The boys in the Park are examining it this morning, so we should get some initial feedback from them around lunchtime.'

O'Rourke looked around the room, taking in the whole team. 'I want to know what happened to that child and how it ended up in the hem of a bloody dress.'

17

Oleander House was in darkness when Zoë arrived.

It was almost ten o'clock but she had expected the Guards to be still here, someone at least to be minding the place, waiting for her, but the house looked abandoned, curtains open, the windows unlit, like the soul of the building had left it. It was strange seeing it unoccupied. As she paid the taxi driver, Zoë realised that she couldn't remember a time when the house had been empty. Even as a child, when a driver had collected her from school and dropped her home, if Lavinia and Trish weren't in then the housekeeper had been, lights on throughout the house, the old building warm and welcoming, often more so than the two women who lived there.

Slamming the car door, Zoë shivered. The rain had stopped but the sky was steel grey, the clouds hemmed seamlessly, meeting the sea on the horizon in a line so sharp it could have been drawn with a pencil. She hoped the house wasn't too cold, that someone had left the heating on. She was sure that Trish would be back the minute she picked up Zoë's message that the Inspector had phoned, and if the place was cold, that would give her something else to complain about.

Would Trish expect to stay now Lavinia was gone? Who even owned Oleander now? Zoë had no idea what was in Lavinia's will, had never thought to ask. She wouldn't be surprised if Lavinia had left the house to Trish.

Lifting the latch on the gate, Zoë sighed. She really should be feeling sad about Lavinia's death, but all she felt was numb. Numb and confused about, well, just about everything.

Pushing open the front door and flipping on the light switches in the hall, Zoë threw her handbag on the spindly-legged chair that stood between the dining room and the study and headed for the kitchen, her footsteps silent on the deep carpet. In Lavinia's study the mantel clock began to chime, the sound familiar but somehow hollow, lonely.

Reaching tentatively in around the heavy kitchen door, Zoë felt for the brass panel of light switches. There was something about a dark room that totally spooked her, and the kitchen was at the back of the house, the two windows that opened onto the garden shaded by shrubbery. A moment later the electric strip lights flickered into life and Zoë breathed a sigh of relief.

Filling the kettle, she turned and looked around the room while it boiled, steadying herself against the counter. It had looked exactly the same for as long as she could remember, the floor a chequerboard of black and white tiles, cupboards painted a dull orange, their long perspex handles catching the light from the fluorescent tubes overhead. She'd sat here at the scrubbed pine table to do her homework, listening to the housekeeper humming along to the radio as she prepared dinner. She had opened her exam results here. Had waited here, listening out for the postman, hoping one day a letter from her mother would come.

But now black footprints trailed across the tiles where the Guards had been backwards and forwards to the back door, and even in the short time that they had been out of the house a fine layer of dust had formed on the Formica counters. Everything was changing. Zoë hooked a long strand of hair behind her ear, trying to focus. She'd thought she'd feel better coming back here but right now she felt like everything was swirling around in her head like a winter sea, cold and threatening to overwhelm her. She didn't know what she should be worrying about first.

There was just so much happening. Her exhibition, and the bones, and Steve and now this, now Lavinia. *And then there was the man in her garden.* Had he been the one who had broken into her house? She hadn't been able to get him out of her head, his shadowy figure growing in her imagination last night as she'd tossed and turned in Steve's spare room. *What had he wanted?* Zoë shivered, crossing her arms tightly around herself.

Out in the hall her mobile began to ring and Zoë's heart sank a bit further. *It couldn't be Steve. His note had said he had a meeting around now.* Was it Trish? She hoped not. Zoë needed a few minutes on her own to, well, just to try and get her head around everything. Steve's face appeared in her mind, full of concern. He'd been so lovely last night, and even this morning had had to go out but had left her a note with a Belgian chocolate beside it – as if chocolate was the solution to all her problems – but it had made her smile, made her feel so grateful that someone cared. The phone stopped as the kettle came to a boil noisily behind her and Zoë turned to pull out the teapot. But before she could make the tea it began to ring again, the ringtone, an old-fashioned telephone bell, insistent, demanding attention. *She had better answer it.*

By the time she got into the hall and found it in her bag, it had stopped once more. Checking the screen, she sighed with relief. It was Phil. Silly, lovely Phil. She hit the dial button.

'Zoë, pet, I was just leaving you a message – how *are* you? We saw the news about Lavinia.' Before she could answer, the line cracked with static. 'Hang on a minute, is that better? The reception is terrible here. You'd think we were in Outer Mongolia, not Donegal. We have to walk up the lane from the cottage to even get a signal.'

Zoë smiled; Phil might spend his holidays looking for driftwood to make beautiful picture frames, but he was a total techy, got twitchy if he couldn't check Facebook at least twenty times a day. It was good to hear his voice.

'I'm fine, really. It's a shock but –'

'I know,' he interrupted. 'It's Lavinia. Selfish to the end. It's like she planned to go out in a blaze of press speculation.'

'Phil!' Zoë almost laughed. Lavinia had been so incredibly rude to him the first time they'd met, Phil had never forgiven her.

'We're coming back, Dan and me, we're taking you out to dinner –'

It was her turn to interrupt him. 'I'm at Oleander, Phil, there was, there is . . .' How did she say it? 'I left a message on your phone. My house was broken into. The Guards found . . . some . . . well they found some stuff they had to examine so I can't go back yet.'

'You left a message? Damn the reception here.' Then Zoë heard him turn away from the phone. 'I told you there was a message, Danny, didn't I say?'

Dan muttered something Zoë didn't catch. They were totally inseparable but were always fighting, didn't seem to agree on anything, even had different sorts of milk in their coffee.

'That's terrible, was much taken? Do they know who did it?' She could feel his concern coming down the phone line, his voice as anxious as she was.

Zoë shook her head. 'I'm not sure if anything was taken. I can't go in to see yet, but there was a man in the garden.' As she said it, she felt the hairs stand up on the back of her neck. 'I don't know . . .'

'We're coming. We'll be back in Dublin by tonight. I'll ring you then, babes.'

Before Zoë could answer, the front door opened behind her, a gust of chill sea air billowing into the hall. She spun around to find Trish standing in the doorway.

'There's a taxi outside with your cello in it, you better go and pay him.'

18

'This is totally ridiculous. We can't keep her here.' Tony Cox put his empty mug down on the granite counter too hard, the sound ringing across the kitchen, and hauled the fridge door open, searching for the milk. He could hear the kettle bubbling to the boil and with it, he was sure, Emily's temper. He'd nipped home mid-morning but was due back for his rounds soon – but not before he'd sorted out the almighty mess Emily had created. How could she have invited this *mad* old woman – Tony hated the term, but let's face facts – into their *home*? He closed his eyes, summoning reserves of patience from the tips of his toes, battling to keep his own temper under control. *He already didn't get to spend half as much time with Emily as he wanted to, and now this?*

Behind him, Emily had gone quiet. *Not a good sign.* Suddenly realising that he was clenching his teeth, Tony consciously tried to relax his jaw. *Sometimes he wished Emily was more like his mother. Just plain loud.* But Emily was so different. She turned everything inward. *Everything.*

The fridge started to peep loudly, its alarm telling Tony he'd had the door open too long. But he still couldn't see the milk, and realised that he wasn't actually looking for it. Every argument he came up with, every reason he had for Mary not staying made him sound like the Grinch who stole Christmas. And Tony already felt like a total shit, his guilt sharp, like someone was prodding him with a pitchfork, whenever he disagreed with Emily. She had been through so much . . .

Emily's voice cut into his thoughts, low but forceful: 'There was no way Mary could go back to that flat on her own after spending half the night wandering the streets, and well you know it, Tony Cox.'

Tony took a deep breath and, giving in to the fridge's manic insistence, let the door fall shut as he turned to face his wife.

'Emily, *it's Thanksgiving.*'

Leaning on the counter, her hands thrust into the pockets of her jeans, shoulders squared ready for a fight, Emily glared back at him.

'Exactly. Thanksgiving. When families get together to give thanks for the harvest and for the safe delivery of the Pilgrim Fathers. Your mother –'

'Oh my God.' Tony held up his hands in surrender, a partial one at least, his tone incredulous. 'Do we have to bring my mother into this?' Tony deliberately opened the fridge again and peered inside.

'Your mother says it's a time for family, for thankfulness.'

Family.

The one thing Emily wanted more than ever. The word was like a kick in the gut.

He turned to face her, conscious of the tension radiating between them across the terracotta tiles. He felt an overpowering urge to hug her, wanted to close the gap yawning between them. Then he realised that the fridge door was still open, and it was peeping again. He slammed it shut and cleared his throat.

'So, what are we going to do with her?'

'Can't we just keep her until after Thanksgiving? It's not as if she's your patient – she's *our* house guest. And can't you have a word with one of your colleagues and get her assessed? I'm sure she'll be better if she gets some medication.'

Emily's voice was imploring, tugging at Tony, notes of the same tune that went around his head every day. Every single day. It was his fault she couldn't have children, his fault she'd been attacked. If only he hadn't been late. If only he hadn't taken that call – if only he'd been there. He should have been with her sitting in the park on their bench, sharing coffee and bagels, swapping hospital gossip like teenagers. But instead he'd been on the phone in his office arranging a meeting that could have waited, and Emily had been alone, wandering aimlessly as she waited for him. The shock of getting the call from the cops had made his world stop turning. He'd thought he was going to lose her, and at that moment he'd realised he couldn't live on without her.

'OK, OK. I'll ask Singh to assess her. He can organise an MRI scan, but you know it could take a while to get a positive diagnosis.'

'Do you really think she's got time to wait? She's started wandering. You know it'll only get worse. Would he not make an educated guess?'

Tony looked at her despairingly. She knew as well as he did that that was a ridiculous question. 'He can guess lots of things, but without monitoring we can never be sure the prognosis is correct – it's hard to be definitive in cases like this . . .'

'But she's rambling, hallucinating – she's hearing voices and keeps saying she can smell cigars, for goodness' sake. And she's disassociated, emotionless, seems to have retreated deep inside herself.'

Tony picked up his cup. 'I know, I've seen all of that, but it could still be Alzheimer's. There's a fine line between a psychiatric disorder and dementia. And late-onset schizophrenia is relatively rare.'

'What if it's not late-onset, what if Mary's been like this her whole life, but no one has noticed?'

'Is that likely? Irrational behaviour, disassociated thoughts, depression? I think someone would have noticed that.'

'Not necessarily. Mary's been on her own for years. She said something about being a governess. I mean, when did people last have governesses?'

'OK, OK, I'll ask Singh to check her out. There are a few things he can try that might help bring her back.'

Emily's smile was warm, like the sun coming out, lighting her face.

'Thank you. We'll let her get over the shock and then I'll take her home. She's so bewildered, she's like a child.'

Like a child. Tony looked at Emily, stunned. It had popped out before she'd even known she was saying it. The words stung, left a dark hole of silence in their wake.

Realising what she'd said, glancing at him, Emily continued hastily, papering over the cracks as fast as she could.

'I don't mean that, I mean she's vulnerable, and she's been alone for so long . . .' She tried to backtrack, but the damage had been done.

Tony came over to her, enveloping her in his arms, pressing her face into his broad chest, resting his chin on her head.

'One day I'll get my hands on that kid and I'll kill him.'

Tony could feel Emily's tears through his shirt, her voice already husky, trying to sound bright.

'That's mad, Tony Cox. It wasn't his fault. He was doped up, probably never even realised he'd cut me.'

It wasn't the mugging that was the problem. It was the infection that had caused the damage. Irreparable damage. Damage so severe that Emily might never be able to have what she wanted so desperately – a child of her own. They'd talked about it so many times, going over and over the same ground, so many rounds of IVF, so many failures. And after the most recent one, just before they left America, she'd begun to talk seriously about adoption. The one thing Tony really couldn't get his head around. It might be for others, but not for him. He wanted above everything else for their child to be a part of them. He'd been so sure IVF would work eventually.

He knew Emily couldn't understand his worries that an adopted child might turn out to have deep-rooted psychological problems that none of them could have foreseen, and of the heartache that might bring. Perhaps he was being irrational, but he saw it every day in work, and it nagged at him like toothache whenever they discussed it. There were so many behavioural difficulties that couldn't be detected with genetic screening, and were they ready for that? Would he, at his age, be able to cope? Would Emily? Would he end up resenting the fact that someone else's child was taking all of Emily's attention?

Without adoption as a possibility, surrogacy was looking like the only alternative, and that was fraught with difficulty, quite apart from the legal issues.

'I know, sweetheart,' he said. 'Really, I know. So I guess we'll keep Mary? As a house guest?'

19

'What are you doing here?'

Cathy hastily shoved her phone back in her pocket and swung around to find Steve Maguire behind her, the wheels of his bike hissing to a stop on the glistening pavement outside Oleander House. He was shaking his head. 'Haven't seen you in months, and here you are for the second time in two days. Anyone would think you fancied me or something.'

Had he heard her on the phone, making the appointment? She tried to hide her anxiety with a glare.

After the briefing this morning, O'Rourke had summoned her to his office, had stood staring out of the window, hands deep in his pockets.

'Zoë Grant knows something about all this, she must do. I want you to go and see her this afternoon. Find out about her mother. Saunders reckons Lavinia Grant's death is from natural causes. A massive heart attack. The bash on the back of her head is consistent with a fall and he's found no evidence to suggest interference.' He didn't sound like he believed Saunders for one minute. 'Though what caused her heart to fail so dramatically on that day of all days remains an issue in my mind.' He'd paused. 'We'll have to release the scene. I'm going to ring Trish O'Sullivan and Zoë now to let them know they can go back to

Oleander House. I want you to meet Zoë there later, ask about the mother. Watch her reactions. And have a good look at that house while you're at it.'

Cathy had nodded to his back, her face pale, reflected in the windowpane like the ghost of someone she used to be.

'Take Jamie Fanning with you. I've got him buckshee from Cabinteely; he needs the experience so keep him busy. He'll get on with your Zoë like a house on fire.'

'You sure that's a good idea? He's a bit of a charmer.' Jamie Fanning, who kept the entire district entertained with his nocturnal adventures, was nicknamed 007 for good reason.

O'Rourke had rolled his eyes. 'He's keen to make a good impression. I'm sure he can manage to take notes while you talk to her. It's not rocket science.'

Standing in his office, she'd groaned inwardly. Having Jamie Fanning hanging about would make it bloody difficult for her to get a moment on her own to make a private phone call – but as they'd arrived outside Oleander House, he'd been complaining about needing a coffee and she'd seen her opportunity and packed him off to the shop. Thank goodness the receptionist at the Well Woman Clinic had picked up on the first ring. The next available appointment was next week. Cathy's sigh of relief had been ragged. It was a step forward, but it still felt like a lifetime away.

So here she was, appointment booked, fresh coffee on the way. And here was Steve Maguire. *Had he heard her?* She'd been careful, keeping her voice low. She shook the thought from her head; he couldn't have done, she was getting paranoid.

Cathy looked at Steve, tuning back in to his question. *What was she doing at Oleander House? What he was doing here was more to the point.* He was still wearing his denim jacket, now with a navy fleece-lined jacket under it, his messenger bag slung over his back, looking like he'd just got out of the shower.

'I'm here trying to do my job, obviously.'

He jumped off the bike, grinning. 'Looking good, girl. This detective business suits you.'

Cathy shot him a withering look, self-consciously yanking her hair behind her ear, wishing she'd tied it back, thankful she'd thrown on a tailored black jacket this morning over her black roll-neck and jeans. *At least she looked professional . . .*

'You on your own? I thought cops always had partners.'

'I do, thanks, he's just nipped to the shop. But never mind what I'm doing here, aren't you through with the knight-in-shining-armour routine?'

'Me? Never . . .' He threw her a cheeky grin.

Cathy rolled her eyes. 'So, what exactly *are* you doing here?'

'Zoë called to say she was here, so I thought I'd check up on her. She's really scared that the guy she saw in her garden might come back. She needs someone to look out for her.'

Cathy looked at him quizzically. Did Steve have any idea what he was getting himself into? She knew he meant well, but she'd always thought he was a bit of a dreamer, more interested in his music than the real world and earning a real living. Pete didn't agree; he reckoned Steve Maguire was as sharp as they came, would make more money than all of them with his various enterprises. And Cathy had to admit he was probably right on that score – the band Steve had managed when he dropped out of med school had gone viral on YouTube, and now he'd started this magazine, was already looking at expanding it across Europe. He thought big, never let anything get in his way. That didn't mean he hadn't had some major disasters, had come to Pete to be bailed out more than once, but he always had another project in the pipeline that could be the next big thing.

Should she warn him about Zoë though? Whatever was going on here could bring everything he'd built tumbling down. The rag press loved a good scandal and to bring anyone who looked like they were doing well back to ground level. Steve Maguire was too young and too successful for a lot of the whiskey-swilling old guard to stomach.

Would she be breaching protocol if she told him to back off? *She and Steve Maguire went back a long way.*

Cathy took a deep breath, trying to impart the seriousness of the situation with a frown, failing miserably. *He wasn't getting it.*

For a moment Cathy felt a blast of impatience – she didn't want to have to spell it out letter by letter but it suddenly clicked that she *was* going to have to tell him. For one thing, if he got in the way of the investigation O'Rourke would go nuts . . . Cathy could hear him now, going on about her not declaring a conflict of interest, forgetting to mention she knew the suspect's boyfriend . . . personally. She glanced over her shoulder to see if there was any sign of 007. He was probably chatting up the girl in the shop, but he could appear at any moment. She'd better make this quick.

'Look, you didn't hear this from me, Steve, but you really need to keep away from Zoë Grant. This is a whole lot more complicated than it looks.'

Steve looked at her, surprised.

'Why?'

'She's not someone you want to get involved with.' Cathy kept her voice low, conscious of a man waiting at the bus stop across the road, the collar of his overcoat turned up against the chill sea breeze. He had his head buried in the *Irish Times* but she didn't want him overhearing their conversation.

'And why exactly would that be? Because she thinks she's being stalked and now her grandmother's dead?' Steve's voice had a sharp edge to it, like Cathy was interfering, like it was none of her business.

She could understand that.

'She just isn't . . .' Cathy tried to reach for words that would paint the picture, but that wouldn't compromise her. *She couldn't give him specifics, but she had to make it clear.* She didn't get a chance.

'You my keeper now, Garda Connolly?' Obviously she'd hit a nerve.

'Of course not.' Cathy shot the words right back at him. 'I'm just telling you that there's stuff going on here you don't know about.'

Steve frowned. 'Zoë's had a tough time. Her grandmother was a total bitch – the last person who should have been bringing up a kid. Zoë's a brilliant artist but she's got a ton of issues; she's terrified of the dark and so frightened of water she can't even take a bath.' He paused. 'She's never had anyone to look out for her.' Then he said, half-teasing, 'You jealous?'

'For God's sake, Steve, have you got a one-track mind? Is it possible that I'm looking out for you here without a hidden agenda? Just listen to me, will you? Keep away from her.' Cathy paused. She was getting annoyed now; whether it was from embarrassment that he'd thought she was jealous, or because he'd been sucked in by Zoë Grant's apparent neediness, she wasn't sure. 'Don't you get it?' She kept her voice low as she tried to control her temper. 'I'm not here for the good of my health. Read my lips, *I'm working.*'

Avoiding Cathy's eye, Steve grimaced, and jumping off the bike, leaned it on his hip, crossing his arms. Tight. Defensive?

'I know. She told me.' Narrowing her eyes, Cathy looked at him speculatively. 'About the bones I mean.' Steve grimaced and rubbed his hand across his face.

About the bones. The words reverberated between them like a bell tolling. A big bell. Ringing loud.

Cathy raised her eyebrows. 'She didn't happen to mention where they came from by any chance?' Cathy had intended it to sound sarcastic, but she half-meant it, the possibility that Zoë Grant might actually have told him the full story at some point after a bottle of wine in the early hours of the morning hitting her right between the eyes in one of those 'duh' moments.

Steve checked out the toe of his Converse, kicked a piece of gravel around the pavement for a moment, *weighing up how much he could tell her?*

'She doesn't know.'

'Really?' Cathy was tempted to say. 'And you believe her?' but bit it back. Was he telling her the truth? Surely the past counted for something, surely he'd be straight with her when push came to shove. But she was a cop and his latest conquest – if that's what Zoë was – was a suspect. Cathy tried to make the next question sound relaxed, casual.

'How long have you known her?'

Steve's sigh was audible. 'About twenty-four hours.'

Cathy did a double take. Was that the truth? If it was, at least it got her off the hook with O'Rourke. It was hardly a conflict of interest if they'd only just met.

'You're not serious. So what's with the boyfriend routine?'

Steve shrugged. 'I didn't ask to be shipped in here last night – that was your boss. Then Lavinia Grant's body gets found – I couldn't exactly abandon her, could I?' Steve paused. 'And that Trish O'Sullivan's nuts. She might be drawing her pension, but for all I knew, she could have topped Lavinia Grant and been after Zoë next.'

Cathy raised her eyebrows: *gallantry or foolishness?* Steve shuffled nervously. 'And she doesn't seem to have many friends – there wasn't anyone else she could call.' He sounded like he was trying to justify himself.

'She must know someone. Everyone has friends.' Cathy was about to say more but suddenly she felt the hair rising on the back of her neck. Glancing up towards the house, she checked the windows, expecting to see a pale face looking down on them. But each window stared out blankly towards the horizon, reflecting the sharp grey line of the sea. *There was someone watching them*, she was sure of it. *Someone hidden.* Cathy looked again. No one there. But the feeling didn't go away.

Turning and leaning back on the railings, crossing her arms, Cathy glanced back down the road. Still no sign of Fanning – how long did it take to get coffee? She frowned, trying to focus on what Steve had said. O'Rourke's idea this morning had been for her to come back and chat to Zoë, to build a picture of her life without dragging her into the interview room and tramping all over what could be a delicate situation with their size elevens. And here was Steve Maguire, someone Zoë *was* likely to open up to, already on the inside . . .

Steve leaned his bike on the railings beside Cathy, one hand on the handlebars, the other stuck in his jeans pocket. 'You'd think she'd have friends, but apart from this guy Phil who frames her pictures and a couple of girls she used to know at school, Zoë seems to have a very limited circle.' He paused. 'It's probably to do with being a Grant. If you're worth millions it's hard to know who to trust.'

Steve frowned, like he was suddenly seeing something for the first time and it was worrying him. 'You'd think that was the answer to all your problems, wouldn't you? A couple of million in the bank.' He looked rueful. 'You know, Pete and me, we're always talking about making it, moving forward, hustling, looking for the next opportunity, and that's a real buzz, but when you see the impact real money has, you start to wonder if that really is the right win. They say money can't buy you happiness.'

If Zoë Grant was anything to go by, he was damn right there. About to answer, Cathy glanced behind her again, looking up at Oleander House's high windows. The feeling of being watched was still there. Like ice sliding down her back. She turned back to him, her voice low, serious: 'Do you believe her, Steve, honestly? How did you meet her?'

'She's doing an exhibition for Max. I was supposed to be interviewing her.'

Of course, *how could she forget?* Max. *Max fecking Igoe.* For a moment Cathy felt like the world had shifted a foot, fast, and in the opposite direction to the one she was going in. This wasn't her day.

'If Zoë knows Max Igoe, she must have friends.' *Keep it practical.*

'That's business. I wouldn't put him down as a friend. He saw one of her paintings in that flower shop she works in, asked her to come in for a chat.'

Cathy was starting to build the picture, although it wasn't the one she'd expected. 'So why exactly did you turn up at her house yesterday? To get the interview?'

Steve nodded, drawing in his breath. 'That's about it. Max had a meeting with her yesterday, was worried when she didn't call back, thought she'd changed her mind about the exhibition. Then the whole thing happened here and . . . well . . . she asked me to help her.'

'To help her?' Cathy looked at him, her eyes wide. What the hell did she want help with that didn't involve interfering with a Garda investigation?

Steve was looking at his Converse again, didn't appear to have noticed her reaction. 'She's lost touch with her mother, wants me to help her find her.'

'Her mother?' Cathy knew she was sounding like a parrot.

'You know that Dr Seuss thing "I have heard there are troubles of more than one kind. Some come from ahead and some come from behind"? Well Zoë certainly seems to have more than her fair share.' He paused. 'She said her mother's in France some-where – Paris, she thinks. Went when Zoë was about three, but they've lost touch. And she really wants to find her – now more than ever, because of the exhibition. Her mum's an artist too.'

'And how are you planning to find her, exactly?'

Steve shrugged like it was obvious. 'Google. If you know how to look you can find all sorts of things. Not just social media, there are lots of ways. If she's an artist she's probably had an exhi-bition. And she went to live with Zoë's father, apparently. Max said the French social security system is pretty thorough.' Cathy shook her head, half to herself: *Max again. As if this was any of his business.* Steve didn't seem to notice. 'If her mother's there,

I'll find her. It's very hard to be invisible these days. Might have to be a bit clever, but you know . . .'

Cathy knew – or rather she didn't want to know. Steve had started coding in school, had hacked into University College Dublin once to get the phone number of a girl he fancied. Some things she was definitely better off *not* knowing. She looked at him meaningfully. He grinned, getting it immediately.

'Sorry, Garda Connolly. Point taken.'

She rolled her eyes. 'So who's Zoë's father?'

Before Steve could answer, the front door slammed shut, the sound making them both jump. Cathy turned sharply to see Trish O'Sullivan barrelling towards them, a cigarette hanging from her mouth.

Across the road, the man waiting for the bus turned to the next page of his newspaper.

20

'Do you think you could work in your study instead of at the kitchen table?'

Emily put a cup of coffee down beside Tony. It was his late day, he wasn't due in for another hour. Looking up, he grinned. 'I won't be a minute, just need to sort these notes and then I'll be off. What are your plans for the afternoon?'

Emily sat down opposite him, turning her own mug in her hands. 'I thought I'd take Mary shopping for some new shoes. I don't think a woman of her age should be wearing trainers. And then I'm taking her to Praxis for a late lunch.'

'Where's Praxis?' Tony pretended to be affronted. 'You've never taken me there for lunch.'

'That's because it's a charity for migrants and refugees arriving in London. On Potts Street next to the church. They have a coffee shop and an Irish group that meet there. You never know, it might stir some memories.'

'Sounds good. The quicker she's back on her feet' – *and out of here*, but he didn't say it – 'the better. It'll take a while for the medication to kick in fully but I think you should start seeing an improvement soon. Singh wants to monitor her but he's confident she's on the right track. It certainly won't hurt at all if Mary hears a few homey accents. So, you won't be lonely?'

Emily didn't answer, instead threw him a weak grin, looked into her cup of tea like she was reading the leaves. Sensing the opening of an uneasy silence, Tony tried to look busy, shuffling his papers. His voice low, Emily could hardly hear him when he spoke.

'We could try IVF again, you know. Might have more luck here. Different doctors.'

Her reaction was instantaneous, a sharp intake of breath. Emily shook her head.

'I can't do it again. I couldn't face setting myself up for another fall. We've tried *seven* times. You know what the doctors said. And the hormones mess with my head as much as my body.'

'I know, sweetheart.'

The sob escaped before Emily could hold it back.

'All I want is a baby ... It's just not fair. There are girls not much more than thirteen giving birth around here – what can they offer a child? Drug addicts and alcoholics and ...' She hadn't meant it to all pour out, but her anguish was molten.

'I know.' What could he say? Tony bit his lip. Why had he brought it up? And he knew what was coming next. He could almost hear her gearing herself up.

'But now we're settled here for a bit, we could check out adoption again. The rules might be different in England ... And I know you're worried about the psychological thing but there's all types of screening available now.'

His sigh was deep and jagged. 'I know, honey, I know.' Tony paused, grappling with his conscience. The possibility of psychological problems was only one part of it. *It was such a big thing.* He could hardly say it to himself, let alone to her, and he'd thought about it a lot, trying to get his head around it, but *how could an adopted child ever be theirs?*

Emily sighed, her eyes filled with tears. 'There must be someone out there who got pregnant by accident, or who just isn't ready for motherhood. It happens all the time. There must be someone, somewhere, who needs a really good home for a baby.'

'You've an old lady to mother for the moment. You could hardly manage her with a baby in the house, could you?'

'Just think about it, Tony. How can we leave this planet with no legacy? You've so much to offer a child. What about junior football, about passing on your basketball skills to someone . . .'

Above them the scrape of furniture stopped Emily.

'Sounds like our guest is on the move. Did you put away all the sharp knives?'

'Christ, Tony – yes, I did, against my better judgement. She must be ninety if she's a day, do you really think she's going to have a psychotic episode and murder us in our beds?'

He held his hands up, stopping her. 'Pays to be cautious. It's our home, we need to be careful.'

'Mary's mind might be wandering but she's hardly going to turn into a serial killer. She was talking about Dior yesterday, the New Look. She was really sweet, laughing like a teenager, telling me all about the dances she used to go to.'

'The New Look, that was the late forties wasn't it?' Tony thought for a moment, his mind ticking through his school history. 'If she was in her teens then, that would put her in her late seventies now. I thought she was older.'

Emily smiled, distracted momentarily from the baby debate by her new charge. 'Mary said she had a dress made of saffron silk with puff sleeves and a huge skirt that twirled when she danced. And she wasn't allowed out in the street without her gloves and her hat, and even if it was boiling she had to wear stockings. Sounds so formal now, doesn't it? She was telling me how they had all their outfits tailor-made.'

'You forget about that in these days of mass production. Had to get everything made then.'

'My family didn't. I don't think my father had new shoes until he was nine and he certainly never had a new pair of trousers until he went to college.' Emily paused. 'From what she says I'm sure Mary is from Dublin, from a well-off family. She said she remembers women coming from the States to buy their dresses, that it was quite a fashion capital.'

'And no rationing.'

Emily sighed. 'It's so sad. She really lit up when she was talking. I could almost hear the chink of the champagne glasses, see the jewels. And here she is with only the clothes she stands up in.'

21

'Zoë's inside, making a load of bloody awful noise.'

Speaking through her cigarette, Trish O'Sullivan pulled open Oleander's black wrought-iron gate with one hand, fumbling in a huge lizard-skin shoulder bag for her car keys with the other. Finding them, hauling them out, she looked from Cathy to Steve, her eyes red-rimmed, spitting contempt. 'You two know each other, do you? Might have guessed.' She looked disdainfully at Steve. 'Zoë told me all about you.'

Cathy held her ground but felt herself retreating inside, shrinking physically. Trish's breath smelled foul, rank with alcohol and nicotine. And the rest of her wasn't in much better shape, her perfectly coiffed hair squashed to one side where she'd slept on it, and in the stark light of day, the blonde was dusted with grey. From a distance she had looked smart in a navy trouser suit, but close up Cathy could see it was creased, like it had been tossed on the floor the last time she wore it.

'We're back in the house anyway, no thanks to your Inspector. I hope you don't want to speak to me, I'm off to the hairdresser's.' Trish paused. 'When do you think we'll be able to bury Lavinia? I need to make the arrangements.'

'I'm sure it won't be long –'

Trish cut Cathy off. 'Find out. Sooner rather than later. It's utterly ridiculous that the pathologist should be involved at all. Undignified. We'll have the press all over us.'

With that she pushed past Cathy and strode off down the road, almost colliding with Jamie Fanning who had appeared around the corner juggling two takeaway coffees, a cellophane bag of pastries and his mobile phone, which was clamped to his ear. *At last, she needed that coffee now.*

Steve watched Trish go, his eyebrows raised. 'Whew, spiky.'

'Sudden deaths are always a shock. People react in different ways.' It sounded more generous than Cathy felt.

'Don't see any sign of the media myself. Reckon she's as bad as it'll get. I'm sure with her contacts she's burying the story . . . Max reckons she's only still working because she's got the dirt on every big player in the country. No one dares suggest she retire.'

Steve paused as Fanning arrived beside Cathy, still on his phone, mouthing the words 'Who was *that*?' at her and nodding in Trish's direction.

'Trish O'Sullivan. She found Lavinia Grant's body.'

Fanning raised his eyebrows and nodded, his attention back on his phone. 'Cool, talk to you later.' He flicked it off, handing Cathy one of the cups. 'Latte for madame.'

'Thanks.' She took a long sip. Lukewarm: he'd obviously found someone to talk to. Then Cathy realised he was looking at her expectantly, his chocolate-brown eyes wide. It took her a moment to work out what his problem was. 'Sorry, this is Steve Maguire, friend of Zoë Grant's.'

'The suspect we're going to interview?'

Tactful. Cathy rolled her eyes. 'The one *I'm* going to interview. *You're* taking the notes.'

They could hear the haunting notes of a cello from the doorstep, the sound fluid and beautiful. Steve reached for the polished brass knocker, the head of a serpent, and rapped twice. Moments later Zoë answered the door, her hair pulled into a wispy tumble on the top of her head, long filigree earrings set with moonstones jangling from each ear. She was wearing a long grey skirt the colour of her eyes, velvet, embroidered in a vivid purple with an intricate pattern of flowers and butterflies soaring up from the hem; a soft purple mohair sweater, sloping off one shoulder; beneath it a white linen shirt. Cathy could feel Fanning react beside her, straightening up, putting on his legendary James Bond smile. *That was all she needed.*

'Steve.' Taking in the group on the doorstep, Zoë said his name with an unmistakable sense of relief. 'Did you get my message? The Inspector called to say we could come back so I got a taxi over – I knew you'd be busy. How did your meeting go?'

'Cool, got the last of the advertising stitched up.'

As Steve stepped into the hall, Cathy lagged back on the broad granite step. Zoë spoke before she had a chance to, her voice suddenly cold.

'You've just missed Trish.'

'It was you we wanted to talk to, actually.'

Zoë's thick eyebrows met in a frown. 'Why?'

Why indeed. Cathy tried to look as warm and relaxed as possible. *Because a baby's bones were found in your bedroom the same day your grandmother was found dead?* Tempted though she was, she didn't say it, instead kept her professional smile in place.

'Would you mind if we came in?'

Cathy was across the threshold before Zoë had a chance to say no, Jamie Fanning right behind her.

In the hall, Cathy could see that Steve was looking for a way to defuse the tension. Putting on his casually sexy grin – the slightly vacant one that made him look like he needed mothering – he slipped his arm around Zoë, giving her a brotherly hug, his tone deliberately cheerful. 'I'd murder a cup of tea.'

Cathy would have found the whole scene – including Steve's choice of words – hilarious, if she hadn't, at that moment, felt a real spike of jealousy. Why the hell was she jealous? The mad Miss Grant was welcome to Steve Maguire, to his Dr Seuss quotations and intensely irritating PR power talk . . . She tried to pull herself together, to focus back on the job. Then Jamie Fanning interrupted her thoughts.

'That sounds like a great idea.' He'd managed to lose their empty takeaway cups outside somewhere, had his hands casually stuck in his jeans pockets like this was a social call, his devastating smile firmly in place. Zoë looked from Steve to Cathy and Fanning, obviously unsure whether she really wanted them as guests. Then, grudgingly, she gestured towards the end of the hall. 'Of course, come through to the kitchen.'

Following them, Cathy threw a look at Fanning, her eyebrows arched. He grinned back, knocking his highlighted fringe out of his eyes, and shrugged, his 'I can't help being amazing' gesture. *Amazing. Right.*

Blocking him out, Cathy took a moment to glance around the hall. Every light was on, including, totally unnecessarily it seemed, the chandelier on the half landing. The house was stiflingly warm and all the doors leading from the hall were open. In the dining room, she could see that the polished mahogany table was covered in papers, a box file flung open. Opposite it, the living room was meticulously tidy, the cello leaning against a carved mahogany dining chair, a music stand beside it.

In the kitchen the story was the same. Lights on. Fluorescent tubes, sidelights, under-counter lights all bouncing off the polished melamine surfaces and orange cupboards, off the linoleum on the floor. A spray bottle of kitchen cleaner stood on the counter, a sponge beside it, the smell of bleach hitting Cathy hard in the gut, her hand instinctively flying to her mouth. She hid it well, rubbed her nose, coughed like she was starting a cold, tried to filter the air through her mouth as she breathed.

Steve hauled his bag off over his head, dumping it on the table, and headed for the counter.

'I'll make the tea, you guys sit down. That cello sounded great. Have you been playing long?'

Picking up the kettle, he filled it noisily, deliberately creating a distraction with hustle and bustle and jollity.

Fanning pulled out a chair from the scrubbed pine table and sat down. Zoë hovered for a moment, unsure whether she should sit; her hand fluttered to one of her earrings, the other crossed protectively across her waist. Cathy pulled out a chair opposite Fanning and sitting, rubbed her hands together, blowing on them. *Hiding her nausea.* 'Whew, it's cold today.'

'Tea's on its way. Warm us all up a bit.'

Sinking down into a pine carver, pulled out from the head of the table like it was waiting to receive her, Zoë turned to Cathy.

'When can I go home?'

'We're moving as quickly as we can.'

Her hand back at her earring, a smile flicked across Zoë's face. 'I wasn't expecting to be staying away for more than the night.'

'Here we are.' Steve brought a huge bone-china teapot to the table and poured the tea. Cathy played with her cup, weighing up whether she should plunge straight in or pussyfoot around the issues for a few more minutes – it didn't take her long to decide. Zoë Grant gave her the creeps almost as much as this too clean, too bright kitchen. Sitting forward in her chair, Cathy hooked her hair behind her ear as she spoke.

'Zoë, what can you tell me about your mother? Did you say she was living in France?'

Across the table 007 finally stopped gawking at Zoë long enough to pull out his notebook.

Zoë put her cup down carefully, angling the handle to her right like the position was important, would make a difference to the outcome of their conversation.

'Why do you need to talk to her? She hasn't been in Ireland for years.'

Cathy kept her voice level. 'It was her dress, wasn't it, in your room?'

'Yes but I don't see –'

'It's just that if you don't know how the bones came to be in the hem, perhaps she can tell us. It's important that we get as much information as possible, as quickly as we can. Then you can get back home and we can tidy everything up.'

Zoë took another sip of her tea, nodding, glancing anxiously at Steve. He put his hand out across the table, rubbed her arm like she was a pet dog. Out of the corner of her eye Cathy could see 007 watching them closely. *Maybe he wasn't a complete waste of space.*

'It's OK,' Steve said, 'you can tell her. I'm sure she can help.'

It still took Zoë a moment to answer, and when she did, Cathy could hardly hear her.

'We've lost touch. I really don't know where she is.' Then, louder, 'Lavinia said she had made her decision to leave and that was that. I want her to come to the exhibition but now I need to find her to tell her about the funeral.' It was like a confession.

Fanning opened his mouth to speak but Cathy threw him a glare before he got a chance. She nodded to Zoë, sympathetically, she hoped.

'Do you have her last known address? Any information at all? I'm sure we can find her.'

Zoë shook her head, a tear forming in her eye. She brushed it away like it was a speck of dust.

'I don't have one. She sent me some birthday cards when I was younger and a couple of Christmas cards but they didn't have a return address . . .' She paused, struggling with the truth. 'I think Lavinia must have burned the envelopes.'

Burned the envelopes? Why? Cathy fought the urge to ask, moving on, her tone deliberately gentle. 'Would Lavinia have kept in touch with her, do you think? She must have had some point of contact in case of an emergency?'

Zoë shook her head helplessly like the whole thing was becoming too much for her to cope with. 'I had a look in her study earlier but I couldn't see anything. And then Trish came in and started shouting, said Lavinia's affairs weren't anything to do with me.'

'Did you tell Trish what you were looking for?'

Zoë nodded. 'She said that my mother wanted to leave, that it wasn't for me to start raking up the past.'

OK . . . Cathy nodded, sipping her tea, said in her 'not a problem' voice, 'If you can tell me your mother's date of birth and full name, it'll speed things up. We'll see what we can do.'

It took a moment for Zoë to reply.

'Her name is Eleanor, Eleanor Grant. I don't know her full date of birth. It must be in Lavinia's papers somewhere.'

Great. 'And why did she go to France?' Cathy tried to sound relaxed, interested but offhand.

'To be with my father. I don't know anything about him except that he was French and Lavinia didn't like him. My mother must have loved him though – she chose to leave me behind and go to him.'

Whew. Silence yawned uncomfortably between them. Cathy could see Steve was trying to think of something to say, something that would make a mother abandoning her child better. Not surprisingly, he wasn't having much luck. And 007, his pen poised in his hand, was keeping his mouth shut – *thank God.*

Giving the statement a dignified amount of time to mature, Cathy said softly, 'How old were you?'

'I don't know. I don't have many clear memories of her.' Zoë sipped her tea, her face screwed up clawing for the half-forgotten pictures in her head. 'I can remember a really hot summer, playing in a paddling pool in the garden. I had this swimming costume with a frilly skirt, bright pink. And a woman with long hair and a patchwork skirt. I remember she was pretty, beautiful, and she gave me ice cream. She had a butterfly necklace. Silver with enamel on its wings, turquoise and pink. I loved it. And a clip in her hair. But something about her was sad. I don't remember her smiling.' Zoë stopped for a moment, her gaze fixed on her cup. 'It's all a bit hazy.'

Cathy nodded again. 'Did Lavinia ever tell you anything about your father?'

Zoë shook her head. 'She never spoke about him – I've never even seen a photograph of him. Lavinia didn't like photos. There aren't any in the house. She probably burned them.'

'Did she burn a lot of things?' Cathy tried to sound casual, to keep the incredulity from her voice, suddenly seeing an image of Lavinia Grant stirring a brazier like something out of *Macbeth*.

Zoë shrugged. 'She was worried the press would go through the bins. Being the head of Grant Valentine has its downside – she didn't want the press knowing anything about her private life. She was always saying to remember what happened to Diana.'

'Diana?' Cathy was beginning to lose the thread.

'The Princess of Wales. Remember what happened with the paparazzi.'

'Of course, of course.' Cathy took a hasty sip of her tea. *Surely Lavinia Grant didn't seriously compare herself to Lady Diana?* She might be one of the in-crowd but she was hardly royalty. And wasn't her best friend a journalist? But perhaps that was the relationship she didn't want the press exploring.

Before she could think of anything intelligent to say to follow that one, Cathy felt her phone vibrating in her pocket.

'Sorry, excuse me.' She pulled it out, checked the screen. O'Rourke. You had to give him full marks for timing.

'Excuse me.' Throwing a stern glance at Fanning, willing him not to speak, she slipped out from the table and headed for the tiny hall that linked the kitchen with the back door. Behind her she could half-hear Steve murmuring something sympathetic to Zoë.

'How's it going?' O'Rourke's tone was loaded.

'Tricky, but we're getting there – 007's playing a blinder.' Cathy kept her voice low, her lips grazing the mouthpiece of the phone. She was sure she was out of earshot, but she wasn't taking any risks.

'Good.' She could hear him smiling. 'I won't keep you. We've had a development.' O'Rourke paused. 'The techs have had a look at those bones and the dress.'

'And?' Cathy could feel his excitement radiating down the phone, cursed him for keeping her on tenterhooks. If she'd been standing next to him she would have poked him in the ribs.

'I need to know if there's anyone out there who might have a grudge against Zoë, an old enemy maybe, someone who doesn't like it that she's finally getting a break with this exhibition of hers.'

'Go on.' *Why?* Cathy felt like shouting it down the phone. O'Rourke could be a pain in the arse when he was being clever, going all mysterious.

'Some of the clothes on the floor in Zoë's room had been slashed, including the wedding dress. That's why it caught on the nail and you found the bones. Someone ran a knife through the skirt from the waistband to the hem.'

Jesus. 'Nice. Anything else?' Cathy knew there was, could tell from his voice. O'Rourke paused before he answered.

'They've found soil traces. In the hem and on the bones. Looks like the bones could have been buried before they ended up in the dress . . .' She could hear him moving, like he was bending over to polish his shoes or dropping something in the bin. 'So we're digging up the garden, see if we can find the rest of them.' It was blunt, no-nonsense. 'You better tell Miss Grant that she's not going to be going home for a while.'

22

The Angelus bell was striking as Cathy headed back into the station, her heels rattling off the chill grey paving stones into the even chillier grey air. She'd walked briskly from the DART station, weaving through office workers heading home, teenagers beginning to gather around the grim 1970s hulk of a shopping centre that dominated the otherwise elegant Victorian seaside town. She could have caught a lift from Monkstown but she'd felt like the walk, had hoped it would clear her head, give her some time to arrange her thoughts. It hadn't helped.

Now it was six o'clock, and bells were ringing out across the country, calling the loyal and devout to prayer, a constant reminder of duty and obligation, a reminder that the Church was watching, waiting, like a great black crow hungry for the weak to stumble.

Boy, had she stumbled.

Shivering involuntarily, Cathy heaved open the steel and plate-glass front door of Dún Laoghaire Garda Station. It sucked closed behind her, sealing out the world, sealing her into a protective bubble of ringing phones and urgent voices, interviews and leads, of laughter and despair, of frenetic teams trying to beat the clock. But today it was a bubble that also stank of bleach, the disinfectant masking cheap perfume and unwashed bodies, last night's puke. The confusion of odours hit Cathy like a slap in the face as she headed across the pale-grey-tiled hall, nodding to the station house officer in the public office, punching her code into the inner door, holding her breath just long enough for her to get to the bottom of the stairs. When she let her breath out, it came in a whoosh. She gagged, coughed theatrically, trying to hide it. *Feck this.*

Her appointment next week couldn't come fast enough.

Upstairs, O'Rourke was in his office scowling at his laptop when she stuck her head around the door.

'You look like you need a coffee.'

'Cruise in the Caribbean more like.' O'Rourke didn't look up, continued to type, two fingers flying over the keys like he was hammering out a tune. Rock or heavy metal.

'What's up?'

'Angel Hierra has vanished off the face of the earth. And he definitely didn't get on the ferry. I've got twenty bloody mules out there checking every bar, every hotel, every bed and breakfast. Nothing. Nada.'

Cathy came into the office properly, closing the door behind her, leaning her back on it, her fingertips tucked into the tight-fitting pockets of her jeans.

'Could he have changed his appearance?'

O'Rourke paused from his typing to look down his nose at her. 'It seems likely.'

'But he's American. He must have a strong accent.'

'He's Mexican American, speaks fluent Spanish. I imagine he's dropped into the Spanish student population.'

Cathy nodded. There were a lot of Spanish students in Dún Laoghaire, in Ireland to study English at one of the many language colleges.

'Are you going to do a press conference?'

'Looks like it, Chief Super's orders. Spread a bit of terror among the residents, have the local gougers turn on anyone who speaks with an accent.' He shook his head, widening his eyes at the implications. A press conference was more likely to spook Hierra into running than anything else, while they coped with the fallout.

'Anyway, the Grant case.' O'Rourke cleared his throat. 'The soil samples' – he said it like he was announcing the best actor award at the Oscars – 'don't match.' He paused, looking straight at Cathy, his hands hovering in mid-air as though if he sat there long enough he could perform magic, solve all his problems with the next keystroke. It was one of those significant pauses, but Cathy wasn't too sure what he wanted her to say, so she kept her mouth shut. She was pretty sure he was going to tell her anyway. He did. 'Wrong sort of sand.'

Leaning over, O'Rourke riffled through a pile of printouts, looking for the report.

'Are there different sorts?'

'There are. And the sort we've got doesn't come from Zoë Grant's garden.'

'How can they tell?'

'Remember Jim Donovan?' O'Rourke didn't wait for Cathy to answer. Everyone knew Jim Donovan's name: the first director of forensic science in the state, who had had his legs blown off by The General. O'Rourke paused, shaking his head, appalled all over again by one of their own taking a direct hit. 'When

Jim worked the Mountbatten case, he did a comparison of sand granules from the beaches around Mullaghmore, the whole way from Sligo to Mayo. And he found out that they're all different shapes. Amazing, isn't it? Sand looks like sand to me . . . So anyhow, our sand didn't come from Zoë's garden.'

'So where did it come from?' Cathy asked.

'That's the million-dollar question. The lab boys are going to take samples from the surrounding area but for all we know those bones could have been buried in Kerry . . .' A sigh of frustration escaped before O'Rourke could stop it.

'So it's going to take a while.'

O'Rourke scowled at the screen of his computer, chewing his lip. Then rubbed his hands over his face, massaging away the strain, the tension.

He hated it when things went wrong. And Cathy knew he wanted to move the investigation forward. If they found the burial site then there was half a chance it would lead them to the crime scene, give them an idea of who it was who had taken it upon themselves to murder a child, bury it and subsequently (*why?*) move the bones to the hem of a wedding dress.

They needed to hide them.

The thought hit Cathy slap in the middle of the forehead like it had been out there all the time but she was too stupid to see it. At some point after burying them, the person who had hidden them had needed to move them, to hide them again.

Obviously.

But why the dress? *It was hardly convenient, hardly the first place you'd think of to stick a pile of bones in a hurry.*

Cathy thought hard but nothing came. Sometimes her subconscious was downright uncooperative.

Crossing his arms tight, O'Rourke forced a grin. 'So how did you get on? Better than me, I hope.'

'So-so.' Cathy moved away from the door, pulled out the chair opposite his desk and flopped into it.

'Sit down, why don't you?'

'Thanks, I –'

O'Rourke cut across her. 'Hope you've had something to eat today. You're looking positively peaky at the moment.'

'Peaky?' The words didn't fit coming out of his mouth.

'My grandmother's favourite word. Has you covered. You coming down with something?'

That was about right. Cathy shrugged. What could she say? How many headaches could you have in nine months without someone smelling a rat?

'Just keep away from me if it's contagious. I've enough problems. So, Zoë Grant's mother. Where is she and when can we talk to her?'

Picking up the dog tag on her necklace, Cathy ran it along the chain as she answered.

'That's looking a bit tricky. She's in France, apparently, but Zoë lost touch with her when she was a child. They haven't had any contact since she was about three. She doesn't even know her date of birth.'

'What d'you mean, no contact? She's her mother, isn't she?'

'Zoë was brought up by Lavinia Grant. She thinks that perhaps Eleanor – that's her mother – might have been in touch over the years, but Lavinia never told her. Sounds like she eloped, reading between the lines. Zoë thinks Lavinia might have burned the correspondence.'

'For pity's sake. So what are we supposed to do, put an ad in *Le Monde*? Jesus. You'll have to get back down there first thing tomorrow and go through Lavinia's papers. Take 007 with you again.' He frowned. 'There must be some record of her mother, a postcard or an email, her birth cert. Something. Anything.' He paused. 'I'll get the lads here to get on to the embassy and Interpol, put out some feelers. I want to know exactly who has had contact with that dress since the day it was made.'

'I'll need a warrant.'

'Obviously, I'll organise it for first thing in the morning. Have an early night and get your beauty sleep. And you'd better get hold of some garlic on the way. Those bloody women are like a coven of witches. Burning? Jeez, they probably nail their men to stakes, leave them in the basement to rot . . . You'll have to keep a close eye on lover boy.'

23

Tony Cox put his head around the living-room door.

'You asleep?'

The fire was dying in the grate, a reading lamp throwing a pool of warm light over the end of the sofa on which Emily was lying, a cat stretched out on her knee. She stretched, yawning.

'I must have been. Have you been drinking? I thought you were at a meeting.'

'I was – it ended up in the Blind Beggar. Did you know a guy was shot in there? It used to be a real gangland pub – the Krays drank there.'

He flopped into an armchair.

More awake than she wanted to be, Emily slipped her hand under her head. 'How did you end up in Whitechapel? I thought the meeting was at St Thomas's.'

'It moved. Right over to The London. Very handy. I walked home.'

'I guessed you didn't fly. You should be more careful. You'll get mugged.'

Tony didn't answer, was struggling to undo his tie in the half-light.

'I swear these things get harder as you get older. So how was your day?'

Emily yawned again. 'Good, actually. I got Mary kitted out, and we had lunch. Met an old guy from Bundoran who knew my parents.'

'What, both of them?'

Emily nodded, turning to face him, curling her knees up, much to the cat's disgust. 'They're from the same village. Ireland's a small country, you know. They say you're only one person away from the person you need to speak to.'

'What's that mean?'

'That everyone knows everyone else, and if you don't know someone, you'll know someone else who does.'

'Got it.' It was plain he didn't, but he wasn't going to dwell on it. 'How was Mary? Any improvement?'

Any improvement? It was hard for Emily to be sure, but sitting in the brightly lit kitchen, the radio tuned to RTÉ 1 and Ireland's favourite morning show, a cup of tea cooling in front of her, Mary had seemed to be emerging from the cloud of confusion that had surrounded her, was almost chatty. And it was a huge relief. Emily knew she had made a fuss of the old lady with the soda bread and home-made marmalade, knew she should be distancing herself, not getting involved, but seeing her sitting there, bundled up in her cardigan, her shoulders hunched, it seemed, through years of shivering, Emily couldn't help herself.

There were still tests Singh wanted to do, but he'd been satisfied enough to try a course of medication, and it seemed to be beginning to work. Which meant that with proper care Mary would be able to function in society without the anxiety, the paranoia, the isolation she had probably been feeling for years. Tears had pricked at Emily's eyes. She blinked them away; *now she was being ridiculous*. She took a deep breath; the years of hormone treatment had left her emotions heightened and, she was quite sure, jumbled, her despair and her failure raw. But right now no one could rob her of the glow that Mary's recovery was bringing her; she might not be able to get pregnant, but one thing she could do was help. And even the prospect of a simple shopping trip had helped, bringing Mary's memories closer to the surface.

'I thought we'd have a look around the shops today, Mary, see if we can't find you some better shoes.'

'Shoes?'

As she lifted her rheumy eyes from the piece of toast in her hand, a shadow had passed across Mary's face, creased like a relief map of the Derryveagh Mountains, as if a shoe-buying expedition was something to be feared. She looked so vulnerable.

'And maybe a new cardy.'

Behind Emily the toaster popped, the wonderful homey smell of brown toast filling the kitchen.

'A new cardy?' Mary frowned, then looked directly at Emily. And for the first time since they had met, her eyes were focused, penetrating, her voice clear. 'I knew you'd come.'

It was a definite statement of fact.

Not entirely sure what she meant, Emily stood up to get the toast.

'We couldn't leave you in that draughty flat now, could we, after you being up half the night?'

Watching her put the plate of toast down between them, Mary shook her head, her voice back to a whisper, but her eyes clear.

'It was so cold. Nowhere to sit. And rough. You can't imagine. Everyone was sick.'

'Where was that, Mary?'

Mary wrinkled her face. 'She told me to pack my case, said it was a holiday . . . until . . . Never even said goodbye. Just gave me the address and the ticket and turned around.'

'Who did, Mary? Who gave you the ticket?'

As if she didn't hear her, Mary took a delicate sip of her tea, her little finger sticking out from the cup as if it was made of bone china and they were taking tea on the lawn. Emily waited, desperate to repeat the question but knowing too that she needed to give Mary space, time to connect with her past.

'I knew you'd come. I knew. You were a determined little thing right from the start. I've been waiting, you know. Every night I thought it could be tomorrow, it could be tomorrow when she comes.' Mary paused and the moment was lost, the glimpse of clarity gone like a cloud scudding across the sky. When she spoke again, it was half to herself, the words almost a mantra, worn like a groove on a record: 'Hard to find. Must have been hard to find.'

Hard to find, like a slipped stitch or a lost button.

'Why did it take you so long?' Not much more than a whisper.

'Sorry, Mary?' Watching her closely, Emily wasn't sure if Mary knew where she was, who she was talking to. But her eyes were still bright, her face animated.

'Why did it take you so long to find me?'

Emily had thought she was talking about them finding her at the police station, but was she? She kept her face straight like she knew what Mary meant.

'I was waiting. Every day I thought it might be the next day. Waiting, waiting. Mrs Hartnett always said I looked like I was waiting – an "air of expectancy", she called it.'

Emily took a sip of her tea.

'Who was Mrs Hartnett, Mary?' It was the first time she'd mentioned anyone from her past by name. And today was the first time she'd talked about the past without living it as she spoke, the first time it was a genuine memory. She must be getting better. The drugs had to be kicking in. In the background, the radio presenter introduced another guest but Emily wasn't listening, her entire focus on Mary.

Trying to sound conversational, relaxed, Emily could feel a tiny bud of excitement flowering inside her. There was something about Mary, something about her story that Emily felt desperate to unravel. She was like she was a character in an Agatha Christie novel, or Dickens, her past a mass of strands knotted together, or the pieces of a pattern jumbled up. All of it locked inside her head. The one thing Emily was sure of was that she was Irish, that she would have family back home. They had a connection, a kinship.

'Who was Mrs Hartnett?' Emily prompted gently.

'She was a dragon.' Mary said it as though the memory left a bitter taste in her mouth. Emily was about to ask why, but Mary continued, her face softening, 'Mrs Lynch though, she was lovely, looked like Rita Hayworth when she was dressed for dinner or the theatre.' Mary smiled, her eyes shining, leaned towards Emily conspiratorially, her toast forgotten. 'But she had terrible trouble with her nerves. Only saw the children after their bath.' Mary shook her head sadly. 'He worshipped her, insisted the children were quiet when she was resting, went mad if there was the slightest disturbance.' Mary nodded as if agreeing with herself, then 'She couldn't believe I was only nineteen and travelling on my own, kept asking questions. All the time, questions.' Mary paused. It was a long pause and for a moment Emily felt like she should say something to keep the memories coming, something to prompt her to keep talking. But there was no need. Almost as if she was trying to justify herself, Mary continued, 'But she needed the help with the two little ones and then another one came along. And then there was the mending. Mrs Lynch was always full of my invisible mending, my fingers were black and blue with all of it, but I didn't mind . . .'

It was the longest speech Mary had ever made. Emily was bursting with questions, but didn't want to interrupt. Mary smiled, the memories obviously happy ones.

Something Mary had said before had made Emily think maybe she'd been a nanny or a governess. Now she was sure. Perhaps if they could find Mary's employers they could find out a bit more about her – the children would be well grown and Lynch was a common name, but . . .

'What were the children's names, Mary?'

'Clara and Tom, and then Benjamin, he came next, and then little Richard, he was on the end. Clara was such a pretty thing, with blonde ringlets, gosh how she screamed when I brushed her hair. And Tom, well he was a devil. Went and joined the Royal Engineers as soon as he was eighteen, but I wasn't with them by then.'

'Where did you go, Mary?'

Mary frowned. 'Where did I go?'

'After Mrs Lynch, after Clara and Tom and Benjamin, where did you go?'

'Mrs Lynch found me a place with the Hartnetts. Great big house in Hampstead. But not like the Lynches at all. I hadn't been there long when she told me little Tom Lynch had been killed in Aden.' Mary sighed, her lip trembling. 'But Mrs Hartnett wouldn't let me have the afternoon off to go and call, to give my respects. They were all going away to the country, couldn't spare me. And of course we were away all summer. I wrote but I never heard back.'

Emily leaned across the table. 'I'm sure they got your letter, Mary, I'm sure Mrs Lynch knew you cared.' She could see Mary was getting distressed, tried to move the conversation on. 'Did the Hartnetts have children?'

Mary looked impatient like it was a stupid question.

'They wouldn't have needed me if they didn't. Twins, girls, and little madams, always scheming to get me into trouble. I didn't stay . . .'

Mary left the sentence hanging, and looked down at her toast, cold now, her face clouding. Reaching for the memories had drained her. Emily was desperate to find out what happened next, to ask if she'd maintained contact with her own family, but she could see Mary was slipping back into the no man's land of her mind. But they were definitely getting somewhere.

'I think she's on the right road,' Emily said, stretching. Unimpressed, the cat had decided to try its luck with Tony, set out across the cream carpet guerrilla style. A log shifted in the fireplace, sending up a shower of sparks.

'When was the Aden crisis? Mary mentioned that one of the children she looked after had joined the army and was killed in Aden.'

Tony pursed his lips, thinking. 'The sixties. Sixty-three to sixty-seven, I think. Pre-Vietnam.'

Emily sighed, there were still so many years missing. She'd said she'd been nineteen when she went to them. 'Mary said she was given a ticket –'

But Tony wasn't listening, instead interrupted her. 'Guess what.' He sounded like a child bursting to tell her what he'd bought her for Christmas.

'What?'

'*I* – Tony paused, trying to make the sentence sound dramatic – '*I* have been asked to give a keynote address to the Irish College of Psychiatrists.' Emily would normally have laughed at the way he was announcing the news, but right now she was too preoccupied to get enthusiastic.

'Sounds exciting.' She yawned, wriggling down into the sofa cushion.

'Actually I wasn't first choice. That guy from Seattle was going to do it but he's had a heart attack.' Tony was working hard to sound sympathetic. 'And guess what – the conference is in Dublin.'

'In Dublin?' Suddenly wide awake, Emily pulled herself up and looked at him. He was slouched in the chair, grinning at her. 'At the Shelbourne Hotel. Five-star – end of the first week in December . . .'

'But that's so soon. What do they want you to talk about?' Tony shrugged. She was missing his point but he knew she'd get there in a few minutes. 'Can you get the time off?' she asked.

'Of course. The great Dr O'Mahony is delighted. Might be able to get the leave that's owing to me too if I play my cards right . . .'

Then Emily got it. 'So we could go home for Christmas?'

'We could. Well, if your parents will have us. Will I have to eat black pudding again? I don't think I could stomach it. Maybe I'd better tell them I'm too busy.'

Emily picked up a cushion from beside her feet and aimed it at him. It fell short, sending the cat behind the armchair in a panic. 'You eejit. We haven't been home at Christmas for years . . .'

'I know. Too many Christmas Eves on the ward. So, do you want to go? They're covering all the expenses and we'll have a couple of days to ourselves in Dublin – I've always wanted to have a look at the library in Trinity, and I bet there are some great antique shops . . .'

'Urgh.' Rolling back, Emily made a sound like a balloon deflating.

'What?'

'I won't be able to come. You'll have to go on your own. I couldn't leave Mary. She's not ready to go back to her flat on her own yet, and it's so close to Christmas.'

It took Tony a moment to work out his response. 'One of the reasons I love you, Mrs Cox, is that you are such a caring soul, but honestly, I'm sure we can find some residential care for her while we're away.'

Even if I have to pay for it personally.

'No, I couldn't dump her in some care home. She's confused enough as it is. I don't think she could cope with being abandoned again.' Tony opened his mouth to speak but she was midstream. 'Unless . . . unless we take her with us, see if visiting Dublin stirs any memories . . .'

'Take her with us?' Tony couldn't hide the groan that escaped. 'Emily, how on earth can we take her with us? You'll be saying we'll have to take the cats next.'

'Don't be silly, next door will feed them. They spend half their time asleep in her front room as it is.'

'"Don't be silly"? Who's being silly?' asked Tony, exasperated.

'It could be the *best* thing. Mary might remember more about who she is, where her people are.'

'And do you think they'll want her back, Em, after all this time?'

'Of course they will. Honestly, Tony, you've no concept of family.'

Tony flopped back into the chair. How the hell was he going to talk her out of this one?

Then Emily's words sunk in . . . *no concept of family*. It echoed around his head, reverberating like a drum roll.

'You cannot be serious. Honestly, Em . . . how can we take Mary with us? It's a conference, it's a five-star hotel . . .' Tony Cox had his back to her, was topping up his coffee cup, a last caffeine hit before he ran for the Tube.

'I can be, totally and absolutely. It's you who's not being serious.'

This whole situation was getting out of hand. He'd honestly thought that after a few days Emily would see the utter lunacy of the idea, would see that carting Mary off to Dublin, while it wasn't an inherently bad idea, was just crazy at the same time as this conference. As if it wasn't bad enough that he had a psychotic patient living in his home . . . Sometimes he wondered how much the assault in Boston had really affected Emily, wondered if it had damaged something deep in her subconscious mind. There were times when Tony was sure she was suffering from delayed post-traumatic stress. He ran his hand across his brow. 'OK, OK. But what I don't get is why it's so important to you now, why can't we take her after Christmas?'

'Because it's Christmas, Tony. Because that's when you spend time with those close to you. How many Christmases do you think Mary's spent on her own? How many do you think she's got left?'

He opened his mouth to speak but Emily didn't let him. 'She hasn't been home since she was nineteen, Tony. That's a hell of a long time. Are you going to be the one who denies her one last chance?'

'Of course not.' Tony took a deep breath. He was having trouble holding it together here . . . how could she be so blinkered? 'You make me sound like the Grinch. But I've got a life too, Em, I thought you'd be delighted to spend a couple of days away from everything, in Dublin of all places. We can have lunch, go to the theatre . . . How are we going to manage that with Mary in tow?' He tried hard to hide the desperation in his voice. 'You're my wife, Em, and I love you and we don't get to spend enough time together . . .'

Tony wasn't sure what he'd said to make her see sense, but Emily suddenly mellowed, her shoulders slumping like she'd been pricked with a needle and all the air that had been holding her up had shot out. 'I know, you're right. You're right . . .'

Pushing her chair back, the sudden noise of the legs scraping across the tiles sending one of the cats tumbling from the counter where it had been making for the butter dish, Emily crossed the void between them. She hooked her arms around Tony's neck, smoothing the collar of his jacket, running her hand over the soft silk of his tie, a mysterious blue-green today, like the sea had been captured along its length.

'I love you, Tony Cox, don't you ever forget that. But it'll be fine, honestly. I'll get it all sorted out. Mary's not a child, she doesn't need a babysitter. We'll have some time on our own, I'll make sure we do.'

Tony's shoulders tensed; he'd thought she was seeing his point – obviously not. 'Mary might not legally need a babysitter, but what if she starts wandering again? Dramatic change can be extremely unsettling for someone of that age, to say nothing of someone in her state of mind. What if taking her there unearths unpleasant memories? We've no idea why she left Ireland – she could have been running away from something, from someone. Maybe she was in trouble or escaping an abusive husband. It could be catastrophic.'

'I've thought about that. I know, I –'

Interrupting her, Tony kissed her hair, pulling her close, resting his chin on the top of her head.

'And even if it's all fine, Em, what'll we do with her when we go to your parents? I can't imagine they'll want her to join them for Christmas.'

Emily sighed. *Could he make her see it was unrealistic, that it was a mad idea?* She buried her head in his jacket.

'Do you think I'm crazy?'

Tony laughed, a deep chuckle.

'Only a little bit. You just get passionate about things, get an idea in your head and feel so strongly that it's the right thing to do that you don't see the fallout. You just have to realise that not everyone sees things from your point of view, that's all.'

'You're right.' Emily paused, digging her head into his shirt, breathing in his aftershave. 'We can't take her to Mum and Dad's, can we? It wouldn't be fair on any of them.' Then, her voice muffled by the angle of her head, 'I just really feel that it would be so good for her, so good to go home and see Dublin again. And she can't go on her own. Argh.' She paused. 'Let's both think about it, see if we can't come up with a plan.'

'Sounds good. The conference schedule's on my desk with a brochure from the hotel. Why don't you ring them and book in for a massage or something while I'm at the conference? I'm sure they've got a spa.'

'Did you call the hotel yet?' Tony's voice sounded distant on the phone, the smooth walls of his office at the hospital always making him sound slightly echoey, like he was inside a box.

'Was just about to.'

Emily stood in Tony's study beside his desk, one knee resting on his chair, cradling the desk phone in her shoulder as she reached for the conference information. Half-reading it, half-listening to him speak to someone who had obviously just walked into his office, she scanned the page.

'How's Mary?' Tony was back to her.

Emily ran her eye down the schedule, flipped over the page. 'She's having lunch. She seems much better, pretty together. I've got my flower-arranging class this afternoon at the community centre. I thought I'd take her along. It'll be good for her.' Emily paused, then spoke half to herself. 'And she was grand when we went out shopping. I was a bit worried going back through the crowds and everything. I reckon that little gurrier mugging her has brought all this on. Everyone I've spoken to said she was a bit muddled before it happened but not nearly as bad as she is now, and she'd never wandered.'

'You said . . .' *They'd had a whole conversation about this . . .* 'It makes sense. Late-onset schizophrenia isn't that common, but a traumatic event would be a trigger. You could be right that she's had mild symptoms for years though . . .' Emily didn't reply, was still only half-listening to him. 'And the hotel, will you ring them?' Tony sounded hopeful.

'I'm looking up the number now.'

'It's on my desk.'

'I know, I know, I've got it.' Emily paused. 'Do you know you're doing the opening speech on Friday evening, then on Saturday you've got a panel, and they've got you introducing someone else later on, and another panel after lunch. You're going to be tied up all day.' She flipped to the next page. 'And there's another dinner on the Saturday, and you've got another speech on the Sunday morning. It doesn't finish until 2 p.m.'

'Damn, I thought it was just the Friday night and a couple of hours on Saturday morning. I haven't had time to read it yet.'

'So . . .' Emily flipped back to the front page again, her mind whirring. 'You're on at seven thirty on Friday. If we flew in on Friday afternoon, you could go straight to the conference. I could take Mary out for the day on Saturday and bring her back here on Sunday morning. If I fly from City Airport I could get the afternoon flight back to you for Sunday evening . . .'

If Emily could have seen him in his office, she'd have seen Tony bury his face in his hands.

24

Lavinia Grant's study was hot and stuffy, the smell of beeswax, furniture polish and cigarette smoke strong. Stale cigarette smoke. Lots of it. Like the windows had never been opened. *Lovely.* Cathy could feel a wave of nausea welling up inside. *Was this ever going to stop?*

Uncomfortably hot, sweat starting to prick at her spine, Cathy stood inside the door and looked around, suddenly feeling at a total loss. It had sounded easy in O'Rourke's office last night, but where should she start?

The place was meticulously tidy, even the ornaments on the mantelpiece regimented. Despite the heat, a shiver ran up Cathy's spine. It wasn't a comfortable room, it was too neat. The walls were covered in bookshelves; beside the fireplace a section was empty where the housekeeper had begun to remove the books for the decorators – not that the room looked remotely like it needed redecorating.

Beyond a Victorian mahogany pedestal desk, tall sash windows overlooked the back garden, the light coming in blocked by an enormous monkey puzzle tree, exotic and bushy. Two filing cabinets stood between the windows, no doubt crammed with more documents.

Cathy thought of her own personal papers, filed in a card-board box under the bed. Everything was there, in one place, clear plastic files keeping the various bits of correspondence together. Organised. *A whole lot better organised than the rest of her life was right now.* But she was twenty-four, worked for the state, rented her house, had one bank account, one savings account, one car, one car loan. Lavinia Grant had been over seventy and ran a multinational business empire. Her paperwork was going to be more complicated. Much more complicated.

Suddenly, Cathy felt her phone vibrate in her pocket. Pulling it out, she checked the screen. O'Rourke. She almost groaned. He'd be phoning for an update and she hadn't even started . . .

'Cathy, that you?'

She winced. 'The one and only.'

'How's 007?'

'Good, he's in the dining room. Zoë's gone to meet Trish at the undertakers.'

'How are you doing on Eleanor Grant?'

'Working on it; haven't found anything concrete yet.' Cathy ran her eyes around the room, looking for inspiration, for something to tell him. Nothing. Nothing at all. Nothing . . . *that was it* – that was the reason why the room felt strange. There wasn't a photo-graph or a personal memento anywhere – on the mantelpiece, on the desk . . . nothing. Not even a photo of Zoë.

'You won't.'

'What?' Still absorbed by the clinical feel in the room, Cathy didn't quite take in what he was saying.

'You won't find anything. No postcards, letters or emails. Nothing. Nada. Diddly-squat.'

'Why not?' *What was he on about?* He was the one who'd told her to come and look.

'We found her. Well, one of the lads did. Easy when you know where to look.'

'Where? Where is she?'

'Guess.' *What had he found out about Zoë's mother? Where was she?*

'Feck that, just tell me.'

'Cathy, sorry to interrupt.' Cathy jumped: Jamie Fanning, his head around the door. 'Hold on.' *What the –?*

Cathy glared at him, just as Zoë appeared at his shoulder. She must have come back.

'How are you getting on? I've got to go out again.' Zoë's voice was hesitant.

'Grand, you work away, we'll be fine.' Cathy smiled reassuringly. Zoë really wasn't getting this search thing, obviously didn't realise that a warrant gave them the right to search the premises without her being present. 'If we finish up before you're back we'll pull the front door behind us. Just leave the number for the alarm and I'll make sure it's all secure.'

'Grand.' Zoë nodded, then her face clouded for a moment like she'd just remembered something. 'I've got to go to the gallery too. I might be gone a while. Max said something about dinner. And Trish said she'd be late.' Then more decisively, she said, 'I'll write the alarm code down.'

Zoë's head disappeared. Cathy could hear her in the hall. The phone back at her ear, she kept her voice low.

'Just a sec, that was Zoë back from the undertakers, but she's going out again.'

'I gathered. Why don't you grab a cup of coffee as well? I've got all day.' O'Rourke was being sarcastic but Cathy could tell he was laughing he knew she was desperate to hear what he'd found out. 'We could talk about the weather, the state of the economy . . .'

Finally the front door closed again, the knocker banging as Zoë slammed it shut, and Fanning was back in the doorway, his mouth open, about to speak. Cathy shot him a look that would have melted ice, making her irritation at being interrupted clear, then turned her attention to the phone. He got the point. Hovering, Fanning shut his mouth.

'She's gone. Tell me before I have kittens.'

'I'd like to see the tom that gets the better of you.'

Feck, why had she said that? She'd left herself wide open. But what was he like? The blush hit her hard and hot. Thank goodness he couldn't see her.

Turning her back on Fanning, trying to focus on the call, Cathy drew in a breath, summoning strength from the musty air of the room, pulled a corkscrew of hair out of her face, tucking it back into her ponytail.

'So?'

'So.' O'Rourke paused. 'She's dead.'

'What?'

O'Rourke spelled it, 'D.E.A.D. Accidental drowning, it says here.'

'What? What do you mean, "says here"?'

'Wake up, Cat, get with the programme. I have the cert in front of me. We went looking for her birth cert, and guess what we found . . .'

'But Zoë . . .'

'Thinks she's in France,' O'Rourke finished the sentence for her. 'More likely Glasnevin Cemetery, I'd say, assuming she made it into the ground. From what I've heard of our friend Lavinia Grant, she's probably dust by now.'

'But –'

'But lots of things.' O'Rourke's pause was loaded. 'So now you're looking for anything, and I mean *anything*, that might relate to Eleanor Grant.' He spelled it out like he was talking to a child but Cathy knew he was working it through in his head, was processing the information as it came to him. Then half to himself, 'There seem to be a lot of unexpected deaths in the Grant household ... We still don't know exactly how old the bones are, but there's every chance they link back to Eleanor, assuming we believe Zoë that it was her dress.' O'Rourke paused again, apparently thinking, then continued briskly, 'We need to build a picture of this Eleanor, talk to her friends, see if there was any hint of another pregnancy before or after Zoë's birth. And look for anything that might suggest hers was anything other than an accidental death.'

Cathy found herself nodding. 'Where did she drown?'

'In the house.' O'Rourke inflected the end of the sentence like he only half-believed it. 'Place of death is Oleander House, Monkstown.'

'Here, at home? But where?'

'I'd guess the bath.'

'How the hell do you drown in the bath?' *That was nuts ... children drowned in the bath, but adults?* 'Unless ...'

'Unless someone holds you under or whacks you on the head. I did wonder that myself.'

'Or you take an overdose.' Cathy could almost hear him thinking, *which you might be inclined to do if you'd recently murdered your child* . . .

O'Rourke continued, 'Exactly. Very tidy. I think we can safely read between the lines. Half the certs right up to the eighties were dolled up to suit the parents' sensibilities. Suicide was still a crime then, don't forget, only decriminalised in 1991.' O'Rourke paused. 'I think I'd better come down and give you a hand.'

'Jesus, it's cold out there.' Bringing a blast of fresh air into the hall, O'Rourke shook the rain from his shoulders in a shower of quicksilver. 'And in here it's like an oven. Christ, it's stuffy.' O'Rourke pointed to the patrol car that had dropped him off, pulled up on the pavement outside, its engine still running. 'Back to base for you, young Fanning. The lads are working on Eleanor Grant. Need a hand with the calls. They'll get you organised.'

Throwing O'Rourke a salute, Fanning hovered for a moment before dashing out into the rain, his jacket pulled up over his carefully gelled head. Rolling his eyes, O'Rourke closed the front door firmly behind him and took a moment to look around the hall, to quickly inspect the dining room with its toppling mound of files. Cathy stuck her head out of the study door.

'Are you coming to help or what?'

'Have you had a look at this lot?' O'Rourke indicated the files on the dining-room table.

'Trish's, I think. They're all press clippings, social stuff, lots of her articles. Seems to be an awful lot here bearing in mind this isn't her house.'

'Perhaps she stays here a lot,' O'Rourke said meaningfully.

Cathy nodded. 'Zoë said Lavinia didn't like being on her own apparently. I'm definitely starting to think they might have been a lot more than friends.' She paused. 'I thought I'd start in the study here and work outwards.'

O'Rourke nodded, throwing his coat onto a spindle-legged occasional chair positioned between the doors of the two rooms. He slipped off his navy pinstripe jacket, loosening his tie to unbutton the collar of his shirt.

'Right, show me what we've got.'

'I've done the two top drawers of that filing cabinet but that's about it so far. It's all bills, house repairs, receipts for everything from the carpets to the kitchen scales – Lavinia Grant even had invoices for dry cleaning in there. Looks like she's kept everything since they launched the Ark. I haven't found her life-insurance policy yet, or any personal papers.'

O'Rourke opened the next drawer down and pulled out a large handful of documents.

After ten minutes leafing through them he gave up.

'This is going to take for ever. We need the Divisional Search Team to do it properly. There might be nothing, but I'd hate to miss Eleanor Grant's suicide note . . .' He looked around. 'Computer?'

Cathy shook her head. 'Zoë says Lavinia Grant was convinced someone would hack into it so she never used one. Her PA handles all the business stuff from an office in town.'

O'Rourke nodded. 'She's on the interview list.' He looked around the room, running his eye over the files packed along the bottom of the bookshelves. 'Let's leave this lot to the team and have a look in her room. If she's worried about people delving into her personal stuff she might have it all at the back of the wardrobe instead of in the study.'

At the bottom of the stairs Cathy stopped, her hand on the scrolled end of the banister. A wave of tiredness had hit her in the study, welling up and overwhelming her before she'd even realised it was coming. She leaned her elbow on the polished wood, rubbing her hand over her eyes, breathing in the cooler air in the hall. Right now she felt like curling up in a small ball on the carpet and sleeping, not rushing up the mountain of stairs.

Ahead of her, O'Rourke was already halfway up the first flight, the broad outline of his shoulders blocking out the light from the window on the half landing.

'What I still don't get is what she was doing at the top of the stairs in the first place.'

Hearing Cathy's voice, realising she was still at the bottom, he slowed, looking at her over his shoulder as she continued.

'It's a hell of a long way up for someone in her seventies. And did you see her shoes? I wouldn't climb all these stairs in those heels. If I knew I was going up that far I'd have kicked them off at the bottom, unless I was in a real hurry.'

Reaching the half landing, O'Rourke turned around to look down at her, put his hand out to lean on the banister as it made the turn for the next flight. *Connecting them.*

Sliding her hand along the polished mahogany of its length as she headed up to join him, taking it slowly, hauling each foot up, Cathy was thinking as she spoke. 'And I know the PM conclusion was that she'd only been dead a few hours when we found her, but could the heat in this house have screwed the results a bit? It's been boiling here all morning, but since you got here it seems to be cooling down. The heating must have gone off.' She paused as if she was testing the air temperature. 'It was pretty chilly when we arrived the other night, and it's a draughty old house, there's no double glazing. If the heating went off it would have cooled fast like today. If she died mid-afternoon, say, when the heating was on, her body temp would have dropped more slowly than normal. We're reckoning she died early evening because of her body temp and the housekeeper saying that she liked to read before she went to bed.' O'Rourke was nodding, letting Cathy finish. It wasn't coming out quite as fluently as she would have liked but he was getting the picture. 'What if she actually died much earlier, closer to the time Zoë's house was broken into? Then there could be a different reason why she was up there. Maybe she'd gone to look for something – or to hide something – in a hurry.'

'Which was why she didn't take off her shoes.' O'Rourke screwed up his face, working it through. 'What made you think of that?'

'Nifty Quinn. I was thinking about Zoë's break-in while I was sorting through all those papers. He's –'

'Got a thing about shoes.'

'Exactly, and I've been boiling until now – the heating thing is a bit of a no-brainer.'

O'Rourke bit his lip to stop from laughing. 'Professor Saunders would be delighted to hear his work described so aptly.'

Full of amusement, his eyes met hers. Blue, very blue. For a split second Cathy forgot why they were there.

Cathy dragged her eyes from his, pulled her polo neck away from her skin like it was irritating her, trying to let some heat out. *Had he noticed?* He had transferred his gaze to the stairs snaking around above him, and was nodding to himself.

'So let's start at the top instead.' Turning to continue up, O'Rourke unclipped his mobile phone from his belt. 'We'll get her phone records, see if she made any calls starting from early morning, and start house-to-house to see if she had any callers. Saunders is in no doubt that she had a heart attack, that there was no interference, but it's all a bit neat for me.' He nodded thoughtfully. 'Well done, Kitty Cat, well done.'

It was years since he'd called her that. Years since . . . a dark night, rain stinging her face, the whap of a bullet leaving the barrel of a Glock . . . the beat of his heart as he held her . . . 'You coming?' O'Rourke threw a grin over his shoulder. Cathy felt it land home somewhere in her middle, glowing, skittering about like a firework trying to take off.

Phew. Focus. She had enough problems . . .

At the top of the stairs O'Rourke pulled a pair of latex gloves from his trouser pocket, shaking them out before snapping them on.

'Right – first things first, we need a bit of light.'

O'Rourke flicked on the single bulb at the switch by his shoulder. It was barely adequate for the space. Striding forward to lean over the pile of cardboard boxes, he threw open a door tucked into the corner of the landing. Even with the door open, the light wasn't much better.

'So she was lying on her back, with her head here.' O'Rourke tapped the beige corded carpet with his foot, indicating the position of Lavinia Grant's body. 'Her feet over there.' He pointed, indicating the angle of the body, recreating the scene in his head.

Leaning her shoulder on the textured wallpaper, Cathy nodded. 'Assuming she didn't perform some sort of mid-air flip, she must have been heading into that storeroom, with all the boxes, or into that room' – she indicated the door O'Rourke had just opened – 'and when we found her she was lying, like she just keeled over. There was no sign she tried to put out her hands to break her fall. So I reckon . . .' Pausing, Cathy moved over to stand where Lavinia Grant's feet had been lying. 'I reckon she was heading this way . . .' Cathy took a step forward into the storeroom, squeezing in beside the box blocking the doorway, looked over her shoulder to double-check the position Lavinia Grant had been found in. Raising her hands to her shoulders, palms out, she glanced behind her again. O'Rourke was nodding. Cathy was taller than Lavinia Grant, but if she fell backwards, her head would certainly be in the right position.

'Looks good. So what was she looking for in there?'

'Let's see . . .' Cathy reached over the box to flick on the light.

The storeroom was the size of a large single bedroom, had a small sash window, smelled strongly of dust and the acidy tang of corrugated card. The floral wallpaper was a drab mustard, the floorboards stained dark brown, thick with dust. A 1930s-style walnut dressing table had been abandoned in the far corner, its mirror catching the light from the doorway, the white of O'Rourke's shirt a blur behind Cathy's black sweater and jeans. Beside it, a pile of chairs had been stacked. More boxes beside them, and more behind the door. Against the wall to Cathy's left, someone had propped an ancient wooden ladder.

She looked around, at the floor, at the layout of the furniture, her mind clicking. It took a moment for it all to fall into place, a moment in which O'Rourke came to stand behind her. Cathy could feel his breath on the back of her neck. She snapped her fingers and took a step into the room. Safer with some distance between them.

'Look at the marks on the floor. See, the ladder's been dragged from the back wall to here' – Cathy turned to look back at the doorway – 'and with that box in the way, it would be a struggle to get it through.' She almost pounced on a shadow in the dust. 'See, the box has been moved, only an inch or so, but pulled or pushed like someone was trying to move it out of the doorway.'

'Surely you'd just twist the ladder and carry it out?'

Cathy bit her lip, went to the ladder, tried to lift it. 'Weighs a ton. You might be able to pick it up, but I'd have to drag it. And I'm pretty fit.'

'So let's say Lavinia dragged the ladder from the back wall to here, realised it wouldn't fit through the doorway . . .'

Cathy cut in, 'So she tried to haul the box onto the landing, to move it out of the way, and pop, her heart gave out. Exertion after the climb up those stairs. Fags, the blood pressure . . .'

It was O'Rourke's turn: 'Fatal combination. OK, I get it. But what was she going to do with the ladder? And how do you know the housekeeper didn't move it when she was stowing the books?' O'Rourke looked at her half sceptically, but Cathy knew from the smile twitching at the corner of his mouth that he was playing devil's advocate.

'We can ask the housekeeper, but I reckon . . .' Cathy brushed past him, her skin jumping at the contact. She was on the landing in a moment, pointing upwards triumphantly. 'She was trying to get into the attic.'

25

'Good evening, Mr Hierra.' The voice was heavily accented, the smell of expensive aftershave hitting him like the first warning tremor of an earthquake.

Half into the doorway of his darkened hotel room, Hierra froze. He'd only been gone a few hours, checking what was happening, keeping an eye on that detective bitch – *how the fuck had they found him already? And how had they got in?* Sweat began to run down his back, cold, as if the barrel of the gun he knew was pointing at him was already on his skin.

He knew the voice. *The big guy;* accent pure Moscow gutter, heavy with the menace of chains and the drip of freezing water running down a cell wall in Lubyanka.

'Why don't you come in and have a chat? We've been looking for you, Mr Hierra.'

To his right Hierra detected a flicker of movement in the doorway to the bathroom. There were two of them. *There were always two.* He'd bet his last dollar the other one was the skinny shit, the Mexican with the mismatched eyes. As if reading Hierra's thoughts, a figure moved into the room, small and lean, confirming his identity without a doubt. *The knifeman.*

'Did you think you could run, Mr Hierra? Did you think we wouldn't find you?' The big guy paused. 'Mr Kuteli isn't happy. It's cost him a lot to send us halfway across the world to find you.'

His mouth dry, Hierra stepped into the room. His foot met something slippery, *what the hell was it?* It felt like plastic. His mind whirling, he took another step forwards. The other foot connected with the same surface and he realised exactly what it was. They'd spread plastic sheeting over the floor. *To stop the blood staining.*

Fear gripped his stomach. Would it be better to run? Die with a bullet in his back? Or try to talk his way out? The one thing he'd inherited from his father was the gift of the gab. Worth a try. Anything was worth a fucking try.

Hierra changed his stance, striving for relaxed.

'I was expecting you. Can we have the light on, or do you feel more at home in the dark?'

The Russian let out a sharp, hissing breath. *That was probably a no to the light.*

'I don't like cheek, Mr Hierra. Mr Kuteli doesn't like cheek. And he also doesn't like people who owe him a lot of money . . . disappearing.'

Hierra's eyes were getting used to the half-light now, he could see the blocky shape of the Russian half leaning on the window-sill, his huge shoulders square in a dark suit. Hierra couldn't see his face, but he didn't need to. It was about as ugly as a human being could get without being branded a freak.

Hierra held out the lapels of his coat as if he was asking the Russian's permission to take it off. The gesture was met with a curt nod. He threw it onto the bed, the face of his watch catching a stray beam of moonlight penetrating the thin curtains. And suddenly it hit him. *His watch. It was the fucking watch . . .*

'I left Mr Kuteli a message. But I had to move fast. Please extend my sincere apologies to him if I have caused him any upset.'

Formal language. Time to think.

'I will of course "extend your apologies".' The Russian's voice dripped with sarcasm.

Hierra continued as if he hadn't noticed. 'I came across a very interesting prospect. Very interesting and very lucrative for Mr Kuteli and the organisation. I had to move fast.'

The shape in front of him moved fractionally – a shrug? The way the guy was sitting, Hierra couldn't see the gun, but he knew it was there, kept his body open like it didn't worry him. He'd learned every trick at the tables, watched the masters shuffling the cards for years as he'd waited for his mom to finish work, observing them bluff and double bluff. *It was all about attitude . . .*

'When I have things stitched up here, Mr Kuteli will be very pleased. He's been looking at diversifying, moving outside Las Vegas. This gig will get him into New York to start with, and after that it goes global. Toronto, London, Dublin.'

The Russian snorted like it was one big joke. 'You know too much about the organisation.'

Hierra shrugged again like he had a personal understanding with the man calling the shots.

'Mr Kuteli can trust me. He knows I'm good for it, and . . .' Hierra took a deep breath. *This was the ace.* 'I'm interested in his interests. That's why I'm here. I could have lost you easily, but I didn't. I know how you work.'

It was the watch, had to be – it was the only thing he'd brought with him. The bastards must have put a tracking device into his watch. Hierra waved his wrist at the Russian, raised his eyebrows like he'd known they were on his tail the whole time. *Bluff and double bluff.*

The big guy didn't answer. Good, that was good.

'I'll be speaking to Mr Kuteli personally, but look in my bag if you don't believe me – over there.' Hierra nodded towards his case lying on the floor at the end of the bed. 'There's a magazine, have a look at the cover and the article inside. You'll see what I mean.'

The Russian paused for a beat, then flicked a nod to the skinny one. Hierra felt his heart rate increase. He'd heard enough about them to know they worked like a scorpion's pincers, each knowing the other's movement, anticipating their victim's next move, perfectly tuned for the kill. They were Kuteli's best men.

Holy fucking shit. But this wasn't the time to lose his nerve. *This was the time to show his hand.* He just needed to keep the trump cards concealed a little bit longer.

The skinny one leaned forward, flipping open the lid of the suitcase. The magazine was tossed on top of the carefully folded clothes, its white cover glowing in the darkness. It was scruffy, the edges curling, obviously old, but the title was unmistakable: *Vanity Fair*.

'So what are we looking at?' Hierra could hear in his voice that the Russian's patience was running thin.

'I'll show you.' Hierra held his hand out, grinning.

The skinny one picked up the magazine and passed it to him, the cover catching the light from the window. Hierra held it up like he was about to read a bedtime story. 'So this, gentlemen, is a very wealthy lady who owns a company worth many, many millions. Grant Valentine has four major department stores in four capital cities. That's a lot of poke for a woman now in her late seventies. It offers a ready-made structure for Mr Kuteli to expand his interests into import/export, and' – he paused for effect – 'I have unique access to the principal decision-maker.' It was a long speech and he was thinking on his feet, but Hierra was pretty sure he'd caught their interest. He tapped the magazine cover. 'It's all in here.'

Below the blood-red title a woman's face stared back at them. Her expression was haughty, unapproachable, her bleached hair drawn back into a severe chignon, pencilled eyebrows arched. Beside her face, the headline read: 'Irish Eyes Smiling on Fifth Avenue'. Lavinia Grant was at least thirty years younger in the photograph than she was now, but when she'd walked into the drawing room at Oleander House to find him leaning on the fireplace, there'd been no mistaking her. She hadn't been smiling much then, but he sure as hell had been.

PART THREE

Tailor's Tacks

A tailor's tack is created by two threads in a needle, drawn through the fabric layer(s) and then snipped, leaving tails of thread on the top and bottom of the fabric as a marker. Tailor's tacks can be used to mark pattern pieces for darts, buttonholes etc. or to hold two pieces of fabric together in preparation for machining a seam.

26

The Tube train shuddered to a halt, the lights flicking off, passengers lurching forward and staggering back again in the darkness. Tony groaned. Overhead the lights began to flick slowly back on, the electricity spitting in the silence left by the thundering of the wheels, eerie, expectant. Then the shuffle of feet, the page of a newspaper turning, the tinny beat of music coming from someone's earphones, sounds magnified. Somewhere further down the carriage someone blew their nose.

The carriage was full. Way beyond full in Tony's opinion. Hot and stuffy, stinking of bodies and wet clothes and the acid tang of fresh newsprint. Somehow, with the tidal movement of Londoners in transit he had managed to get stuck in the back corner of the carriage, his back to the single sliding door, head bowed where the roof of the train curved, just that bit too low to allow him to stand straight. There were days when he wondered if he should buy a bike. He could imagine Emily's face as he wobbled off down Cambridge Heath Road, his pants legs clamped in bicycle clips, briefcase strapped to the pannier.

Emily. *Emily.*

Tony's sigh escaped before he had a chance to catch it. Self-conscious in the silence, he shifted uncomfortably, unbuttoning his heavy wool overcoat, still damp across the shoulders, his mind wandering over their conversation this morning. In front of him, a guy with an earring was labouring through an article about climate change. Tony had skimmed through it, leaning discreetly over his shoulder to catch the last paragraph, had been waiting for him to turn the page since Blackfriars. Tony took another peek. *He must be reading it over.*

But whatever about being trapped in a Tube train a hundred feet underground, or the threat of a global climatic catastrophe – what the hell was he going to do about Mary? She was sweet enough, inoffensive, but he could feel her presence in the house, found himself tiptoeing to his study, dreading meeting her on the stairs. He came home to get away from work, goddammit, and fascinating as Mary's mental condition was – as *she* was: Tony was taken by her air of mystery too, even if he was reluctant to admit it – he needed a bit of space at the end of the day. *And now Em wanted to take her to Dublin . . .* Deep in thought, he shook his head unconsciously. On the other side of the carriage, an African woman in a colourful batik jacket who had been studying him intently looked away, afraid perhaps that he might turn to meet her eye.

Tony shifted within the few spare square inches surrounding him, tried to twist to lean against the end of the carriage. His knees were beginning to ache, the oppressive heat soporific. How the hell were you supposed to cope with this transport system if you were on the edge? Mildly psychotic, claustrophobic, smelly-people-phobic? He was amazed more people didn't have psychotic episodes.

Jesus. The more Tony thought about it, the worse it got – if Em had her way with this trip, with this all-expenses-paid, five-star hotel trip, then being stuck in a Tube train was going to be a stroll in the park compared to spending at least an hour on a plane with Mary – several hours, if you included travel and checking in. Several hours with a confused elderly lady who was unlikely to have ever flown, and who, from what Emily had told him, wasn't keen on crowds. Several hours in which he and Emily would normally have enjoyed a coffee, browsed the bookshop for something fresh to read, whiled away the time speculating about the lives of the people around them. Tony's head began to ache. They'd have to clear passport control, security; would she even be able to walk as far as the gate? *Boy, he hoped she wasn't incontinent.*

Then it hit him. Passport control.

Tony felt a peal of hope. He reached inside his coat to check for his phone – there was no signal down here, but as soon as he got to the surface, he'd better ring Em. Maybe they would be able to have a weekend in Dublin on their own after all. He put his hand out to steady himself on the window as the train lurched, shuddering into life, the relief amongst its occupants almost tangible.

When he finally reached his stop he emerged blinking into the daylight and took out his phone.

'Em?'

'Where are you?'

'Walking up from the Tube. It's not raining here . . .' Why did she always ask where he was whenever he phoned?

'I thought you had rounds this morning.'

'I do, I just phoned in. Tube got stuck. Look, have you checked those flights yet?'

'Just about to. It's just as well they're paying, they'll be expensive this close to us going.'

'Right.' Tony tried to sound like he was listening, then decided to jump right in, fighting to keep the smile off his face. He'd once read that if you smiled when you spoke to someone on the phone they could tell. And right now he didn't want Emily to know he was smiling. 'I was just thinking, does Mary have a passport?' There was a pause, a long pause. 'Em, you still there?'

'Damn, I never thought of that. She must have somewhere but even if we find it, it probably won't be in date. Damn. I'll have to ask her. I'll call you later.'

Tony clicked off the phone and slipped it into his inside pocket. He hated to be the bringer of bad news, but . . .

From the living room, Emily could hear the radio, could hear Mary humming. Why hadn't she thought of the passport? Putting down the phone, Emily scooped up the cat, who had sneaked in to curl up in the rocking chair, and headed for the kitchen.

Mary was sitting at the table, dressed in a new navy-blue cardigan, a pretty cotton blouse buttoned to her neck. She had brushed her hair, smoothing the short silver strands from her face into a sort of a style. Working intently, she had emptied out several of the bags of old clothes that Emily had collected at her flat, had spread them out in front of her, the fabrics undulating over the polished wood, satin threads reflecting the lights from the overhead spots like the tips of waves. Holding an enormous pair of kitchen scissors, the only ones Emily had been able to find, she was cutting the fabrics into neat squares, the rasping snip of the blades regular, methodical.

Realising Emily was there, Mary looked up. Her soft skin was creased in concentration but for a moment Emily was sure something fluttered across her face, a strange look. Fear? Guilt? Emily wasn't sure.

'Those colours are wonderful, Mary, what are you making?'

It took Mary a moment to answer, a moment in which her gaze flicked from Emily to the fabrics and back again, anxious, like a child expecting to be scolded.

'Patchwork. A bag. For all those plastic carriers' – Mary nodded towards a drawer beside the Belfast kitchen sink – 'you'll be able to pull them out more easily when you need them.'

Smiling, Emily pulled out a chair on the opposite side of the table, twisted one leg underneath herself as she sat down, her elbows on the edge.

Selecting another piece of fabric, Mary brought the scissors down on it, her eyes as bright as a bird's, completely absorbed.

'That's going to be lovely. Do you enjoy patchwork?'

'Keeps me busy.'

Emily waited to see if Mary was going to say more, but she was focused back on the fabric.

'Where did you learn to sew?'

A smile lit Mary's face, glinting like the sun off the sea. 'Nanny taught us embroidery, but our housekeeper showed me how to mend and do patchwork. She used to stitch every night, sitting in front of the fire.'

Hoping for more, Emily waited, but Mary seemed to be content that that was all she needed to say. Emily picked up a piece of fabric, a Liberty print of roses and ivy, smoothed it flat, her voice casual. 'Us? Was that you and your sisters?'

Mary bit her lip, the scissors still, her brows meeting in a frown, shoulders tense. It was like a door had closed inside her head. Then, ignoring the question, she said: 'I liked making clothes the most. Dresses and skirts. Drawing the designs and cutting out the patterns. Books and books of sketches, so many ideas ...'

'And the rag dolls, Mary, did you make those as well? They were lovely.'

Mary nodded, muttering, 'Do you like them? They were for you.'

She said it so quietly Emily almost missed it.

'For –?' Emily started to say it, but stopped herself. Mary was obviously getting confused again, and she didn't want to lose her.

Not right now, not when she was about to ask her about the trip.

'Mary?' How should she put it? 'Have you ever thought about going home?'

'Home?' The word came out as a whisper, slipping and sliding, sad. When she spoke again, Mary was shaking her head, muttering more to herself than to Emily, 'Can't go home, can't go back . . . what would they say?'

Emily's heart took a swoop towards the floor. What had she expected? A smile, a laugh, excitement? *Maybe Tony was right, maybe it was a bad idea . . .* She tried again. 'I don't mean home exactly. I mean back to Dublin, back to Ireland?'

'Why?' It was raw, harsh.

For a moment Emily didn't know what to say – *wasn't it obvious?*

'Well, just to see the place, maybe. Do you remember you were telling me about the dances, about the hotels? Would you like to go back to Dublin and look at the hotels again?'

Watching Mary frown, Emily desperately tried to think of something that would persuade her.

'It's just that Tony's been asked to talk at a conference, in Dublin, and I thought you and I could go.' Mary's face was changing, as if memories were flicking through her head like cine film. 'Just for the day, or overnight maybe. We could have some lunch in a nice hotel, have a look at the place. It's years since I was in Dublin too. There's the Ha'penny Bridge and the Custom House, and Trinity College. Lots to do.' Her eyes on the table, Mary picked up a piece of sea-green taffeta, laid it down carefully beside the others. 'It's just we could go by plane but you'd need a passport. Do you have one?'

Mary picked up another piece of fabric, blood red, a seam running across its centre like an artery. 'An aeroplane?' Her voice was tiny, incredulous.

'Have you ever been on an aeroplane?' Mary shook her head, her lip beginning to quiver. Oh God, what had she said? Emily wanted to reach out, to hug her, to take her in charge and tell her she'd be fine, that they'd look after her, that it would be fun. But she knew that was the wrong thing to do. And Tony had told her to be careful stirring the memories . . . Her voice soft, she tried to move away from the whole aeroplane thing.

'Can you remember how you got here, Mary? How you left Ireland? Did you come on a ferry?'

Mary leaned over to pick up a tiny scrap of fabric, silver threads running through it like water. 'On the mailboat.'

The mailboat. Mary had said something before about tickets, about everyone being sick. Had she been talking about the ferry from Dún Laoghaire to Holyhead? If Emily was right and Mary was from Dublin that would made sense. Before she could say anything, Mary spoke again, her eyes watery.

'The mailboat. Came every day. We could see it coming in from the hall window.'

Emily drew in her breath – *they could see the mailboat?* Was she from Dún Laoghaire? 'I always thought it was so exciting, all those people going over to England and people coming home. Romantic, girls waiting for their chaps by the pier. So romantic.'

'So what did she say, has she got a passport?'

It was late, after nine. Now, with Mary tucked up in bed, they were sitting in the living room, the TV turned down, the fire lit, curtains drawn against the night. As he waited for Emily to answer, Tony lifted his plate off his knee onto the coffee table and reached for his glass, the liquid ruby red, rich and fragrant. He held up his glass to meet hers, the sound of their rims meeting like a bell tinkling. Emily took a sip.

'Actually, it doesn't look like it. Just as well you thought of it.'

He reached for the bottle beside the arm of the sofa. Emily was staring into the flames, nursing her own glass, the foot resting on her knee, drawn up on the sofa.

'Shame. But maybe it's as well.' Tony worked hard to keep his face straight.

'Well, I was thinking about it, and the whole air-travel thing would have been very traumatic for her, so . . . I had another idea.' Tony put the bottle down on the polished boards with an unexpected crack.

'Go on . . .'

'Well, it's obvious really. The ferry. We were talking about it today. She said she could see the mailboat from her hall window. That's what the ferry was called then, the mailboat – even my parents talked about people catching the mailboat to England. So she must have lived somewhere around Dublin Bay.' Tony could feel Emily's excitement like an electric charge, could see her eyes glowing as she explained the plan. 'That's what gave me the idea. I need to check it's still running – they've been talking about closing the route – but we can get the train to Holyhead and get the ferry. I'll hire a car when we get there, drop you and the bags off at the hotel and we can go back to Dún Laoghaire or on into Dublin, whatever she likes. I'll bring her back to London the next day, then I can fly back to you as soon as I've got her settled here.'

'Get the train to Dublin?' Tony turned to look at her, his brown eyes open in wonder.

'Why not?'

'It'll take hours for one thing. You'll be exhausted, and so will she. She's too old for that sort of travel.'

'Well, maybe I'll take our car, drive up. She'll be sitting down all the way. But the point is, she won't need a passport for the ferry. They rarely check. And she has an Irish accent. It's not like she's an asylum seeker.'

An asylum seeker? He'd be seeking asylum if this kept up.

'Em, do you honestly think this is a good idea? It's not like you're Mary's family, you only met her by accident . . .' Why had he said that? Tony could feel Emily's good spirits evaporating, could feel her withdrawing into herself. He grasped for something to dig himself out of the hole, but she didn't give him a chance.

'She hasn't got any family, Tony, that's why. Mary's not got anyone. She's not even got her memories.'

'But does she want them, Emily? Home sounds like a great place but there has to be a reason why she left. What if she doesn't like what she finds when she gets there? What if it stirs something she's spent years trying to forget?'

27

Her head thrown back as she scrutinised the trapdoor leading to the attic, thumbs stuck in the back pockets of her jeans, Cathy could feel O'Rourke's eyes on her, studying her closely. Hot, searching. She tried to ignore him, subconsciously drew her stomach in. *Maybe she was imagining it.*

'What?' Finishing her inspection, she looked back at him, one eyebrow raised in question. He was still watching her, leaning on the door frame, his tie loose, the day's stubble already shadowing his chin. He looked good, tired but good; George Clooney with a broken nose.

'Nothing.' Shaking his head like he was trying to dislodge a memory, O'Rourke turned to look back at the ladder, taking a moment to think.

'Wait here, I'll see if I can find a torch.'

Before she could speak he was trotting back down the stairs. Moments later he reappeared with a steel-cased torch in his hand.

'That was quick.'

He smiled. 'Thankfully Ms Grant's housekeeper is a very logical woman. It was under the kitchen sink.'

It only took him a second to put the ladder in place, extending it to reach up the twelve feet to the high Georgian ceiling.

'Hope you're not scared of spiders.' She scowled at him. 'Ladies first.'

He stood slightly back from the foot of the ladder, steadying it. 'Thanks a bunch.'

'Well, there's no point in me going up first, is there? If I slip and land on you I'll kill you. At least if you slip, I can catch you.' His mouth twitched.

'I bet. Right, move over.' She pulled a pair of latex gloves out of her jeans pocket and pulled them on. For a split second, her hands on either side of the ladder, Cathy wondered if she should really be doing this. She was *pregnant*. Surely she was supposed to take things easy, sit about drinking tea, not go around climbing ladders. But she wasn't exactly in a position to back out now. She took a deep breath, pushed the worries away.

It only took her a second to get to the top. Her gloved hands flat on the hatch, Cathy pushed gently.

'It's stuck.' Cathy pushed harder, then, balling her fist, gave it a thump in one corner. Yielding with a squeak, it moved. 'We're in.' She levered the flat wooden panel upwards and slid it into the space beyond, darkness gaping above her. A musty, damp smell hit her, coating the back of her throat. Stale. Fetid. Her stomach reacted immediately. *Fantastic*.

'Here you are.' Passing up the torch, O'Rourke stood with his hands on either side of the ladder, his foot on the bottom. Trying to focus on something other than nausea, for a split second Cathy wondered if she should test his skills and slide down into his arms. Sliding down ladders was one of her party tricks, perfected in lightning attacks on her brothers' tree house when retreat was as important as the element of surprise.

Brushing aside the thought, she switched the torch on, swinging the beam around the roof space. The light bounced off a chimney breast of crumbling red brick, illuminating the rafters above, the steep pitch of the roof vaulted like a church. She moved up a step until her head and shoulders were inside, running the beam around her in a slow arc. The attic was floored, at least partially, raw wooden boards reaching away towards a huge water tank at the back of the house, beside it a pile of trunks and boxes, a travelling rug, thick with dust, slipping off one end. Levering herself up to sit on the edge of the hatch, Cathy looked down.

'There's a load more boxes up here. They all look pretty old.'

'Are there boards over the joists? Can you climb up?'

'Yep, all looks pretty safe. It's freezing though. You'll need a jacket.'

Cathy swung her knees out of his way as O'Rourke followed her, his head appearing as she stood up. 'What, and ruin an Armani suit clambering around an attic? I'll risk the cold.'

Moments later they had wedged the torch onto the top of the water tank and were looking at the boxes.

'These haven't been touched for years. Look, there are steamship stickers all over this one, *Cobh to New York*, *Dublin to Liverpool*. Whoever they belonged to certainly got around.'

O'Rourke tried to lift the catches on the trunk. The hinges protested, squeaking. Kneeling down, levering the lid with both hands, he lifted it, sending an ancient umbrella slithering onto the boards. He hardly noticed, immediately intrigued by the contents. Inside was what looked like hundreds of twists of tissue paper. He picked one up, unwrapped it.

'Lead soldiers. Good God, there must be thousands in here. They're worth a fortune.'

Kneeling on the edge of the pool of light, Cathy looked up from her contemplation of a black Gladstone bag.

'Should we get a team up here to do this properly?'

O'Rourke didn't turn as he answered, was still absorbed in the soldiers. 'We're OK for now. No point in dragging a load of lads out on a hunch. It'll cost a fortune for one thing. Let's keep going.' He looked up, scanned the attic, his eyes adjusting to the darkness. 'There's not that much here. Only really this pile. I doubt she was up here to get a set of golf clubs.' He nodded towards a bag leaning against the side of the chimney breast, the woods hooded, webs dripping with dust linking them together like power lines.

Finally getting the catch on the Gladstone to open, Cathy sat back on her heels, her bubble of excitement bursting unceremoniously. She sighed audibly.

'You're right. I can't see anything she'd be after up here. Look, this is full of medical instruments, must have been a doctor's bag. Who do you reckon it belonged to?'

'Shouldn't be hard to check. Does it look like it's been used recently?'

Cathy shook her head, closed it, dusting her hands together. Despite the gloves she was feeling uncomfortable, dirty. 'Feck it, I was so sure she was coming up here.'

'Don't give up yet, we've only just started. Look, there's a paraffin lamp over there, see if it'll light.' Indicating a lantern hanging from a rafter, he rooted in his pocket and threw a book of matches at her.

She caught the matches deftly and stood up, her legs tingling with cramp.

Unhooking the lamp, she tipped it forward, the thin metal handle cold against her glove. 'How do you do this? The glass is filthy. I can't even see whether it's got a wick.'

'Here, give it to me. God, haven't seen one of those in years. My gran had them all over her house, didn't hold with electricity.'

Standing up, brushing down the knees of his trousers, O'Rourke grabbed the torch and strode over to her, his footsteps loud, echoing. Turning the lamp around, with a deft twist he tweaked a lever at the side with his thumb. Miraculously the glass moved, grating on the rusty body, lifting to allow the candle inside to be lit. The match flared, lighting both their faces, now only inches apart, uniting them in a warm pool of light. Cathy played it in under the edge of the glass, trying not to get distracted by his closeness, by the heat of his arm through the fine cotton of his shirt, by his aftershave, a scent out of place in the damp air. After a moment the wick spluttered into life.

'That's better. Very cosy.' O'Rourke waited for a moment to make sure the wick had caught light properly. 'That's not going to last long. Have a quick look around behind the chimney while I go through these boxes. If there's anything interesting we'll get Thirsty to drop in some decent lights, and come back with the right gear on.'

Cathy lifted the lantern by its handle as she moved back towards the boxes. 'I feel like Florence Nightingale.'

O'Rourke shook his head, amused. 'Not in those boots, more like Pussy Galore.'

She turned, arching her eyebrows, feigning shock, opened her mouth to point out that she was a good little convent-school girl, quickly changed her mind. *Better not to go there.* Instead she said, 'Us girls have to hang on to some semblance of femininity in this job, you know . . .'

O'Rourke turned to look at her over his shoulder. Up and down. Like he was looking at her naked. Checking out just how feminine she was? She felt herself blushing again. Cathy lowered the lantern, hoping her face would be hidden in the shadows. She carried on hastily, as if she hadn't noticed, 'And, these boots have rubber soles – ideal for running in – and steel heels . . .'

Wide-eyed, O'Rourke threw a look at her, trying not to laugh. 'Got the picture, I definitely don't need an illustration of the benefits of steel heels, thanks.' His smile was teasing. 'And for God's sake don't drop that thing or we'll both be toast.'

Heading around the chimney breast, any excuse to beat a retreat, Cathy stepped carefully, making sure the planks were sound before she put her weight on them. Behind her, she could hear O'Rourke closing the lid of the trunk and sliding the first of the boxes onto it. Cathy glanced over her shoulder: he was fully absorbed, pulling open the interleaved flaps on the top. *Maybe it was all in her head.* A cobweb danced across her cheek. She brushed it away, shivering involuntarily. Whatever about her satisfying her curiosity, this place was seriously creepy. She was starting to get that feeling she'd had as a child when she'd woken at night and discovered that the landing light had been switched off.

There wasn't much to see behind the chimney breast – a box of china, blackened with grime and spiders' webs; a rug, rolled inside out, its hessian backing pale in the lamplight. Ducking as the rafters sloped, Cathy lifted the lantern as high as she could to

check out the corners of the attic. To her right the floor board-
ing ended abruptly, the joists running away to the corner of the
house, the spaces between in shadow. She caught a whiff of dead
mouse, the odour pungent, unmistakable. Why had she been so
sure Lavinia Grant was coming up here? Why on earth would
she have wanted to?

She swung the lantern to her left, the light falling on the arm
of a bucket armchair, its seat sagging, holes in the faded brocade covering, its horsehair stuffing teased out. Mice again, or
rats. *Lovely.* About to turn back to O'Rourke, Cathy lifted the
lantern again. Something had caught her eye. Something solid
and squat stuck in behind the chair. Cathy paused – why stick
something there when you had the whole attic to store stuff?

Moving forwards, Cathy bumped her head. Hard.

'Argh, shit!'

'You all right?'

'Fine, fine. Just hit my head. There's something here.'

Cathy put the lantern down a safe distance away from the
armchair and, crouching, shuffled into the corner. She hesitated
before touching the chair, half expecting a flurry of movement
as its residents ran out. *Nothing, thankfully.* Her gloved hand
on the arm, she tried to slide it forward. It was heavy, the legs
catching on the uneven edges of the boards, unwilling to move,
unwilling to reveal its secrets.

'I think I've found something.' This time Cathy's voice was
positive, definite, brought movement from behind the chimney
breast. About to try the chair again, Cathy suddenly thought
better of it. Whatever about scrambling around attics, she was
pretty sure wrestling with heavy objects was a no-no when you
were pregnant.

'Give me a hand, will you?'

O'Rourke was right behind her. 'Move over, what are we doing?'

'There's a suitcase crammed in behind the chair, right in under the eaves. You'd never see it unless you were really looking.'

'Well done, Sherlock.' Laying the torch on the floor, O'Rourke grasped the arm of the chair, and heaved it out – it was wedged hard under the roof joists. Obviously whoever had put it there hadn't intended it to be moved. He leaned over the arm as Cathy crawled in behind to retrieve the suitcase; she could hear him breathing above her, hear her own heart loud in her ears.

Was this what Lavinia Grant had been after?

It was small, old, an ordinary overnight case, or one that might have held a travelling salesman's samples: brown leather, scratched and battered like it had been well used, the corners rough, worn even though they had been reinforced. And the whole thing was thick with dust.

'That's not been touched for years, phew,' O'Rourke said, sneezing as Cathy pulled it out, anticipating weight, but it was lighter than she expected. Disappointment welled inside her.

'Feels empty.'

'Lay it down, let's have a look. Hang on though, I'll get some newspaper to put under it. Don't want to lose anything.'

In a second O'Rourke was back with an old newspaper, still folded where the reader had turned the pages. Shaking it out like a tablecloth, he fanned the sheets over the boards. Normally Cathy would have pored over it, fascinated, but right now she wasn't going to stop and read the headlines. Holding the case by the thick leather handle, she laid it gently on its side.

'OK, catches, two; brass. Very, very rusty.'

Using her thumbs, Cathy tried to push them back, her face creased in concentration.

'Nope, you have a go.'

O'Rourke's hands were strong, but he still had to apply some pressure.

'There we are.' One flicked open suddenly, the other rising more slowly, bizarrely, as though it was in slow motion. He looked up at her, meeting her eye. Cathy could read his mind, could feel the tension zinging between them. He eased back the lid, the leather groaning.

The smell hit her first. Instantly she recoiled, her hand over her mouth and nose. Feeling her move behind him, O'Rourke glanced over his shoulder, surprised.

'It's not that bad, just a bit stale.'

Cathy shook her head, her stomach turning. It was worse than bad, deeper, something much more sinister. Like a bully's whispered threat. She put one hand out unconsciously to lean on O'Rourke's shoulder. Warm, safe, solid. And drew in her breath.

The bones. It was like the smell she'd got in the bedroom, musty fabric, old perfume and – she was sure – something else.

O'Rourke's voice brought Cathy back to her senses.

'So this is where all the family photos are. She didn't burn them.'

The case was lined with green tartan shot with red – cheerful, jolly even. An elasticised pocket at the back was apparently empty. But the main section was anything but. It was crowded with a tumble of black-and-white photographs, different shapes and sizes, some with frilly edges, some plain-cut. One, much larger than the others, was in a dimpled, once white card presentation cover, silver scrolling catching the light of the torch. Bundled up to one side, like it had been stuffed in, in a hurry, was a piece of fabric – *part of a scarf or a shawl?* Dark purple, cashmere or wool, a fine weave, the pattern lacy. But Cathy's eyes were on the photographs.

'What are they of?'

Reaching for the torch, O'Rourke held it up, playing the beam over the first photo in his hand. It showed two girls standing side by side, squinting at the photographer as if the sun was bright behind him. One was a few years older than the other, much taller, slimmer, her bones sharper. Both wore summer dresses, pin-tucked with puff sleeves. Cathy had never been much good at history but the dresses looked pre-war at least. The older girl's expression was serious, a half-smile on her lips like the whole episode was a test. In total contrast, the little one was smiling broadly like someone had just told a joke, her hair a halo of curls pulled into a pair of haphazard plaits. There was very little background, but from the foliage it looked like they were in a garden.

'Who do you reckon that is?'

Cathy fought to concentrate, unable to move any closer, unable to really give the photos her full attention. She shook her head. Neither girl looked familiar. Still hanging on to his shoulder, she felt her thoughts getting jumbled. *The smell. And the strength of his muscles as they rippled beneath his shirt.*

O'Rourke tossed it back into the pile, reached for the fabric, turning it over gently. Cathy recoiled, the movement releasing the smell, jangling like keys in a door.

She was going to puke. She felt him tense.

On the underside of the fabric was a dark stain. Black, like tar.

'We need to get this examined.' His voice was urgent.

'Is it blood?'

He shrugged and Cathy's hand recoiled at his movement, suddenly self-conscious. She pressed her clenched fist into her breastbone. *She couldn't puke now.*

'Could be. Doesn't look like paint, that's for sure.' He leaned forward. 'It's on the lining of the case too, looks like it soaked through.' Gently, O'Rourke lifted the photographs to one side, inspecting the base of the case. 'But it doesn't seem to have got onto the photos, so perhaps they were put in later.' He paused, quiet for a moment, the silence dignified, respectful. 'At least it's one step up from a plastic bag in an alley . . .' He trailed off, replacing the fabric carefully. About to close the case, he picked up another photograph, the one in the white folder, flipping it open.

'Whoa, recognise her?'

It was a wedding photograph – the bride smiling broadly, her hand on her headdress as the wind lifted it; the groom, dashing in a bow tie and tails, had his dark hair slicked back, a pencil moustache twitching above a steely smile. *Like Rhett Butler in* Gone with the Wind. It took Cathy a moment, recognition nagging before she twigged. It was Lavinia Grant. Much younger, more attractive, her dark hair curled around her face in a forties style.

'Jesus.' Cathy's hand fell away from her mouth.

'What?' O'Rourke looked up at her, then back to the photograph.

It took her a moment to spit it out, but the more she looked, the more she was sure. It had been tangled on the floor and she hadn't seen it for long, but the fabric, the lace . . . 'That's the dress. She's wearing Zoë's wedding dress.'

28

'That you, Cat?'

'Who else would be answering my phone at eleven o'clock at night, Steve Maguire?'

Wrapped in a towel, her mobile to her ear, Cathy flicked off the bathroom light and headed for her bedroom. The lads were all out – Decko down in Templemore on a course, the others either in the pub or working. For once Cathy had been glad of the peace and quiet, had made herself a bowl of cornflakes and watched a repeat of *Friends* after O'Rourke dropped her home. Then taking advantage of the rare moment of privacy, she'd taken her phone and Bluetooth speakers into the bathroom and had a very, very long bath.

For the first time in what felt like ages she'd relaxed, really relaxed. With the appointment booked at the Well Woman Clinic she had suddenly felt that she didn't have to obsess about the mess she was in – at least not until next week. She'd always believed firmly that there was no point in worrying about stuff until it happened, and the relief of having the appointment booked was, well, just that: total relief. She knew it wouldn't give her all the answers, but it did give her some breathing time. Breathing time she *really* needed. At last it felt like she had a plan, wasn't just freewheeling headlong into God knew what. *If only it was that easy.*

There would be plenty of time for worrying when she'd spoken to the doctor.

She heard a car accelerating somewhere close to where Steve was standing, laughter in the background. Where on earth was he calling from?

'So how can I help you, Steve, or is this a social call?'

'Just touching base.' Steve sounded breathless, like he was walking fast. Probably on the way home from the pub himself.

'So how's Miss Grant?' Cathy fought to keep her voice offhand, to give the impression that her interest was purely professional.

'As cool as you can be when your house is swarming with coppers. Sometimes you hit the slump.' Cathy almost groaned. *Oh, the Places You'll Go!* was Steve's favourite Dr Seuss, quoted and misquoted at every opportunity. At the other end of the phone Steve continued, 'Have you had any joy finding her mother? I've been flat out. I'm going to start looking tonight, but there's no point if you've already tracked her down.'

Half-listening, she reached for her bedroom light, took one look around the box room, at the heap of laundry tossed in the corner, and turned the light off again. She wasn't in the mood for clearing up, or facing the reality of being on her own. On her own in a rented house. Single. Very single. Cathy spent as little time in her room as possible, and this evening, she knew precisely why . . . *sometimes you hit the slump.*

Pulling down her duvet, grabbing her Bagpuss hot-water bottle, Cathy sat down heavily on the edge of the narrow single bed, hugging the heat to her. *Boy, she was tired.* She tried hard to focus on what Steve was saying.

'Whose mother d'you mean? Zoë's?'

'Are you looking for anyone else's mother at the moment?'

'Less of the sarcasm, thanks.'

The retort was quick, but then Cathy paused, unsure what to say next. She knew there was no way she should discuss the progress of the investigation with him, but she knew it wouldn't take Steve long to find exactly the same information O'Rourke had, and just as quickly. Even so, she hesitated. 'Zoë definitely thinks her mother's in France?'

'Yep. Paris. You know that.'

'OK . . .' Cathy paused, lingering on the edge for another second before she decided to take the plunge. If she brought Steve into her confidence then he might do the same, give them something on Zoë. 'Has she thought about the possibility that she might not be in Paris?'

'Eh, no.' Steve's voice was cautious. 'She's convinced she's there somewhere. I haven't had a minute to start looking yet; we go to print in a couple of days. Have you found her?'

'You could say that. If she was still alive.'

'Ah, shit.' He said it with passion, then again with a hint of despair. 'Ah *shit*. Jesus, I don't think she can take much more bad news.' He continued before Cathy could say anything, 'When did she die? Bloody hell, it's a classic headline, "Daughter Loses Mother Twice". How's that for shit? If she'd looked for her sooner, had some help, she could have met her. Now all she's got is a gravestone somewhere in France.'

Cathy chose her words. 'It doesn't look like she got to France.'

She heard Steve stop, his breathing steadying, the sounds around him – engines accelerating – clearer. 'What do you mean? She's been living there for years, hasn't she?'

'Not exactly. The only reference we've found is her death certificate. She died in Ireland.'

'In Ireland?' His voice was laced with incredulity, like Cathy had pulled a loaded Smith & Wesson out of her hat instead of a rabbit. 'You must have the wrong Eleanor Grant.'

'Nope, definitely the right one.'

'Shit, Zoë was sure she went to France . . .' Steve paused like he was thinking about it. 'What happened? How did Eleanor die?'

'It says accidental –'

Steve interrupted her, his voice confused: 'Did she get hit by a car or something?'

Cathy paused significantly. 'It's looking like drowning, actually. At home.'

'What do you mean, "at home"? How do you drown at home?'

'My thoughts exactly.' Cathy sighed – it was too late to be having this conversation. Right now she just wanted to get out of this damp towel and into a warm pair of pyjamas. 'We'll have to tell Zoë.'

'Not tomorrow though, eh? That's why I'm ringing. Her grandmother's funeral is at eleven o'clock in Monkstown. They want to keep it private, no press.'

'Good of them to let us know.'

'I expect she forgot.'

'Expect so. Expect it'll be me that gets to go, too.'

'Good. You can keep me company. That Trish will be there – she gives me the heebie-jeebies. I don't think I'm her favourite media mogul right now.'

'Media mogul?' Cathy's tone said it all.

'Brains in my head, feet on my feet. One day, girl.'

'Yeah, like I'll be Commissioner.'

'"Kid, you'll move mountains."' There was a strange strangled beep. 'Shite, battery's flat, gotta go.'

Steve clicked off before Cathy had a chance to ask more, like who else would be going, like *have you slept with Zoë Grant yet?* Not that it was any of her business. Cathy knew it was irrational but she felt bizarrely possessive of him, irritating habits and all. They'd known each other a long time.

Cathy put her phone down beside the photo on her bedside table, and picked up the slim silver frame, angling it towards the light spilling in from the hall. The colours had faded, but the memories were still there as though it had been taken yesterday. Her three brothers: Tomás the youngest, Pete and Aidan; and Steve Maguire, of course, all hanging out at the tree house. The only picture of them all together. Beside Pete, Steve grinned like there was some big joke, his blond hair tousled, *always a mess*, two fingers making rabbit ears behind Pete's head. Like they were about eight years old.

Steve Maguire. What was it about him that reeled her in over and over again? Maybe it was his total lack of respect for authority, his self-confidence, or the charm, the cheeky grin . . . Cathy sighed, slipping her legs into bed, pulling Bagpuss to her. Whatever it was, she'd be seeing him again tomorrow. And he'd be with Zoë Grant. Was she a child-killer? The thought arrived like the howl of a steam train coming through a tunnel. Cathy pushed it away, shocked at its force, at the speed it had shot into her head. Behind it she could hear O'Rourke's voice echoing through the dark . . . *could be a victim herself* . . . innocent until proven guilty . . .

The church was almost empty when Cathy arrived at Lavinia Grant's funeral service. She checked the time on her phone. It was bang on eleven. And Steve had been right when he said they wanted to keep it small.

Right at the front, Zoë sat with Trish to her left, Steve a bum shuffle away on the other side of her, nearest the aisle. In the pew behind them two young guys with trendy haircuts, both in overcoats, were sitting close together, one wrapped up in a Doctor Who scarf. The one with the scarf reached forward to rub Zoë's shoulder affectionately. *Her friend, the picture framer?*

On the other side of the church, a blonde sat leafing through the prayer book, a paisley silk scarf over her navy trench coat, and beside her a man, balding, the collar on his tweed shooting jacket pulled up. Lavinia's PA and the manager of the Grafton Street Grant Valentine store.

Cathy slipped into the back pew, pulling her good black coat around her, trying to retreat into its high Cossack collar. The scent of incense was strong, even at the back of the huge church, biting at the back of her throat, making her stomach contract. *God she hated funerals . . .*

O'Rourke had been all smiles when Cathy had shown up at the station this morning fresh from the gym, had thrown his arm around her shoulder as they'd headed up the corridor, filling her in on the preliminary reactions from the Technical Bureau, with that smug look of someone who knew they'd made a breakthrough. He'd already put up scans of the photographs they'd found in the suitcase. There weren't as many as Cathy had thought, and seeing them spread out, well lit this time, she'd almost forgotten about the funeral had become absorbed, with him, in the faces that looked back at her.

'That's definitely Lavinia Grant. She was quite a looker.' O'Rourke had put the wedding picture centre stage. 'And I think this could be her as a child' – he indicated the picture of the two little girls they had looked at the night before. 'It's about the right period, but I've no idea who the other one is.'

'Could be a cousin or a friend from school?' Cathy stared at the picture. 'They don't look much alike.' O'Rourke had nodded. 'And this must be Eleanor.'

Cathy had put her finger up on the board, let it linger for a moment, trying to make a connection. *If only the photos could talk.* It was a small black and white snap of a girl with waist-length hair, parted in the middle, a clip pulling one side off her face. She looked about eighteen, was pulling a stripy shawl or blanket around her, had a deep fabric holdall slung over her shoulder, was wearing flared jeans, a long bead necklace. But the most striking thing about the picture was her beauty, thick eyebrows and haunting eyes.

'You can see where Zoë got her looks.' O'Rourke was standing back, his hands in his trouser pockets.

Cathy nodded, scanning the rest of the board. 'There don't seem to be any of Eleanor as a child, or of Zoë for that matter. What happened to the rest?'

'These are the only ones with people in them. All the rest are location shots – mainly of a garden, some of a city, could be holiday snaps.'

'Lavinia Grant's garden?'

O'Rourke shrugged. 'Maybe; it's hard to judge. They were taken a long time ago, that's for sure – it looks different now. There was a pond and a birdbath, lots of paving, sort of split-level. Here.' He indicated a photo on the edge of the group, a man sitting in a deckchair wearing a straw boater and stripy blazer. It was hard to tell if the man was smiling, his face hidden by a huge moustache. 'This was taken in the same place. Could be Oleander.'

Cathy pulled a face, looking hard at the picture. She hadn't spent a lot of time in Lavinia Grant's garden but there was something familiar about the photo.

'I think it is – I've no idea what an oleander bush looks like but see this tree in the border? It's a monkey puzzle. It looks tiny here but there's a big one in the garden beside the wall – you can see it from the study. If the lads at the bureau can blow it up they might be able to match some of the bushes around it to what's there now and confirm it's Oleander House. There's a guy up there who specialises in plants and seeds and stuff, isn't there? He'd know about trees and bushes ...' She paused. 'How long before they can tell us what that stain is?'

'A day or so. They were being cagey when I phoned.'

'It only takes a few seconds to test for blood.'

O'Rourke nodded, grimacing. 'They want to do more tests before they confirm anything. You know what the lab's like, has to be black and white.'

'Shouldn't we be sealing the house?'

O'Rourke chewed his thumbnail for a moment. 'I've been thinking about that. Trish doesn't know we have the suitcase, so she's not likely to do anything she couldn't have done between Lavinia's death and us finding it ...'

'Like moving the rest of the bones.'

'Exactly. I'd prefer to keep an eye on her, see what she does while we wait for the test results.'

It was at that moment that Cathy remembered the funeral.

'Think you can handle it on your own?' O'Rourke asked. 'You don't have to stay, just show your face and see who else is there, make sure there's no one hovering with malicious intent.'

Cathy nodded, sighing. It was part of the job and she couldn't think of a good reason why she couldn't go. Apart from the fact that it was bloody freezing ... and the chance of being hit by a bolt of lightning if she set foot in a Catholic church.

'Just keep your phone on vibrate.' O'Rourke's face was serious. 'I'll ring as soon as I have any news from the lab.'

'What the hell are you doing here?'

Trish's voice was like barbed wire. They were outside the church, after possibly the longest funeral service Cathy had ever had to sit through. She'd hung back as the organist had finally struck up something resembling a dirge, catching Steve's eye as he'd escorted Zoë, leaning heavily on his arm, out towards the door, the guy with the scarf on her other side, his arm around her shoulders. Despite Cathy's attempt to melt into the granite walls of the church, Trish had spotted her the moment she came through the huge oak doors, rounding on her like it was Cathy's fault that Lavinia Grant was dead. Her breath reeked of gin.

Cathy took a step backwards, smiled like the question hadn't been some sort of challenge, like it was the most normal thing in the world.

'Paying my respects, Ms O'Sullivan.'

Trish's eyes were red-rimmed, her face blotchy. 'You're like vultures you lot, hovering over the kill. As if it's not enough that you've turned Zoë's house upside down. Come to have a good gloat, have you?'

Cathy opened her mouth to speak but Trish cut across her, advancing, her voice rising with every step. 'What gives you the right to come here? How dare you?' Cathy took a step backward, trying to keep the smile fixed to her face. 'Don't you think you've done enough damage already with all your questions, poking and prying?'

'It's procedure, Ms O'Sullivan. If there was any interference in Mrs Grant's passing, you would want us to find out, wouldn't you?'

'Interference?' Trish's voice went up another notch. She was almost shrieking now, had drawn the attention of the other mourners. Cathy could see them over Trish's shoulder looking embarrassed, pretending they couldn't hear.

Now Trish was almost on top of her, and Cathy could feel the gin-soaked spit hitting her face. She winced and felt herself gag, her stomach turning over in an agonisingly slow roll. She put her hand to her mouth.

Trish didn't seem to notice, was at full throttle.

'Interference? *You* are the only ones interfering. There are criminals out there robbing banks, kidnapping children – why aren't you out there catching *them* instead of wasting taxpayers' money sullying the name of highly respected citizens with all your bloody questions?'

Cathy was sure Trish could have continued indefinitely, but at that moment the undertakers appeared, the coffin between them supported on a wheeled trolley, clattering across the tarmac. Distracted, Trish pulled herself up straight, turned to watch them.

Cathy drew a breath, deep and slow, closed her eyes for a second as she tried to calm her stomach. A moment later the coffin was loaded into the back of the hearse. As the under-taker pulled the boot closed, Trish turned back to Cathy, hissing under her breath: 'Don't you dare come to the grave, do you hear me?'

Cathy smiled benignly – the smile she saved for suspects in custody, the ones they were about to throw the book at. She wouldn't be at the grave, but she had every intention of going to the graveyard.

A second car drew up, the driver opening the rear door ceremoniously. Turning her back on Cathy, her trouser legs and the skirt of her black coat flapping in a flurry of icy wind, Trish climbed in. Zoë and Steve followed her, pulling the door behind. Cathy could see Trish open her handbag, rooting for a mirror and lipstick. Behind them the guy with the scarf and his friend, the PA and the store manager climbed into a third car.

Cathy waited until the cars were out of sight, and then climbed into the unmarked DDU car she'd purloined, to follow them. When they reached the massive car park beside Shanganagh Cemetery, Cathy reversed into a side bay well away from the cortège. The heater on full, she waited until the Grant group had all got out of the official cars, pulling their coats around them, setting off into the sea of headstones towards the family plot somewhere in the middle. There was no way she was going to get cornered by Trish O'Sullivan again today.

Cathy looked around her. This place always depressed her. It was too regimented, too organised, too flat. Even the trees, naked now, pointing towards the sky with arthritic fingers, were strategically planted in unnaturally tidy rows. To Cathy's right, a much larger party was lingering, straggled untidily across the graveyard. Slipping out of the car, Cathy headed towards them, her good black winter coat blending in seamlessly. They didn't notice her arrival, were discussing the funeral, the weather. Keeping within their shadow, tiptoeing along the shale paths between the graves, trying to avoid her heels sinking into the mud, Cathy moved in as close as she could.

Ahead of her Trish and Zoë had reached the freshly turned grave, were standing opposite each other on either side of it, with their heads bowed, Zoë flanked by the men in her life. Trish had her back to Cathy. Steve, who had managed to find a dark jacket for the occasion, a dark striped scarf knotted tightly around his neck, had his arm around Zoë, was glancing around him, looked cold and tired and bored. Suddenly Steve looked Cathy's way. Cathy shook her head, willing him to ignore her. He got the message, turned back to Zoë, pulling her closer to him, smoothing her hair.

On the other side of the graveyard a crowd of rooks took off, creating a black cloud obliterating the sun, their cries startling, loud. Cathy shivered, looked around her, then, hastily, over her shoulder. *What was it about graveyards?* She was getting a creepy feeling like she was being watched. Very creepy. She looked around again. It was the same feeling she'd had outside Oleander House that had sent a shiver down her spine.

Cathy was supposed to be watching them, but the feeling that she was being watched was growing with every minute. She checked around her again, her hands in her coat pockets, tried to look like she was supposed to be there, like she wasn't getting creeped out.

She scanned the borders of the cemetery, could see nothing strange or unusual. But it was so big, and the feeling wasn't going away. Anyone could be hiding behind a tree, behind one of the larger headstones, one of the sculptures. She fingered her mobile, wondering if she should ring O'Rourke ... but how could she say she had a feeling?

29

'Why on earth are you bringing that thing?' Emily Cox threw her basket into the front seat of Tony's car. In reply Tony pulled his head out from the back seat of the battered Mercedes E220 Estate and lifted his eyebrows in mock surprise. 'It's my briefcase. Obviously.'

'But it was washed up with the Ark. Don't you want to bring that one your sister gave you?'

'Nope, I like this one. Freud had one like this. Think of all the patients' stories it's heard, the world events it's witnessed.'

'It's a bag, Tony.' Emily tried not to smile.

'Yep, but it's a *doctor's* bag, a real black Gladstone.'

'That you found in a pawnbroker's. Are you sure that's a good omen?'

Tutting, Tony shook his head. She'd never understand. No matter how often he explained it, Emily couldn't understand that he'd found this bag the day before his finals, a day when he should have had his head down studying. Instead, feeling distinctly frazzled, he had taken the bus downtown, only to see this bag, *this very bag* sitting, waiting for him in the corner of the pawnbroker's window. It was a wonderful bag, always made Tony think of Vivien Leigh in *Gone with the Wind* sending Prissy on that mad dash through the burning streets of Alabama. And it might be old and battered, but it had got him through his finals, and it would, Tony knew, bring him luck at the conference. But he wasn't about to start telling Emily all that again – right now they had other things to worry about.

'Have you got everything packed? We can drop your bags at the hotel and then you'll be free to wander about with Mary.' Tony stuck his head back into the car, flipping open the brass catch on the top of the Gladstone, double-checking his notes were there. Then, reappearing, he said to Emily, 'What are we doing about the Christmas presents for your lot?'

'All done, wrapped and labelled in the boot. They can stay there, they'll be safe enough. I want to get a fishing rod for Dad, but I'll get that in Dublin, or on the way up.'

'Cool.'

'And thanks.'

'What for?'

'For driving. It'll be much easier than the train.'

Tony rolled his eyes. He wasn't sure at what point he'd apparently volunteered to drive, somewhere between Emily getting out the map and him realising that getting the train at all was fraught with potential problems. If there were any delays he'd miss giving the opening speech, and one thing was for sure: if he was late, he'd never be asked back again. He'd weighed up his flying and Emily going by train but between traffic on the way into the airport, check-in and security checks and then waiting for his luggage (even if Emily brought most of it by car, Tony knew he'd still need a suit for the speech and one for dinner, to say nothing of his notes), the trip would, in fact, take almost the same time as the drive from London to Holyhead. Tony had

Googled it: the 289 miles would take approximately five hours seven minutes (he'd wondered about the seven minutes). And he'd never seen Wales. And the route would take them around the edge of Snowdonia National Park, which had to be pretty spectacular. Even if it was raining. And if he was doing the driving, Tony had quickly realised he wouldn't have to make conversation with Mary, would have complete control of the CD player. It wasn't a hard decision.

'Come on. We need to get going.'

'Just making sure I've got my hairbrush.' Emily's head was back inside the front seat, her fuchsia lambswool sweater glowing against the dark navy interior of the car, her blouse a flash of white at its V-neck. Finally convinced she had everything, she threw her book back into her basket. 'Are you *positive* Duncairn Court will be able to take Mary while we're away over Christmas?'

Tony rolled his eyes again. He hadn't wanted to tell her the whole story, but if she asked him again ... 'Look, I pulled a few strings. One of their residents needed a hospital bed, so I phoned around. Nothing complicated, I just moved things along a bit faster than they normally happen. And I spoke with the superintendent myself. They have a bedsit apartment available and the Toynbee Hall Elderly Care people will keep an eye on her, check she's eating.'

Emily hovered by the open door of the car, ran her hand through her hair, still damp from the shower. 'Do you think she'll be OK?'

Tony swung the back passenger door closed and slipped his arm around her as they headed back into the house. 'We've done the best we can. If she'd never met you, she'd be a lot worse off. Think of it that way. And you've organised for her to be collected for the socials at the community centre so there will be loads of people checking up on her. You can phone every day if you want to.'

'But what about cooking for herself?'

'Actually, I've looked after that.' He picked up the map book and ferry tickets from the kitchen counter and grabbed Mary's bag, pulling his brown leather aviator jacket from the back of the kitchen chair. 'The bedsit's not furnished, so I've arranged for the furniture to be moved from Mary's old place and I've ordered a freezer and microwave. Should be delivered today. One of the nurses at work knows a woman who'll fill the freezer full of food for her, show her how everything works and do her cleaning. She's a widow, from Saint Lucia originally. I met her yesterday, she's very warm and she never stops talking, so she'll be ideal.'

Amazed, for once Emily didn't know what to say. It was at times like these that she knew exactly why she had married him. She hugged him instead. 'Thanks.'

'So when we get back she should be very well settled and you can visit her whenever you like.'

'Good. That's great. Thanks.' He could see a tear welling up.

'Go on, don't be an eejit, as your dad would say. You better go get her. She'll think we've gone without her ...'

'Have you turned off all the lights? And the immersion?' Emily spoke to Tony's back as he disappeared out of the kitchen back towards the open front door, Mary's bag in his hand, his jacket slung over his arm.

'All done. We need to get moving ...' His voice trailed behind him as he trotted down the steps to the car, the last words lost in the sounds of traffic pulling up at the lights on the other side of the slip of green beyond the front door.

'Now, Mary, have you got everything?'

'I think so, dear. Where are we going?'

Sitting in her new maroon wool coat, her legs crossed at the ankles, feet smart in navy leather brogues, Mary smiled approvingly at Emily. 'That colour pink suits you, dear, gives you a bit of a glow.' Emily couldn't resist a smile.

'To Dublin, Mary. On the ferry. Do you remember we talked about it?'

Mary nodded, but Emily could see from her eyes that she didn't know what she meant. 'We have to go in the car first. Tony's waiting.'

Emily put out her arm like an usher at a wedding and Mary grasped it, manoeuvring herself out of the chair. 'Will it rain, dear? I don't want to get wet.'

'It'll be grand, Mary. Don't you worry about anything, I'll look after you.'

Her arm looped through Emily's, Mary patted her hand. 'I know, dear, I know you will.'

'Is she asleep?'

Flipping back the corner of his paper, Tony looked over at Mary dozing beside him. They'd only been on board the ferry for about forty minutes but the gentle roll of the boat and the long journey were obviously having their effect. Her chin almost rested on her chest and she was snoring quietly, her eyes closed, bottom lip slack.

Looking up from her book, Emily brought her finger to her lips. 'She's just gone off.' Emily leaned back, looking around her. 'Will you be OK if I go for a walk? I'll get rid of these on the way.'

Tony nodded, folding his paper, helping her to pile up the paper plates and styrofoam coffee cups, the remnants of a not particularly auspicious meal, onto the tray.

Emily stood up. 'Won't be long.'

Settling back in his chair, his arms folded across his stomach, Tony watched her go, her pink sweater bobbing as she weaved between the other passengers towards the coffee dock. It was tricky to walk with the swaying of the deck. He watched as she swerved around a mother and child who were coming towards him, and disappeared around the corner towards the on-board shops.

Laughing, the mother and child fell into a free table at the end of the row of window seats, their backs to Tony, shimmying over so the mother could point at the waves, at the ship's wake curving away beyond the outer rail of the deck. The little girl wasn't much more than four, had glossy mahogany hair brushed into intricate French plaits, each one tied with a bright band. She'd been hiding her face in her hands on the way down the corridor, guided by her mother, enjoying the sensation of the movement of the boat, and as Tony watched her, she put out her arms, mimicking a bird, maybe a seagull. He couldn't resist a smile. She was evidently thrilled with the trip, every angle something new and exciting.

Several people turned to look at the pair as they passed. They glowed like a beacon, their bond, their completeness, wonderful, refreshing. The mother smiled, pointed out of the window again. The child's laughter was high-pitched, contagious, tingled with excitement like the first page of a new book. She clapped her hands in delight at the bird and threw her arms around her mother's neck, hugging her hard, her face buried in her hair. Tony felt a tug deep inside. *That should be Emily, sharing the joy of new experiences, feeling the warmth of a child that needed her love in her arms.* They separated and the mother began to kiss the little girl, silly, playful sloppy kisses all over her face. The child put her arms around her mother again, her chin on her shoulder, her deep brown eyes meeting Tony's in a moment of absolute clarity.

She had Down's syndrome. Her flattened face, the shape of her eyes, the ruddy glow of her cheeks were unmistakable.

Tony felt the impact like a freight train.

She had a serious disability.

With alarming clarity Tony was back in school, in junior-high biology, prepping for the SAT, their geeky weirdo teacher explaining the syndrome. 'Not expected to live beyond twenty-one years . . . often born with serious heart defects . . . an extra chromosome 21.' The prognosis had improved dramatically over the years – kids with Down's nowadays outlived their parents – but it didn't alter his shock, didn't alter the stab of pain Tony felt for her, for her mother. The little girl giggled again and her mother turned to kiss her. Even from her profile Tony could see she was smiling, was totally infatuated. And the little girl *was* beautiful, a little bundle of energy, a bundle of joy . . .

Taking a deep breath, Tony linked his hands behind his head, pretending to stretch, could feel his shame festering like heartburn. *Who was he to play judge and jury? Who was he to play God with Emily's life? To allow his fears to interfere with what she wanted beyond all else?* Watching them, Tony realised that all the reasons he'd come up with that were stopping them from embarking on the adoption process were hot air, a confusion of excuses. It was having to share Emily that he was frightened of, worried that a child, particularly one that could have problems, would take her love away from him. He could see now that the real thing holding him back was his fear of the unknown, of what *might* happen if they brought a child into their family, what might happen if that child had issues – but how did anyone know how their kids were going to turn out, even if they were their own flesh and blood? Living with Emily, he'd learned that the world wasn't all black and white – it never ceased to surprise him when she explained the flip side of a situation or an issue that he just hadn't seen – when she pointed out all the shades of grey. Perhaps it was her Irish upbringing. But this was another one of those times when he *had* to open up to seeing all sides of the argument. Until now it had been completely black and white to him – over the years he'd come across so many cases where hidden psychological issues had only come to light as a child had got older, had seen the heartbreak, the stress, destroy marriages. But Emily was right, it didn't happen in every case, there had to be hundreds of children who, with a bit of help, grew up to be normal, well-adjusted adults.

Bringing a child that wasn't theirs into their home might not be easy, but they'd never know if it would work unless they tried. A mother's love was different from the love they had for each other; surely their lives would only be enriched taking the next step? And if they didn't try, would Emily's sadness and resentment eat away at their relationship, would it always be the elephant in the room? Looking at this mother, Tony was suddenly sure that Emily had more than enough love for them all, that they had to take the risk.

'OK, darling?' Tony jumped at Emily's hand on his shoulder. 'Did you survive without me?'

30

'I don't honestly know what I can tell you that's going to be of any assistance.' Sitting in Oleander House's elegant drawing room, flames licking hungrily at the logs in the fireplace, Trish O'Sullivan was working hard to be polite, her voice like cut glass, every syllable pronounced perfectly, *like they were stupid.*

'We're just covering all the bases, Ms O'Sullivan, wanted to check a few things out with you.'

O'Rourke could do painfully polite when it suited him. Sitting beside him on the sofa, Cathy rubbed her nose, hiding a smile behind her hand. They were well matched.

Trish's look had said it all when she'd opened the door to them. O'Rourke had decided to surprise her, given her enough time to get up and about ('Don't think I'm ready for her in a bathrobe'), but had stood firm as she'd prevaricated about appointments and arranging Lavinia's affairs and being exhausted after the funeral. O'Rourke had made it clear that he was going to question her, and he was going to question her now, regardless of her commitments, and if she preferred to do it at the station that was fine by him.

'I still don't understand what this is all about.'

Showing them in, Trish had collapsed into a huge armchair, legs crossed, one finger making circles on the heavy brocade of the arm while she waited for them to sit, like this was all a waste of time. She was wearing black again, a long knitted thing with frilly bits at the collar over trousers and wedge-heeled boots. It might have been intended to be feminine with its clever stitching and soft yarn, but Cathy thought she looked more like a member of the Stasi.

Seated on one end of the huge velvet sofa facing the fire, O'Rourke leaned forward, his elbows resting on his knees.

'As I explained, and as I'm sure Zoë has told you, we made a discovery at her house. The bones of a baby. Obviously we are very concerned. We are keen to establish the identity of the child and the cause of death in order to establish whether a crime has been committed.'

'But unless you have proof that death occurred after a live birth, and that death was instigated by the mother, surely there can be no prosecution for infanticide?' Trish stood up abruptly, went to the fireplace to pick up a small ivory box, took out a cigarette. Her back to them, Trish held it in her teeth, picked up a barrel lighter, lit up, took a drag, letting the smoke curl from her thin lips before she turned back to them, arching her eyebrows.

Infanticide? Cathy exchanged a look with O'Rourke. Trish O'Sullivan seemed to have got from A to C without passing B. And she certainly knew her law.

'Indeed. But not every child mortality is infanticide. We have to consider the possibility that the child may have been murdered by someone else,' O'Rourke said.

Trish let out a scathing grunt. 'Or it died of natural causes.'

There was that phrase again. Cathy shifted on the sofa, trying not to breathe too deeply. The cigarette smoke was burning the back of her throat, sending her constant feeling of unwellness a step closer to pukesville.

'I still don't see how I can help. I've never been to Zoë's house.'

'But you did know Lavinia Grant?'

Trish nodded, leant back on the fireplace like a cowboy leaning on a saloon bar. Looked at him like it was an utterly ridiculous question.

'Obviously.'

O'Rourke paused a beat, hiding his irritation.

'How long did you know her?' He made it sound offhand like it wasn't that important.

Trish rolled her eyes. 'Years. We were at school together.'

'So you've known her all her life.'

'Yes, certainly sounds like it, doesn't it?' Abrupt. *What was the problem here?* Was she getting sensitive because she was worried they might stray into exactly how close her relationship with Lavinia had been?

'You maintained your friendship when she got married?'

'I was in London, at a secretarial college.' Trish took a drag on her cigarette, blew the smoke out slowly.

'Did you attend her wedding?'

'Obviously. Is this going to take much longer? I do have things to do.'

Cathy glanced at Trish. *It could be a whole lot quicker if she gave them something to work with.*

O'Rourke nodded, acknowledging her hectic schedule, then leaned over the arm of his chair pulling his briefcase towards him. 'I'd like you to look at some photographs, tell us what you know about them.'

'Photographs?'

O'Rourke clicked back the catches, the sound surprisingly loud. Trish was watching him, the toe of one foot jiggling in time to some tune going around in her head. He produced a sheaf of photocopies, each one contained within a plastic cover. Half-standing, O'Rourke leaned forward to hand the first one to her.

'Can you tell us who is in the picture?'

'Lavinia, obviously.'

'And the man with her?'

'Her husband.'

Helpful. Cathy could tell he was starting to lose his patience.

'That would be a Charles Henry Valentine?' O'Rourke prompted.

'If you already know why are you asking me?'

O'Rourke ignored her. 'Tell me a bit about him.' *He was looking for her to loosen up, to let something slip about the dress.*

'I didn't know him well – he died quite soon after they were married, a car accident in France.'

O'Rourke nodded slowly. 'What was he doing in France?'

Trish shrugged. 'He came from somewhere near Paris. It wasn't long after the war, France was in a mess, he went back to see if he could salvage anything of his family estates.'

'What year would that have been?'

'Nineteen forty-nine, nineteen fifty, I don't know, around then.'

'Five years seems a long time to wait before going back.'

'Lavinia said he was something in intelligence, that he had to escape. I think it took him a few years to come to terms with everything.'

O'Rourke nodded again. Cathy could almost read his mind. *Eleanor was supposed to have gone to France.* O'Rourke moved on, but she could feel him parking the questions in his mind for exploration later.

'And the dress Lavinia's wearing, what can you tell us about that?'

Trish shrugged again, twirled her cigarette around.

'It's her wedding dress.'

Cathy slid forward in her seat. The heat in the room was getting to her, making her palms sweat.

'Do you know how the dress ended up in Zoë's possession?'

'It was given to her, obviously.'

'Zoë thinks it belonged to her mother . . .' O'Rourke left the sentence hanging.

'It was a very expensive dress, passed down. That happens, you know.'

'But we don't have any record of Eleanor Grant getting married.'

Trish scowled. 'You can own something and never wear it, can't you? Zoë's not married but it didn't stop her having it in her wardrobe.' *She was getting defensive now.*

O'Rourke changed tack. 'Can you tell us who this is?'

Trish glanced at the picture of the young girl with the jeans, handed it straight back to him like it was hot. 'That's Eleanor.'

Cathy felt like cheering, giving Trish full marks for cooperation.

'Zoë told us she went to France.' Cathy tried to sound innocent, like it was a question.

'She was young, headstrong. Lavinia never knew where she was from one day to the next.'

'Do you know where she is now?' Cathy asked.

Trish shrugged noncommittally, was about to speak when O'Rourke interrupted her.

'We have found evidence that she never got to France.'

Trish lifted her eyebrows again, took another drag on her cigarette. 'Really?'

'What can you tell us about that?'

The shrug again. Cathy felt the impulse to stand up and grab her cigarette, to shout at her, *just tell us.* O'Rourke tried again.

'Why did Lavinia tell Zoë that her mother had gone to France?'

'It was probably the first thing that came into her head. Charles was French.'

Cathy felt a burst of impatience. *He didn't mean why did Lavinia tell Zoë that Eleanor had gone to France, he meant why did she tell her she'd gone anywhere? Why didn't she tell her the truth?* The *truth* – did they even know what that was in this house? Then Trish's actual words hit Cathy like a slap in the face. *The first thing that came into her head?* How could you spin a tale like that for your granddaughter and keep it up for her entire life? *How could anyone be that spiteful?*

Cathy could tell from the tension in his jaw that O'Rourke was thinking something similar. Before he could say anything his mobile rang from the depths of his inside pocket.

'Excuse me.' Reaching for it, he stood up, an energy in the movement that conveyed his mood, his pent-up anger. He headed down the room to the window, the phone clamped to his ear. Cathy was aware of him nodding in her peripheral vision, was focusing on Trish. She seemed completely unaffected by his questions, uninterested as if they had nothing to do with her. *She was some piece of work.*

A moment later, O'Rourke turned back to them.

'That was the lab, Ms O'Sullivan. We have reason to believe that this case *is* one of murder, whether infanticide or not, and that the body of the child was hidden in this house. We know that the bones were buried for a period of time before they were concealed in the hem of the dress, and we know we don't have the full skeleton . . .' He paused significantly. 'So we're going to have to examine this house and garden in order to locate the rest of the remains.'

Trish looked at him like he was mad. 'Surely if it was buried here it would have been dug up by an animal? Would have degraded? The bones you're missing could be anywhere.'

She'd obviously given the whole issue some thought.

'Perhaps, Ms O'Sullivan' – O'Rourke said it with some satisfaction; he could do the eyebrow thing too – 'but we will need to establish that for ourselves. We're going to need you and Zoë Grant to vacate the premises immediately.'

They had to wait for Trish, lethally silent, to throw her things into an overnight bag before she left the house. Cathy had watched her stamping around her room from the door, her arms folded, fighting a smile of satisfaction. Thankfully the scenes-of-crime lads from Dún Laoghaire had arrived promptly to secure the house for the Technical Bureau crime-scene techs, but Trish's glare had been acidic as she had stalked off down the front steps of Oleander House to return to her own apartment.

'What did the lab say?' Cathy could hardly contain the excitement in her voice as they walked fast towards O'Rourke's car, parked in a side lane off Longford Terrace.

His keys in his hand, O'Rourke turned and grimaced at Cathy, his teeth gritted.

'Come on, tell me.'

He flicked open the central locking. 'In the car.'

Cathy almost ran the last couple of yards.

'So?' Breathless, Cathy pulled the car door closed behind her.
'They've found meconium.'

'What the hell's that?'

'Faeces. I'm no expert but apparently it's the stuff a newborn passes first – the by-product of whatever it absorbed in the womb.'

Cathy shivered, put her elbow on the window ledge, her fingers gripping the roots of her hair. There was a newsagent's right next to them, busy, a gang of kids looking at magazines just inside the door, a builder, his overalls splattered with paint, juggling a cup of coffee and a sandwich, trying to get the plate-glass door open. *Ordinary people with ordinary lives going about their business.* There were days when Cathy wondered why she was in this job, days when the crap that people went through, the stuff they did to each other was just too nasty. *This was one of them.*

'So the – it – *was* in the suitcase.' Cathy tried to keep her voice level.

O'Rourke nodded, watching the builder cross the road to a battered Transit abandoned on the double yellow line. 'Wrapped in the shawl.'

'And the stain was this meconium stuff?'

'Yep.' O'Rourke sighed, ran his hand across his eyes. 'The guy at the lab said meconium's composed of the materials ingested during the time the baby spends in the uterus. They're sending the full detail, but it contains intestinal cells and amniotic fluid – they're going to try for DNA. The thing is that it's only passed in the first few days of life.'

Cathy could feel herself pale, her stomach turn over. It had been shut up in the case. A tiny newborn baby had been wrapped up and stuffed in a case. It took a moment for her to get back on track. When she did, her voice was weak.

'So it was alive?'

O'Rourke glanced at Cathy, patted her on the knee like he felt the need for contact. She sure did. Right now she needed a lot more than a pat . . . but he was way too professional for that.

'They still don't know for sure.' O'Rourke paused. Cathy looked across at him. He was staring out of the windscreen, eyes fixed on a car ahead of them turning at the T-junction, its indicator flashing orange like a warning light. 'If it was dead when it went into the case the meconium would have leaked when the body started decomposing. If it died *in* there, the same thing would have happened.'

'And they think it was moved from there to the garden, and then at some stage, what was left of the bones was moved to the dress?'

O'Rourke nodded, biting his lip. 'Looks like it.'

'Will we find anything in the garden though, after all this time?'

'A baby's bones are soft. They may have degraded so much there will be nothing left to find. But we still have to look.' O'Rourke paused, his voice low. 'The fact is that a baby was stuck in a bloody suitcase.' He turned his key in the ignition, firing the engine. 'And from the traces they've found, the techs think it was in there for a while. I don't know about you but I can't leave it there. I reckon we'll find out the rest when we find out who owned that suitcase and who the child was.'

31

Inside the newsagent's, Angel Hierra twirled a stand of greeting cards like he was looking for something particular, one eye on the road, watching them through the window. The guy – O'Rourke was it? – seemed to be giving the girl bad news. She was shaking her head. She looked good, had her crazy hair dragged back today like it had been when he'd seen her in the cemetery, but she had a good body, lithe and young. *Cathy, Cathy Connolly.* He twirled the stand again, lifted out a card, watched out of the corner of his eye as the unmarked car pulled out of the parking space, headed towards the junction.

Why were they back again? He'd been surprised that the pair of them had got to Oleander House so fast the other night. They'd shown up moments after the cop car had pulled up, its blue strobes penetrating the darkness and that fucking awful misty rain.

Hierra twirled the carousel of cards, thinking. The old bitch's death had been reported as a 'tragic loss'. *It was fucking tragic all right.* If Kuteli's pair hadn't appeared, he'd have collected enough to see him right and shot through, left the bastard whistling for his fucking money. But now he had company, and he knew Kuteli's guys were watching his every move. Just because he couldn't see them didn't mean they weren't there. He knew they'd stick to him like shit on his shoe, and he needed to come up with something fast to make it all work. He'd come too fucking far for it to go tits-up now. He was owed, owed big time, and he was going to collect.

Plan A had been to get a down payment, as much cash as he could to get him started and clear through, then set up something more regular. Keep it simple. When you had money you could do anything, change your identity, vanish. And vanishing was what he needed to do right now. But then the bitch had croaked and Plan A had become Plan B. Still simple, still with the same end goal, just not quite as fast as he would have liked.

Then Kuteli's guys had shown up and he'd pulled Plan C out of the hat, pretending he was here to get a grip on the Grant Valentine empire for Kuteli. Not that he'd be telling them about Plan B; he'd be keeping that one to himself. And when it all came together he'd be out of this stinking country so fast – and this time they'd never find him. Plan C would keep Kuteli and his lot happy, all the balls in the air, while he got himself organised to move on through.

Hierra smiled to himself. It had taken a bit of persuasion, but he'd been pretty impressed himself as he'd leafed through *Vanity Fair* explaining who Lavinia Grant was, showing them that painting of the boats that was worth a fortune. He'd always been good at thinking on his feet and it had sounded plausible even to him – that he'd found a way to get control of the Grant Valentine machine, giving Kuteli an opportunity to develop the biggest money-laundering operation in the world, one that spanned continents. But it wasn't the hired help he had to convince – it was Kuteli himself.

Hierra rotated the card stand again, his mouth going dry as he thought about it. When they'd got Kuteli on the phone he'd thought he was going to shit himself, but he'd kept his voice level, had outlined the plan, the background, practical, business-like; explained what the fuck he was doing in Ireland. He'd even cracked a joke with him at the end. Some joke. When he was finished the joke would be on the big man.

Outside the shop, Hierra could see O'Rourke was getting ready to leave, had the engine of the BMW running, was check-ing his mirrors. Hierra smiled to himself. It was time to get the ball rolling on Plan B.

Zoë was next. And she'd be a pushover compared to her grandmother.

32

'I brought you another coffee.' Wobbling slightly with the motion of the ferry, Emily set a takeaway cup on the table and bent down to kiss Tony on the cheek, the scent of her shampoo, roses blooming, like a caress. 'What have you been doing?'

Tony smiled up at her on automatic, watched her slip into the chair opposite, dropping her basket into the spare seat. But it was like she was moving in slow motion, like he had somehow got disconnected from the here and now and launched into the complicated world of his subconscious. Thoughts were flowing, weaving themselves together like the threads in a piece of fabric, *the little Down's girl, Emily lying in a hospital bed, the little girl's mother* . . .

Behind Emily, the mother and child were still looking out of the window, the little girl tracing patterns with her finger on the glass, her mother adding in imaginary detail. A butterfly, a boat. *She looked like she was telling her a story.* Both of them were smiling, locked into the moment, oblivious of everyone around them.

What had he been doing? Tony didn't know how he should answer that one. Truthfully, he'd been thinking – thinking and realising what a selfish idiot he'd been.

'Are you OK?'

'Me? I'm fine . . .' Hauling himself back to focus on Emily's face, Tony tried to shake himself out of it. 'Tired, I guess. Long drive.' Tony picked up the coffee cup, took a sip. *He needed it.*

'And perfecting your speech at midnight.'

Tony grimaced. The sound of Emily's voice, the taste of the coffee, began to penetrate the layers in his head, bringing him slowly back to a seat on a ferry crossing the Irish Sea.

'Yep, *mea culpa.*' Tony held up his hands. 'You're right.' He smiled. 'You're always right.' Tony's eyes flicked to the child again, still absorbed in her game. She had pressed her cheek to the window, feeling the chill of the glass, her eyes alight with mischief.

'What have you been up to?' Trying to divert Emily's attention away from him, from his strange mood, Tony nodded towards her basket and the carrier bag sticking out of its open top.

'Perfume for Mum, aftershave for you. Didn't you go into the shop on your walk? There's an offer on Tommy.' Emily reached over and pulled the cellophane-wrapped box from the bag, showing him the label.

Tony shook his head, catching the twinkle in Emily's eye. He didn't shop – she did that for both of them, knew full well he'd rather jump off the boat than get trapped in the aisles of a gift store.

'No, I managed to avoid it.'

Emily laughed, the sound golden, like a peal of bells. Beside him, Mary snorted in her sleep.

'Oh goodness, I've woken her up.' Emily's hand shot to her mouth. As if caught in suspended animation they both watched, waiting to see if she would wake.

A moment later Mary opened her eyes.

Raising her hand to her forehead, smoothing the soft silver waves of her hair back from her face, Mary looked around her, unfocused, confused. They could both see that she couldn't remember where she was.

'It's OK, Mary, you're on the ferry, the mailboat. Almost home.' Emily put her hand out across the table, took Mary's hand in hers. It was light, more bone than flesh, her skin soft and dry, paper-thin.

'The mailboat? Home?' A flash of fear crossed Mary's face, knotting the creases in her forehead tight. She shook her head again and looked around her, at the passengers gathering at the windows for their first sight of land, at the bright colours of the ferry's 1930s-inspired asymmetric interior.

'Not the mailboat exactly, don't worry.' Seeing her anxiety, Tony joined in, his tone relaxed, jovial. 'It's a ferry, Mary; it's changed a bit since you were last on it. A bit more comfortable, isn't it? And it doesn't carry the mail any more, just lots of trucks and cars.'

Mary looked from Tony to Emily fearfully, still not quite awake. 'But I can't go back. She said she'd send for me when it was time. Did she write? I don't remember a letter.'

Emily glanced at Tony anxiously.

He knew Emily was worried that Mary would slip back, experience a psychotic episode like the one she had before, a flashback triggered by a smell or a sound. But Mary was still half-asleep, and Tony could see that recognition was slowly beginning to dawn, that she was aware of them, of her surroundings. He nodded for her to continue.

Emily spoke confidently, keeping her voice low.

'It's OK, Mary, you're with me, with Emily. We're going back together.'

At the sound of her name, Mary's confusion appeared to lift, like the cards were slipping back into the pack, this time in the right order. She grasped for Emily's fingers.

'You came to get me, didn't you? You found me.'

'I did, Mary, and you're safe now.'

The old lady nodded, still not entirely focused. 'And we're on the boat. Going home.'

'That's right.'

Turning to look out of the window, taking in the guard rail on the deck outside, the sea, Mary took a deep breath. *To calm her nerves?* Then her bottom lip began to quiver.

The distinct outline of a mountain range darkened the horizon. Tony followed Mary's gaze, surprised himself to see that they were nearing land.

'Almost there now. Do you remember those mountains, Mary?' Mary nodded.

'I didn't know they had mountains so close to Dublin.' Tony peered out of the window with interest.

Her reply was barely a whisper: 'The Wicklow Mountains. They're the Wicklow Mountains. We used to go for picnics in the summer. To the Sugarloaf. You can see the sea from the top.'

Emily glanced at Tony, her eyes wide with excitement. He shot her a warning look, mouthed the word 'careful'. Behind them a gang of schoolkids were testing each other's mobile phones, the ringtones merging like someone was trying to tune in a radio. But neither of them heard it.

'Was that when you were a child, Mary?' Emily kept her voice low, gentle, encouraging. Mary nodded slowly, concentrating, her eyes still fixed on the dark shape of the land. 'Who were you with, Mary – who did you go on the picnics with?'

It took a few moments for the words to come.

'Nanny when we were little . . .' Mary brought her fingers to her lips in an unconscious movement, her elbow catching Tony's Gladstone bag. Looking down at it, she paused. Tony and Emily could almost see the wheels inside her head beginning to turn, slowly, creaking with the effort. 'Working . . . he was always working . . . too busy to come.' Mary looked across at Emily, but it was as if she wasn't seeing her, as if she was looking straight through her. She frowned, the effort of remembering painful, difficult.

Then suddenly Mary smiled, the years of hardship slipping away, like a veil had been lifted, like a cloud had moved away from the sun. Focusing on Emily's face, she leaned forward, her tone conspiratorial. 'Once, one of the fellas gave us a lift in his car.' Mary's eyes lit up. 'A car! It was his father's. I've no idea if he should have had it. We were very naughty. We were supposed to be at the regatta . . . at one of the yacht clubs.' Mary paused, searching her memory for the name. It wasn't coming, but that didn't stop her. 'I can't remember which one, but it was near to the pier. It was a beautiful day, so hot. We were going to watch the races, but he was driving past and hooted and . . . ooh it was such fun.'

'Who were you with, Mary?' Emily's tone was gentle, coaxing. *Were they getting closer to finding out where she had come from, who her family were?*

'Connie.' The name was crystal clear, no hesitation, the memories coming now like the tide, each wave gaining strength. 'She was a devil, it was her idea. We left our bicycles on the pier. It was such a long drive, right up to the mountain. The boys had a picnic. We took the basket up along the path.' Then, Mary's face creasing with a smile, mischievous, she lowered her voice. 'And do you know, Connie took off her stockings and went paddling with him. Can you imagine? The water was crystal clear, beautiful. We got into terrible trouble, we were home so late.'

'Who was Connie, Mary?'

Emily had inched to the edge of her seat, could feel the hard-lipped edge of the table cutting into her stomach as she leaned forward.

'Connie was my friend. We were like two peas, everyone said. We met the first day at work. Hadn't she forgotten her gloves, but I had a spare pair in my bag. She was always in trouble – so bold. Always late for work, ready with a string of excuses, you should have heard them . . . She could have written a book.'

Mary trailed off. Itching with questions, Emily waited to see if she would say more, but Mary was looking out of the window at a point far out to sea, her eyes glazed, enjoying the memories.

Emily glanced at Tony, her eyes anguished, eyebrows raised in question. Tony looked around the boat. People were gathering their possessions together, but looking at the distance they were from land, he was sure they had a few more minutes. Enough time for Mary to talk without them having to interrupt her and bustle her out. He gave Emily a discreet nod.

'Where did you work, Mary?'

'Oh, at Arnotts. On the Estée Lauder counter.' Mary's voice was warm. 'Goodness, I couldn't believe it when I got the job. Everyone wanted to work for them. It was so glamorous. They only took girls from good families, you know, it was nearly as hard as getting into the bank. Connie always said I got in because I looked like Olivia de Havilland . . .'

'Arnotts, the department store? On O'Connell Street?'

'Oh yes. We had to go on a training course, find out what colours suited different complexions, find out how all the products worked. We quite often got actresses coming in, real film stars. Goodness me, it was fun.'

Emily drew in her breath, stole a look at Tony. He was nodding to himself, listening intently. Emily crossed her fingers under the table.

'And did you live nearby? Did you live in Dublin?'

Emily's mind was working fast. Mary had said she could see the mailboat coming in from her house, but the curve of Dublin Bay was huge, ran from the south side of the city right around to the north. She could have lived at any point along the bay and still have been able to see it.

'Live near?' Mary shook her head. 'No, I had to get the bus to work. Connie lived nearer, in Ballsbridge. We always went to her house when we went out, to get changed and do our hair. Much closer.'

Closer to Dublin. And Mary got the bus to work. And she'd taken her bicycle to the yacht club regatta. Emily was beginning to feel like Miss Marple. She was sure the yacht clubs were all in Dún Laoghaire, on the south side of the city. So had Mary lived between Dún Laoghaire and Ballsbridge?

'Where did you go out? To the dances you told me about?'
Mary nodded. It was all flowing freely now, happy memories.
'What was the name of the hotel?'

It took Mary a moment. 'The Gresham. That was it. We went
to the Gresham. There were always dances on. The university
boat club or something like it. They all had committees to organise the dances. Connie's sister was doing a line with a lad in the
boat club so we were invited to everything.'

Mary half-smiled to herself, looked out of the window. The
mountains were clearer now, shaded in purple, sharp against
the sky.

'That was before . . . It was a long time ago.' Like a bubble had
burst, Mary gave a sad half-smile, the happy memories washed
away. 'Before . . .'

Emily opened her mouth to ask another question, but caught
a warning look from Tony.

They were out of time and Mary was heading into dangerous waters. Her whole manner had changed, the smiles
gone. Tony didn't want Emily to push Mary any more – they'd
learned a lot, and he was sure they would be able to coax out
some more when they got her settled in the hotel, but right
now it was time to stop. As if agreeing with him, a disem-
bodied voice came over the tannoy: *Would all drivers please
return to their cars.*

'Time to go, ladies.' Tony stood up, stretching, stiff from sitting for so long. He picked up his coffee cup, knocked the last of
it back. Behind him the high-school group were grabbing their
backpacks, jostling into line to head for their bus. Tony glanced
ahead – the mother and child had disappeared, gone to find

their bags perhaps, to head for their car. He caught Emily's sigh of frustration as she reached for her basket, put out her arm to help Mary up. Tony knew what she was thinking – *they had come so close.* Mary had said *before*, all the happy memories had been *before . . . before what?*

33

'Steve?'

It took Zoë a moment to realise that she was speaking to the answer service. She hesitated, unsure whether she should leave a message, then, as his recorded voice was followed by a sharp pip, said, 'Hi. It's me, Zoë. I'm back at home. They've finished . . . so I'm back. Give me a buzz if you get the message . . . I wondered if you'd like to come over.'

Ending the call, Zoë put the phone down on the kitchen counter and pulled her hair back out of her eyes, rotating her neck. She was tired. Exhausted. It had been an utterly draining week. *Thank God the Guards had gone and she was home.*

Turning her back on the kitchen window, on the night creeping in, Zoë sighed, the sound loud and ragged. She might be home, but it wasn't quite the same as the home she'd left when she'd packed her paintings into the back of her car and headed into Temple Bar and Max's gallery. When the Guards had finally called to say she could come back, she'd naively assumed that they had tidied up. *Well they had – a bit.* They'd tidied up their stuff, but when Zoë had arrived and gone upstairs to unpack, the reality had hit her smack in the face, together with the realisation that it wasn't the Guards' job to tidy up the mess the burglar had left behind, to pick her clothes up off the floor, to tidy her make-up back onto her dressing table.

That detective, Cathy, had tried to prepare her, Zoë knew, had explained that whoever had been here had gone right through her bedroom, but it didn't stop the shock bouncing around Zoë's head like a wasp in a jar.

Even with all the lights switched on upstairs, Zoë felt a shiver run up her spine at the sight of the room. Whoever had done this had literally chucked her things out of every drawer, had taken every neatly folded garment and slung it across the room.

Why? Why had someone broken into her house and gone through her things? What could she have possibly have done for this to happen? Had it been the man she'd seen in the garden?

Zoë had always felt safe in this house, safe and secure even though she lived alone. She'd shared a house when she was at college, had needed to get away from Lavinia's constant inter-ference in her life. Lavinia had let her do the textiles course, expecting her to come back full of ideas, ready to slip into the family business. When she had realised that Zoë wanted to be an artist, that she wasn't interested in fashion design, or busi-ness, or running shops, that all she wanted to do was paint, she was furious. There had only been one word – apart from 'ridiculous' of course – that seemed to apply to everything Zoë did, and that was 'failure'. Zoë was a failure to her family, a failure as a granddaughter and, in fact, as far as Lavinia was concerned, a failure as a human being. And getting the job in the florist's had been both degrading (apparently) and another sign of her failure – Lavinia hadn't wasted any time connecting

Zoë wanting to work, to actually communicate daily with the outside world, with her failure to be a successful artist.

In fact, the only places where Zoë didn't feel like a failure were the studio and at work, where she could create beautiful displays that her clients loved. They didn't think she was a failure. And Phil didn't either – he had been telling her for years that she should have a solo show, that her work was good enough.

But now the excitement of the show, of Max loving her paintings, was tainted by the break-in, by someone coming into her space.

How could so much happen in such a short space of time? It was like she'd been safe in the calm eye of a storm when she was at the gallery with Steve and Max, while everything else outside, her house, her family, had been pounded with rain, rattled around. Hard. Till they shattered. The break-in. The dress . . . *The bones.*

No matter how much she thought about it, she couldn't work it out, work out how they had got there, let alone who they belonged to. But then there were often times when Zoë felt like she was living her life by candlelight, that there were things in the corners hidden in the shadows, that, no matter how hard she tried, how hard she strained her eyes, she couldn't see.

And then Lavinia . . . Zoë felt a fleeting sense of loss. *Lavinia Grant.* Her grandmother. More like her governess. In the past few days Zoë had tried to remember a time when she'd loved Lavinia, a time when her grandmother had loved her, taken her in her arms and hugged her, or even given her a peck on the cheek, a smile of encouragement . . . She'd had more warmth for Trish than she'd ever had for her own flesh and blood.

Looking around her at her bedroom, Zoë wondered where she should start. There was so much mess. She suddenly felt panic pricking at her. Someone had been through her things, had touched her stuff, her clothes, *her underwear*. The solution came faster than Zoë expected, swift and sure. She'd put everything through the wash. Everything. Every last thing that was out of place, that had been moved, she'd wash, dry, iron and fold back into its place, as if nothing had happened. Perhaps it was time to have a really good sort-out.

Leaning over the bed, Zoë scooped up an armful of clothes and dropped it into the tall laundry basket beside the door, reached for another, bundling everything in, bent to pick up a shirt from the floor.

Even from the road Angel Hierra could tell Zoë Grant was back home. The cottage blazed with light in the gathering dusk. Walking up the last of the hill, his loafers crunching on the uneven surface, Hierra pulled a box of matches from his pocket, paused to light up. The match flared, lighting his face for a moment. Shaking it out, he took a drag on the cigarette. *It was time to get things sorted.* He put his free hand into his coat pocket and felt for the key: cold, smooth, its edges still sharp.

Struggling down the hall with the laundry basket, Zoë didn't hear the handle on the back door easing down or the squeak of the hinge as the door opened. Didn't hear footsteps crossing the kitchen. But she did feel a rush of cold air around her ankles as the door was opened, and for a moment was sure she caught the sound of the waves pounding at the end of the garden.

Zoë stopped, listened, the ticking of the hall clock suddenly loud. Had she left the back door open?

A whiff of cigarette smoke.

Her mouth dry, heart drowning the sound of the clock, Zoë put the washing basket down as gently as she could, and peered down the narrow hall, trying to see into the kitchen. She'd left the door to the hall open, all the lights on, but the room ran into the extension at the back – Zoë couldn't see much more than the narrow strip of terracotta tiles running away from the door, the corner of the kitchen table. *Maybe Steve had got her message and dropped in after all, was waiting to surprise her?*

But surely she'd locked the back door?

Edging up to the kitchen door, Zoë put her hand out to push it wider. The tang of smoke grew stronger. Bitter. Acrid.

She'd definitely locked the door. She remembered throwing her keys onto the counter, her bag in her hand. Her head had been full of what she might find upstairs, with the relief at finally getting back inside. But she was *sure* she'd locked it.

Taking another step forward, she pushed the kitchen door further open.

'Good evening, Zoë.'

The cry escaped before she had time to call it back, her hand flying to her mouth. *Who was there?*

Zoë pushed the door wide until she could see the whole room.

Leaning casually on the counter opposite the back door, Hierra took another drag on his cigarette, blew out the smoke with a twisted grin. Zoë felt her mouth drop open, fear clutching at her chest. She took a step backwards, grasped the door frame for support.

There was a strange man in her kitchen. In her kitchen. Her mind slowed by shock, Zoë grasped at details. She noticed his coat first. It was long, dark grey, good quality. He was young, tanned, hair cropped tight to his head. He raised his eyebrows, thick, expressive, his eyes amused.

Payne's grey.

His eyes were grey.

'Who –?'

Hierra interrupted her, his smile revealing sparkling white teeth. 'Who am I?'

He had an American twang to his accent, but it wasn't pure American, had something else blended in, she wasn't sure what. He waited to see if she would reply, took the cigarette out, flicking the ash into the sink. *He was wearing latex gloves.*

Zoë watched him like it was happening in slow motion.

Then she nodded, tried to speak, tried to look like she wasn't scared witless, pulling her cardigan around her with one hand, the other plucking at her necklace. *The phone was on the counter on the other side of the kitchen.*

'You don't need to know who I am.' The man's voice was relaxed, calm, like walking into someone's house through a locked door was the most natural thing in the world. Zoë shook her head, too hard, her earrings swinging with the movement, catching in her hair. 'What do you want?' The words finally came out as a croak.

Zoë felt her knees wobble, steadied herself against the door frame, her back to the sharp edge of the architrave.

'I was doing some business with your grandmother. She wasn't able to complete it.'

For a moment Zoë thought she was going to be sick. She felt cold even though sweat was forming under her arms, sticky, unpleasant. *Who was he?*

'What business?' She could hardly hear herself.

'Business that, if it's not settled, will cause you problems. A lot of problems.'

She could feel his eyes boring into her as he left the words hanging there like a flag waiting for a gust of wind to lift it.

'I don't understand –'

'Look, you're a pretty girl . . .' Before she realised what was happening, he was standing in front of her, too close, running his fingertip down her cheek. His touch was icy even through the glove. She tried to pull back, but the wall was in the way – she flattened herself against it as his finger continued slowly along her clenched jaw, down her neck towards her breast. 'You've got a lot going for you.' Shuddering, she didn't dare meet his eye, could feel his gaze burning her, stripping her naked. 'Your grandmother owed me. We were discussing a down payment. A hundred k.'

Terrified, Zoë opened her mouth to speak but no sound came out. She tried again, her senses overloaded: his breath hot on her face, the sound of her heart thumping in her ears, his aftershave strong, spicy, catching in her throat. Her voice came out in a whisper. 'I don't have that sort of money.'

He grabbed her jaw, his fingers pinching hard, hauled her face around until she was looking him in the eyes.

'Get it, honey. Sell the painting in the front room, if you have to. The one of the boats. We both know it's worth at least 100k. You've got twenty-four hours.'

'I can't . . .'

'You can.'

Her face still in his grip, Zoë suddenly saw a flash of steel, recognised the shape of a blade. She drew in her breath, her eyes widening.

'A hundred k. In used notes.' Her eyes fixed on the blade, she missed his smile, the dead look in his eyes.

'No cops. Do I need to say that?'

She shook her head, winced at the pain as he tightened his grip. She felt the prick of the knife, heard something skitter to the floor.

'You don't want the cops, do you understand?'

She nodded, tried to at least.

Hierra smiled, a half-smile, released her face. The blade vanished as quickly as it had appeared. Zoë fell to her knees, her hair tumbling over her face. *He'd cut her.* The top button of her blouse was gone, revealing the satin edges of her pale pink bra, the curve of her breast. A pinprick of blood oozed where the tip of the knife had nicked her skin. Pulling her cardigan across her chest, she looked up as he spoke again.

'Good. We don't want anything to come out in the papers, do we? The shit would certainly fly. And there's plenty of it, let me tell you, plenty. You wouldn't want that exhibition of yours to be trashed by the tabloids, would you?'

'What do you mean? What would come out in the papers?' It came out as a whisper. *Did he mean the bones?*

'You've a very interesting family. And a very helpful neighbour. Stupid but helpful.'

Zoë didn't speak, couldn't move, felt her stomach constrict. *What did he know about her? About her family?* But she didn't get time to find out. He was on his way to the door.

'You just worry about the cash, darling. I don't have much time. Got a plane to catch, as they say. I'll be in touch to collect it.'

'I still don't understand.'

'We don't want anything nasty to happen, do we? A hundred thousand in cash now, a down payment.'

34

'Cathy? Are you at work?'

'I am. What's up?' Cathy put her finger in her ear, trying to block out the noise of the incident room. There was a note of urgency in Steve's voice, urgency or fear, she wasn't sure which, but neither was characteristic.

'Zoë just rang.' Cathy could tell he was fighting to keep his voice level. 'There was a man in her house – I think he broke in. She's not making much sense. I'm in a cab on my way there. Can you meet me?'

Slipping off the desk she was sitting on, heading for O'Rourke's office, Cathy kept the phone clamped to her ear.

'I'm on my way. Did she know him?'

At the other end she heard Steve clear his throat. 'He had a knife.'

'Thank God you're here.'

Steve jumped physically as Zoë threw open the back door, falling into his arms, her sobs jumbling her words until he was hardly able to understand what she was saying. 'Oh my God, I was so scared . . .'

Half-carrying her inside, trying to kick the door closed behind him, Steve yanked out one of the kitchen chairs from the table, lowered Zoë into it, trying to free himself to see her face, to get a clear idea of what had happened. But she wasn't letting go, was clinging on to his jacket, still sobbing.

'Did he hurt you? Zoë, listen to me, did he hurt you?'

Struggling to keep his voice calm, Steve squatted in front of her, gripped her shoulders. He wanted to shake her, wondered for a moment if he should slap her face to calm her down. She was pale, wild-eyed, staring at him like he was an apparition, like he was part of the nightmare. Zoë opened her mouth to speak but nothing came out.

'I've called the Guards, Cathy's on her way. You're safe now. Tell me what happened.'

Zoë interrupted him, suddenly getting her breath. 'No, no, he said not to call the Guards. The man. I don't know how he got in. Tell them not to come.' Her words were tripping over themselves, her eyes wide with fear.

'It's OK, I called Cathy. She's a friend, it's different. Did he do anything to you? Did he hurt you?' She'd been incoherent on the phone, babbling about the exhibition, about the break-in, obviously deeply shocked.

'He cut me.' Her voice was little more than a whisper.

'Jesus, where?'

'He grabbed my face. He had a knife, he cut me.' Zoë began to sob, the sound raw, unnerving, pointing to the wound on her chest, blood clotted around it.

'Does it hurt?' She shook her head, held on tight to his jacket as she continued, 'He said he knew my grandmother, that she owed him money.' Zoë's whole body was shaking, her fear like static.

'Was he someone who worked for her?'

Zoë shook her head, taking a deep breath, her eyes brimming with shock, bleak as a storm-tossed sea.

'No, I don't think so. He was American – he had an American accent.'

Steve pulled Zoë towards him, holding her tight. *She was so fragile, so vulnerable.* Behind him, Steve heard the door open, realising at the same moment that it hadn't closed when he kicked it. *Christ.* He felt a gust of cold air in the warmth of the kitchen. Had he come back . . . ?

His eyes met Cathy's as she pushed the door firmly closed behind her, her warning about getting involved with Zoë Grant suddenly ringing in his ears like a klaxon . . . *but it was too late for warnings.* In the short time he had known her, Zoë Grant had become imprinted in his subconscious like a watermark. For a split second he felt like he'd been caught with his trousers down.

'Cathy, thanks for coming.'

Cathy nodded curtly, and he could see she was taking in the set-up: the distraught heroine, the knight comforting her – *the only thing they were missing was the horse.* Cathy didn't need to speak. Steve could feel his cheeks flushing. She raised her eyebrows meaningfully.

Pretending he wasn't reading her disapproval, Steve disentangled himself and sat back on his heels, lifting Zoë's chin so she was looking at him.

'Cathy's here. Tell her what happened.'

Zoë drew in her breath, the sound sudden, like a rent in a piece of fabric, her voice when she spoke not much more than a whisper. 'But he said –'

'I know, but Cathy's different.' Steve turned to Cathy. 'He said not to call the cops.' She nodded curtly. 'Just tell her what happened.'

Zoë drew in a shaky breath. 'I was upstairs, tidying up. I came down with the washing and . . . and he was here, in the kitchen. But I locked the door. I *know* I locked the door.'

The strength of Zoë's words left a void of silence in the room, a void filled by the sound of a clock ticking faintly from somewhere down the hall, by the rasp of her breathing. Cathy nodded towards the kettle.

'Why don't I make us all a cup of tea, and you can tell me exactly what happened.'

It took Cathy a few moments to find the mugs, teabags, milk, a few moments she knew would give Zoë time to calm down. As the kettle boiled, Cathy pulled open a drawer, looking for teaspoons. Beside the cutlery tray were about a dozen keys, each one meticulously labelled in neat black ink, plastic tags creating a rainbow of colour against the dull rubber matting in the bottom of the drawer. *Zoë was sure she'd locked the door . . .*

Sliding it closed with her hip, Cathy put a large scoop of sugar in each of the mugs. They all needed it today.

'Here we are.'

Pulling out a chair, she sat down opposite Steve, Zoë between them at the head of the table. Cathy cradled the cup in her hands. 'Tell me what he looked like.'

It took a moment for Zoë to reply.

'He had a tan, short hair. An American accent. And a knife, he had a knife.' Zoë sniffed loudly. 'I just don't understand. He said Lavinia owed him money.' Abandoning her cup, Zoë put her face in her hands, then looked up, straight at Cathy, her voice little more than a whisper: 'He said I didn't want anything to come out in the press, that it might ruin my exhibition. What did he mean?'

Cathy sat back, her mind whirling. *An American.*

Then, so quietly that Cathy almost missed it, 'He had grey eyes.'

Cathy sat forward. *Freaky eyes.* 'Do you think you'd know him again?'

Zoë nodded, her face saying it all, *how could she forget him?*

'So what did she say?' O'Rourke looked up from his desk the second Cathy put her head around the office door.

'Like Steve said, there was a guy in her kitchen. He pulled a knife on her.' Cathy closed the door firmly behind her.

'Did she know him?'

Cathy shook her head, drew in a breath. 'He was American. Six foot, clean-shaven, grey eyes.'

'What?' O'Rourke paled about three shades. 'Is she *sure*?'

Cathy pulled out the chair opposite him and sat down, sighing, rubbing her face with her hand. 'It's the eyes. She said he was tanned, dark, but he had grey eyes. And he wants 100k in cash.'

'Hierra. It has to be Hierra. Jesus Christ. How the hell did this happen?' O'Rourke was shaking his head, didn't wait for her to answer. 'How many men have I had out looking for him? And what does he do? Turns up in bloody Zoë Grant's bloody kitchen.' He looked like the thought was giving him a physical pain. And Cathy knew she was about to make it worse.

'He seems to know something about Lavinia Grant. Said she had a lot to hide.'

O'Rourke closed his eyes for a moment, ran his hands over his face, then looked back at her. 'He'd be right there. He didn't happen to mention hastening Lavinia Grant's departure from this world, did he?'

Cathy put her elbows on the edge of the desk, playing with the band holding back her ponytail. 'He said he'd been talking to her about a deal, all right. Think it's likely?'

'With his record? More than likely. Can you die of shock?'

'If you've got a weak heart. Zoë's always saying Lavinia hated publicity, that she was paranoid about the press.'

O'Rourke nodded slowly. 'But what the hell is Angel Hierra's connection to Lavinia Grant?'

Cathy ran her fingers through her ponytail. 'Honestly, I don't know that there is one. I reckon he's trying it on. I was thinking about it all the way back here. He's a con man, we know that; he's violent, and he's on the run. He must need money. I don't know that he ever met Lavinia Grant. I reckon he saw the obituaries in the paper . . .'

O'Rourke interrupted. 'And put two and two together?'

Cathy nodded. 'Zoë said he had spoken to her neighbour. He knew about the exhibition, but he could be winging it on the history. There's every chance that Zoë's neighbour caught wind of the bones being found, could have overheard something the lads said . . .'

'And maybe she let something slip to Hierra that fitted neatly with his plan, and he thought he'd try a bit of blackmail.'

Cathy nodded. 'The FBI said he was a charmer.' She paused. 'I reckon that there's a good chance Hierra is our burglar. Zoë was sure she locked her back door this afternoon, and he managed to get in without a sound – but she's got a load of keys in a drawer in the kitchen. I think when he broke in, he borrowed the back-door key in case he had to go back.'

O'Rourke nodded, weighing up Cathy's words. 'And presumably she had a key to Oleander House. Is that still there?'

'I'll have to ask her.'

He frowned, obviously thinking, then said, 'But why would he have had a slash at that dress?'

'Maybe he was just trying to give Zoë a fright, thought it was her dress. Or maybe he's got a problem with marriage.'

O'Rourke nodded again slowly. 'He certainly had a problem with his father, so maybe. God knows . . .'

He paused, as if he was turning it over in his head. 'She'll need protection. I'll get a team on the house.'

'He insisted no cops so they'll have to be invisible.'

'We can do invisible. We'll need someone on the inside plus a team outside. She on her own?'

Cathy shook her head. 'Steve Maguire's with her.'

'The boyfriend? He won't be much help if Hierra reappears. The lads will have to go in through the back in case he's watching.' O'Rourke paused. 'I'll call the FBI, let them know. You get down there with his picture, see if Zoë can identify him. I don't think we need to tell her who we think her visitor was yet, she's had enough of a fright tonight.'

Cathy pushed her chair back, but O'Rourke wasn't finished. 'The lab was on. The soil samples from the bones aren't one hundred per cent conclusive but they reckon there's a fighting chance they came from Oleander House.'

She raised her eyebrows. 'So the lads are going to start on the garden?'

He nodded. 'They're having a good look at the fireplaces and the drains right now; nothing yet.' O'Rourke drifted off for a moment, looking over Cathy's shoulder, spoke half to himself. 'Jesus, Hierra. That's all we need.' Then coming back to her: 'You getting an early night?'

Cathy leaned back in the chair, stretched. 'Trish O'Sullivan left a message with the front desk. She wants to collect the post from Oleander. I explained we're processing it but I said I'd meet her to give her what I could. Don't trust her one little bit. Thought I'd check in and see how the lads are getting on at the same time.'

'Grand. Then go home, you look like shit and you're going to need your beauty sleep.'

'Thanks a million.'

O'Rourke shrugged. 'You look knackered. And we're going to be busy if this does turn out to be Hierra. Could be the last full night's sleep you get for a while.' Cathy half-nodded. He was right; she needed an early night. 'Is Zoë getting the locks changed?' he asked.

'I called the locksmith from Dalkey when I was leaving.'

'Good. Wouldn't want her turning up dead. We'd look right prats.'

Cathy couldn't resist a smile. 'You're all heart.'

O'Rourke's eyes met hers, lingering for a moment before he looked back at his laptop, shaking his head. 'Mind that Trish one, I think she bites.'

35

'Do I go right here?'

Tony swung the car out of the Stena terminal. The signs for Dublin were straight ahead of him, positioned high, but he was concentrating on the car ahead that had been lurching erratically since they rolled off the ferry. He'd thought at first the driver must be dazzled by the floodlights illuminating the port after the darkness of the ship, but now the driver had stopped at the traffic-light-controlled T-junction. *Which was fine. But the lights were green.* Tony flicked the wipers on to max, trying to clear the rain from the windscreen. It was like someone had turned on all the taps and left them running.

'Do you think he's waiting for a train? What colour of green does he want?'

'What is the matter with you? Calm down, they're probably lost.' Emily looked at Tony out of the corner of her eye, surprised, his exasperation electric in the confines of the car.

'They've only just got off the boat, how can they be lost already? Jesus . . . The sign is there.'

Tony smacked his forehead with the heel of his hand and pointed ahead of him at approximately the same time the other driver spotted the sign. The car swung into the narrow two-lane feeder road just as the lights changed. Tony opened his mouth to say something and shut it again, bottling his anger. This wasn't the time or the place.

Tony knew damn well it wasn't the car ahead that he was mad with; it was himself. The image of the little girl on the ferry flashed before him again, the bond she had with her mother stronger than anything he'd ever seen. Their love, their closeness, despite her disability, *because of* her disability, *because she was just a wonderful child*, was so strong it didn't look like anything could break it. And right now he was standing right between Emily and any hope she had for ever feeling like that, for them both as a couple to ever experience that joy. And they had so much to offer a child. Tony could hear Emily's words echoing through his mind. They had so much to offer.

'This bit's all new.' They both jumped at Mary's voice in the back of the car. Like a comic double take they looked at each other and then back at Mary. Her face was passive, her tone matter-of-fact. She didn't seem to notice their surprise. 'There were never that many yachts. Look at all the masts.' Sitting behind Emily, Mary pulled her safety belt out a fraction so she could lean forward and get a better view out of the rear window, nodding towards a long, low granite building to their right, Palladian pillars guarding elegant steps. In the gathering darkness the front was bathed in pools of light thrown up from concealed spotlights. Even in the rain it was pretty impressive. 'But that's the same – the Royal Irish Yacht Club, that's the same. It was *very* smart . . . Lots of doctors.'

Tony took a deep breath. Christ, how mad was this? He'd denied his wife a child and what had he got instead? An old lady, crazy as a coot. For a moment Tony felt like laughing.

'Will we stop for a coffee, Mary, check it out?' Keeping one eye on the traffic light, Tony looked at Mary in the rear-view mirror.

'Oh no, you have to be a member. They have a doorman and everything.'

Tony nodded sagely, the lights changing to green before he could think of a suitable reply.

'Did you go there, Mary? Do you remember you were telling us about watching the yachts race at the regatta?' Turning in her seat, Emily spoke over her shoulder.

Mary nodded slowly. 'They all had regattas – bands outside during the day and then dancing at night.'

She trailed off, craning her neck to look behind her as they passed the single-storey building. Tony almost groaned as he pulled up at another set of lights. At least the rain seemed to be lessening. He knocked off the wipers.

'Right again here, for the city?' Leaning over to look at the map, open on Emily's knee, Tony traced the edge of the coastline with his finger.

'Yep, through Blackrock, then it's pretty much a straight drive into the middle of the city, to Stephen's Green.'

'Goodness, look at those.' Mary again, this time dipping down in the back seat, looking out of the window at a huge glass and steel apartment block on their left, every window lit to a view of the harbour.

'Has it changed much, Mary? Do you remember Dún Laoghaire?'

'Oh yes, none of those buildings were there. You could see right through to the church from here.'

Tony glanced at Emily, his eyebrows raised. The memories were obviously flowing freely, Mary was speaking as if they'd never been missing. Maybe Emily had been right, that a trip home was exactly what Mary needed. Maybe it was what they all needed.

'It's a neat area.' Tony glanced over to his right towards the sea. In the darkness it danced with the wind, wavelets tipped with white catching the light from the moon as the clouds passed. High up across the bay he could see white warning lights flashing, the faint outline of huge chimneys.

The lights changed.

'Jesus!' Eyes back to the road, Tony slammed on the brakes, the map sliding off Emily's knee, hitting the floor hard. The car ahead had stopped suddenly in front of them, its brake lights blazing, a queue of traffic snaking ahead of them.

'You OK?' he asked.

Emily nodded, reaching for the map, looked over her shoulder at Mary. She was frowning hard, her hand on the seat belt where it had restrained her.

'There can't be *more* traffic lights . . .' Tony sat up in his seat, craning his neck to see what the hold-up was. A white van was parked at the side of the road, a constant stream of oncoming traffic preventing the first car in the queue from getting around it.

'At this rate we'll never get to the hotel on time.' Tony let out a sigh of exasperation, glanced at his watch. 'Is there a back route we can take?'

About to tell him this was the most direct route, behind her Emily heard a seat belt unclick. Turning to check on Mary, she realised that the rear door had swung open.

'Dear God! Pull over. It's Mary, look, she's got out!'

Still focused on the traffic ahead, now drumming his fingers on the steering wheel, Tony turned at the sound of Emily's voice to find her unclicking her seat belt, her door already open.

'What?'

'It's Mary, look . . .'

'Jesus Christ.'

'I'll get her . . .'

'I can't park here . . .'

Emily ducked her head back inside the door. 'Pull over in the next side road, I'll catch up with you.'

'This is ridiculous. How much longer is this going to take?'

Standing outside the gate of Oleander House, Trish O'Sullivan lowered her umbrella, shaking the rain off as she closed it. The street lamp threw shadows across her face, made the umbrella look like a weapon.

'It's hard to tell. Obviously we don't want to tie up resources any longer than absolutely necessary, but the lads are very thorough. They need to be satisfied that the search is complete.' Cathy resisted a smile, enjoying the look on Trish's face. The muscles around Trish's mouth had tensed like she wanted to spit. Sometimes Cathy loved her job.

Her eyes cold, Trish grabbed the few envelopes Cathy had in her hand – bills, a magazine – and shuffled through them. But Cathy was pretty sure she was too angry to read anything. If they'd been in a cartoon strip there would have been smoke coming out of her ears. Cathy couldn't resist laying it on a bit thicker.

'As DI O'Rourke explained, we've found the partial skeleton of a child. We're going to find the rest.' It was a definite statement of fact.

'After all these years, how the hell can you expect to find anything?'

Cathy smiled. 'You'd be amazed what can turn up . . .'

Trish shivered theatrically. 'Lavinia would hate the idea of having her garden dug up. Do you have any idea of how much it cost to landscape?' It was more of a snarl than a statement. Cathy nodded like the cost of the landscaping was relevant. 'Just you make sure you put everything back exactly as you find it . . .' Trish drew a breath. 'I'll be back tomorrow for the rest. This is hardly everything, is it?' She waved the letters in the air, perilously close to Cathy's face. Holding her ground, ignoring the intrusion of her personal space, Cathy frowned.

'We can only give you what's been checked while the investigation is ongoing. We wouldn't want to miss finding out that someone was blackmailing Lavinia Grant by post now, would we?'

Her eyes glowing with anger, about to make a cutting remark, Trish stopped herself, catching sight of an elderly woman standing on the pavement staring at them.

'What the hell are you looking at?'

'Please don't speak to her like that.' Arriving beside the old lady, catching her breath, a younger woman in a bright pink sweater put her arm around her protectively. 'She's a bit muddled. Come on, pet, let's get back to the car.'

But the old lady wasn't moving. She was starring fixedly at Trish.

And Trish's face was creased in a look somewhere between shock and amazement. It was a cliché but she looked exactly like she'd seen a ghost. And as Cathy watched, Trish's eyes widened, *in recognition?*

Who was she? Who could have this effect on the impervious Trish O'Sullivan? It was the first time Cathy had seen her stuck for words. One eye on Trish, Cathy bided her time, waiting for the old lady to speak. When she did, her voice was fractured like broken glass, sharp-edged.

'Patricia? Trish? Is it you?'

The old woman paled, swaying as she spoke. Supporting her frail shoulders, her minder looked in amazement from her to Trish and back again. It was possible that the old woman and Trish could have been around the same age, but with the layers of make-up and jewellery and her hair perfectly done, Trish looked at least twenty years younger.

'Do you know each other? Mary, do you know this woman?'

To Cathy the minder's accent sounded like Donegal, but with an American twang. Trish opened her mouth to speak, closed it again. When she finally got the words out they were whispered, her voice incredulous, laced, Cathy was sure, with a large measure of horror.

'Grace?'

'Where's Lavinia? Is Lavinia here?' The old woman stepped forward, reached out to grasp the spikes of the fence, her voice getting stronger, her eyes locked on Trish, unwavering.

Cathy felt the hairs stand up on the back of her neck. Who was this? Trish had turned ashen, was leaning on the gatepost, her voice shocked.

'Grace? I thought you'd never come back. Thought you'd left.' Then, realising she'd been asked a question, recovering a little, Trish said, her voice harsh, 'She's dead, Grace. A heart attack, a few days ago.'

'Dead?' The old lady's mouth fell open. 'No! . . . Dead?' Laden with disbelief. 'Why didn't anyone tell me?'

'We didn't know where you were, Grace –'

The answer came back like a bullet. 'But *she* knew. Lavinia knew. She must have done. She must have told you.'

'I thought Lavinia had lost touch with you . . . years ago.' Trish faltered. 'It's been so many years. You upped and left so long ago.'

So long ago? Cathy's mind was racing.

'But dead? How can she be dead?' The old woman's voice was thin, disbelieving.

'It was her heart, Grace, it gave up. She'd had high blood pressure, high cholesterol.'

The old lady staggered, the shock written across her face, raw, painful. Trish didn't move, appeared to be stuck to the spot. But the old lady looked like she was about to fall. The woman in the pink sweater tried to steady her, her face flushed; a second later Cathy was supporting the old lady on the other side.

'Are you OK there?' Cathy's eyes met the younger woman's over the old lady's head. *Was she a relative, a carer?* Turning to Trish, she kept her voice level, calm. 'Do you know her, Trish? Is this lady a relative of Lavinia Grant's?'

Trish didn't answer, just nodded, seemed to be in some sort of daze.

'What's going on? I managed to park around the corner.'

Cathy looked up to see a dark-haired man arrive behind Trish, a set of car keys dangling from his hand. American. Fifties, professional despite the jeans and impractical lemon cashmere sweater. The minder was obviously relieved to see him.

'Mary knows this lady. She recognised her.' The minder sounded amazed, nodded towards Trish.

Cathy's eyes flicked from the old lady to Trish. Why was Trish calling her Grace when the other two were calling her Mary?

'She's in shock, we need to sit her down.' The American turned to Trish. 'I'm sorry about this. Tony Cox.' He stuck out his hand. 'I'm a doctor. We need to get her into the warm, calm her down. She's been ill.'

Juggling the mail in her hand, sticking the umbrella under her arm, her face confused, Trish automatically returned his handshake, not really registering what he was saying. 'This is my wife, Emily. Mary's been staying with us.'

It took Cathy less than a second to make a decision.

'There's a restaurant around the corner. Why don't we pop in there and get you a nice cup of tea?'

But the old lady wasn't having any of it.

'No. No. I'm not leaving. This is my home. I want to go inside. I'm not going –'

Her home?

The American, Tony Cox, interrupted Cathy's thoughts. 'Now Mary, a cup of tea's exactly what you need, that sounds like a plan to me. And we can find out who's living here now while we're at it. It's been a long time, it's probably changed hands several times since you lived here.'

'No, no it hasn't. I live here.' The words were out before Trish realised their implication.

'You?' The old lady's face contorted. 'You're living in my house? Why? This is my house, my father's house.'

'I . . .'

One eye on Mary, on her increasing distress, Tony spoke again. 'Could we go inside? I really think we need to get her out of the street. And it's going to rain again any minute.'

Trish opened her mouth to speak, but it was Cathy's turn to interrupt.

'I'm afraid the house is sealed. There is no way you can go inside.'

'Sealed?' Tony looked at her like she was mad. Then, like the pieces were falling into place, he looked from the white Garda Technical Bureau van on the pavement to Cathy and back again, his brows creased. He opened his mouth, about to ask what was going on, she was sure, but he thought better of it. *Just as well.*

Damn it – Cathy felt frustration pricking at her – there was no way they could go inside the house. Even if she kept everyone together, stuck to Trish like flypaper, letting *anyone* inside could contaminate the scene, prejudice the final case when it came to court. The defence would chew them up and spit them out. *But the old woman obviously knew Lavinia, knew Trish – had LIVED here. What if she knew something about the bones?*

'I think we should go and get that cup of tea.' Cathy steered the old lady around. Dazed, she finally allowed herself to be moved. 'She's had a shock.'

She wasn't the only one.

Cathy glanced behind her to see Trish following them like she was on autopilot, like the world had just stopped turning. It was time to get O'Rourke down here.

PART FOUR

Binding the Edges
Encasing the raw edges of a blanket or quilt with another piece of fabric. Binding also refers to the fabric itself that is folded and used to encase raw or fraying edges.

36

'Hey, Cathy, what's the craic?' Only a step away from the gate of Oleander House, Cathy turned at the sound of her name. Thirsty was skipping down the steps of the house, a cigarette already between his teeth; he waved to her.

Thirsty. Someone must be smiling on her today . . .

'I'm sorry, I won't be a second.' Cathy untangled herself from the old lady's arm and slipped back inside the gate.

'The old lady used to live here. She's just found out about Lavinia. I want to talk to her, but I can't take them all down to the station yet, she might have a coronary. And I can't bring them into the house. I thought we could all get a cup of tea around the corner.' Thirsty grimaced. She read his mind. 'I know, it's not ideal.'

Thirsty took a puff of his cigarette. 'Want me to talk to the guys inside? You'll get more out of her here than somewhere public, and you never know what she might say when she walks back inside the front door.' He paused, exhaling the smoke. 'They've pretty much finished at the front downstairs. Still have the kitchen and upstairs, but . . . let's see what we can do.'

Not daring to look at him, Cathy worried at a loose piece of gravel with the toe of her boot, shaking her head, smiling to herself. *Sometimes Thirsty was such a bloody gem.* Cathy knew he watched her back, had heard on the grapevine that he'd sung her praises more than once to the Super in Dún Laoghaire, had, Cathy was sure, been the one who'd got her out of uniform and into the detective unit in the first place. He and John Lacey the Super went way back, had been stationed together in Ronanstown – bandit country – when they graduated, blood brothers. *What had she done to deserve this?* Cathy looked up, met his eye. *He knew what she was thinking.*

'Reckon you could? If we can get her inside, spark some memories, she might let something slip.'

'Consider it done. We'll need the seal of approval from Lacey, but I'll have a chat to him. Give me five minutes. I'll call O'Rourke too, fill him in.'

Moments later, his fag stubbed out into an empty matchbox in his pocket, Thirsty was on his way back into the house, his mobile clamped to his ear.

Back on the pavement Tony Cox was getting restless, looked cold, was jangling his keys in the pocket of his jeans. Cathy threw him an apologetic grin.

'Sorry about that. I think we might be OK to go inside. The scenes-of-crime team are just getting clearance. You'll have to keep to the taped areas, but they've finished the drawing room. It'll be more private.'

Before Tony could open his mouth, Emily stopped him. 'Why don't you go on? I can catch a cab with Mary later. I think we ought to let her see the house again if she can, and you don't want to be late.'

Tony checked his watch. 'OK, I'm sure Mary wants to see inside. Are you sure you'll be all right?' Tony turned to Cathy expectantly. She realised she hadn't introduced herself.

'Detective Garda Cathy Connolly.'

He lifted his eyebrows, and turned back to Emily. 'Perhaps the detective can help you get a cab when you're done.' Then, to Cathy, 'We're staying at the Shelbourne Hotel. I'm speaking at a conference . . . they're expecting me.'

'We'll be fine, honestly.' Emily threw him an encouraging smile. 'You'd better get moving, the traffic's terrible.'

'Cat?' Cathy heard Thirsty's voice behind her. He was at the top of the steps, beckoning. 'You're grand. Permission granted. O'Rourke's on his way.'

The smile on her face said it all.

'Careful there, Mary, mind the mat. Perhaps I should be calling you Grace.' Emily Cox held Mary's arm, steadying her as she struggled up the steps and across the threshold. Trish, her face pale, was bringing up the rear, the umbrella passive at her side, mail stuffed under her arm.

'Here, the sofa's comfortable,' Cathy said, guiding Mary and Emily into the drawing room. The old lady was looking around her like a child in a sweet shop, her eyes glazed, mouth open.

'It's a beautiful room.' Emily helped Mary to sit, perching on the sofa beside her, looking around at the magnificent chandelier, the thick drapes.

Trish came in behind them, headed for the fireplace, flipping open a cigarette box on the mantelpiece, picking up her lighter. Watching her, Cathy sat down on the arm of the easy chair beside the fireplace.

'Now, isn't this cosy?' Trish took a drag on the cigarette, her voice dripping with sarcasm.

Glancing nervously from Cathy to Trish, Emily rubbed Mary's arm. 'Was this your house, Mary, I mean Grace? Is it the same as you remember it?'

Cathy shifted slightly to get more comfortable, thinking of Thirsty's advice as he'd shown them in. *Let them talk.* He was right. Whatever was going on here, Trish was wound up like a spring. And she wasn't the type to keep her thoughts to herself.

'Where's my painting? The one of the harbour, where is it?'

Startled, they all turned to Mary. The old lady's voice was barely a croak but her face had flushed. She glared at Trish. 'What have you done with my painting? Daddy gave me that painting for my birthday. It should be there, over the fireplace.'

Trish didn't answer immediately, instead paused to pick something off her lip. *A piece of tobacco?* Then, offhand, like it was no big deal, said, 'Lavinia gave it to Zoë. A house-warming present. She wanted something more modern in here.'

The picture now hanging over the fireplace was a wild scene of the sea, charcoal and pastel, impressionistic. Predominantly grey.

'But it was my picture. She had no right.'

'Did you live here when you were a little girl, Mary? Did your parents live here?' Emily put her hand on Mary's knee, her eyes alight with excitement. Mary frowned, like the memories were coming back in pieces. 'My father. I don't remember my mother.'

'She died. Giving birth to you.' Trish's voice, cold and hard and matter-of-fact. Like it was Mary's fault her mother had died. 'I don't think Lavinia ever forgave you for that.'

Even Cathy felt the sting of her words. Emily glanced at her, her eyes dark.

'I'm sorry, are you a relative?'

Trish looked at her like she was dirt on the floor. 'A close family friend. Lavinia's friend.'

'But you live here?'

Before Trish could enlighten her, Mary turned on Emily. 'Why didn't you tell me? Why didn't you tell me Lavinia was dead?'

'I'm sorry, Mary, I didn't know, honestly. Who was Lavinia, pet?'

'My sister. She was my sister. You know who she was.'

Cathy drew in her breath, trying to hold on to the questions bubbling up inside her. She was Lavinia Grant's sister, and there was no love lost between her and Trish, that was for sure . . . she must know something . . .

'I don't, Mary. I'm Emily from London, I don't know Lavinia.'

'Of course you do. She sent you, didn't she? Sent you to find me. And why do you keep calling me Mary? I keep telling you, my name's not Mary.'

Emily threw a concerned glance at Cathy, suddenly unsure whether this had been a good idea. 'Because that's what we thought your name was . . .' Emily took it slowly. 'Social Services found a letter in your pocket addressed to Mary. You told them you had to move out of the place you were living because it was being sold. You didn't have any documents.'

Feeling the need to explain, Emily turned to Cathy. 'We think she was in rented accommodation somewhere in London, then something happened. She was very confused. They found her a place in a residential unit. I'm an occupational therapist, I work for Tower Hamlets, the local authority.'

Cathy nodded but before she could comment, Trish had taken another drag on her cigarette, was stubbing it out in the lid of the box.

'The *Virgin* Mary was it, Grace? Were you getting mixed up?' Her tone was loaded with vitriol. Cathy felt a shock wave cross the room, but Trish wasn't finished. 'Did you spin them a story, Grace? Did you tell them that you were misunderstood, that you were a good little girl?'

Before Cathy had realised quite what was happening, Emily was on her feet, had crossed the room.

'I'm sorry, I don't know who you are, but how dare you speak to her like that? How dare you? Can't you see how difficult this is for her? She hasn't been well, she's very confused.'

Taking the cigarette from between her lips, Trish laughed in Emily's face.

'How dare I? She was a little tart, didn't she tell you?'

Emily delivered the slap before any of them anticipated it, least of all Emily, who took a step back, watching Trish recoil, her hand covering the red mark on her cheek. For a second Emily looked like she was about to follow it up with a comment, but then, with her point made clearly enough, she sat down again beside Mary, catching Cathy's eye, wide open with surprise.

'You can't just sit there and let her do that – that was assault!' Trish's voice was shrill. Her hand still at her face, she looked angrily from Cathy to Emily. Cathy shifted her position on the arm of the chair, silently considering her options. If the truth were told, that slap was long overdue.

'Thanks, Trish.' Cathy's tone said it all: *that's enough*. 'I think we all need to calm down, don't you?' Cathy managed to include Emily in the statement without actually looking at her. 'Try and keep this polite. How do you know this lady, Trish? How did she end up homeless?' Cathy glanced at Emily for confirmation. 'In

London?' *While Lavinia stacked up the cash in Dublin . . .* Cathy was sorely tempted to say it, but bit it back.

Still stunned, Trish shook her head. 'Why the hell should I tell you anything? You saw what she did.'

'You'll tell us because I asked. If you'd prefer to talk to DI O'Rourke down at the station, under caution, that's fine by me.'

'Me under caution? What about her?' Trish pointed an accusing finger at Emily, who looked like she wanted to bite it off. Emily's face was set, eyes flaming, but Cathy could tell she knew she'd already overstepped the mark, was working hard to keep quiet.

'Would you like to file charges, Trish? Explain to the court exactly what is going on here? I think we'd all like to know.'

Trish stubbed out her cigarette, reached for another one. She took her time lighting it. When she finally answered Cathy's question, nodding towards Mary, her voice was bitter. 'She left. Got a job as a governess and went. She always was headstrong, did what suited her without a thought for anyone else, left Lavinia to pick up the pieces.'

'When would that have been?'

Trish shook her head like the date was irrelevant. 'Late forties, early fifties? I don't know.'

'Around the time that Lavinia got married?' Cathy kept her tone innocent. *Now that was a coincidence.*

'Around that time.'

Mary drew in a ragged breath, a tear spilling from her eye, her voice little more than a whisper. 'It's lies. It wasn't like that . . .'

'Come here, pet, I've a tissue . . .' Emily bent down to pull a tissue from her basket, but Mary pushed her hand away, looked up at Trish. 'Is he here?'

Behind her Cathy heard the door open and O'Rourke slipped into the room. She knew Thirsty had briefed him. Now, catching Mary's question, he raised a questioning eyebrow to Cathy. *How's it going?* Her nod was almost imperceptible.

The others hardly seemed to notice his arrival, their focus on Mary.

Trish snorted and threw her head back like she was trying not to laugh, like the whole situation was farcical. 'Who? Charles? He died, Grace. Went back to France and got killed in a road accident years ago.'

Mary grasped Emily's hand.

'Why didn't you tell me? Why didn't you tell me he was dead? I'd never have come back . . .'

'I'm sorry, Mary, really I am, I didn't know.' Emily smoothed the back of Mary's hand.

'Why not, why didn't you know? Lavinia sent you, didn't she? She must have told you where to find me.'

'I didn't know Lavinia, Mary . . .' Cathy could tell Emily was fighting to keep her voice level.

But Mary wasn't having any of it. 'Don't be ridiculous, she was your guardian, wasn't she? Of course you knew her.'

Emily glanced anxiously at Cathy again, noticed O'Rourke standing behind her leaning on the wall. A glimmer of recognition passed across her face and Cathy could tell Emily knew he was a senior officer. But now wasn't the moment for introductions.

'Mary – sorry, Grace – you're getting a bit confused. It's all been a shock. I think maybe we should come back tomorrow when you feel a bit better.'

Trish's words cut across her before Mary could reply. 'This woman's not Eleanor, Grace. She didn't know Lavinia.' Her voice was harsh.

Mary shook her head, glaring at Trish. 'I don't believe you. You always were against me. You and Lavinia. Always against me . . .'

'She's right, Mary, I'm Emily – Emily Cox, from London. Who's Eleanor?'

The old lady sobbed, the sound raw, uncontrolled, her shoulders shaking violently. 'Eleanor's my daughter.'

Stunned, Cathy and O'Rourke exchanged glances.

Emily pulled Mary to her, hugging her tight, her eyes meeting Cathy's over her head, beseeching. But O'Rourke had already read the situation. He stepped forward, throwing a hard look at Trish. *Christ, she had some explaining to do.*

'I'm Detective Inspector Dawson O'Rourke. We're in the middle of an investigation here that you might be able to help us with, Mary – sorry, Grace – but I think you've had enough for one day, there's a lot to take in.' *He'd said it.* Cathy stood up as he continued, 'I think Mrs Cox is right, it would be wise to adjourn until tomorrow. Will we say 2 p.m.?'

Cathy bit her lip. She was desperate to find out more but Grace obviously had a fragile grip on reality, and they couldn't afford to lose her now.

37

In a third-floor suite in the Shelbourne Hotel, Tony Cox was standing in front of a huge walnut armoire, flipping his tie into an Oxford knot. It was 7 p.m. Emily was stretched out on the bed beside him, while Mary had a lie-down in the adjacent room.

'Have you got your speech?'

'In my briefcase.' He grinned over his shoulder at Emily. 'Honestly, you don't have to worry. I'll be fine. There's not much they can throw at me that I can't handle . . .'

'I know.' Emily wrinkled her nose apologetically. 'Do you mind me not coming to the dinner? I really don't think I've got the energy.' Glancing over at her, he shook his head as she continued, 'Will you be tied up all day tomorrow?'

'I guess so. But you're going to be busy now. You won't need me.' Tony grimaced, double-checking the navy silk knot, easing out his collar. *The tie looked good. The suit looked good. And the line-up for the conference looked even better.* When he'd finally had a chance to read through the paperwork, he'd spotted some big hitters he really wanted to meet. Which meant, thankfully, he really would be tied up all day.

Tony smoothed his shirt into the top of his trousers and turned to face her as she spoke.

'I still can't believe it all came back so fast. Dear God, if we'd come by plane we might never have known.'

Tony shook his head, disagreeing. 'No, it was inevitable. You had an idea she was from Dún Laoghaire – you would have taken her out there. The memories started coming back as soon as she saw those mountains, then with the yacht clubs, the boats ... I guess, leaving like she did, she held on to her childhood memories – they grew in her mind, images became cemented if you like. Seeing the place where she grew up brought all the missing bits back.'

Emily nodded, hitched herself up on one elbow.

'You're right. She was just so upset. Thank goodness that inspector stepped in– I don't think she could have taken much more of that awful woman.'

'Just keep an eye on her and call me if there are any problems. It's all coming back a bit *too* fast for my liking. Mary's been through a lot over the years, and now when she finally finds her family, her sister's dead and the cops are all over her house.' Tony paused, frowning, his hands on his hips in an unconscious medical-practitioner stance. 'I reckon Mary gave a false name way back when because she was trying to disassociate herself from the real Grace, from whatever trauma made her leave. She may have been Mary for years, it's only now the memories are surfacing.'

'I'm really worried about her,' Emily said. 'She seemed more mixed up than ever – it was like everything was scrambled in her head.'

'Exactly. She found herself face to face with everything she'd blanked out.' Tony paused. 'At least she isn't hallucinating any more, that's something. But remember there's a strong possibility that she's suffering from the onset of dementia as well as everything else. It's only when we're controlling one psychosis that we'll be able to distinguish the symptoms of the other.' Emily nodded, sighing, as he continued, 'So what's your plan?'

'To go back to the house tomorrow like the inspector suggested. They need to talk to Mary – I mean Grace – I can't get used to calling her that – some more. I know they'll be gentle with her; that young Guard is very nice. I'm sure Mary wants to find out exactly what happened to her sister, and there may be other family members still alive.'

'Watch that Trish O'Sullivan if you meet her again. I still can't believe you slapped her.' Tony smothered a grin. He'd been amazed when Emily had slightly sheepishly explained what had happened. Emily drew in a sharp breath, her face flushing. 'I felt like taking her bloody umbrella and bashing her over the head with it – I couldn't believe anyone could be so rude.'

'The bit about the Virgin Mary? No love lost there. But remember Mary is your first priority. Antagonising her family probably isn't the *best* way forward.' Emily rolled her eyes pouting, as Tony sat down on the edge of the bed. 'Just go easy– whatever's been going on in that house, you don't want to get involved.'

'I think we already are. What did the Garda say to you when she called? That they'd found the bones of a baby and were looking for the rest of the corpse? Dear God ...' Emily shivered, paused for a moment. 'Mary couldn't have had anything to do with that, could she?'

Bile burned the back of Cathy's throat as she heaved again. *Surely her stomach had to be empty by now ... and what the feck was it with 'morning' sickness that she puked almost every bloody evening?*

She pushed her hair back out of her face, hooking it behind her ears, hastily rubbed the tears from her cheeks with the palms of her hands, her stomach curling again. *Oh God, how long was this going to last?* But the last retch was dry, a reflex action. Both hands on the edge of the toilet seat, she hung her head forward and breathed a sigh of relief. *It was over. Thank God it was over.*

Cathy took a moment to breathe, the taste of vomit bitter, overwhelming, reached for the flush, banishing her misery in a cascade of lurid blue. The water in the glass balancing at the back of the tiny bathroom's single basin was tepid but she didn't care. Swishing it around her mouth, Cathy turned the tap on full, the jet of water loud in the silence of the empty house, refilled the glass, leaning heavily on the basin's cold hard edge as she did so. Her knees were wobbly. Another sip and Cathy straightened, caught sight of herself in the bath-room mirror. *Jesus.*

She looked like a macabre Pierrot, her skin alabaster against the black of her hair, half of it dragged back into a ponytail, the rest hanging around her face. Two long black streaks of mascara bisected her cheeks like scars. *She looked like shite.*

What a day.

The whole scene at Oleander House played out in her mind again. O'Rourke had been right to intercede – they really couldn't afford for the trauma to unsettle Grace's mental stability – but, boy, Cathy had so many questions jumping around her head she'd have to write them down. But at least now she'd be going into tomorrow's interview fresh. And she wanted to have a chat with Zoë first, would have loved to have called over to her this evening, but O'Rourke had been right (again) – they needed a break to work through the new information and she'd needed a workout and a good night's sleep.

It had been worth the trip over to Ballymun. It didn't matter how bad or tired she felt going into a session, she always felt better coming out. Although she'd feel a damn sight better if she could stop puking.

Jesus, this was crap.

And this was just the start.

Cathy knew now, for sure, that this was just the start. Booking the appointment at the Well Woman Clinic had given her the space she needed to stop panicking and get her head in gear. And as she'd pounded the bag this evening she'd realised that whatever happened when she talked to the doc, she knew she couldn't have an abortion. Had known it from the start if she was honest with herself. It had just taken her a while to face it, to recognise it. She had one option and one option only – to have the baby. What happened after that was a whole different problem.

She had no idea how the hell she was going to explain going from a size ten to a . . . God only knew what. Whatever about morning sickness, a bump couldn't exactly be passed off as food poisoning. Even if she wore baggy tops – which she never did, so that would arouse suspicions for a start – Cathy knew she couldn't hide it. She stared at the ceiling, at the spiky white peaks of Artex coating it. Maybe she could leave the country – take all her leave in one chunk and some unpaid, tell everyone she needed to go on kibbutz or picking grapes or something. The idea appealed for a moment. But where could she go, where could she afford to go, for how long? Months. And then what would she do? Turn up at her mum's with a baby in her arms and pretend she'd found it on the doorstep?

Jesus. One night. *One fecking red dress.* One too many glasses of champagne. Or maybe bottles, it was hard to be entirely sure. Memories of the night flashed through her mind yet again – Steve's cheeky grin, his hair dark blond, tousled like he'd just got out of bed, her brother Pete's dark head bent over the bar, deep in conversation . . . There would be time to work it all out, had to be – but right now, more than anything else, she needed to get to bed before she collapsed.

38

When she arrived at the station the next morning, fresh from the gym, O'Rourke looked almost as bad as Cathy had felt the previous evening.

Staring blindly out of his office window, he acknowledged her arrival with a nod at her reflection in the glass. His own reflection was pale, strained.

'Were you here all night?'

'Does it look like it?'

'Same suit, same tie, same creases. 'Fraid so.'

He turned, a stoic smile flitting across his face.

'No flies on you, Detective.'

She shot him a one-eyebrow-raised attempt at a withering look. 'Any news on Hierra?'

O'Rourke sighed, ran his hand over his eyes. 'A couple of techs up at the Park have been updating his mugshot. They've taken off the beard, given him a good haircut – I've got a copy for you to show to Zoë.' Cathy sat down on the edge of his desk, one foot on the visitor's chair, as he continued, 'We're circulating the new photo to every Bus Éireann driver and all Iarnród Éireann employees. If he tries to catch a bus or a train we should be covered. And it's going out to all the cab companies in a twenty-mile radius. *And*' – he paused – 'I've called a press conference for lunchtime. We know for sure he's here now and we need to get him before he makes any more house calls.'

Cathy nodded, contemplating the toe of her boot. She felt she should say something intelligent. Or helpful. Neither came. She'd slept well, felt a damn sight better than she had all week, but realistically nothing she could come up with was going to solve the Hierra problem or make O'Rourke feel better. Sometimes it was better to keep your mouth shut.

'So you're going to talk to Grace again this afternoon?'

Cathy nodded; safer ground. 'Yes, all organised.' She paused. 'Emily Cox is bringing her back to the house. I can talk to them in the front room again.'

'With Trish there?'

'Christ, no. Emily Cox's husband is a doctor, Tony Cox, he's an American, a consultant psychiatrist, he wants us to keep things as calm as possible.'

'That makes sense.'

'I called to check on Grace last night and spoke to him at the hotel, outlined what had happened, that we'd found the bones and about Lavinia Grant croaking. Not in those exact words obviously.' O'Rourke smiled, his amusement lifting the fatigue in his face for a moment. Encouraged, she continued, 'He's pretty sound, he's the main speaker at some international psychiatrists' conference on in town. They're staying at the Shelbourne.' Cathy paused, playing with her chain, running the flat oval pendant across the bridge of her nose. 'Trish was a real bitch to the old lady last night. I think it's better to keep them apart for the moment. Trish might be tempted to hit back next time and then we'll have a fight on our hands.'

'And the old woman definitely said she was Lavinia's sister, and Trish didn't dispute that?'

Dropping her pendant, Cathy nodded, picked up his pen from the desk, began playing it through her fingers.

'You OK?'

'Me? Yes, why?' Cathy looked up startled.

'You're very fidgety, don't seem quite yourself. Did you sleep properly?'

Cathy nodded. 'I did.' She put the pen down, patted it, smiled at him. 'Sorry, lot on my mind.'

O'Rourke nodded, watching her. 'Join the club. But you're right, it's one of those cases.'

Missing the calculations going on behind O'Rourke's sharp blue eyes, the expression of concern that crossed his face, Cathy screwed up her nose, picked up her pendant again, running it along the chain, said, 'Trish made some crack about Grace pretending to be the Virgin Mary. Talk about vicious. That was when Emily whacked her. Then the old lady got all mixed up. She started saying that Emily Cox knew Lavinia, that Lavinia had sent her – Emily, I mean – to find her.'

O'Rourke moved over to his desk, collapsed into the chair. 'I caught that bit. So Eleanor was her daughter. Not Lavinia's.' He reached for the pen and rolled it slowly across the desk, deep in thought. 'Sounds like she may have had an unplanned pregnancy, and because she wasn't married, Lavinia stepped in to take the child.'

An unplanned pregnancy . . .

'Something like that.'

O'Rourke didn't appear to notice her blanch, continued, 'It happened more than you think. Do you know some convents used to have a slot in the wall for unmarried mothers to leave their babies in?' Cathy shuddered – she'd seen the movie about the Magdalene laundries, knew how 'fallen' women were treated right up to the seventies: incarcerated, abused, their babies taken from them. O'Rourke kept going, warming to his theme. 'Having a baby out of wedlock was about as bad as it got.'

Cathy nodded, trying to move on, to shift up a gear, *didn't she know it?* 'It all seems to tie in. We know Eleanor was born the year Lavinia got married.'

O'Rourke grimaced. 'And Trish reckoned this old lady, Grace, went off to London around that time? Was sent there, probably, as her punishment for bringing disgrace on the family. Wouldn't have been the first time.' He paused. 'I still don't know how it helps us with the bones. Could Lavinia have had a child as well? Maybe she got pregnant while Grace was pregnant, realised someone would smell a huge rat if she supposedly had two children a couple of months apart.'

'That would be some rat. Do you think she'd murder her own child over the other one?'

O'Rourke shrugged. 'To save the family name, who knows? . . . She was prepared to send her sister away, sever all ties apparently . . . It does all keep coming back to Lavinia.'

'I still think Zoë could be good for it. *We* know her mother wasn't married, but *she* didn't know that. As far as she's concerned the family are paragons of respectability. Maybe Zoë got pregnant and she was terrified of what Lavinia would say if she found out, thought she'd cut her out of the Grant Valentine fortune?'

Before O'Rourke could comment, the phone rang on his desk. He looked at it for a moment as if he was hoping it would ring off. It didn't. He picked it up.

'O'Rourke.' He paused. 'Hallelujah. Put him through.' He put his hand over the mouthpiece. 'It's the lab in the UK – the one we sent the bones to.' Cathy hopped off the desk and pulled the chair around so she could sit facing him as he spoke on the phone. A moment later he hung up, frowning.

'Come on, out with it, don't keep me in suspense.'

'It was a boy. They can't say conclusively at this stage that Zoë Grant is the mother, but' – he paused – 'there *is* a very close familial relationship; they share mitochondrial DNA.' Cathy nearly said *told you so*, but held it in. 'So' – O'Rourke pulled a face – 'that puts the whole lot of them into the picture, Grace included.' He rolled his eyes. 'I had rather hoped it would clear things up a bit.'

'How about the timing? Can they give us an idea how old the bones are? That would move us along.'

'They're still working on it. The process is called carbon-14 dating and they reckon they can be pretty accurate if the bones are from the nuclear age . . .'

Cathy raised her eyebrows, her face sceptical. *Like he knew what he was talking about.*

O'Rourke smiled, caught out. 'The bones have been sent up to Oxford University. Their expert is on holiday so that's holding things up a bit, but he's the best, so we have to wait for him. Don't want the evidence blown apart in court. And until we hear otherwise, we do have to assume Zoë is still in the frame.' O'Rourke leaned back in his chair, made a pyramid with his fingertips, his forefingers resting on the end of his nose. Then he said decisively, 'You'd better get down to Zoë's place now, show her some mugshots, see if she can pick Hierra out of a line-up and tell her about this Grace one turning up. She'll want to meet her, presumably. Get Zoë to call over to Oleander House after you've spoken to the old lady. We're going to have to give them all a bit of a shake. Someone in that house knows what happened, how those bones ended up in that bloody dress.'

39

'So do you train *every* day, or were the lads winding me up?'

Cathy threw Jamie Fanning a withering look, wondering why she'd thought it was a good idea to catch a lift to Zoë's house with him. 'Twice a day when I'm coming up to a tournament. You have to, to stay on top.'

'Like in the gym?'

'Gym or pool every morning, sparring and training at the club about four times a week, more if I can get there.'

'Impressive.' *It was the way he said it.* He'd been trying to chat her up since they'd interviewed Zoë Grant, was failing miserably, not that he'd noticed. *Thank God it was a short trip.* He was good to look at, but she had some serious doubts about his morals. The word 'jackrabbit' sprang to mind. But what was she worrying about? She might be the Women's National Full-Contact Kickboxing champion but she'd bet she wouldn't see him for the dust if he knew she was pregnant.

Feck. Pregnant. The word still made her want to curl up and hide. Whatever about deciding she was keeping this baby, she knew she still had a long way to go before she accepted the cards fate had thrown her way.

Pulling up outside the neighbour's house, Fanning let the car roll towards the corner of Zoë Grant's property, stopping short of it by a whisper. *Why couldn't he just stop outside?*

'Want me to wait?'

'No, I'll be fine, thanks.' Cathy's sarcasm was wasted on him. 'I'll walk back to the station.'

Fanning tipped his forehead in a salute. As she slammed the door of the unmarked Mondeo, he took off into a spin, turning the car around in the narrow lane in a shower of dirt. Cathy brushed down her jeans, drew in a deep breath, looked over at Zoë's house and felt her spirits sink another notch.

Zoë's car wasn't in the drive and the house looked empty. She checked the road. No sign of the surveillance team.

Why the feck hadn't she rung to say she was coming, to check Zoë was in? There were times when her brain just didn't work. And she could have checked with the surveillance team. *Jesus. She just had too much going on in her head.* It was only a fifteen-minute walk down to the DART station, but there was no way she could go back to O'Rourke without at least trying the doorbell.

Cathy heard the door chime echo through the house. She could almost see the sound bouncing off the black and white tiles in the hallway, heading up the narrow stairs, echoing into the back kitchen. *Maybe Steve was here and they were in bed ... Maybe they'd been out last night and decided to leave the car in town, got a cab home ... Maybe the surveillance team had followed her to work or sloped off for a piss. They definitely weren't around now.* Cathy stuck her hands in her pockets and waited. It was cold. Even wrapped up in her leather jacket with its thick down lining, she still felt chilled. She rang again. Waited. *Was anyone there?*

Still nothing.

Cathy took a step back from the front door, had another look at the expressionless windows. About to bend over to get a look in the letter box, Cathy caught a movement out of the corner of her eye, a shadow, something reflected on the inside of the living-room window. *Someone was in.* At last. She wasn't in the mood for a wasted trip today.

But a moment later the front door was still firmly closed. *Where the hell was Zoë Grant?*

Climbing into the flower bed under the living-room window, Cathy leaned on one of the small glass panes, put her hands around her eyes so she could see into the gloom. There was no one in the room – it looked pretty much the same as the last time she'd seen it. A rug was screwed up on the easy chair, like someone had meant to come back to straighten it, a cushion tossed on the floor. Cathy strained her eyes trying to see into the hall. *Nothing.*

She was just pulling away when she noticed something.

Her hands back around her eyes, Cathy took another look. The last time she'd been here, there had been a huge oil painting leaning against the wall, a dust sheet or something half-hiding a marine landscape. *Was that the bloody painting that everyone kept going on about? The one of the yachts in the harbour that Grace had asked about?* Now the heavy gilt frame was leaning against the sofa, the bit she could see. *But it was empty.*

Jesus, what the hell? *What had Hierra said to Zoë? Sell the painting* . . . but surely Zoë would have taken the frame as well . . . The spectre of worry, like a sleek black cat, stretched inside her, sharpening its claws. *The picture had gone.* And if he had come back for it and Zoë had been in . . . What the hell had happened? Could he have got past the surveillance guys?

From the rear of the cottage, Cathy heard the crunch of gravel. *Holy feck.*

Cathy crept to the corner of the house, her hand on her gun. Hanging back, using the wall as cover, she took a look down the side towards the studio and the garden. Nothing. Was the back door open? Cathy couldn't tell from this angle. She bit her lip . . . She'd definitely heard something – someone – a footstep on the gravel. Maybe whoever it was had come out and then gone back into the house?

A second later she heard the back door close and the crunch of footsteps. She peeped again. A clean-shaven guy with a tan. Six foot, hair close-cropped. Glancing furtively towards the road, he turned, tugged the back door closed, one hand up against it like he was trying to deaden the sound. Cathy dipped back behind the wall, her heart racing.

Cathy knew exactly who the man was – he answered Zoë's description precisely, was the dead spit of the mugshot the techs had dickied up. *Angel Hierra.* Cathy drew in her breath. She was on her own, and there was no way she could make a call for backup without him hearing her. And he must have heard the doorbell, knew someone was standing on the door-step. Cathy thought fast. She didn't have a lot of choice – she'd just have to create her own surprise and keep her fingers crossed. With any luck he'd be expecting the busybody from next door, or the postman . . .

A moment later she heard Hierra's footsteps on the gravel, this time heading towards her. Walking briskly like he had somewhere to go. Cathy pressed her back hard into the wall of the cottage, grateful for the creeper that was growing up the corner, its foliage pulling at her hair, offering cover. *What the feck was she doing?*

As Hierra appeared around the side of the house, he seemed to be adjusting his overcoat, getting it settled at the front.

'I knocked. Nobody's in . . .' He grimaced like they were both inconvenienced, like he had every reason to be there.

Cathy cut across him. 'Armed Gardaí, stop right –'

Hierra reacted even before the words were fully out of Cathy's mouth, broke into a run, dipping left, out of the drive, heading for the woods and the narrow footpath leading up to Killiney Hill.

Jesus. Cathy set off after him, her boots slipping on the mucky ground, wet from the rain, the gravel churned to mud by the vehicles that had been parked there.

This was *not* part of the game plan.

Pregnant women weren't supposed to chase suspects up muddy paths. Keeping his back in sight, Cathy did her best to watch her footing, terrified she might trip over a root or a rock. Mud splashed up her jeans as her foot landed in the centre of a puddle, brambles clawing at her jacket, scratching at the thick leather as she pulled away. The path was slick with fallen leaves, rotting in drifts at the sides. She was sweating, breathing hard, the loamy scent of the place catching in her throat. Her arms pumping, she used her whole body to get herself up the incline.

Ahead of her, Hierra rounded a bend in the footpath, disappeared behind the bushes for a moment. *Christ, he was fast, but she was closing the gap on him*, her circuit training paying off. Panting, her feet flying, she leaped from dry patch to dry patch, trying to avoid the slippery puddles. *He had to stop soon, was wearing loafers, had to be struggling with the mud.* Cathy knew she was fit but Hierra had the advantage and was moving like his life depended on it.

Suddenly Hierra broke out of the woods at the top of the path, slipped, went down on one knee. It was all the break Cathy needed. Puffing up the last few feet, her sides splitting with the effort, Cathy came up behind him, grabbed his arm, twisted it up behind his back.

'Gardaí, stop!' Out of breath, it didn't come out as loud as she hoped. Cathy fumbled for the handcuffs on her belt. Hierra yanked his arm free, scrambling away from her, slipping in the mud. She reached out for him, tried to grab his coat, but whipping around, he threw a punch up at her, catching her shoulder, the impact sharp, hard, knocking her back, knocking her off balance. Using the second he'd gained to pull away from her, Hierra was off again. Cathy lunged for his wrist, missing it. Then he slipped again, landed on his knees in the mud with a grunt of pain. Cathy registered a flash of silver at his ankle.

Feck, a knife. This wasn't funny.

Taking a step back to steady herself, Cathy drew her gun, holding it two-handed. She was breathing so hard she almost couldn't speak. *Only draw when you intend to fire. And remember, you shoot to stop, there are no second chances.* The instructor's words went through her head like a flash of light. *Fecking right she intended to fire.*

She caught her breath. 'Armed Gardaí. Drop your weapon.' The words were clear.

Hierra hesitated for a split second, moved his left hand away from his leg, raised it, turning to face her as if he was about to stand up, to surrender. He smiled, his grey eyes meeting hers, and in less than a beat his right hand was at his ankle, the knife was out of its sheath, sweeping for her thigh. Skipping out of his range instinctively, in one fluid movement Cathy was back with a powerful snap kick, her boot connecting with the bones in his wrist. With a sharp crack the knife flew from his hand and Hierra collapsed to the ground with a cry of pain, cradling his arm, his eyes spitting.

'Bitch, it's broken. I'll wipe you.'

Cathy could feel the blood pounding in her ears, hardly had the breath left to speak.

'Face down. Hands behind you.'

With her gun still trained on him, it took Cathy a moment to pull out her handcuffs. Hierra moaned again.

'It's broken. You've broken my arm, you fucking bitch.'

Cathy glanced at Hierra's wrist. It was starting to swell all right, but she hadn't hit him that hard. In training she went in harder than that and there was no damage. *Admittedly she didn't wear leather boots, but Hierra was lying, had to be.* Ignoring his protests, she clipped the steel handcuffs onto his wrists, took a step back, her gun trained on him.

Out of the corner of her eye she caught a movement in the trees, took a sharp intake of breath. *All she needed now was a do-good dog walker barging in on things . . . at least she hadn't shot him.* Cathy delivered the caution, loud and clear. Loud enough for anyone on the hill to hear it, to make it perfectly clear that this wasn't a gangland hit or a drug deal going bad.

'You are under arrest. You are not obliged to say anything unless you wish to do so but anything you do say will be taken down in writing and may be given in evidence.'

The trees were silent. *Maybe she was imagining it.* Her knees trembled with the exertion, with the adrenalin pumping around her body. Pulling out her radio, Cathy hit the call button.

'I cannot believe you did that.' O'Rourke shook his head slowly. He was so angry he could hardly speak, had been glaring at Cathy for what felt like half her life, trying to find the words to express himself. The door to his office was firmly closed but she knew, if he yelled, half the station was going to hear what a fecking idiot she'd been.

Cathy took a breath, trying to keep her voice steady. 'I didn't have time. He was coming out of the house. He'd already heard me at the door. I must have spooked him.'

'You spooked him all right. Then you chased him halfway up Killiney Hill *on your own.*'

Cathy winced. He was right. She should have called for backup, but . . .

'Didn't you learn anything in Templemore? How can you not have had time to make the call? You could have pretended you were canvassing for the election, smiled sweetly and followed him AT A SAFE DISTANCE down the road. You could have pulled out your mobile and CALLED ME.'

O'Rourke was yelling now. Cathy could feel the whole floor stopping what they were doing to listen in. She drew a breath, the urge to defend herself almost as strong as the urge to chase Hierra had been.

'I would have lost him.' But Cathy knew she sounded stubborn, petulant. Stupid.

'And *we* could have lost *you*. Did you think about that?' O'Rourke paused, cleared his throat, conscious of the tremor in his voice, trying to hide it. 'What if he'd turned on you halfway up the hill? He'd have had the advantage, been above you, could have stabbed you and left you there and when would we have found you, hey? An hour later, maybe two. How long do you think it takes to bleed out from a stab wound? He's killed two people already, do you think one more would trouble his conscience?'

Christ, he was right. Why was he always right? Suddenly O'Rourke wasn't her superior officer any more, he was Cathy's friend, and she'd got it wrong, and she felt like shit.

'You're not made of Teflon, Cat, you were fucking lucky the last time. *You don't have nine lives.*'

O'Rourke was leaning forward on his desk now, his knuckles white. Cathy could feel the tears pricking at her eyes. She wanted to scream at him, *I know, I was a fecking idiot, how do you think I feel?* She took a deep breath but before she could think of anything sensible to say, O'Rourke shook his head like he didn't know what to do with her.

'I can't do this without you, Cat.' He said it under his breath. Cathy almost missed it. O'Rourke paused like he was struggling with his own emotions, then said louder, like he was trying to qualify it, 'I need to be able to trust you. I need you on the team.'

Her eyes on the floor, Cathy nodded.

'I got it wrong.' She could feel her face flushing. 'I know I got it wrong. We never go in without backup, I know.'

'Urgent assistance required. Three small words.' O'Rourke paused, a hint of desperation in his voice. 'You give your location, and *urgent assistance required*. And do you know what happens?' O'Rourke could see Cathy was cringing but he paused again, driving his point home. 'Do you? We come. All of us. Every uniform, every detective in the area. All of us. A member in danger is absolute priority.'

Cathy felt herself nodding. She'd been there before, could still hear his voice on the radio, *'Assistance required, member shot. Urgent assistance required.'*

What could she say?

O'Rourke let out a sigh like a steam valve opening. 'You aren't a one-woman army. Don't do it again.' Then more softly, 'But well done, girl, you played a blinder.'

40

'What are the red dots for?'

Standing beside the reception desk in Max Igoe's brilliantly lit, airy gallery, Zoë pointed to the vibrant wooden frame of one of her pictures, a small circular red sticker in its bottom left-hand corner. The picture looked fantastic on the rough white stone wall, the lower half panelled in pine, also stark white. Above them, bright spotlights were angled to illuminate the cobalt blue of the sea raging in the painting, the light drawing out the movement, the hidden depths of the subject. Classical music was playing from hidden speakers, making the whole thing . . . *exactly as Zoë had dreamed it would be* . . .

But what were the red dots all about? Zoë knew Max was smiling at her like she hadn't a brain in her head, but she just wasn't getting the red dots. Steve had laughed when she'd confessed she was just a little bit frightened of Max. Well maybe not frightened, but completely in awe of him. He was just so sure of everything, so confident, so successful, and Zoë didn't want to make a huge blunder on the opening night.

'The dots show it's sold.'

'What, already?' Looking at Max in amazement, Zoë opened her mouth, forgetting completely about trying to look professional and confident. 'It couldn't be.'

Throwing his head back, Max laughed, shaking his head. Then putting his arm around Zoë's shoulders, said confidentially, 'It's a trick of the trade, makes people think that they have to buy fast before everything is sold.'

'But what happens if someone really wants that one?' Zoë's thick eyebrows knotted; Max chuckled, charmed. 'Sales fall through . . . maybe an interested party can't come up with the finance . . . and then it's back out on the open market.'

Zoë nodded, like it was making sense, but her eyes were still puzzled.

'Let me worry about that end of things. You just have to circulate and chat and smile for the cameras. If anyone looks like they want to buy, pass them on to one of the girls. OK?'

She tried not to grin. 'OK, got it . . .'

'Now come and have a look at the end wall, it's pretty impressive.' Steering her towards the back of the gallery, where the triptych was hanging, Max watched her face. It was the first time Zoë had seen everything in place, the first time she had seen the collection hung together.

'How do you think it looks? Pleased?'

'It's fantastic. Really, it is.'

The show brochure in her hand, Zoë looked around, mesmerised, so absorbed in fact that she was oblivious to the commotion erupting behind her.

'I'm sorry, madam, but we're closed. The private viewing for the press is tomorrow evening.'

One of Max's staff, a tall willowy girl with pink hair and a turquoise knitted dress that barely skimmed her behind was at the glazed door, trying to block a woman in black from entering. Obviously not prepared to wait, the woman was about to push

her physically out of the way when Zoë turned around. And realised who it was.

'Trish!'

The girl turned to Zoë in surprise, dropping her arm to allow
Trish to enter. Straightening her jacket, throwing a barbed look
at the assistant, Trish marched into the middle of the shop like
she owned it.

'I need to speak to you.'

'Now?' Glancing anxiously from Max to Trish, Zoë looked for
a moment like a deer caught in the glare of a high-power lamp.
Max stuck his hands in the back pockets of his jeans, regarded
Trish with one eyebrow raised, waited for Zoë to speak. 'Trish,
I'm busy. We're getting ready for the press viewing tomorrow.
Everything needs to be right.'

'I'm well aware of that. This won't wait. Not now.'

Confused, Zoë looked at Trish, waiting for her to continue.
'It's private.'

Seeing Zoë's discomfort, Max stepped in. 'Why don't you use
my office? I've some calls to make. I can do them down here.'

'Thanks, I'm sorry . . .' Realising she hadn't introduced them,
Zoë shot him a grateful look. 'Max, this is Trish O'Sullivan,
Trish, Max Igoe.'

Trish nodded curtly. 'I don't have much time.'

His eyes steely, Max made a sweeping gesture towards the
door to the office. 'It's all yours, call me if you need anything.'

Zoë strode up the stairs, waiting at the top for Trish to
catch up. She had gone from mildly irritated to annoyed, very
annoyed. *How could Trish just barge in like this . . . Who did she
think she was?*

'What's happened that's so important we need to discuss it right now? I told you this morning that I'd be home later, that I'd be able to talk then.'

Slightly out of breath, Trish reached the top step and put out her hand to take the door. 'It won't wait.'

'Will we sit down?' Moving inside, Zoë pointed to the sofa, taking a step back, her arms folded. Trish shook her head. 'I think you're the one who needs to sit.'

'Why?' Zoë marched over to the sofa and plumped down in the middle, making no attempt to hide her irritation. 'What can possibly have happened now?'

Taking a moment to scan the office, the bright white walls, the untidy desk, Trish bit back the retort that leaped to her mouth. Instead she pursed her lips, adjusted her handbag on her shoulder and coiled her arms together protectively like she was cold.

'A lot has happened this week. Things have changed. Changed a lot. I've got some news for you. There's no easy way to say this, so, well ...' Trish paused for a split second, but the hesitation didn't last. 'Look, Lavinia had a sister. I should say, *has* a sister. She ran away to London years ago – to be honest I thought she'd *died* years ago, but ... well ... she's come back.'

Zoë's mouth dropped open. 'A sister ... how ... why did she never say?'

'They had a falling-out.' Trish pursed her lips again, then focused on a point on the floor like something foul was crawling towards her. 'The thing is, she's actually your grandmother. I mean, she was Eleanor's mother, not Lavinia.'

Falling back on the sofa, Zoë looked at her stunned. 'What? What do you mean?'

Trish smoothed the polished boards with the toe of her boot as if she was trying to rub something out.

'She is. She just is. It's a long story, she . . .' Trish sniffed, screwing up her nose. 'She got herself pregnant and, well obviously, you just didn't do that then. She couldn't bring the child up, she wasn't married, so either Lavinia brought Eleanor up as her own or the child would have gone to the Sisters of Charity.'

Lavinia wasn't her grandmother.

It took a while for the information to register with Zoë, and even after she'd said the words to herself a few times, it still didn't make any sense. *Except, except . . .* one thing Trish had said struck home. As swiftly and surely as if she had stuck a knife in her.

'Does she know where Eleanor is? Does this woman know where my mother is?'

Trish sighed, rolled her eyes to the ceiling like Zoë was being stupid.

'Now how would she know that? She's been gone for sixty years.'

'How do you know Eleanor didn't find out all this and go and look for her?' Zoë's voice rose a notch, her face flushed. 'And don't look at me like that. How do *you* know what happened?'

How dare Trish treat her like a complete idiot – how dare she? It wasn't her mother that had gone missing . . .

Zoë stood up, took a step towards Trish, her hands outstretched, begging her to understand. 'I want to find her. With the exhibition and everything, I *need* to find her . . .'

There was a pause. A pause in which Zoë could hear a clock ticking somewhere over by Max's desk, heard a jet engine, its roar softened by the distance, pass overhead.

'You won't find her.' Trish spat the words out.

Shocked, Zoë took a step backwards towards the sofa. 'What do you mean, I won't find her? Have you heard from her? Do you know where she is?' Zoë almost whispered, her eyes wide open in horror. *Had Trish known all this time where Eleanor was? Had Lavinia kept in touch with her after all?*

'She's not coming back.' The words were final, spiteful. Zoë opened her mouth to speak but before she got the words out Trish said, 'She's dead. She died years ago.'

'What?' Zoë's voice wavered. Her knees giving way, she sat down with a thump on the sofa. 'What do you mean she's dead?'

'You heard me.'

'But how? How did she die? Why didn't Lavinia tell me?'

Trish shook her head like it didn't matter. 'It was an accident. She drowned. Maybe she drank too much, or took some pills, I don't know. She had a row with Lavinia and then the next thing you were running down the stairs screaming . . .'

'Me?'

It took a moment to sink in, then Zoë's face drained of colour. She clamped her hand to her mouth, the need to retch overpowering. Trish didn't appear to notice, or just didn't care.

'Yes, you. You found her. She was in the bath. You couldn't wake her, you –'

Trish didn't get a chance to finish. Bolting from the sofa through the door into Max's private bathroom, Zoë reached the toilet just in time, bent over the white porcelain, her stomach muscles screaming as she vomited over and over again.

A girl lying in a bath . . . her hair like seaweed, soft fronds floating around her face. Her skin wrinkled . . . one arm limp over the side. The water was cold, so deep, so cold . . .

Zoë heaved again, tears streaming down her face, nose running, her hair falling into her eyes. Behind her she heard the door slam.

Downstairs Max was leaning on the reception desk, his mobile to his ear, as Trish barrelled out of the door to the office. Alarmed, he looked up.

'She'll need something stiff to drink. She's had a shock.'

From above them a scream of pain ripped through the calm of the gallery, through the classical music, bouncing off the pure white walls, off the polished boards.

Max didn't hear the door close on Trish, was already taking the stairs two at a time.

41

'It seems you're much sought after, Mr Hierra.'

In the small cream-painted interview room in Dún Laoghaire Garda Station, Angel Hierra leaned back in his chair and cocked his eyebrow as if O'Rourke was confusing him with someone else. His smile was charming, teeth unnaturally white, grey eyes twinkling like this was all some sort of joke. *Like he'd been in an interview room before, and wasn't fazed in the slightest.*

Cathy had caught his aftershave as she came into the room. She noticed now that despite their scramble in the mud, his nails were clean, manicured, his hands soft. The duty doc had strapped up his injured wrist, leaving his fingers free. He was wearing a black roll-neck and cords. And a heavy gold wedding ring. *Cathy didn't remember reading anything on his sheet about him being married.*

O'Rourke straightened the papers in front of him as he spoke, meeting Hierra's eye.

'Indeed, Angel, much sought after. There are two FBI agents on their way right now who are very interested in having a chat with you.' O'Rourke checked his watch. 'Their plane lands in four hours.'

Hierra paled, but keeping up the pretence, said, 'So?'

All innocence. Jesus he was good. Cathy had to give him marks for his acting skills.

'So? So there is the small matter of a man being shot dead at the Holiday Inn near JFK, and his credit card being used to hire a car at Dublin airport. And the murder of your father with a bullet from the same gun.' As soon as the words were out of O'Rourke's mouth, Hierra was shaking his head like it was all a big mistake. O'Rourke ignored him, continuing, 'And before our friends from the FBI arrive, there are a few things we need to discuss.'

'Not me, you've got the wrong guy. I haven't shot anyone.'

'Angel, crimes committed in the United States are really not my problem. What interests me is what you were doing coming out of Zoë Grant's house with a valuable oil painting rolled up in your coat, and then assaulting one of my officers, so let's get on with the interview, will we?'

It only took a few seconds for O'Rourke to load three DVDs into the recording unit on the wall between them. He glanced up to check the video camera was functioning as he began.

'For the purpose of the recording, those present are DI Dawson O'Rourke and Detective Garda Cathy Connolly. Can you confirm your full name and home address for us, please?'

'Angel Hierra, 221 Golden Sands Apartments, South Bay Street, Las Vegas.'

'You are aware this interview is being recorded and that you are not obliged to say anything unless you wish to do so, but anything you do say will be taken down in writing and may be given in evidence?'

Hierra nodded.

'For the recording, please.'

'Yeah, yeah, I've got it.'

'So can you tell me why you are here in Ireland?'

'Business.'

O'Rourke nodded slowly. They had been a long time getting to this point and Cathy could see he wasn't in the mood to be messed about. *There was something about Hierra that rubbed him up the wrong way.*

'And what sort of business would it be that brings a man like yourself from Las Vegas, Nevada, to South County Dublin?'

There was a pause before Hierra answered. Cathy watched him closely. *Was he getting O'Rourke's measure, seeing how far he could push him?* Then the answer came, surprising them both.

'Family business.'

Family business?

'More specifically, Angel?'

Rubbing his forefinger and thumb together, Hierra looked from one of them to the other, *buying time?* When he spoke, it was offhand, like the answer was obvious.

'Like I said, it was family business. Lavinia Grant owed me.'

Cathy caught her breath. *Lavinia Grant? How the hell was he related to Lavinia Grant?*

'How did she owe you exactly?'

Cathy tucked a stray curl behind her ear, shifted slightly in her seat, keeping quiet as O'Rourke spoke.

Hierra shook his head like it was simple mathematics. 'My father knew her, she owed him. It was time to get things settled.'

'You're going to have to paint the picture for us here, Angel.' O'Rourke made it sound like he was talking to a child. 'How did your father know Lavinia Grant exactly?'

'They were married.' Hierra looked at them like it was obvious. 'She made it. He gave her his name and she made it.'

Jesus Christ. Cathy felt her jaw drop, closed her mouth as fast as she could. *But it didn't make sense – everyone they had spoken to had said Lavinia's husband had been killed in an accident in France.* Unimpressed, O'Rourke checked his notes.

'Your father's surname was Henry, Angel. I'm not seeing the connection.'

'My father's name was Charles Henry, Charles Henry Valentine. When he got to the States he dropped the Valentine – it's not helpful having a memorable name, in his line of business.'

That was for damn sure.

'So your father was French?' *O'Rourke sounded like he didn't believe a word Hierra was saying.*

'No, he was British. Deal went sour in London and he came here. Met the Grant sisters. Suited him to tell them he was French.'

'He told you this, did he?'

There was a pause. 'Eventually. He told my mom. When she died I wanted to find out if it was true.'

'And how did Lavinia Grant owe him exactly?'

Hierra sat back, folded his arms like he wasn't prepared to discuss anything to do with Lavinia Grant. O'Rourke took it in, changed his tack fractionally.

'You might as well tell us. We will find out, one way or another.'

'My mom was a croupier at a casino, Inspector, my dad was thirty years older than her. He had this big win and convinced her he was the business, but he was a lowlife piece of shit. We lived in a trailer. There were nights when I went to bed hungry.' Hierra drew in a breath. 'Lavinia Grant used my father's name to help build her business, Grant *Valentine*, a business that is worth, what, fifty mil today, a hundred mil? Shops in Toronto,

SAM BLAKE | 327

New York, London. He married her so she could get her first bank loan. They never divorced. So he was her next of kin, and I'm his. She owed him. She owed me. Period.'

O'Rourke nodded like he was taking it in. *It was a lot to take in.*

'You arrived in Ireland the day before Lavinia Grant's sudden death. Can you tell us anything about that? It seems rather coincidental.'

'Story of my life. It was a bad beat.'

Hierra made it sound like a joke. *As if he was in a position to be funny.*

'A what?' O'Rourke picked up his pen, began feeding it from one hand to the other.

'That's a card player's term, isn't it?' Cathy leaned forward. *A bad beat.* She'd heard that before from her brother Tomás. He was poker mad, had played his way through college. Which was just as well – he'd done a lot better at the card table than in his exams.

Hierra smiled at her like she was top of the class. Lots of teeth. 'I suppose it is.'

'And it means . . . ?' O'Rourke's irritation flared.

'It was bad luck. I should have gotten here sooner. Would have liked to have got to know the old bird better.' Hierra checked out his nails for a moment, twisted his ring straight. 'It's the way the cards fall.'

'I bet. So you reckon you're due part of her estate, do you?'

'Obviously.'

Cathy could see that O'Rourke had his own thoughts on that. His tone said it all. 'And how were the cards falling this morning exactly? When you sliced that oil painting from its frame in Zoë Grant's living room? An oil painting valued conservatively at a hundred and fifty thousand euro?'

'They owed me. The Grants owed me. I needed cash. In the end I had to move quicker than planned.' Hierra's face changed, going hard. As he spoke, Cathy could suddenly see how he could be capable of killing two people and frightening the wits out of Zoë Grant. *Why the hell had she gone after him? Why hadn't she just walked away?* Something deep inside her flipped over. Under the desk she was very glad she could feel O'Rourke's knee next to hers.

'Why didn't you take the painting the first time you broke into Zoë Grant's property?'

Hierra looked mystified for a moment. 'The first time?'

'Zoë Grant's house was broken into the day Lavinia Grant was found dead. Zoë's bedroom was ransacked.'

'So?' Hierra shook his head, folded his arms. 'Nothing to do with me.'

'Perhaps you can explain then exactly how you knew Zoë had the painting, that it was an original. Are you an art critic?' O'Rourke raised his eyebrows, enunciating his point. *They had no evidence that Hierra had been present the first time, but if they were lucky . . .*

'There was an article in *Vanity Fair* about Lavinia Grant opening up a store in New York, all about Zoë and her mother disappearing. My father kept it. The painting was in one of the photos. Guy who wrote the article kept going on about it.'

'Angel, we aren't stupid. The only way you could have known that Zoë, specifically, was in possession of that painting was if you saw it in her house.'

Hierra shrugged and rolled his eyes. 'You can see it from the front window.'

'Half of it. If you're standing in the flower bed,' Cathy chimed in. 'The only way to identify it is as an original is to see it close up.'

O'Rourke glanced at his watch. 'I think you're wasting our time, Angel. I don't think you have any connection to the Grants. I think you read Lavinia Grant's obituary in the paper and thought you'd have a crack at Zoë while she was weak and vulnerable.' O'Rourke moved to stand up like he was finished, like Hierra had nothing to tell him worth hearing.

'Wait.' Hierra's response was fast. 'If I can help you, what can you do for me with the Feds? I can't go back to the States. I'm a dead man if I go back.'

O'Rourke coolly shuffled his papers together. *Cathy could almost hear him thinking – Hierra was spinning them a line, had to be.* But Hierra's next statement stopped him in his tracks.

'I can help you with the bones. Zoë's neighbour said you found bones. It was a baby boy, wasn't it?'

42

Steve Maguire had just sat down at his desk with a fresh cup of coffee when his mobile rang. He'd only been in the office ten minutes, had a lot of catching up to do before he headed over to the gallery to meet Zoë. Focusing on the document open on his laptop, he was only half-listening as he answered.

'Maxie boy, how's it going?'

'We've got a problem.' It was the urgency in Max's voice rather than the words themselves that made him put his cup down with a crack. 'That Trish O'Sullivan came to see Zoë – I don't know what she said to her, but Zoë's hysterical.'

'Jesus. Where is she now?' Standing up abruptly, sending his chair rolling back into the specimen Swiss cheese plant his mum had given him as a house-warming present, Steve was heading to the front door before Max had a chance to reply.

'Here in my office. She's been vomiting, but now she's just catatonic. Do you know who her doctor is?'

Weaving through the traffic coagulating on the main arterial road heading into the city, every spit of rain hitting his face like a needle, Steve could feel the adrenalin pumping around his body, mixed with a potent blend of fear and guilt, his stomach twisting. *He bet he knew exactly what Trish had said to Zoë. It had to be about her mother.* The bitch. Ahead of him the lights changed to amber, the stream of traffic continuing like they were still green.

Almost there. Shite. SHITE. *Why the hell had she decided to tell Zoë now, right before her big night? Jesus, he knew she was dangerous, but . . . Jesus.*

Barrelling in through the door of the gallery, ignoring the pink-haired receptionist, Steve didn't bother to try and get his bike up the stairs, instead threw it down in the middle of the floor and headed up, taking them two at a time, leaving the door banging behind him.

'Where is she?'

Hardly able to speak, his breath coming in short bursts, Steve burst into the office, looking around wildly. Max was on the phone at his desk, pointed towards the sofa.

Zoë was curled up into a tight ball in the corner, foetus-like, her face buried in her arms, her knees pulled to her chest. Someone had taken off her boots, put a glass of water on the low table beside the arm of the chair.

'Christ.'

'Thanks, that's great, soon as you can.' Max hung up.

'Doc's on her way. She's an ex, works with an on-call service. I think y'one needs a sedative.' He nodded in Zoë's direction.

Slipping in beside Zoë, Steve pulled her into his shoulder, rocking her. She moaned as she felt his arms around her, nestled into him. Steve's eyes met Max's over her head.

'You've got to give that Trish marks for timing.' Max's face was pale, he was chewing his thumbnail. *Having his star collapse right before her opening night wasn't part of the plan.* And the opening of an exhibition like this wasn't the type of thing you could postpone. They'd pulled out all the stops to get the international press on board, had spent a fortune on advertising and the timing was perfect to pick up the Christmas spend. You only got this sort of chance once.

'Zoë, are you OK, love? What happened? What did she say?'

Steve felt some of the tension leave her at the sound of his voice, felt Zoë mould into his side.

'My mother. Trish told me what happened to my mother.' It wasn't much more than a whisper.

Jesus, he knew it. What should he say? Did he ask her to tell him what Trish had said? Pretend he didn't know? Would repeating it be cathartic, or make her live through the shock all over again?

Steve didn't have a lot of choice.

'What did she say? Tell me, love.'

Zoë made a noise that made the hairs stand up on the back of his neck, a wail, like an animal wounded, dying. Then she sobbed again and again, trying to catch her breath to speak. Finally she did.

'Trish said she was dead. She's known all this time.' Zoë pulled away to look at him, but her eyes were unfocused. Steve smoothed a tear from her cheek. Her face was blotchy, eyes and nose red. A moment later the distant look went and she was back. *Back with a whole heap of information she didn't need right now.*

'Trish said . . . she said I found her . . .' The wail came again as Zoë clung to him, hid her face in his shoulder. 'I found her . . . I didn't know. But when she said it, it all came back. I remember now . . . I remember.' Zoë gulped back the sobs. 'She was in the water . . . in the water.'

In the water. It all clicked in Steve's head. *The paintings, her morbid fascination with the sea, with water. No wonder she was terrified of it.* And Cathy had been right about the drowning, about it happening in the house. But Zoë finding her? She must have been a child. Steve's mind clicked again. Zoë must have been three or four. Zoë Grant had been three years old and she'd found her mother dead in the bath. No wonder she'd suppressed the memory. She'd hardly had grief counselling at the time, was probably lucky if she even got a cuddle from either of those two witches.

The sound of heels skipping up the wooden stairs was loud even over Zoë's breathy sobs, her body vibrating with each one. Steve looked up sharply.

'Sally, am I glad to see you. Thanks for coming so fast.'

A statuesque blonde rounded the top of the stairs, a briefcase in her hand. Shaking raindrops from her cropped hair, she threw Max a grin. 'Long time since I've heard that from you, Max Igoe. Where's the patient?'

Max couldn't hide the relief on his face, came out from behind his desk, pointed to the sofa.

'This is Sally – Sally, Steve Maguire. I'll leave you to it. I'll be downstairs.'

'Great.' Unbelting her raincoat, Sally's eyes met Max's as he hovered for a moment at the door to the stairs.

'She'll be fine, I'm sure.'

'Thanks. Thanks, Sas, I owe you one.'

Slipping her coat off, Sally laid her briefcase gently on the floor beside the sofa, bobbed down on her haunches to get a look at Zoë, unbuttoning her tweed jacket. It was soft green, out of place somehow with their denims and the bright white walls of the studio. She was wearing a cream silk shirt that set off a pair of huge brown eyes, high-heeled boots and brown jeans. *Just Max's type. Brainy and good-looking.*

Brainy enough to be reading his mind. She flicked a grin at Steve like she could see inside his head. He could feel a flush rising, but she had already turned away, speaking directly to Zoë.

'My name's Sally, I'm a doctor. Max says you've had a bit of a shock. Do you mind if I ask you a few questions and we'll see if we can't make you feel a bit better?'

No movement. It was as if Zoë hadn't heard her. She still had her knees drawn up on the sofa, her face hidden by the crook of her arm and her hair, her hand tucked in behind Steve's shoulder. *Like a bird with a broken wing.*

'What's her name?'

Sally's voice was so low, Steve almost missed the question.

'Zoë, Zoë Grant. I'm Steve Maguire, her . . . boyfriend.' It was a split-second pause but Steve was sure Sally picked it up. *Doctors were trained to read all the signals.* He continued hastily, 'I'm a pal of Max's. They're Zoë's pictures downstairs.'

Sally nodded. 'They're fabulous . . . Zoë?' She raised her voice a notch. 'Zoë, I need you to answer some questions. I know you've had a shock, love, but I just need you to talk to me for a few moments.'

'Will I . . .' Steve moved fractionally, suddenly realising that Sally might want him to go. But Zoë grabbed him, unfolding, her face appearing from behind her arm.

'No, stay. I need you to stay.'

'That's fine, Zoë, he can stay. Don't worry.'

Sally reached for her briefcase, clicking open the catches. 'Before I give you anything I need to get some basic information, check your pulse and blood pressure. Is that OK?'

Zoë sniffed, nodding. Gathering her to him, Steve slipped his arm around her shoulders, steered her to face the doctor.

The first few questions were standard: full name, address, date of birth. Still crouching, Sally jotted them down into a pad on her knee.

'Whew, I'm getting stiff. Mind if I grab a chair?'

Standing up, she headed for Max's desk, pulled over the chair opposite it.

'She's nice, isn't she?' Steve whispered into Zoë's ear, kissing the side of her head, smoothing her hair away from his face. Zoë managed a small smile, a sigh, ragged but without a sob. Steve felt himself relax, realised he'd been so tense his back was aching.

'Must be the weather, I'm like an old crock.' Squaring the chair off next to the sofa, Sally sat down, pad on her knee, bent down to pull her case towards her. 'Nearly there now.'

Sliding up the sleeve of Zoë's blouse, slipping the blood pressure cuff around her upper arm, Sally smiled. 'There, that's not too bad is it?'

Zoë shook her head, not meeting Sally's eye but definitely calmer.

'Blood pressure's grand.' Sally pulled off the Velcro, the ripping sound making them both jump. Bundling the cuff into her case, she picked up her pen.

'Now any allergies? Penicillin, that sort of thing?'

Zoë shook her head.

'And are you taking any sort of medication?'

Again the shake. Sally's eyebrows twitched for a second. 'Nothing at all?'

Zoë shook her head.

'I'm thinking of paracetamol for a headache, the pill, even iron tablets, anything like that?'

The shake was definite.

The pill? The words roared through Steve's head like white water. She wasn't on the pill. SHITE. DOUBLE SHITE. Why the hell was he finding that out now? How stupid was he? Steve felt his mouth dry, sweat breaking out down his back. He could see the next question coming like a steamship heading for an iceberg, its horn howling fit to burst.

'And is there any chance you could be pregnant?'

'I ... I ... no ... I don't know ...' Finally Zoë spoke, her voice tiny, raw with emotion. But the doctor had seen the look on Steve's face, watched him pale until his only colour was two bright circles in the middle of his cheeks.

'I need to be sure before I prescribe anything. Do you think we ought to do a test?'

Her eyes flicked to Steve.

'Zoë, you better do a test. It only takes a minute.' *Like he was an expert.* Steve unwrapped his arm from behind her, turning to face her. *Why didn't you tell me?* He felt like shouting it, but now wasn't the time, she had enough on her plate ... 'It's really easy...'

Sally was already rooting in her case.

43

'Bones?' O'Rourke looked puzzled. 'Now what would you know about that, Angel?' O'Rourke laid his papers down on the interview-room table and looked straight at Hierra, a direct challenge.

'There's no way I can go back to the States. You have to guarantee you'll look after me. They'll kill me if I go back.'

Cathy could feel O'Rourke's tail twitching, like a cat watching a mouse, assessing the kill.

'We need to know if there's something to play for. What do you know about the Grants?'

Hierra shifted uncomfortably in his seat. 'I know there was a baby boy. I know it died. I know how it died.'

Jesus. How the feck did he know that? Cathy forced herself to look blank, not to react, didn't dare take a look at O'Rourke but she knew him well enough to know that the hairs were standing up on the back of his neck, just like they were on hers.

Apparently unruffled, O'Rourke switched gear. 'Who will kill you? You needed the cash, the painting, was it to settle a debt?' Hierra nodded. O'Rourke paused for a beat. 'So who do you owe?'

Cathy could almost feel the cogs turning inside O'Rourke's head as Hierra's eyes darted between them, *weighing up his hand.*

'Guy called Kuteli. His operation runs the big games out there, in Vegas. Runs everything. You don't mess with him.'

'So why did you?'

Hierra shrugged like he was exhausted, worn out with it all. 'The first time? There was a big game. I'd had a bad streak, reckoned I could turn my luck around. And it was a dead cert, I paid them back no problem. Then one of their guys gave me a tip-off about a private game – high stakes – said he'd do me a favour and talk to the boss about getting me in, loan me the stake.' Hierra grinned ruefully half to himself, shaking his head sadly. 'I was broke, thought it would be an easy play – but the game went wrong. Thought I'd square it with the next game, bigger stake, but it didn't happen.' The shrug again, the hesitation. 'Then I found out about Lavinia Grant. It was time to get out. I thought I could get enough cash to set myself up somewhere else. I'd nothing to keep me in Vegas.' A sigh caught in his throat. 'They were really breathing down my neck.'

'I'm surprised they let you out of the country.'

It sounded like a fairy story. Cathy could hear it in O'Rourke's voice. Out of the corner of her eye she could see him studying Hierra, looking for the tell. Most people had a habit that came out when they were lying – a twitch or the compulsion to scratch their ear, a small unconscious action that put what they were really thinking up in lights. Hierra hadn't moved. But then he was a card player, had either mastered his poker face at the tables or was a born liar. And Cathy knew which she'd go for.

Hierra's pause was heavy, loaded, the whir of the DVD suddenly loud, punctuated by the dull sound of O'Rourke's pen tapping on the page of notes in front of him. Hierra cleared his throat.

'They didn't let me go. Thought I'd given them the slip but they found me all right. Tracking device in my watch. Sent two stooges to make sure I delivered.' He paused. 'I had to tell them the whole story, convince them I was here to help Kuteli expand. It was all going great until Lavinia Grant croaked. I was going to wait for the cash but Kuteli's guys were getting restless. I thought I could use the painting as a sweetener while I worked out what to do.'

O'Rourke nodded slowly. 'This Kuteli must think you're valuable to send two guys halfway around the world after you.'

Hierra shrugged again. 'I know how he works, who his key people are.'

O'Rourke nodded, accepting the answer. 'So why didn't you take the painting the first time? Wasn't that why you broke in?'

'No.' A stubborn look flashed across Hierra's face, but it was fleeting. He shook his head. 'I wasn't planning to stick around long enough to sell it – I don't have the contacts out here. I broke into Zoë Grant's place to give Lavinia Grant a bit of a scare. And I reckoned Zoë would have keys to her grandmother's place. I'd heard she'd told everyone my father was dead, reckoned if I showed up again she'd have a bit of explaining to do, would see me straight. But she might have slammed the door in my face. I needed to show her I meant business.'

Had Lavinia Grant known who he was? Had he called in and frightened the life out of her? After all these years, hearing Hierra's story, Lavinia Grant would probably have had a heart attack. The thought was through Cathy's head before she realised it. She took a glance at O'Rourke. She was sure he was thinking the same thing.

'I'm getting the picture.' O'Rourke sat back, his elbow over the back of his chair. For the first time since they had come in, he looked relaxed, taking control.

'So why did you slash Zoë's clothes, the dress? To frighten Zoë? To frighten Lavinia Grant?'

'That's about it.'

'And did it frighten Lavinia, did it work?'

Hierra's face went hard again, his jaw set firm. 'I never talked to her.'

O'Rourke nodded like he didn't believe a word. 'So tell us what you know about this baby, Angel.'

Hierra laughed. 'I'm not stupid. What can you offer me?'

O'Rourke paused before replying, letting the silence grow like he was trying to decide. 'Assuming your information is useful and can assist us in a prosecution, which I have to say I rather doubt, there might be something we can do.'

'I've got written evidence. I can back it all up.' Hierra sat forward in his chair, grabbing for the glimmer of a lifeline.

Cathy felt O'Rourke stiffen beside her, but he continued to look relaxed, sceptical. '*Assuming* the information is bona fide, we can talk to the FBI on your behalf, see if we can't come up with a plan. I'm sure they would be interested in your helping them with this Kuteli character.'

There was something about his tone of voice that made Cathy glance at him. *What had he been discussing with the FBI?*

Hierra's voice interrupted her thoughts abruptly. 'No way. Are you mad? I gave his guys the slip this morning, but if those two creeps have any idea I'm here, they'll know I coughed.'

'I doubt they know you're here. If they'd been watching you today, don't you think they'd have stepped in to grab the painting?'

Cathy's blood ran cold. In that second she was back there, at the top of the hill, her gun drawn. *Had there been someone else there? Had the movement in the trees been her imagination?* Hierra might have thought he'd lost them, but would this crowd really have let him out of their sights? She didn't want to admit it, but she doubted it.

Her mind reached for an answer. She'd only caught the movement out of the corner of her eye, had been sure it was a dog. Surely there couldn't have been anyone watching, could there? O'Rourke had to be right about them intervening to get hold of the painting. *But what if whoever was following him didn't know he had the painting?* It had been well concealed under his coat. Cathy almost crossed herself. *Why the hell hadn't she called for backup?*

Unaware of her thoughts, O'Rourke continued, 'Worst possible scenario – assuming they saw you coming in – you can call them, spin them a line about helping us with our enquiries, pretend you hid the painting before we caught up with you, that you outsmarted us.'

Hierra was still shaking his head. But it was slower, less convinced. 'They won't buy it. They'll think it's a sting.'

'So reassure them. Why would we be interested in them? Las Vegas isn't our jurisdiction. You contact them, tell them you got the painting, had it hidden before we showed up. I'm sure the FBI will be interested in picking up whoever turns up to meet you in LA when you go back to deliver it.' Cathy flicked O'Rourke a look, impressed. *He had it all worked out.*

Weighing it up, Hierra shook his head slowly. 'It would be suicide.'

'I think your options are rather limited at this point, don't you? Why don't we take a break while you think about it, and we'll see what can be done?'

44

Back in the office, Cathy passed O'Rourke a steaming mug. The coffee was hot, fresh. Just what she needed. It had been one hell of a day and she was wiped. O'Rourke didn't look much better, his skin pale. He took a sip.

'Phew, that's good.' O'Rourke leaned back in his chair, loosened his tie, unbuttoned his shirt collar.

'So are you going to tell me what's going on, or do I have to beg?'

O'Rourke shot her a grin, like it was a tempting proposition, then said, 'Most of what Hierra was saying is the truth, well, so far anyway. Kuteli is a big player. The Feds have been after his gang for years, are working with the LVMPD to close in on them.'

O'Rourke took another slurp of his coffee, cradling the cup in his hands. 'They want us to turn him, to implant the idea at least that if he helped them get Kuteli, they could help him out of the other stuff. Time's running against them – there's a big case about to start, and with Hierra's testimony they can put Kuteli away for ever.'

'But they reckon he's killed two people.'

O'Rourke nodded. 'I know. He'll have to do time for that, but the key for them is that this Kuteli has been implicated in a rake of unsolved crimes – murder, armed robbery, money laundering, witness intimidation, human trafficking. The whole lot.

And he doesn't take law enforcement seriously either – he's nob-
bled juries and there's evidence suggesting he was involved in an
explosion that almost killed a judge.'

'And they're sure Hierra can give them Kuteli?'

'He's the missing piece they need to be sure they nail him.
They want Hierra to testify against Kuteli and go into their witness protection scheme.' He took another sip. 'The idea is that
we put someone on the plane with the painting. Hierra will have
to come up with a story to explain why it's not him making the
delivery. Shouldn't be too difficult. Then they're going to raid
Kuteli's premises all over the state, as it lands.' O'Rourke paused
like he was considering the proposition. 'We need to pull in the
two guys on Hierra's tail, keep them quiet while it all goes down.'

'How are we going to find them?'

'We've already got tabs on them – they turned up when the lads
were checking the hotels for Hierra. The FBI gave us the heads-up
that they might be coming our way. They aren't exactly invisible –
they're a pair of real characters.' He took a sip of his coffee. 'Special
Branch have been keeping an eye on them.'

*Obviously not a close enough eye or they would have come to
help her on Killiney Hill.*

Cathy leaned forward. 'And in exchange for helping Hierra,
we get the information we need.'

'Assuming there is any information.'

O'Rourke checked his watch. 'We can hold Hierra for six
hours; we've already wasted five, so we better get a move on.
Lacey's primed to give Super's permission to hold him for
another six, and the Chief can give another twelve. The FBI guys
will be here by then. We won't have any trouble with extradition
because he entered the country illegally, should have been stuck
on the next plane home the moment he arrived by rights.'

Cathy opened her mouth to speak, but O'Rourke was already sorting through the messages on his desk. He picked up one, studied it for a moment and reached for the phone.

Cathy sipped her coffee considering what he'd said, as he introduced himself to the person on the other end. It took a moment for him to be put through to the right department, a few moments in which O'Rourke played with his mug, slowly turning it around with his fingertips. He nodded. 'Thanks, you're very good to process it so fast.'

From his face Cathy could see that it was good news.

Hanging up, O'Rourke rested his hand on the back of the phone like he was about to pat it.

'That' – he paused for effect – 'was the carbon dating man. He's back from his holidays, very apologetic. Reckons the bones are approximately forty to sixty years old. He thinks he can get a bit closer but wanted to give us his initial thoughts in case we were in a hurry.'

'Forty to sixty?'

'Yep, so . . .'

Cathy continued for him. 'That puts Zoë out of the picture . . .'

'And it puts Lavinia and the sister right back in, and maybe Eleanor too . . .'

'And Hierra's father?'

O'Rourke threw back the rest of his coffee. 'Charlie boy? Hard to tell, but let's face it, he knew both women, and he was obviously no angel, if you'll forgive the pun. Let's see what Hierra has to say. It's a long shot but it's possible he knows something.'

Back in the interview room, Hierra was nursing an empty styrofoam cup, the smell of sweat clinging to his clothes. He'd hardly spoken to the duty solicitor according to the custody sergeant, was obviously going it alone. He looked up sharply as they entered. O'Rourke glanced at him icily as he loaded three new DVDs.

'Right, Angel, we've had a chat to our opposite numbers in the FBI. To make this work they want some help from you.'

'Do you think I'm mad?'

'I'm sure they'll look after you. The FBI has an excellent witness protection scheme and you'll be worth more alive to them than dead. You'll need to discuss it with them, but I'm sure you won't find it difficult to assume a new identity.'

'Right.' Hierra obviously hadn't considered this possibility. O'Rourke didn't give him much time to think about it.

'So just to recap, you freely admit that you entered Zoë Grant's house this morning and removed a painting' – O'Rourke checked his notes – 'A *View of Kingstown Harbour*, from its frame, with a view to taking it out of the country and passing it to a contact in Las Vegas in payment of a debt.'

Hierra thought for a moment, *ducking and diving, looking for a way out* . . . but there wasn't one.

'That's about it.'

'And do you admit to assaulting Miss Grant at her home last night?'

'I bumped into her.'

'Right. And you admit to assaulting Detective Garda Connolly when she attempted to apprehend you with this painting?'

Cathy's face twitched. *O'Rourke was on a roll.*

Hierra was about to protest his innocence again but he took one look at O'Rourke's face and changed his mind. Cathy could see Hierra's mind clicking, wondering if he'd still get the witness protection deal if he didn't admit the assault, considering his options. Finally he said, 'Maybe there was a tussle.'

'A tussle in which you punched Detective Garda Connolly and threatened her with a knife?'

It took Hierra a moment. 'Yeah, maybe.' He sighed. 'Yeah, that's about it.'

'Good, glad we got that straight.' O'Rourke lined up the papers in front of him, squaring them off.

'So, tell us about this baby. What do you know?'

Under Hierra's eye, a muscle twitched. Just once but Cathy caught it. He cleared his throat.

'There was a letter.'

O'Rourke interrupted him. 'There was, or there is?'

'There *is*.' Annoyed, Hierra emphasised the word.

'And who was it addressed to?'

'Do you want to hear this or not?'

'Just want to get the facts straight.' O'Rourke threw him a charming smile.

'Yeah, right.' Hierra twisted in the chair. 'There was a letter in my father's stuff. With the *Vanity Fair* story and some other crap. It was addressed to Lavinia Grant. I can't remember the date but it was years ago, right before my father met my mom. He was down on his luck around then, was smashed broke.'

'How is this letter written?'

'What?' Hierra looked surprised, like it was a stupid question. 'With a pen, obviously.'

'Signed?'

Hierra could suddenly see where O'Rourke was coming from. 'Yes, it's dated, signed by my old man, handwritten. It's the real thing. Stamp is on the envelope.'

'Grand, just want to be clear.'

Hierra ran his tongue across his lips. 'So this letter says that Grace Grant – Lavinia Grant's sister – that she had a baby.'

'Eleanor, we know.'

Hierra shot O'Rourke a look. 'It was his baby, my old man's. He said he was seeing her, Grace, before he married Lavinia.'

A penny dropped in Cathy's mind. *Hierra had grey eyes . . . Zoë's eyes.* It was obvious. Cathy had known there was something about him . . . if his father was Eleanor's father that made them cousins, or second cousins or something . . . *Jesus . . .*

Hierra sniffed. 'Well my old man was there that night, when Eleanor was born. He doesn't trust Lavinia, see, and he was mad about this Grace. So he hears the baby cry, goes in to see what's happening, and there was some bitch called Trish there, in the room with Lavinia Grant and the sister, and aren't there two babies? It was twins.'

Cathy caught her breath. *Twins. Jesus, why hadn't they thought of that?*

Hierra continued, 'Lavinia's standing there holding one baby and this Trish has got the other one. There's so much fuss going on, Trish doesn't hear him come in, and doesn't he see her holding a scarf or something over the baby's face? Then she turns around, sees him and gets into a panic and says it isn't breathing.'

'So what did your father do?' Cathy could feel the edge of the chair digging into her jeans as she sat forward.

'Nothing he could do. Lavinia Grant didn't see it, and she wouldn't have believed him over this Trish – they were best pals he said. Maybe Lavinia told her to do it, he didn't know, maybe they were going to do the both of them and he interrupted. He couldn't go get the doc, so he hit the brandy.'

'And you're sure this letter was written by your father?' *O'Rourke, practical to the last.*

'Yep. You can get a handwriting expert to look at it if you like, fingerprint it, but he wrote it all right, I'd know his writing anywhere. Like I said, he was broke. He wanted money. From them both, Lavinia and Trish. He said in the letter he'd go to the cops if they didn't pay up.'

'So why didn't he post it?'

'He had a win. Must have been the next week. Big one. Big enough to convince my mom he was worth something. They got together and maybe he forgot about it, maybe he thought it was like an insurance policy if he ever got stuck again.'

Cathy cut in, 'But you said you went hungry when you were a child. He must have needed money later – why didn't he post it then?'

Hierra shook his head. 'Right after he met my mom he started working for Kuteli, had plenty of money. We had no food cos he was mean as shit. My mom had to go beg every week to get anything out of him.'

'And where is this letter now?'

'Here, with me. Well, with my stuff.'

'You were planning to blackmail Lavinia Grant with it?' Cathy could see the whole picture now.

Hierra shrugged. 'It was an insurance policy. She knew what happened. I reckoned as soon as I told her who I was she'd pay up.'

'And did you? Did you tell her who you were?'

Hierra's face went hard again. 'I told you, she died before I got there.'

Cathy could feel O'Rourke tensing, fighting to keep the sarcasm out of his voice. 'So you did. Did your father happen to mention how he ended up marrying Lavinia, not Grace, or why he didn't report the death?'

Sighing, Hierra smoothed his hands over his hair.

'It was her idea to get married – Lavinia Grant's. She found out Grace had gotten pregnant ... there was a showdown.

She'd found out that he wasn't who he said he was, that he'd left a load of shit behind in London. She threatened him with the cops.' Hierra paused, could see them looking for more. 'He'd told everyone he was some French count and they all fell for it.' Hierra shook his head like he almost couldn't believe it himself. 'He'd had enough trouble in London, reckoned he'd do better marrying her and sticking around where he could keep an eye on Grace than running again. Lavinia Grant had a good little business going – clients coming from the States to have dresses made, the whole lot – but she had plans to build it. She knew that being married, she'd do better with the banks, and with his name, the title, she'd attract the type of high-paying customers she wanted. He wanted a piece of the action.'

Looking at his son, for a moment Cathy caught a glimpse of Charles Valentine as a young man . . . *the chat, the movie-star looks* . . . she could see how he'd be convincing.

'But why didn't he marry Grace, run it as a family business?' She was curious now.

'He reckoned it was all about control. Lavinia Grant needed to be in charge. She took over the family finances when their father died, thought she controlled everything the sister did . . .' Hierra smirked. 'She got that wrong.' He paused. 'My old man said Lavinia always hated the sister – she didn't want her to be happy. And there was no way this Lavinia wanted people to think she was left on the shelf. So she came up with this idea that he should marry her, and when the baby was born they'd pretend it was hers.'

'But why did he go through with it? Why didn't he take Grace and the baby away?' Cathy fought to keep her voice level, practical. *He'd watched Trish murder his child and he'd stuck around?*

Hierra laughed, put his head back to check out the ceiling before continuing, 'Fuck knows. He was a shit, I told you. I'd say he thought he'd be more comfortable living off Lavinia Grant than trying to make it with Grace and a child in tow.'

O'Rourke cut in. 'Did he say what happened to Grace after she had the baby?'

'Lavinia Grant sent her away somewhere, said she'd disgraced the family. That's when he left, when she sent Grace away. He took what he could and came to the States.'

O'Rourke was nodding. 'We need to see this letter.'

'The message wasn't very coherent. I reckon Steve was on his bike from the sound of the traffic, but he said Trish just turned up at the gallery and blurted out the whole story.' Cathy set her coffee spoon down with a clatter.

'Who needs enemies when you've got friends like her?'

Sitting opposite her in his office, O'Rourke took another bite of his bacon sandwich. Cathy could see it was cold, pretty crap-looking in fact, but then she knew he'd missed breakfast, had to be starving after the session in the interview room. He'd already sent a couple of men to pick up the letter from Hierra's hotel, another team to pick up the two characters trailing him. Hierra was downstairs in a cell of his own contemplating his future, his shoes lined up neatly outside the door.

Cathy shifted uncomfortably in her seat, the smell of the sandwich making her stomach roll. 'That Trish is unbelievable. She was categorical that Charles was dead, that Eleanor had gone to France. I remember the look on her face, like she had stepped in dog shit or something.'

'Such an elegant turn of phrase for a young lady.'

'You know what I mean.'

'I do, I know exactly what you mean. I think Ms O'Sullivan has a lot of explaining to do. Aren't you going to drink that coffee? Whatever about not eating, you'll get dehydrated if you don't drink something. How are you feeling, anyway?'

Cathy grimaced. 'Grand, not a bother.' She shrugged like she got into a scuffle with an armed suspect every day, like it wasn't a problem.

O'Rourke nodded slowly, watching her as he took another bite.

'Do you reckon Lavinia told Trish to kill the baby? Maybe she didn't think she could cope with two.'

He replied with his mouth full, 'One of them stitched the bones up in a dress, so, really, I'd believe anything.'

Cathy shivered. 'Any joy on the sewing thread?'

'They're confident. The dress was dry, no mould, so there should be something with a bit of luck – DNA from saliva if the dressmaker licked the thread. My gran always did that when she was threading a needle. Or skin cells. We'll see. They can be fairly quick when there's no backlog.'

'But there's a backlog.'

'Isn't there always?'

'If this was *CSI* we'd have had it weeks ago and wrapped all this up.'

O'Rourke shoved the last of the sandwich into his mouth, spoke with his mouth full. 'Time for a chat with Trish O'Sullivan, don't you think? See what she has to say about Hierra's evidence. Here this time.' He swallowed hard. 'We haven't got enough to arrest her yet, but it's only a matter of time. You better tell Emily Cox that you've been held up again, reschedule your chat with Grace for tomorrow – they're here for a while, aren't they?'

'Yep.' When Cathy had spoken to Emily this morning to change their meeting she'd sounded relieved, had been worried about Grace getting upset again. Cathy was sure another delay wouldn't be a bad thing. 'You going to get the lab to test the scarf in the suitcase for Trish's DNA as well?'

O'Rourke nodded. 'The tech boys have it in progress – they got some good samples from a hairbrush in her room at Oleander House and a pile of cigarette butts. She'll probably admit it was her scarf but claim that anything we find is circumstantial, but you never know, it might spook her into a confession. Stranger things have happened.'

45

'Can you please state your full name?'

Sitting opposite them with her arms crossed tightly, Trish O'Sullivan rolled her eyes and sighed theatrically like this was all a waste of time. Cathy could feel O'Rourke tense beside her, coiled like a panther about to pounce. They'd had enough trouble bringing her in; she would have slammed the door of her apartment in their faces if O'Rourke hadn't wedged his foot in it.

'*Why the hell would I want to talk to you lot? I've told you, I don't know how many times, I can't help you.*'

'*We just have a few small ends to tie up and then we can release Lavinia Grant's house . . . if you could come down to Dún Laoghaire for a quick chat it would be most helpful.*'

Cathy had almost laughed – despite having his foot in the door, O'Rourke had managed to make it sound casual, like it hadn't occurred to him that Trish might be desperate to get back into the house. *He knew how to push everyone's buttons.* What did they say, possession was nine-tenths of the law? The look of realisation on Trish's face, the subtle change in her attitude as she realised what he'd said, was a classic. Cathy could almost see the cogs in her head whirring – Lavinia's will would take at least a year to go through probate and who knew if she'd even left a proportion of her estate to Trish? If Trish moved back into Oleander it could take Zoë years to get her out, indeed she might not even bother.

And some people just didn't think the law applied to them.

'This is utterly ridiculous. My name's Patricia O'Sullivan, as you well know, and I have things to do, Inspector.' Cutting through Cathy's thoughts, Trish glared at both of them. O'Rourke didn't reply, instead tapped the end of his pen on the corner of his pad, his eyes on the typed pages in front of him. The main file on the Grant family was at least two inches thick. The team had been thorough, as far as was possible, ferreting into Trish's past as well as Lavinia's, Eleanor's and Zoë's. So they knew Trish was an only child, that her parents had both lived to ripe old ages, that her father had been first a journalist and later the editor of a provincial newspaper. *That she had a creative approach to the truth.*

'I'm afraid it is far from ridiculous, Ms O'Sullivan. As I explained, we have a few last issues to wrap up before we can release Oleander House.' Cathy bit her lip as he paused, his voice deliberately relaxed, the George Clooney charm turned up to full blast. *They didn't have enough evidence to arrest her, yet. But she didn't know that.* If he was clever he might get her to trip up. And one thing Cathy knew about O'Rourke was that he was clever.

'We have reason to believe' – Cathy could feel him choosing his words, drew in her breath sharply as she realised that he was going to go for it – 'that you concealed the death of an infant and that you played a part in that death. At the very least that you are an accessory in the instigation of that death through wilful neglect. It is also a criminal offence in this country to conceal the birth of a child.' O'Rourke's voice was clear, precise.

Trish's mouth dropped open. 'What the hell's that supposed to mean – *wilful neglect?*'

'Assuming the child died of natural causes, it was born without medical intervention and as a result died. If that is the case, at some point shortly after its birth it must have become distressed and yet no doctor was sought. We must also consider the possibility that the child may have been smothered – wasn't that a common method of disposing of unwanted children in the 1940s and 50s?'

Cathy shifted in her seat. Whatever about them knowing that Trish had lied to them about Charles being dead, about Eleanor's disappearance, whatever about them knowing that the baby was a boy, they had nothing to substantiate Charles Valentine's claim in the letter. *And his statement to Angel Hierra, most likely with a gun to his head, would hardly stand up in court . . .*

'Oh please, Inspector. You have evidence to support this supposition, do you?' As Trish recovered, shaking her head, her upper lip curled in a look of disgust. 'It's guesswork, Inspector. Absolute guesswork. And if I decided to leave right now you'd have no evidence to keep me here, would you?'

O'Rourke looked straight at her, meeting her eye.

'We have arrested a man named Angel Hierra. I believe you knew his father – Charles Henry Valentine? We had a very interesting conversation.'

At the mention of Charles's name Trish went white, licked her lips quickly. It took a moment for her to gather herself.

'You've spoken to Charles?' Leaping to her own conclusion, Trish looked at them in disbelief, then snorted. 'And you believed what he said? Good God, he'd say black was white if he thought he could make a few pounds out of it.' She paused, her eyes flicking from O'Rourke to Cathy and back again. Cathy stared back, *she wasn't about to put Trish right, to tell her Charles had died*. Almost sneering, Trish continued, 'Did he tell you how he convinced Grace and half of Dublin that he was a French count? Had the accent and everything, the cigars, the stories. The poor girl was completely infatuated. He was after her money, you know, thought she was a soft touch. He hadn't anticipated Lavinia. But she saw through him pretty quickly, found out he was some East End wide boy, a spiv on the run.'

'Thank you, we know.'

'Oh, *excuse me.*' Pretending to be affronted, Trish fired O'Rourke a scowl designed to wound.

'What we're interested in is why you lied about his death, and the death of Eleanor Grant.'

'Charles left, ran off with half of Lavinia's jewellery box. There was no way he was coming back. It wouldn't have looked good if people knew he was a crook. She had a *reputation*, Inspector.'

O'Rourke deliberately ignored the implication that he didn't have a reputation. 'And Eleanor? I seem to recollect you told us she had disappeared as well, had gone to France. I believe you told Zoë Grant something rather different this morning. Why did it take you so long to remember?'

Trish's hand fluttered to the chains at her neck. She was wearing a silk trouser suit, a murky no-colour somewhere between vomit and peanut butter, a cream silk T-shirt underneath it, her hair lacquered so heavily that each hair appeared to be glued in place. And she was still wearing the huge solitaire diamond earrings that had turned Cathy's stomach the first time they had met.

'Well, what was I supposed to say? Eleanor had gone, hadn't she? Did it really matter where to?' She paused. 'With Grace coming back it was time she knew. I couldn't have Grace spreading lies about Lavinia. She needed to hear it from me.'

There was a pause. When O'Rourke spoke his voice was low, a rumble like a dog growling.

'The truth, Ms O'Sullivan, isn't always nice, but it is nonetheless the truth. Knowing the truth mattered to Zoë Grant, don't you think? It took you a long time to tell her.'

The truth . . . Cathy shifted uncomfortably in her seat. *He was right. The truth wasn't always nice, but striving for the truth was what it was all about, wasn't it?* That's why they came into work every day, why they sifted through other people's shit. *To find the truth . . .*

'We couldn't tell her before.' Trish interrupted Cathy's thoughts, looking at O'Rourke like he was stupid. 'She was too young to understand, would have blurted it out somewhere. She was traumatised after it happened, kept asking where her mother was. So we told her Eleanor was fine, that she'd been playing a game, that she'd had to go away for a while. Lavinia gave her birthday cards, Christmas cards the first couple of years, so she wouldn't miss her.'

So she wouldn't miss her? Cathy felt her face form a look of horror, would have interrupted if she'd been able to think of anything to say, but Trish continued like it was all fine. 'Zoë was three or four, her mother was gone. She accepted it in the end, stopped asking.'

If O'Rourke shared Cathy's revulsion at this statement he didn't show it, concentrated icily on the facts. 'She was traumatised? So tell us: what happened to Eleanor exactly?'

Trish shook her head like it was irrelevant. 'I was at the office. Lavinia called to say that they'd had a row, that Eleanor had taken something, pills or booze, and that Zoë had found her in the bath. She must have fallen asleep.'

'Eleanor and Lavinia had had an argument?' O'Rourke kept his voice calm.

'They were always arguing. Eleanor was very difficult, up and down. She'd stay out all night, going to parties with the layabouts she'd met at art school, then when she eventually came home, she wouldn't come out of her room for days. And then she got pregnant. Christ, the rows then . . .' Trish paused, let out a sigh, a blast of irritation and anger. 'It was Grace all over again. The stupid girl. We ended up looking after Zoë more than Eleanor ever did. She never seemed to connect with her.'

'And Zoë's father?'

'God knows. Probably some doped-up student. Eleanor was the one who wanted to go to art school, said she needed to express herself, although I don't remember her ever actually painting anything. Lavinia thought it was all ridiculous. Eleanor could draw all right, had a great eye for colour, but it was all peace and love and free sex then. She wasn't able for it.'

'So Eleanor argued with Lavinia and then took her own life?'

'It was an accident. She fell asleep.'

'Right. And who certified the death?'

'The family doctor.'

'He understood the situation, did he? Looked after everything.'

Trish rolled her eyes like it was obvious.

'You understand that when Eleanor's death occurred it was also an offence to conceal a suicide.' Trish didn't respond, instead focused on her nails, looking at them speculatively like she was considering whether she needed a manicure.

'Why the lies, Trish?' Cathy sat forward, hardly able to believe what she was hearing. 'Why didn't you tell Zoë what happened when she was older? Attitudes have changed to suicide. Surely Zoë had a right to know.'

'It was an accident.'

There was something about the way Trish's face had shut down, about the way she had moved from her nails to start playing with her rings, twisting them straight until the gemstones caught the light, that made Cathy's skin crawl, a shiver shoot up her spine. *What if it wasn't an accident, what if Lavinia had held her under the water? Would they ever know?*

O'Rourke cleared his throat. 'Let's just backtrack a bit, can we, and ask you about Grace. What exactly happened there?' O'Rourke voice was tense. Trish seemed to have forgotten that she was here voluntarily, but he hadn't.

The sigh again, but this time Trish's jaw was set. *Had they hit a nerve?*

'It was a long time ago. What does it matter now?'

'Let us be the judge of what matters, Ms O'Sullivan.' O'Rourke shifted in his seat, adjusted the cuffs of his shirt, his cufflinks blue and gold, the Garda crest. 'We have evidence that that you were present the night Eleanor was born, and that Charles Valentine was also present.'

There was a short pause, the silence laden with half-truths. Then Trish snorted like a horse refusing to go into the stalls. 'I'm surprised Charles can remember.'

'Why would that be, Ms O'Sullivan?'

'Because he got hold of a bottle of vintage brandy, Inspector, several bottles in fact. He passed out.'

O'Rourke nodded silently. 'Apparently he was able to remember enough.' He left it hanging out there. 'So, tell us what happened. Let's start with how Charles and Grace met.'

'It was at some dance at the Gresham. He was very attractive, I suppose, suave. Once he realised that Grace and Lavinia were living on their own, that their father was dead, he thought all his Christmases had come together. He seduced her, Inspector. She was a silly girl, flighty, easily led.'

'So Grace discovered she was pregnant, and . . .'

'She thought Charles loved her, thought he was going to marry her – well he might have done if Lavinia hadn't found out the truth about him. She told him if they got married she'd cut Grace off without a penny. That changed things a bit.'

'And then, despite his background, she decided to marry him herself?' Even with Hierra's version of his father's story it sounded nuts. But, Cathy knew, Ireland in the 1950s was a very different place from today; society had very strict rules about what was acceptable and what wasn't, found ways around the issues that defied belief.

Trish's face twisted like there was a bad smell in the room.

'It wasn't that simple. He was useful to Lavinia – he had a name, a title, even if it was in his head. Married to her, he gave her business huge credibility; married to Grace, he was a total liability – he could have talked the stupid girl into anything.' Trish paused for breath, waiting for O'Rourke to speak. He didn't, continued to look like he thought she was making it all up.

'Look, Lavinia worked really hard after their father died. *She had dreams*, she couldn't risk Charles taking it all away if he married Grace. She wanted to open a shop, to build the business, but it wasn't easy for a woman on her own back then. She needed finance, needed the bank to take her seriously.' Trish paused. 'And we had to do something about the child, couldn't have it leaking out that there was an illegitimacy in the family. It made sense all round.'

To everyone except Grace.

There was a pause. A long one.

'So take us back to the night Eleanor was born.' O'Rourke was frowning, obviously trying to get his head around the logic . . .

Trish's voice was hard. 'Nothing to tell. Grace went into labour.' She shuddered. 'Lavinia delivered it.'

'The doctor wasn't called.'

'Of course not. Women gave birth at home all the time back then, without doctors fussing about.'

'And many of them died.' Trish shook her head like O'Rourke was being ridiculous, like it wasn't relevant. 'And was Eleanor a healthy baby?'

'I suppose so. She screamed a lot, but don't they all?'

'And the boy?' O'Rourke's tone was light, conversational. Beside him Cathy froze. He was fishing, but it was slick, calculated.

'What boy?' Trish tried to look mystified, but she had paled several shades, reached up to twist her earring. The tell. It was a good act but not quite good enough.

'The boy, Ms O'Sullivan. We know about the boy.'

O'Rourke let the silence between them grow, sat back waiting for Trish to speak. Eventually she shook her head, her face angry.

'Look, he died. So what? He was too small. Grace wasn't cut out to carry twins. And Lavinia could never have managed two of them.'

O'Rourke nodded, continued, his face deadpan. 'Is that what happened? Really? He was too small?'

'We didn't even know Grace was having twins. Eleanor came first. Lavinia thought she was finished and then there was this other one.'

'Did he breathe, Trish? Did you hear him cry?'

'I was downstairs.' Her voice was hard, razor-sharp.

'Really? We have reason to believe that you were in the room, Trish, that you held the child.' Trish blanched, her eyes flicking between them as he continued, 'We have evidence to suggest that you were helping Lavinia, that Charles didn't start on the brandy until much later that night, that he went up to see Grace, to see his baby, and he saw everything. Did you know he was there, Trish? Did you know he was right behind you?'

'It's lies, it's all lies.' She spat the words across the table, her voice rising to a scream. 'Charles is a liar. I was downstairs.'

O'Rourke raised his eyebrows, but kept quiet. *Waiting to see if she would say more?* She didn't. The outburst seemed to have exhausted her. The silence grew, filled with disbelief.

'And what did you and Lavinia Grant do with the body?'

'*I* don't know what Lavinia did with it – I was downstairs. I expect she buried it, what else could she do?'

'Before she buried it, what did she do with it, Trish?'

Trish looked noncommittal, like she wasn't sure. 'Wrapped it in a scarf, I think . . .'

'A purple scarf?'

Trish's face froze. She opened her mouth to reply but nothing came out.

O'Rourke continued, 'And concealed it in a suitcase, perhaps?'

'I don't know, I wasn't there.' Stubborn, not moving. *But she knew about the scarf.*

Transfixed, Cathy had to clear her throat to speak. 'Where did she bury it, Trish? Where did she bury the body?'

'In the garden.' *Like it was obvious.*

So why hadn't they found anything yet? And how the hell had the bones ended up in the dress?

'Can you tell us exactly where? It will save our lads digging the entire place up.' There was a hint of sarcasm in O'Rourke's voice.

'I don't know exactly. It's changed a lot over the years.'

A light went on in Cathy's head. 'Lavinia had it landscaped, didn't she?'

'We were in Italy. When we came home the gardener had half of it dug up. A surprise for her, he said. Lavinia went nuts but he had to finish the job. All the neighbours were calling in to see what we were doing – she couldn't stop it in the middle.'

'Did one of you move the bones then? Did Lavinia dig them up?' Cathy knew she was on to something. In the photo they'd found of the man in the straw hat, the garden had looked totally different, but the monkey puzzle tree had been there . . .

'I don't know. The next day the whole business with Eleanor happened. It was all a bit fraught. She was such an inconsiderate little bitch; honestly, we were only just back from our holidays. Lavinia was devastated.'

Eleanor died the next day? Had Lavinia and Eleanor argued about the bones? Had Eleanor seen her dig them up, challenged her? Cathy's mind was racing. *If Eleanor was unstable, erratic, had this pushed her over the edge? Or had Lavinia lost her temper and held her under the water?*

Before Cathy had a chance to say anything, a tear rolled down Trish's cheek. 'They all let her down. All of them.' Suddenly she sobbed. 'I was the one who loved her, who stuck by her. They all let her down. I was the one who was there for her.'

Cathy could feel an anger growing inside her, an anger that had started that first day, and now, with Trish snivelling in front of her . . . As if he could sense it, O'Rourke cut in.

'And the dress, Trish. Tell us about the dress.'

Trish was crying hard now, was difficult to understand through the tears. It took her a moment to find the words.

'It was Grace's. It was made for some woman whose wedding fell through – she never collected it – but Grace always loved it. Lavinia gave it to her years before Charles even appeared on the scene. It was beautiful, the best silk, French lace, had taken days to make.' Trish drew in a breath, rough, torn at the edges. 'Then with everything, it seemed stupid to leave it hanging there and for Lavinia not to wear it herself – Grace certainly had no use for it. Afterwards Lavinia kept it for Eleanor, thought she'd wear it.' A sob ripped through her. 'They all let her down. Lavinia had such hopes for Eleanor, hopes for a good marriage, hopes that she'd be able to take over the business, to continue everything she'd started. Then Eleanor . . . the stupid girl.' Trish's eyes glazed over. 'It was that night, the night Eleanor died. I couldn't sleep, came down for a glass of whisky. Lavinia hadn't even gone to bed, was still dressed. She had the dress spread over the dining table, had her workbox beside her, her scissors out. She said the dress had brought her nothing but bad luck – I thought she was going to cut it up but she told me to take it to the undertakers, to have Eleanor buried in it.'

Cathy realised she'd been holding her breath, let out a silent sigh. She could feel the sweat breaking out on her palms. *Was this the truth?* At last? Had Lavinia Grant been forced to move the bones from the garden, then, with Eleanor's death, come up with the perfect hiding place? *Burying the baby boy with his sister* . . . like there was some sort of symmetry in the madness of it all . . .

'So you took the dress to the undertakers?' O'Rourke kept his voice practical, conversational.

'I planned to, but so much was happening. We'd managed to get Eleanor's body out of the house into the doctor's car earlier in the evening. He took her to the undertakers, sorted it out with them. I put the dress into the car but just as I was going out the next morning the bloody priest turned up on the doorstep, asking how our holiday had been, asking about the plans for the garden. I couldn't get away. When I finally got there the undertaker was busy with some other family. Lavinia had made me promise to be discreet – I couldn't just waltz in with it.' Trish shook her head. 'I meant to take it back later but then Lavinia told me they'd done it – they'd cremated her, I mean. I didn't know what to do with the bloody thing then – I couldn't tell Lavinia I hadn't got it to the undertakers, so I shoved it in the back of a wardrobe and . . . and forgot about it.'

'Didn't Lavinia realise? Didn't she notice that Eleanor wasn't buried in it?'

'We didn't go to the funeral. We couldn't. And Eleanor was cremated anyway. Nothing to see.'

There was a pause. O'Rourke broke it, his voice low. 'And then what happened to the dress?'

Trish shook her head like it didn't matter.

'It was years later. I was having a clear-out. I'd forgotten all about it – it was in a cupboard under a load of other stuff. Zoë had just bought her own place so I gave it to her, told her Lavinia wanted her to have it but never to discuss it, that it would upset her too much . . .'

46

'How are you feeling?' Steve glanced at his watch, one eye on Zoë. She looked pale, was a bit distant, but seemed to have brightened since they had arrived at the gallery. Max was upstairs trying to get more wine delivered and finding out what had happened to the champagne, giving them a welcome few moments to themselves.

'Grand.' Zoë flicked him a smile, pulled her hair back over her shoulder, took a deep breath.

'You look fabulous, you'll knock them dead.' Steve leaned over to kiss her, pulling her towards him, running his hand around her waist, the velvet of her dress rich purple, soft, sensuous, her cleavage emphasised by rows of sparkling sequins and crystals, sea green, turquoise and silver. Made her look like she'd just risen from the depths.

Zoë took a short quick breath. 'What time did Tony and Emily say they'd be here?'

Steve hugged her again. Finding out about Eleanor, about Grace, had been more than he'd thought Zoë could cope with, but meeting Emily and Tony had helped smooth the waters. When Cathy had introduced them it had been like they each held part of a puzzle – only when they brought them together had they been able to find the whole. And Zoë had connected with Emily from the moment they'd met.

'Around now. They're staying to eat with us and Max, and Phil and Dan, after we wrap here.'

'I hope Grace isn't too tired. It's been a terribly traumatic time for her too.' A sad smile passed across Zoë's face as if blown by the wind. 'I still can't believe it. Hearing everything ... I can't believe that Lavinia didn't tell me about Eleanor, about Grace.' Steve nodded again, *right now they were all dealing with the unexpected* ... He'd never felt about anyone the way he felt about Zoë and part of him had been shocked when he'd realised that he felt a tiny bit disappointed that she wasn't pregnant. In a very short space of time he'd been doing more serious thinking than he had ever done in his life before. 'And Trish knew all the time. I'm glad they've arrested her. I don't think I ever want to see her again.'

Zoë had said it a hundred times today already, but she was working through it.

Steve said nothing – they might have arrested Trish as an accessory, for not informing the authorities about the death of the baby, but after all this time he wondered if they'd be able to prosecute, if her confession to being in the house that night was enough. He knew that they were waiting for DNA results, that Cathy was hoping when they questioned Trish again that she'd confess to her true part in the whole mess. He knew Trish would get a lighter sentence with a guilty plea – which would keep the whole thing much simpler all round. Zoë hadn't thought about it yet, but if Trish didn't plead guilty, she might have to give evidence, to tell the whole story to the media. And he didn't know if she was up to that.

'She's going to need some professional help; I'll get a name for you. I can brief them.'

Tony Cox's words lingered in Steve's consciousness. Despite being the keynote speaker at the conference, he'd managed to escape from his duties, albeit briefly, to join them for lunch in the Shelbourne Hotel's bistro. *A chance for Grace and Zoë to get to know each other.* It had been busy, a hubbub of voices punctuated with the tinkle of china, with refined laughter, but they'd managed to get a table beside the window overlooking Kildare Street.

After lunch, Zoë and Emily had vanished to the bathroom with Grace, one of them on each side of her, both mothering her, holding open the double doors, making sure she didn't slip on the marble floor.

'Zoë's going to need some professional help; I'll get a name for you. I can brief them.'

Nodding towards Zoë, Tony had reached for the milk jug, topping up his coffee. Sitting forward in his seat, Steve had been nursing his own coffee – black. *He needed it.*

'It's the betrayal that's the worst, all the lies. It's like her entire childhood has been washed away, all her points of reference gone.' His face serious, Steve kept his voice low.

Tony rolled his eyes as he spoke. 'That Lavinia Grant sounds utterly charming.' He grimaced. 'But looking at Grace, hearing what you guys are telling me about Lavinia's paranoia about the press, the highs and lows, I'd guess Lavinia was bipolar – a manic depressive. A lot of her behaviour would be symptomatic of the condition. It fits with Grace's psychosis, the schizophrenia. The two are closely related, have common traits. And Zoë's mother Eleanor, too – if it was suicide as the cops are suggesting . . . it all fits.'

'Do you think Eleanor was bipolar?'

Tony grimaced again. 'Impossible to say for sure. I'd guess it was more likely she shared Grace's symptoms, was schizophrenic. There's a strong genetic link in these illnesses.'

A strong genetic link?

Steve had felt his train crash, the carriages concertinaing into each other, glass shattering. *Whoa . . .*

Unaware of the impact of his words, Tony continued, 'Zoë should be assessed. I'm sure some of the issues she's struggling with could route back to a diagnosis similar to Grace's. She mentioned feelings of isolation and depression, her need to be in control over her surroundings. She'll feel much more level once she's taking the right medication – at least we know what we're dealing with.'

'We do?' Steve had stopped himself, then repeated it, trying to sound positive. 'We do.'

'And it will be great for Zoë to have Grace near her; they've got a lot of catching up to do. I was a bit concerned initially that the negative associations Grace has with that house would throw her off track, but she seems very happy at the idea of moving back home. And Emily's going to stay as long as she can, help smooth things along. I'm sure she'll be backwards and forwards checking on them both.'

Steve nodded. Zoë had been the one to suggest Grace move back to Oleander House, had just sort of assumed that she would want to, pointing out that by rights the house was hers. It would take the solicitors months to sort out Lavinia's will, but one way or another Grace would be looked after for the rest of her days, Zoë had assured Tony she would see to that. Steve grinned. 'The housekeeper will probably find Grace a walk in the park after having to look after Lavinia for so many years. From what Zoë said, she was pretty difficult.'

'You could say that. She was a classic case from the sound of things.' Then Tony's voice brightened. 'Here they are, back again.'

Tony stood up, grabbing his napkin to stop it from falling off his knee, pulled back Zoë's chair to let her sit. She was smiling.

'Emily just told me your news. It's great.'

Tony rolled his eyes, smiling, threw Emily a look as she slipped into her own seat.

'I couldn't keep quiet, sorry.'

He shook his head, like it didn't matter, a smile creeping onto his face. 'We've left it a bit late to start a family, my fault entirely. But we should be OK if we get a reputable agency to help, look to adopt in China or Russia maybe.'

'It's a wonderful thing, giving a child from somewhere like that a home, a future.' Zoë sounded almost wistful.

'I hope so.'

Emily met his eye. 'It is. It's a wonderful thing.'

'Here they are.' A knock on the gallery's street door jolted Steve from his thoughts. He put down his glass on the reception desk beside a pile of copies of *Scene*, Zoë's face smiling from the front cover. With everything going on it was a miracle they'd got it out in time, but the girls in the office had been great, had got the whole issue to print pretty much on their own, had thrived on the challenge, showed just how good there were. *Which was a total blessing.* Looking at Zoë's face on the cover, Steve knew that from now on he was going to have to get serious, was going to have to start running the magazine like a real business, a business that could support both of them.

The girl with the pink hair was already opening the gallery door when Steve felt Zoë hesitate.

'What's up?'

'Will it be OK? Tonight . . . everything . . . will it be OK?'

He put both hands on her shoulders, kissed her forehead. 'It'll be fine. You've got your friends all around you.' He nodded to the back of the shop, where Dan had his arm around Phil's shoulders as he pointed out something in one of the paintings. The pair of them had been beaming since they arrived. '*This is your day.* Trust me. Everything will be fine. Everything.'

Zoë's smile was like the sun coming out. She put her hands on Steve's arms, still resting on her shoulders.

'I love you.'

Steve kissed her again, this time on her lips. 'Good, cos I think you're pretty wonderful yourself. And you're going to be seeing a lot of me.'

The drizzle was clearing as Cathy headed out of the car park into Temple Bar. Dublin was busy, early-evening Christmas shoppers mingling with students and the occasional out-of-season tourist. She zipped up her leather jacket, glad of its thick lining. She felt cold, uncharacteristically nervous. Passing into the cobbled pedestrian area, she glanced upwards at the Christmas lights glittering in the darkness, chains of stars, blue and white, this year's colour, guiding her towards the gallery. *Christ, why was she here?*

Outside the gallery a crowd was already beginning to gather, women in high heels and expensive coats, men in blazers and tweeds trying to look like they weren't cold, several photographers, their cameras swinging from their shoulders. Cathy hesitated for a moment. *The timing was crap . . . worse than crap . . . but she was here and there was a chance that she might not have the courage to get here again . . .*

In the depths of her pocket her phone rang. Cursing, fumbling for it, she checked the screen as she answered. *Number withheld.* The voice on the other end was male, heavily accented.

'We don't like –'

'Feck off Decko, I'm busy.' Cathy ended the call. Decko was still in Templemore on the training course. No doubt he was in the bar bored out of his brain but she really wasn't in the mood right now.

Slipping through the knot of expectant guests outside the gallery, Cathy rapped on the door with her car keys. Thick blackout blinds had been pulled down on the inside of the door; opposite the window, one of Zoë's canvases dominated the display space, brilliantly lit – a splash of colour in the darkness of the street. The blind didn't quite meet the edge of the door and through the gap Cathy could see flashes of movement, of light and colour. She rapped again, harder this time, more insistent. A moment later a girl with pink hair and a ring through her nose pulled back the blind, drew back the bolts, opened the door an inch.

'We're closed; Zoë Grant's opening is at seven o'clock.'

Cathy flipped open her badge. 'Gardaí, I need a word.' Reluctantly the girl pulled the door wide. 'Is Zoë here?' The girl nodded but Cathy had already spotted her, willowy and elegant at the back of the gallery talking to Grace, Steve's arm protectively around her. Emily and Tony Cox were looking at another painting, holding hands *like love's young dream*. 'I need a word with Max Igoe.'

'He's upstairs in the office, he'll be down any minute.'

Cathy smiled, the muscles in her face working but leaving her eyes cold. 'It's private. Show me the way, I can go up.'

Steve glanced over his shoulder as the door closed behind her, raised an eyebrow, was obviously about to say something when Cathy shook her head. He got the point, turned back to the painting Zoë was explaining, slipping right back into the conversation, waving the glass of wine in his hand towards it. The girl with the pink hair opened a door concealed in the panelling, curiosity written all over her face. 'It's straight up.' Behind her the phone started ringing.

'Thanks. You better get that.' Cathy looked up the stairs, steep and narrow, dark after the bright lights of the gallery.

It was a long climb.

At the top, Cathy paused, her hand on the door handle, taking a moment to breathe, to gather her wits. She could hear Max on the phone, smell the unmistakable tang of paint – the same smell she'd got in Zoë's studio that had made her stomach churn. *But she couldn't puke now.*

Cathy was through the door before Max looked up, the phone clamped to his ear. He raised his eyebrows, but his grin of greeting was broad, genuine. *That was something.* Max gestured for her to come over to the desk as he finished speaking.

'Yes, tonight. It should have been here at six. And it better be bloody chilled when it gets here. You've got about five minutes.'

He hung up, tossing his mobile onto the desk, sitting back to look at her, drinking her in, *from the top of her head to her boots,* his eyes alight with mischief. For a second Cathy hadn't a clue what to say, smoothed her hair behind her ear, avoided his gaze, had a good look around the office. *Like she was relaxed, like she wasn't dying inside.*

'Cathy Connolly. And how are you? To what do I owe the pleasure? This isn't an official visit, I hope?'

'Hi Max.' The words stalled in Cathy's mouth, her mind going blank. She had rehearsed this so many times.

The truth. The words loomed large in her head. *Max needed to know the truth.*

Sensing Cathy's discomfort, seeing she was struggling, Max stood up, slipped out from behind the desk, a moment later was there beside her, his arm around her shoulders like it was the most natural thing in the world.

'Come on, sit down, spit it out. You pissed with me because I didn't call?' He kissed the top of her head. 'Mm, you smell good.'

Cathy felt her knees wobble, leaned in to him, closed her eyes in exasperation. 'Max . . . !'

'I know – I'm a dog. Here, sit, I'll get coffee or maybe a glass of wine? Bloody champagne's stuck on the quays somewhere.'

'Don't, I'm fine.' Max was already heading back to the desk, looked back at her in surprise. She'd put her hand up like she was stopping traffic. He crooked an eyebrow, then turned around to face her, crossed his arms, his eyes narrowed. *He'd copped it, knew something was wrong. Something big.*

'What is it? What's happened?'

Cathy sat down on the sofa with a bump, could feel a hot flush working its way up from somewhere in her middle. She put her head in her hands, massaging her temples with her fingertips.

'What is it? Jesus, Cathy, what? Has something happened to Pete?'

Cathy shook her head, resisting the urge to laugh.

'Pete's fine . . .' *Pete was always fine* . . . There wasn't an easy way to say it. 'It's me. I'm pregnant.'

There, she'd said it. *For the first time out loud.* Now it had to be real. Cathy waited for the bells and whistles, the trumpet fanfare. It didn't come. Nothing came. Cathy moved her hands from her face. Max was looking at her, his mouth open. Wide open.

'Fuck.'

His face, his choice of words – it was all ridiculous. Cathy smiled, hysterical laughter trying to fight its way out. *Max looked exactly how she felt: shell-shocked.* At least she wasn't on her own in that.

'Fuck.' Max said it again, more quietly this time.

And the tears came.

Cathy tried to stop them, catching them with her forefingers before they headed down her cheeks, but there were too many. A moment later Max was at her side, pulling her to him, cradling her head against his shoulder.

'How long? When?'

Cathy sniffed. 'You know when. Pete's party. I'm six weeks.'

'Fuck.'

'Will you stop saying that?'

Max looked frightened. 'Sorry' – he moved one hand to massage her stomach – 'we need to remember little ears.'

Cathy shook her head, *God he was an idiot*. 'What am I going to do?' All the anguish, all the worry was wrapped up in that one sentence.

There was a long pause. Laughter drifted up from the gallery below, the gentle strains of a piece of classical music, she didn't know what. *Why didn't he say something?*

'What do you want to do?' Suddenly focused, practical, Max leaned back, tipped Cathy's chin, his eyes meeting hers, searching like radar. 'What do *you* want to do?'

Cathy blinked away the tears, trying to look at the floor. 'I don't think there are that many options. I've thought about . . . about everything . . . but I couldn't get rid of it, or give it away . . .'

'OK. Fine. That's fine. I mean great,' Max corrected himself hastily. 'That's great.'

'It is?'

He kissed the top of her head again, smiling sheepishly.

'It is.' Max sounded surer than Cathy thought possible. 'We'll work something out.' He paused. 'You don't want to get married or anything, do you?'

'Christ, no.'

'Cool. I mean that's grand.' Max shook his head like the words weren't coming out right. 'OK, OK . . .' For once it seemed like he didn't know what to say, was struggling with it himself. Then, as if he had made a decision, Max said, 'Eh, there is one thing.'

'What?'

It was the way he said it. *He was married and she didn't know; no, he was gay . . . as if this wasn't bad enough already.*

'Erm, I've got another kid. Well, he's not exactly a kid, more like a teenager now.' Then, seeing Cathy's face, Max said hastily, 'I don't see his mum, we're not together or anything, weren't ever, really. Well it's a long story . . . she's been in and out of rehab.'

Feck. Feck. Cathy's gut twisted. *Her baby already had a half-brother . . . and his mother was what? An anorexic, a drunk . . . a junkie? Rehab? There was no way she'd thought this could get any worse . . .*

'But look, don't worry about that now. Let's get you sorted out. Money's no problem. You'll need somewhere to live.' Then, half to himself, 'And you could work here part-time after it's born.'

'What?'

Max wasn't really listening. 'When you've had it, you'll need something part-time.'

'But I've got a job.' Cathy moved away from him on the sofa.

'You can't work those hours with a kid.'

'Of course I can . . .' She looked at him in disbelief.

Her job was her life. She loved it, everyone knew that. She socialised with Guards – she lived with Guards for God's sake. She'd spent Christ knew how many evenings grafting for her criminology degree, was about to take her sergeant's exams and he wanted her to work part-time in an art gallery . . .

'I am *not* leaving my job.' Max looked at her, picking up on the finality in her tone. 'No way.'

'Don't worry, you don't have to decide now.' He paused. 'You'll need to think about that kickboxing stuff too, all that training . . .' He shook his head.

What? Cathy's mouth fell open. Before she could say anything more, Max stood up, heading for his desk.

'You'll need a house – with a garden, for swings and things. And a dog. Every kid needs a dog. We never had one, always wanted one. And schools, we'll have to think about schools. St Andrew's maybe . . .'

Max was firing ideas at Cathy like she was his secretary, his voice excited, like he was planning a new project, but she was still reeling from the idea of giving up her job, her *kick boxing* . . . was hardly listening. Suddenly realising Cathy wasn't responding, Max turned back to look at her. 'What?'

Cathy shrugged. What should she say? Thanks? *Thanks for what? For taking responsibility? For not demanding she had an abortion? Or thanks for screwing her on a fire escape when he already had a permanent connection to his junkie ex-girlfriend? Feck* . . . It was all swirling around inside her head like she was caught in a whirlpool, the water deafening. Right on cue, Cathy's phone began to ring again. Wrestling it out of her pocket, she looked at the screen. Number withheld. Jesus, she didn't need Decko acting the maggot again now. She turned it off. He could leave as many messages as he liked on her voicemail.

Ignoring the distraction, Max said, more to himself than to Cathy, 'Steve's always saying, *your day will come.* I'm forty on the 29th of December. Reckon this is mine . . . I never saw Zac grow up, I don't even really know him.' His voice was suddenly serious. 'Maybe this is my chance to make that right.'

'Maybe.' Sighing, Cathy ran her hands over her face.

47

Cathy heard the car draw up just as she put the key in her front door.

It was eight o'clock. She'd left the gallery just as the flash-bulbs started popping, slipping out of the door behind the crowd listening to Max's introduction of 'a sensational new Irish artist, who will be making a huge imprint on the inter-national art scene . . .' He was in his element, his excitement contagious.

And now she was home. And a very new, very shiny navy-blue BMW had pulled up outside her house like it had been hov-ering at the end of the street waiting for her.

O'Rourke.

Half turning, Cathy watched as he slipped out of the driver's seat in that easy way he had, looking at her over the roof of the car. He leaned his forearm on it, the other hand on the open door.

'Your phone flat?'

She paused a beat. *Had he been trying to ring?*

'The lads were messing.' She nodded back towards the house. 'Turned it off.'

Even from this distance, in this light, she could see him cock one eyebrow.

'You eaten?'

Cathy shook her head, hesitating, realising at the same time that she was starving.

'Come on then.' O'Rourke was back in the car before she could refuse.

'They're going to get them.' O'Rourke spoke as Cathy pulled the door closed behind her, slipping her bag into the foot well as the courtesy light faded gently. O'Rourke loved this car. Everyone said he was mad using it for work but with his back he reckoned he'd spend more time at the physio than behind his desk if he didn't.

'Going to get who?'

'Kuteli, Hierra's mafia pal.' O'Rourke said it like she should know exactly who he was talking about. He was smiling like he'd got a gold star – *probably had*. 'Hierra is going to testify.' O'Rourke made it sound like he'd won the lottery. 'The two FBI guys arrived and took him straight to the airport. The lads picked up the two honchos following Hierra no problem – they were in the Patriot Inn.'

'Making friends with the Provos? That would be right.'

O'Rourke nodded. 'The international brotherhood of gougers. Surveillance have a guy on the inside, they've been in and out a few times, apparently, seemed very friendly with the locals. Perhaps Kuteli was thinking of expanding his operations over here. Anyway, they're in the Bridewell for the night. More secure than Dún Laoghaire. The FBI is sending someone to collect them tomorrow.' He glanced at her again, a *you won't believe this* expression on his face. 'They've got six separate teams ready to close in on Kuteli, DEA, LVMPD, FBI, the whole lot.'

'Whew, they must want him.' Cathy's eyebrows shot up.

O'Rourke nodded. 'Apparently so far every case they've tried to bring against Kuteli and his cronies has fallen apart. He specialises in witness intimidation, from the judges right through to the prosecuting cops. If they can keep him alive, Hierra's testimony will be the clincher.'

'And then he'll go into witness protection?'

O'Rourke grimaced. 'He will. He'll have to serve a few years first, but it will be somewhere secure. I still reckon he had something to do with Lavinia Grant's death, but with Saunders convinced it's natural causes the Director of Public Prosecutions won't entertain it.' O'Rourke paused, decisively flicking the car into drive.

'And Trish O'Sullivan?'

O'Rourke scowled like he had a pain. 'She's admitted being present on the night the babies were born and that she knew one of them had died but failed to report it. We've charged her with wilful neglect, but much as I would like to, unless we can get a confession that she smothered the child, we haven't got enough to charge her with murder.' Cathy could see O'Rourke was clenching his jaw.

'Going on her past form, I don't think Trish's the type to break down and admit it. She's already realised she's gone too far saying she was in the house that night.'

'She has, which gives us enough to get her into court. We'll see how she copes in front of a judge when she's asked about Valentine's letter. She's got a lot of explaining to do.' O'Rourke's voice was hard. 'At least the FBI is happy.' He checked his rearview mirror. 'Hierra was really playing with fire; this Kuteli is a big player.'

'Weird name.'

'That's what I thought. Albanian, apparently. I thought he was Italian.'

Albanian? Cathy felt a shiver go up her spine. *That stupid accent had sounded vaguely* . . . why hadn't it occurred to her earlier? She shook away the idea. Decko was always messing, winding them up. There was no way . . .

'So you hungry?' O'Rourke interrupted her thoughts.

'Bit.'

It must have been the way she said it. O'Rourke flicked the car back into park, twisted round in his seat to look at her. 'OK, so what's up?'

What's up? The words ricocheted between them, gathering weight with every deflection. Cathy shrugged, her face a picture of innocence, eyebrows raised like she had no idea what he was talking about. *Had he guessed? Surely not . . . he was a bloke . . .*

'Come on, Cat. We go back a long way.'

A long way. A long way to a cold dark night, to a Section 49, the driver of the car they'd stopped so pissed he couldn't even walk, to an armed robbery at a warehouse on the other side of the street, to being in the wrong place at the wrong time.

'You can talk to me, Cat. I owe you, girl. You took that bullet for me – that gouger didn't even know you were there, you know that, don't you?'

Cathy sighed, looking at the roof of the car. O'Rourke continued like the words had worn into a groove in his head: 'You were on the other side of the car looking in the guy's glove compartment. Bent over. The shooter didn't even know you were there. If you'd have kept quiet, not yelled, he'd have wiped me out. He had a clear shot.'

O'Rourke was right. They both knew he was right.

'*Gardaí. Put your weapon down!*' Cathy's voice had reverberated off the walls of the warehouse, off the road, echoed inside her head like it was yesterday.

Distracted by her sudden appearance over the roof of the drunk's car, the shooter had gone wide, the bullet shattering the driver's window, heading straight through the interior, straight for her. She still heard it in her dreams. Bang. Bang. The Glock discharging, the windscreen exploding. Like the explosion of pain as the bullet seared her side, leaving her ribcage on fire.

'Anyone would have done the same.'

O'Rourke laughed, shaking his head. 'What, anyone would have put themselves in the line of fire? Yeah, I bet. You stuck your head up there like a coconut on a fecking shy.' Cathy wrinkled her face like she was about to say something, but O'Rourke didn't let her. 'You put your life on the line for me, Cat. I had my back to them. Wouldn't have known what hit me.' She was shaking her head, but he kept going. 'Anyway, what I'm trying to say is you're stuck with me now. I'm your guardian angel, girl.'

Laughter bubbled up inside her as Cathy shook her head. 'Won't wings spoil the suit? You're some eejit.'

'I am? I'm the eejit? What about you?'

'What do you mean?'

'Are you going to tell me or do I have to guess?'

'Tell you what?'

'That you're pregnant.' O'Rourke inflected the end of the sentence like a belligerent teenager. Could have added a *duh*. He shook his head, disbelief all over his face. But it wasn't disbelief that she was pregnant, she knew, it was disbelief that she hadn't told him. 'Apart from the fact that we've known each other for what – years? – you're operational, Cat, we both know what that means better than anyone else. It's the type of thing I need to know.' O'Rourke said it like she was five years old.

Feck. FECK.

'Have you told anyone?'

Cathy shook her head, her elbow on the window ledge, fingers locked into the roots of her hair. Turning away from him, she stared at the straggly patch of grass in front of her house, at her beautiful laser-blue Mini Cooper gleaming under the street lights, avoiding his eye.

'The father?' O'Rourke's voice was incredulous.

'Yes, I told him.' Cathy couldn't bring herself to inject any enthusiasm into the statement. *He wanted her to give up her job . . .*

O'Rourke let out a sigh like gas escaping. 'Well, that's something, I suppose.' Then, 'I didn't know you were seeing anyone.' The comment was loaded.

'I'm not.'

'Right.' O'Rourke's voice brightened. 'So no one's going to get upset if I take you out for dinner then?'

'Nope.' Cathy turned back to look at him, their eyes meeting, connecting for a split second before she looked away quickly, a smile twitching at the corner of her mouth. 'No, you're grand there.'

O'Rourke pushed the car into drive, pulled away from the kerb.

'Good, that's good.' Then, embarrassed, trying to hide it, 'So what do you think about the Russian mafia, or Albanians or whatever they are? Reckon we've won a major feather there. Yanks are singing our praises already. They've been working on nailing Kuteli for over a year.'

'Good, it's good.' Cathy bit her lip, *she'd better say it*. 'Look, I got this weird call. I thought it was one of the lads messing, but the accent was . . . Maybe it was Eastern European, sort of Albanian, maybe?' O'Rourke slammed on the brakes, the car lurching to a halt in the middle of the road.

'What?'

Cathy looked at him out of the corner of her eye, wincing. *She was going to get a bollocking for not telling him, she knew it. Another bollocking . . .*

'I'm sure it's nothing. That's why I turned the phone off. It sounded like Decko but I wasn't really concentrating. Maybe they left a message . . .' Reaching into her bag, she rooted for the phone. 'Shit, I left it in the car. I'll get it.' Cathy had the door open before he could protest.

The explosion was instantaneous, lit the sky like it was the 5th of November, the sound shattering windows at the end of the street.

Watching her through the rear window, O'Rourke had already hit reverse, was about to take his foot off the brake when the flash blinded him. The force rocked the BMW, shattering the windows, detonating the airbags, knocking him senseless for a split second.

'Cathy!'

His own cry still ringing in his ears, O'Rourke came to, dizzy, the interior of the car filled with white smoke-like powder. He heaved open the door.

The air outside was rank with the smell of burning, bitter, acrid, catching in his throat. Falling out of the car, he staggered, then ran towards the drive. All around him car and house alarms were going off. The Mini was blazing, the heat searing his eyebrows, drying his lips, smoke billowing into the night. He could see a body lying across the neighbour's lawn.

Covered in blood. Not moving.

'Cathy . . .' It came out as a croak.

O'Rourke fell to his knees beside her. Cathy was lying on her back, arms thrown above her head where the blast had carried her backwards, her face blackened, blood running from her nose, her ear, down her forehead. Her leather jacket had taken the brunt of the blast, was in tatters, shards of glass embedded in it, catching and reflecting the flames. O'Rourke ripped off his own jacket, balling it, pressing down to stem the flow of blood from her side. Then, slipping his fingers under her chin, he searched for a pulse. He held his breath, the sound of his heart hammering in his ears. Finally he found it, weak, fluttering like the wings of a butterfly. Fading with every beat.

He heard his own voice shouting into his phone like it was someone else's.

'Member down. Ambulance. I need an ambulance . . . Corbawn Lane, Shankill . . . Fast. I need it fast.'

Cathy's eyes were closed, her skin china white. Bending over her, he kept up the pressure on the wound in her stomach, not allowing himself to think about anything else except keeping her alive. In the grass beside her head his eye caught something familiar, something metallic. Holding his jacket in place, he reached for it with his free hand. It was her necklace, the chain broken, the silver dog tag hot, searing his palm. But O'Rourke hardly felt it, clutched it tight. *'If found return to Tiffany's'*. *She'd loved it. She'd bought him aftershave.* He scooped her into his arms, cradled her head on his knee, his tears hot, falling freely.

'Cathy . . .' He heard his own scream, echoing in his ears like a banshee.

Then the road was filling with people. Far away he could hear the wail of a siren, quickly joined by more, heading towards them.

Acknowledgements

No story comes together without a massive contribution from a huge variety of people – it is their expertise and patience that turns an uncut idea into something tangible and shiny, and that shiny thing into a book. A lot of people have helped as this story developed and if I have missed anyone, *mea culpa*, but trust me, I am truly grateful for all your support.

First and biggest thanks go to my awesome agent Simon Trewin, whose faith in this story has brought it to your hands. Joel Richardson, my editor at Twenty7, has been amazing since day one and has made that early manuscript into something real.

Cathy owes her sporting prowess in its entirety to Glen Heenan at Elite Martial Arts in Dún Laoghaire, who has had the incredible patience to teach me the basics of kickboxing. Glen has trained many, many real champions and introduced me to the national champion Damian Darker, who was invaluable in explaining exactly what it takes to get to the top. Massive thanks to you both – and to all the guys for not hitting me too hard! Thanks too to Jason Flynn at the Glenview Health Club for keeping me in shape, or I would never survive Glen's classes!

Any police procedural relies totally on the experts who share their experience, knowledge and stories to ensure that every detail is plausible and correct – any that aren't are entirely my doing (and that includes a few liberties taken with geography and ferry timetables – it *is* fiction after all). My husband, Shane O'Loughlin, was a member of An Garda Síochána for thirty years and I hope, as a result, I bring a sense of what the job is about to Cathy, O'Rourke and the team.

Garda Joe Griffin and Garda Dave O'Sullivan have endured my writing efforts from the very beginning (I hope it's getting better, guys!) and are always at the end of the phone when I've needed to fact-check. Detective Inspector Frank Keenaghan lent Dawson O'Rourke his tie and Irish State Pathologist Dr Marie Cassidy has been inspirational from the first draft of the very first (terrible) book I wrote, and she kindly critiqued. I still have my own copies of the books she lent me, way back then, in my 'black library'. Thanks, too, to Jenny Hynes in the State Pathologist's Office for all your help.

Garda Steve Monaghan and retired Special Branch Detective Colm Dooley were utterly invaluable in ensuring the final drafts of this book rang true. Thanks also to Roger Robson of Forensic Access for his assistance in clarifying detail.

My sister Louise Fox is the real creator of the fabulous triptych that features in this story. Trained in textiles, she is an incredibly talented artist, gallery owner and event curator, currently director of the Cornwall Film Festival – thanks Lou for letting me borrow one of your most epic pieces. (She wrote the words that are embroidered on it too – not me.)

Getting a half-Jewish American consultant psychiatrist right required assistance from many sources, including the immensely helpful Ellen Rovner in Boston, whose PhD on American Jewish ethnicity, food, gender and memory helped inform Tony. Bonnie Sashin of the Boston Bar Association, Dr Rohilla at Newcastle Hospital here in Ireland, Consultant Psychiatrist Brendan Kelly and Mary Igoe (whose surname I borrowed too, thank you!) were all essential in developing this part of the story.

Thanks too to Elizabeth Murray, now published as E. R. Murray, who helped with the poker references, and to Professor Gabriel Cooney of University College Dublin and Linda Fibiger of Oxford University for their expertise on carbon-14 dating.

Kristi Thompson, Mary Igoe, Sally Clements, and Sophie and Paul O'Rourke Walker all read early drafts – I cannot thank you enough and I hope you can see an improvement in the finished product!

Without my amazing writer friends Sarah Webb, who gave me the best advice *ever*, so long ago – *just keep writing*; Niamh O'Connor, my partner in crime, who is always on the end of the phone, truly thank you for everything; and the fabulous Alex Barclay, who was instrumental in this book happening in more ways than one, plus many, many more, I wouldn't be a writer at all. So THANK YOU GIRLS *chink*.

My wonderful family, husband Shane and two beautiful children, Sophie and Sam, have a lot to put up with (no writer has a tidy house) – huge thanks to them for all their support since I started this writing thing.

And last but by no means least, a massive thank you to all the Inkwell writers and visitors to Writing.ie who colour my days with your fabulous stories and successes – this book is for all of you.